The Consequences of Loving Syra

❧ ❧ ❧ ❧ ❧ ❧

For Nina and Herman —
Gratefully, and
with love —
Peggy

September 16, 1990

Novels by Margaret Freydberg

The Bride
The Lovely April
Winter Concert
Katherine's House
The Consequences of Loving Syra

The Consequences
of Loving Syra

by Margaret Howe Freydberg

The Countryman Press

Woodstock, Vermont

Library of Congress Cataloging-in-Publication Data
Freydberg, Margaret Howe.
The consequences of loving Syra / by Margaret Howe
Freydberg
    p.   cm.
  ISBN 0-88150-168-9 : $18.95
  I. Title
    PS3556.R448C65 1990
    813´.54--dc20   90-33267
                                     CIP

Manufactured in the United States of America

To my son

PART ONE

❧ I ❧

NOBODY was in a hurry here.
Syra said this to herself and as she did so felt it to be a fact that she thought of as fat—an abundant, very fleshy fact—something that had an existence of its own in this place it belonged to. It was other than anything she had every experienced. It lifted her up and filled her out as she strolled slowly and without purpose along the tropical street in her soundless ballet slippers.

She stopped and stuck her nose into a thick scarlet rose, the bush flaunting out over the sidewalk. Drawing away from it with a pleased look, she sauntered on—a short young woman with dark hair swinging wide to her shoulders, wearing a sleeveless shift of tiny-flowered calico.

The fragrant little glossy-leaved street opened up onto the sudden fanfare of a boulevard with elegant shops and restaurants. At first Syra was goggle-eyed, then left abruptly cold by it. Then, with a feeling of adventure, she began to be interested. The wealth! Window after elegant window of perfect slacks—slacks,

slacks, and more slacks–of French and Italian perfect sweaters, of silk and sequined and cotton and satin and flower-splashed perfect party dresses, of perfect, high-arched beautiful shoes, of perfect elegantly boxed candies, of great, incomparable lakelike diamonds, of perfectly, intricately woven, threadlike gold. Perfect, perfect, everything perfect. The wealth! And the succession of ageing men in the world's most beautiful clothes (did some of them wear corsets?), their feet in immaculate white, their faces high-blood-pressure and alcoholic purple, plump and disdainful and looking as though they might burst and deflate at a pinprick.

A very old man in red trousers gave Syra a quick, frightened, covetous glance. He had the fuzzy unsubstantiality of a dandelion gone white and tremulous, to be blown away at the slightest puff. Why do I scare you, old beau, she wondered, and what on earth do you see in me, who am not Marilyn Monroe?

There was suddenly something about this parade of misused maledom that troubled Syra, a feeling she did not wish to have on vacation. She thought of Lewis and for a vivid second she saw him as an elegant and decadent old man wearing perfect red trousers and perfect white shoes.

She wished she had not seen these old men.

Not wanting to think about this at all, she stopped to lean against a lamp post while she took a pebble out of her slipper, delighting for a moment in wriggling her damp warm bare toes, now free, letting them enjoy the air before she imprisoned them again.

She performed this small intimate job with complete unconcern, and with an unexploited joy. Rather a spectacle. So that more than one person stared at her, obliviously holding her slipper away from her foot and smiling to herself. The old man, the others, saw no particular beauty of face or form–just a short, plainly dressed young woman with large private dark eyes, no longer a girl. Yet they stared.

4

Shoveling her slipper back on, she resumed her stroll, turning off the thronged boulevard into another shopping street that led soon to quieter streets. She began looking for a clock (she didn't own a watch), trying to keep in mind her "complete absence of any time sense" that Georges was always rebuking her for. Damn, I wish time weren't in such a hurry, she fumed. I do hate to flurry like snowflakes, here of all places. At home I may have to, but not here.

All at once a feeling begun in Syra's gut rose up into her head and was words: But *here* was home! The *name* of home was Auburn, but the *truth* of home was here. Mildly surprised to find herself having some sort of profound idea, she lifted her head like a proud child (she was devoid of the reasoning process, she believed, and was often troubled by her lack of it, since it seemed to be the process by which other people lived successfully). Oh, yes, yes, she thought, I love this air. I am a balloon. She laughed out loud, and then noisily and ecstatically pulled a long draught of fragrant warmth into her lungs.

It was then that she was suddenly obsessed with the knowing—a total final sense-knowledge evolved gradually through mind and body this past week of vacation—the knowing that she needed, vitally, to live in a climate that could cause such a flowering of her being. This heat, this air, makes me sexy, she thought. This is a glory. I am knocked out of, no, I mean into, my senses. I feel as though I'm budding, bursting out from little buds into flowers, she thought, for she could feel the tightening of her nipples that did feel to her like budding buds. And she was delicately conscious of a tingling, a swelling-out and opening of her sex, that felt to her like a flowering too.

Would it be possible to move to the south to live? she began to ask herself. Everything seemed possible today, she felt like a sun-colored sphere floating through blue air, and this brilliant, obvious climate was the air for her, not the seasons of the north, where nature withheld itself, where nature was proper.

There was some meaning, some message here that was declaring the life she lived at home to be neuter, contained, closed, shriveled.

She reminded herself that she must find a clock. She was in a street of glass-fronted, dazzling-white apartments, their driveways disappearing behind glossy hedge-walls of such an unnaturally *green* green that Syra plucked a waxy leaf and rubbed it to reassure herself that it was real.

For a while she stood rubbing the leaf between her fingers, thinking about how awful it would be to live in a condo—all round, open letters *condo* was, o's and c and d, spelling something that was so closed. I would shrink into a fig of fright if I had to live in a little box like that, here in this Garden of Eden, she thought. Oh, I hope many who live in those little boxes find their bit of sky absolutely enormous. They may even fly through the window into it. She began to laugh, imagining people zooming around—fierce body traffic.

She meandered on, realizing finally that the leaf was in her hand and putting it into her bag—a bit of the tropics to come across later. She snapped the bag shut on the chaos within it—small seashells, bobby pins, sand, a paperback of haiku poetry and a paperback mystery, car keys clanking against a miniature bottle of rum for Lewis, a tube of sunproof cream gritty with sand, combs, tiny hairbrush, lipstick, sunglasses not in a case—a miracle they hadn't broken in that shifting sea of hard objects—leaflets handed to her on street corners, she never refused one, a bulging tattered wallet. The leaf could perfectly well remain there for six months, or even for as long as the life of the bag.

There would be no clocks on residential streets like this, she realized at last. And so she turned reluctantly and began to walk back the way she had come. Soon she came again to the thronged boulevard, and this time, walking rather more quickly along it, she did not really enjoy it. She acknowledged it, she let it be, because there it was, but it had nothing to do with her and so she had no interest in remaining with it.

Now, though haste was unnatural for Syra, she began to walk still faster, thinking of Georges who would be waiting for her, watching for her. And soon, there was the little seaside street and the little pink stucco hotel with its extension of palm-shaded patio, where, of course, Georges *was*, sitting at a table under a green-and-white-striped umbrella, an expression of blank discontinuity on his decent face, both elbows braced expectantly on the arms of his chair. He saw her and waved, his face loosening, his short body subsiding with relief into his chair.

She stopped and waved back–a languid movement as though she were slowly smoothing the air around her–and went then into the hotel.

After the heat of the street, the lobby was pleasantly cool. As Syra crossed it toward the door to the patio, she heard someone calling her name. Turning, she saw Mrs. Raab, the proprietress–transparent mountain of sprayed-stiff, platinum-blond hair, kindly eyes in a forest of fake eyelashes–leaning over the desk and waving an envelope heartily. "Mrs. Gachet," she sang out, "we have a letter for you, dear."

❧ II ❧

IN some part of her she didn't mind leaving, even welcomed leaving. She fingered her coffee cup and stared across the tropical street to the hot bright beach and the sea beyond. Lewis's letter lay open on the table. She had just read it a second time, and now she folded it and stuck it in her bag with a great sigh. "I'm worried about my cousin," she said to Georges, turning to look at him with steady eyes.

Beneath the umbrella's shade, Georges shifted comfortably.

"Really worried," Syra said with care.

"Oh." Georges was lazy, dreamily detached, only partly concerned. "Poor guy." But then Syra's tone made him look at her sharply.

"I've got to go," she said firmly. "Right away. Today if I can get a flight. I am sending up all sorts of novenas–I love that word, though I am not exactly certain of its precise meaning. I'm praying for a flight, is what I mean."

"*Today!*" She could see his disbelief, and then, next, see his buoyancy subsiding–a visible deflation. A small man, he seemed to her to grow smaller and to become condensed, heavy, solid with melancholy. He sat for a few moments with a deliberating, deductive, mildly suffering air, then rammed his thumbs into the pockets of his new Madras shorts, drummed his fingers against his thighs, and said abruptly, "May I see the letter? Let me see it."

Syra opened her bag and fished for the letter. "I think I've lost it in this hideous beat-up bag that loses everything. Oh, here it is!" She handed it, fluttering in the hot breeze, over to Georges, who took it in his square kind hands and opened it.

Dearest Syra,

Here I sit on a gloomy wet day, imagining you and Georges in hot sun. I really envy you. I'd love to be with you. I really long to see you, dearest cousin.

Spring is of course lovely here, as it always is. The redwings are back I'm glad to report, glad for my sake I mean. But somehow this year they don't fulfill their mission, which is to make me jubilant. I can't seem to be jubilant, only melancholy. Forgive me for writing you in this vein. I know I shouldn't. But to be able to write to you makes me feel better, if such a thing is possible. I'm urging myself to stop but I'm going on. I shouldn't be writing you this on your vacation, but having started a letter to you, this seems to be the only thing I have to say. Actually what I have to say is that I want to see you, more than anything I can think of. The trouble is, I've been sick for a long time (the opposite of spring fever), can't seem to shake it, a virus I think, and I'm sure that's what's bugging me. "Bugging" indeed.

How about you and Georges stopping on your way back and paying me a visit? Or just you? You have to come via New York anyway, so you've no excuse for not coming out to the Road on your way home. I'm thankful though, during these confined days, that I live on the Road. Neighborliness is a great thing. Mrs. Alexander, what a sane light in a crazy dark world she is, has been taking wonderful, straightforward care of me, and Anne Knight has been bossy with lots of good will. All of them have been showering me with attention. Rupert as well. Bernice has been baking wonderful things, even casseroles for the invalid, and of course *chicken soup*! Anne tried to sneak a doctor in on me, but I nipped *that* plot in the bud. There's no reason to see a doctor, everyone has this thing, flu I guess it is, and there's nothing to do for it but rest, they say. Rest! How can one rest if there is no rest *in* one? Lying in bed isn't resting, reading a book isn't resting. And least of all,least of all, the long nights provide no rest *at all*.

Well, dearest Syra, I want to see you very much, so give a thought to stopping by on your way back. You and Georges have a good time. And send me a postcard of palm trees with your handwriting on the back.

Much love, Lewis

P.S. Heloise has finally decided to break it off.

P.P.S. Seriously, come and see me on your way back. For at least a day, if not longer. If I have that to look forward to I'll be considerably picked up, I know it. I *really mean* it, Syra. *Ausec!*

Georges folded the letter and pushed it across the table to Syra, looking elaborately away from her. "I'll tell you what I think," he said at last, fretfully. "*I* think you're going to wreck our vacation for a hunch."

"Hunch? Why, this letter's naked. How," she asked with a particular carefulness and a focus of all of her attention, "could you miss that? It makes me weak inside. There's no subtlety about it. It's just stark naked miserable. And it's only three days earlier than I was going anyway. That won't wreck it. We've already been here a whole week and a half, for heaven's sake. Oh murder Georges, when we planned this vacation, we both knew you'd stay a week longer because of my having to be back at school to help William get ready for his recital, so if I leave today, I hope, I hope, it's only three days before I was going to leave, anyway. If I wait to go home as planned, I won't be able to stop and see Lewis."

"It's mad."

"Really, Georges? You think it's mad?"

"I do."

"Maybe it is. Maybe I'm a mad creature. But I have to go. That's all I can tell you. I'm partly very sorry."

"Not wholly though," he pounced. "Not wholly!" He hunched up one shoulder and glared away from her, out to sea.

"No, not wholly." She tossed her head, for she was uncomfortable, unhappy. Though she was not disturbed at any depth, nevertheless she felt, with Georges, as now, that she was always being thought of as behaving badly. How simple her mother had made behavior sound, and be: Life was not to be lived for the reflection of one's good behavior in the eyes of others. Behavior was neither good nor bad, it was simply behaving in the way one knew how to behave.

Syra knew absolutely that this was true. And yet, even though her mother had made behavior seem simple, Syra had long ago learned that it was not. It was simple to *be* simple, but it was not simple to be approved of for being simple.

She gave a great, exasperated sign. "I want to go to Lewis, that's what. I can't not go. I have to look after Lewis."

"Not me, though, eh?"

"Well, you look so carefully after yourself, don't you?" This was mean. She shook her head slowly, as though to shake away the feeling of meanness. She looked away from Georges, towards the palm tree thrashing languidly in the wind. It was not in her to cheat with apology.

"If you'll excuse my saying so," he said drily, "it's not like you to rush off looking after people."

"Lewis. I look after Lewis."

Georges made an embarrassed sound, and he sat quiet, seething, sucking ceaselessly at the corner of his mouth. "What makes you think you can get a plane reservation just like that?" he muttered, but without conviction, and in the next breath called out sharply, "Waiter, coffee here, please," this being his capitulation.

"I do, though, hate for you to be left alone. And oh, how I'll miss" (she knew the word shocked him) "all that fun fucking. In fact, I'll miss just about everything here."

And she would. In one way she hated to leave all this, to have to cut short, even for only a few days, this vacation she and Georges had set so much store by, particularly since Georges was having such a good time. He had seemed to give himself up to the whole thing from the minute the plane door had opened onto all this vivid warmth. He had even, amazing for him, let Syra persuade him to drink rum, deviating from his careful habitual count of one glass of wine with dinner and no hard liquor ever–careful Georges who counted calories, who took high potency vitamins, who jogged, flat tan hair plastered down his forehead, perspiring face agonized. He had even brought with him on this trip, to guard against possible hyperacidity, his own inflatable wedge-shaped pillow.

But he hadn't had to use it. In no time he ceased to be a short, square pillar of melancholy and had turned impish, kicking up his heels. Literally. He was continually waltzing in and out around the beds, as though this narrow space was his own little dance floor, rising on mincing ballet toes, waving his arms, singing, leaping; leaping and prancing into the ocean with his arms flailing, whooping and shrieking with the bravado of a child, wearing what Syra called his satyr's grin. He was a bit of a sissy about the cold water and the surf, hence all the hullabaloo. Georges had two sides, and this was his seldom-used one. He sank often, suddenly, from the heights of gaiety into a heavy, care-laden silence, as though he had come to his senses. But then again he would be lighthearted and euphoric for hours on end.

So, because of Georges's occasional infectious joy, and because of a humming-as-of-beehives sexuality she hadn't felt in a long time, so that lovemaking gave promise of becoming something heretofore unexplored–because of this excitement, and because of an undefined urgent sense that there could be more between them than there was, that because of her capacities which she felt to be infinite, and because of his which she trustingly believed to be infinite, too, there must be something more, something fuller, deeper, different, that they could bring into flower; and because she was driven by the sense that this vacation was the great chance, had to be, for if not, the future might be a continuing downhill mediocrity, a blur of cotton years, her thirties and then her forties and so on, muffled, thick, no vibrations, lifeless; because of all this, she was divided about leaving.

The truth was that Syra found herself wondering more and more frequently, more and more uneasily, what she was doing being married. Often she had a panicky sense of something happening to her, some process going on that was calcifying her in such a slow, day-by-day, imperceptible way that it was indistinguishable from the passing of time, or from the normal shift and growth and change of any woman's development. She sensed that marriage had not been a continuing natural growth for her, not a further true development of her own self, but a distortion, as though an alien substance were always being rejected by her psychic system, disabling her.

This was a question, a feeling, that disturbed the flow of Syra's life recurrently now, and for which she had no answers, at least in words. Did Georges bore her? Had he bored her right from the beginning?

She had married him on impulse, that much she sensed, at a time when she was newly alone—her mother had just died, Lewis, her closest friend, was far away in Italy, her thirtieth birthday was past. And too, her second long love affair had failed to bring the ultimate in sexual happiness she had seen with her own eyes on that summer Sunday afternoon so long ago, and she was gradually growing uncertain about her search for it and disillusioned about its promise of radical ecstacy.

Alarmingly alone in a way she did not know how to deal with, she suddenly said to herself that since it was married love she had witnessed that summer Sunday, then doubtless it was marriage itself that was missing. So why not marry this charming, decent Frenchman, Georges Gachet, the new French teacher and basketball coach in the school where she taught music—this new lover who was really so kind and who adored her so dramatically and who begged her without letup to be his wife? Why not? To be sure, his hypochondria troubled her, and his piety about marriage, which she found unreal–Georges had absorbed the curious alchemy of a New England mother's ferocious belief in the single standard and a French father's uncomplicated living out of the double. Nevertheless, he did have an intense though unimaginative and self-centered sexuality that she was always hoping would develop into what she was searching for.

They had been lovers for only two months when Syra woke up in his bed one morning–in fact, a Sunday morning–and decided she had better stay there.

The waiter, after a while, came slowly with his tray and set down two cups of steaming coffee, mopping the table indolently, while Georges snatched up his cup and held it to his lips, taking sip after small sip, quickly, and drumming on the table with the square helpless fingers of the other hand.

"I'll try to go standby," Syra said. She probed a finger down the front of her dress, down between her breasts, where a trickle had developed. "Whew, today's really hot, and *that* I actually love." She smiled privately and put up her chin. She was meeting herself again, as she did every hour of every day here on this leave of absence from home. Do I inhabit other exotic places on this globe, she wondered? Would I meet myself on the roads of Marrakesh? Or Bali?

"I'd like to live in the tropics," she said, suddenly grave. "On the subject of the tropics I am quite delirious."

Georges leaned forward and swatted a mosquito, violently. "You'd get tired of it," he said. "You'd miss the seasons."

"No." Quietly and firmly. How little he knew her.

The hot breeze blew suddenly strong, rattling the palms that framed the entrance to the street. From somewhere beyond the pink stucco wall of the patio, perhaps from the bar, Mrs. Raab's fat long lazy chuckle bubbled up, and then slowly, lusciously, subsided.

Syra threw back her head and burst out laughing. She was remembering the jounce of Mrs. Raab's full, pointed breasts in the tight pink blouse as she swayed around to get their room key out of its cubicle, turning back with it, rattling it coyly like a little bell and sweeping Georges with the comradely suggestiveness of her fringed eyes before putting it with her warm hand into his warm hand.

"That soars my spirits exceedingly," Syra laughed. She looked across at Georges and shrugged, then smiled faintly, inquisitively. "Mrs. Raab's spirits are soaring too," she murmured. "That fun woman's spirits are always soaring."

Georges's eyes softened and crinkled at the corners into the kindest of lines, and he drew a long sigh of defeat, and acceptance of Syra, and pensive humor—his way of facing trouble, and wasn't most of life trouble? He put a blunt finger to the letter and tapped it twice, hard, and said, sternly, as though it were his discovery, "He's clearly in a depression. A real depression."

"It feels as though—is that the word, depression?—it feels as though he's all on the wrong side of himself. And that P.S. about Heloise!"

"Yes. I'd hoped he'd marry this one."

"Lewis'll never marry."

"Why do you think that? I've never heard you say that."

Why had she said that? She was surprised. "Well," she said. She was quiet for what seemed to Georges a very long time. Then finally she said, "I've always known he wouldn't ever marry."

"But why? He loves women. He's very domestic. He's lonely. Why do you think he's such a confirmed bachelor?"

"I just know. That's what. I can't imagine him marrying any of those women he's slept with. What I mean is, I feel in my bones he's never been serious about women. I mean his women have never been women he'd want to *marry*."

"Well, he seems to be upset about losing Heloise."

"Maybe his pride has been arrowed. But I doubt if he's really way down deep upset. I doubt if he really loved Heloise."

"She's such a really nice woman."

Syra shrugged. "Maybe. But for Lewis?" Her eyes were proud and cool and skeptical.

"Syra, now look here, dear," Georges said abruptly. "Take a look at yourself. Isn't this too drastic, going there? Bad for him, too. Scare him to death?"

"Oh no." She looked at Georges with an imperturbable assurance that seemed to deepen and darken and focus her eyes. "Oh no. He wants me to come. Why won't you see that? Look at his neighbors, look at Mrs. Alexander, and Mrs. Knight. He's spelling it out that *they've* been concerned about him. I feel there's cause for concern. I can feel it. I wish I didn't have to keep repeating and repeating that. I'm getting a headache from this being hard, not easy." With her hand she snatched her hair from the back of her hot neck, angrily, as though she would like to toss it away. "He'd never have sent a letter like this unless he needed me. It's a desperate letter. Absolutely unlike cool, sophisticated Lewis. He's lost his cool, he has. Look." She opened the letter and turned it over. "Some of the words are so underlined the pen has gone through the paper."

"I see. So. What does this word 'ausec' mean, for goodness' sake? I've never seen a word like that."

"No, you wouldn't have. It's our private word, Lewis's and mine. We made it up. When either of us was in a fix, we'd manage to get our password across to each other. It's short, mon mari, for 'au secours.' If I'd get stuck dancing with someone I'd steer us near the stag line and say 'ausec' to him, not out loud but just moving my lips, and he'd cut in right away and save my life. Things like that. We were always saving each other that way, with good old 'ausec.' But we never used it without needing to. That was part of the pact. We always meant it. He means it now. He's calling 'help,' and he means it."

Syra was feeling a fresh vivid surge of love for Lewis as she spoke, wanting, needing, right now, more than anything else, to be not here but with him. And sitting with Georges under the canvas umbrella that rattled in the hot wind, bringing her cup toward her parted lips, suddenly she remembered peeking, long, long ago in her childhood home, through the keyhole into the guest room where Lewis had slept during his visits that summer, peeking because the closed door in the middle of the day aroused her curiosity, her newly born seven-year-old sexual curiosity—what could Lewis be doing that he must close the door at two o'clock in the afternoon? Could he be doing anything like what Mother and Father had been doing when she'd spied on them? And there he was, rewardingly in line with her limited view through the keyhole, standing beside the dresser, naked, a frightened little boy away from home, holding a hand mirror underneath his behind and peering down over his shoulder with curiosity and dread at the reflection of a large, suppurating boil. Without a second thought she had opened the door and walked in.

What had he done then? Tilting her coffee into her mouth, she couldn't recall. He must have been humiliated to be caught both frightened *and* naked. But she couldn't remember. All she could remember was the sight of his loneliness and fright, and in addition, the fascinating group of little dangling shapes between his legs that was what she had been hoping to have a glimpse of when she peeked, but had found so singularly disappointing, so comical, and yet so disturbing. The sight of it, so utterly silly looking, and of Lewis, so helpless with his boil and his dread, had been her first sure knowledge of Lewis, and neither he, nor her knowledge that he was in some kind of danger, had ever grown to be otherwise.

"I've got to go to the bathroom," Syra said, springing up suddenly. "Also, I think I'll ask Mrs. Raab to call Pan Am. She will be very glad to do that, because Mrs. Raab loves to be helpful."

Georges watched her walking across the patio, weaving in and out among the tables with her indolent hips switching. His eyes, following her, were wistful, guarded, perplexed, defeated.

When after a while she reappeared, he stared at her with a new intentness, at her hair swinging against her shoulders–how it shone–at her cool calm wide-apart dark eyes, and he noticed particularly something he had never noticed before. Her face, her body, the way she held herself, the way she walked, all of her was, oddly, both calm and reckless.

He felt a sudden helplessness and an unfamiliarity with everything, everything.

"Mrs. Raab got me a reservation, with *ease*," Syra called out to him when she was halfway across the patio. She came to the table and sat down. "The flight leaves at one, so I guess soon I will have to start pulling myself together. And I *mean* pulling together, since I feel absolutely dismembered from this lovely laziness."

"It's ten thirty," said Georges, accusingly. "*I'll* say you'd better pull yourself together. Pronto."

She took a wadded pink handkerchief from the pocket of her dress and dabbed at the moisture on her upper lip, her temples, the back of her neck. "The mugginess of this day makes a person float." She sipped cold coffee with one hand, she dabbed with the other, as though not knowing which was more important. Then she put her cup down, and holding the handkerchief in a tightened fist she said, "I really hope you understand that I have to go." She spoke quietly, even pleadingly, as though she had returned from the making of her plane reservation reinforced but gentled in her determination.

Georges, grateful for this tack, shrugged self-consciously and poked a cheek out with his tongue, but then all at once leaned across the table and wistfully, eagerly, put his hand on hers.

She let her hand lie passive under his for a polite moment, then slowly drew it away. At the same moment she observed, on the other side of the street, sauntering in the crowd of strollers and hurriers, a boy and a girl with arms loose across each other's backs. The boy would glance away from the girl, but then turn to look down at her, and her face would linger a moment toward something else, but then longingly, needily turn up to the boy's like a flower toward the sun.

But they were haloed, it seemed to Syra, by some luminous quality they were generating together, and this was what attracted her attention–this quality, beyond the open display of affection, of being unaware of everything but each other. Their sides touched and moved with occasional rapturous slowness, and Syra could feel the fire of it in herself, and knew that for those moments, the boy and the girl were grown together as though they were one flesh.

She was suddenly struck, completely seized and enveloped by the thought that man is born to be alone. And at once she was pityingly filled with the sense of the happiness of these two and of its being so fragile, so fleeting–doomed. She was achingly aware of this declaration of a man and a woman's need of each other, of two together in a crowd of distracted, *single* people, as though, without knowing it, they clung together as a protection against the singleness around them.

Was this what love was? Syra marveled. Was love only a protection against singleness? And where had that strange recognition come from? Had it, on many levels, been accruing in her for years, to be suddenly revealed today by a young couple in love?

For a moment Syra was in a sudden reversal of mood that was disturbingly unfamiliar, and that frightened her as it sadly and strangely thrilled her. And she thought that this couple was miraculously there to tell her of the subjective, poignant nature of loving. She thought that her eyes had selected them at that very moment, in conjunction with a slight movement in herself like a minuscule shifting apart of densities that let in for a second a crack of illumination, so that she might see the tenderness, the vulnerability, the helplessness of human life. These two were not simply sauntering in carefree love. They were clinging to each other because this would help postpone the last, lonely breath before extinction.

She was greatly moved. Startled. What was happening? But then she remembered the sun and felt it on her arms. The couple, she saw, had vanished. Had they ever been there?

She put a hand across onto her arm, and rubbed the warm flesh slowly. She sighed. But then she smiled and said to herself with awe: When such large thoughts enter my lazy brain, I feel the possibility of light. I do. I do.

PART TWO

THE pain was like two brutal arms flung around his chest from behind. They tightened slowly, crunching his bones, crushing his breathing. He was standing in his driveway, next to his sign, which swung slightly in a movement of air. He could hear it squeak as it swung once, then, in a moment, once again. He sat down suddenly and weakly and leaned against the post and said, softly, "Jesus Christ."

He sat for a long time. Slowly, as his pain and his panic faded, he began to laugh quietly. He looked up at his sign. "Fool's Paradise, Antiques, Lewis Cavanagh Lewis," he said aloud, in a mocking voice. "That's good. That's really good. That's it in a nutshell," he said to himself importantly and bitterly. "I'll tell Syra to have that carved on my gravestone."

A breeze had sprung up, a fresh, green-earth fragrance. Sitting there in the cool April sunshine, underneath the lofty branches of the maples in which redwing blackbirds chucked and trilled, Lewis, because of some quiet, some clearness left in him by the blessed going away of the pain, was watching and appraising a procession of thoughts that were coming into his mind surprisingly. The word *unreal* appeared. He let it grow big, and felt it taking control. *Unreal*, that was the word. Not only for himself, but for the Road, which was after all, wasn't it, only an illusion of real country, an antique hemmed in on all sides by proliferating development. Pretendy, Syra's word. Pretendy, the whole shitting thing, he thought unemotionally. The sign squeaking above him in the breeze looked as though it had been there since revolutionary times, the way he had intended it to look. Shit, he thought matter-of-factly, it's all shit. The sign might just as well be *Ye Old Antique Fhop*, with an F for an S. Crazy kid, he thought of himself, sadly and anxiously seeing the silliness of it all.

Well, enough of this, he said to himself suddenly. And then, suddenly too, he jumped up and went over to the mailbox for his mail, which was what he'd come out here for in the first place, and then he strode back over the neat white pebble driveway to the comfort of his house.

❧ II ❧

NOT daring to postpone the visit another day, Rupert Knight was on his way down to call on Lewis, taking along the incredible letter from his agent and a book on Vietnam that Anne felt Lewis should read. He had not seen Lewis in over a week, relaxing in the knowledge that Anne and Mrs. Alexander were taking care of him like two mother hens, and now he was on his way down to call, more than belatedly, he knew with guilt, and with not much anticipation he also knew uneasily, for Lewis, as Mrs. Alexander put it, had been a handful since his illness. The truth was that Rupert, fearful of the sickroom, of illness, was torn between wanting to call on Lewis in order to show him the letter, and not wanting to call on him because he was sick.

He noticed everything as he strolled along—the fragrance of last night's rain, the cheerful persistent busyness of robins, constant, pervasive. The Road, as everyone called it—Deer Valley Road was its name and had been for the two hundred years of its existence—was a winding, tree-shaded, and only recently surfaced country way, with abrupt, sweeping, scenic surprises, with meadows and woods and streams along its borders and here and there an authentically restored old house. Its turning and twisting course had not been altered since its beginnings in revolutionary times, nor had its character changed to any large extent since then. Seven hundred acres of it belonged to Mrs. Alexander, who had lived all her life on the Road, in the house her father, James Ogilvie, had built in 1880 and in which she had been born and married and widowed. And her homestead, her barns, her ample undulating meadows, her woodland where swamps were black and still, gave a good deal of the Road the look of "estate country," a pleasant illusion for the other residents whose acreage was not nearly as extensive.

There had been some division of land and a few new houses built during the past twenty years, each one eliciting from the old-timers an initial curiosity and a flurry of criticism that didn't last, but the unspoiled look of the land, chiefly because of Mrs. Alexander's holdings, remained gratifyingly the same.

Rupert and Anne Knight were the newest comers, having moved here five years ago, though they had not built a new house for themselves, but had remodeled an old barn with a silo at one corner, in a meadow they had bought, along with ten acres of land, from Mrs. Alexander. She had relinquished ownership of this little bit of precious land because she was charmed by Rupert Knight and felt he would be good for the Road.

Rupert swung pontifically along, a massive, gray-haired man, ecstatic in the April morning. His deliberate pace was his own, lazy and ruminative, papal in its processional way, the dignity of it being a combination of arrogance, elegance, and a seriousness born of the occasional reminder to himself that he had once had, might still have, integrity. Within the boundaries of vanity, of perpetual excitement over himself, within the dream, he was his own man, clearly defined to himself. Beyond that lay a reality he had had little contact with, or little will to have any contact with.

His appearance, too, proclaimed his way of life and his occupation. Anyone seeing Rupert walking down the road this April morning would have known, if only because of his beret, that he was some sort of an artist, a refugee from the world of business that throbbed and thrived so few miles away.

The letter in his pocket glowed in him like wine, it detached his spirit from his body so that he scarcely knew he was walking. The feeling of joy unlimited reminded him of his youth, and he felt he was experiencing the high point of the fifty-nine years of his life. At last, at long last, he was going to have a book published! At last he could be known for the man he knew himself to be! He felt not only at one with the world, but on top of it. He felt huge, godlike. The world had at last given him to himself. Now he could exist in the knowledge that he was exceptional, knew finally that he was because the world had told him so. He felt his entire existence at last clarified and justified.

He passed the Moores' and stopped to look up ecstatically at the yellow blur of the weeping willow by their stream, where two redwing blackbirds perched, that joyous sound–*conkereee*–the first song of spring, coming from their exuberant throats. The stream pursued its musical, oblivious way. In the sloping meadow across the road, narrow and glittering, it appeared once more, winding through rocks and mossy tufts into the pond, whose whole ruffled surface was in motion toward the dam, over which April water poured loudly.

Beyond the Moores' the road curved down, then leveled off, and Rupert was in the valley. And gratifyingly now, the church came into view. There were daffodils just opening in the churchyard—spots of thrilling yellow that gave Rupert another surge of joy. He stopped, for this was a loved place. The white church was a pure Greek Revival rectangle with its four fluted columns insubstantially, it seemed, standing on the timeworn waviness of the marble portico. All its large, many-paned windows stood open, perhaps because it was being cleaned by the volunteers, Rupert decided.

Lewis'll be behind that, he thought indulgently. Lewis had recently formed a committee to clean up the church—a "clean-in," he had called it on the mimeographed notice he had sent around to all the neighbors. This out-of-the-way little church had had a long period of disintegration and disuse, and Lewis had finally been the one to believe that it could and should be revived. "It's a sleeping beauty!" Rupert had heard him enthuse to Mrs. Alexander. "We can wake it up! God isn't dead!"

"My dear, I was christened in that church," she had replied, "and married in it, and I'll love you dearly if you'll go ahead and fix it up so I can have my funeral there."

Rupert walked on, thinking about Lewis reviving the church, wondering whether avowedly irreligious Lewis really did believe that God was not dead. He had stood holding a hymnal with Lewis at the last Christmas carol service and Lewis had had to stop in the middle of "Silent Night," choking, unable to make a sound, and then had blown his nose. "I get emotional in church-es," he had confided to Rupert afterward. "In country churches," he had added. "I guess it brings back our childhood." Rupert knew that the "our" meant Lewis and his cousin Syra Gachet.

He hesitated by the old lilac bush at the end of the churchyard, remembering suddenly a hymn of his Sunday school days, hearing it as distinctly as though organ music and choir voices were actually pouring out to him from the stale air and the hypocritical piety of all that sacramental red plush and dead white. He could hear those soaring words, "There is a happy land, far, far away, / Where saints in glory stand, bright, bright as day."

He began to walk again, thinking exuberantly that the Happy Land was *not* far, far away but was right here, and soon he was approaching Lewis's house, an elegant small maroon-painted saltbox with pompous ivy-filled urns flanking the never-used front door, and behind it a barnlike extension that was the shop. The sign that hung on its post beside the driveway—a weathered, knotty board lettered in faded earth reds and greens—was rocking slightly in the new breeze, and Rupert could hear it scrunch, as though it were proclaiming itself, as he passed it.

A chipmunk appeared out of a stone wall and seeing Rupert, sat up, clasped its paws across its throbbing white breast in consternation and indecision, then was uncannily gone. "Oh you're a great one," Rupert cried out to it, brandishing his arm, his face like a radiant child's, his velvet eyes gentle. "And I'm your friend but you don't know it!"

At the same moment he smelled wood smoke mingling with the fragrance of spring air. He was transported. Outdoors it was spring, and indoors were firesides, and in his pocket was the letter. Suddenly he felt a serene saturation of joy, as though it were not possible for him to feel more joy than this.

I am as happy as I will ever be in my life, he told himself with awe.

❧ III ❧

LEWIS had ground out his fourth cigarette of the day and was standing indifferently at his window when he saw Rupert turn into his driveway.

He was suddenly, desperately glad to see Rupert, and was already hospitably at his open door when Rupert crossed the lawn to the porch. Shiningly bald except for a monk's fringe of light brown hair, handsome young face pale, long thin body graceful in good tweeds, Lewis leaned against the bulky Jacobean chest in his narrow hall waiting, with a display of cordiality and also true eagerness, for Rupert to come up onto the porch. His smile was forced.

Not Rupert's. His was real and warm as sunshine, showing straight white teeth. As he advanced he wriggled, once, like a happy puppy. He was both stately and, as he tipped his gray head to one side, coy, murmuring, "Lewissss, Lewissss," in a long-drawn-out, expressive way. Though his smile was genuinely warm, it was also faintly diplomatic. He rubbed his hands together and said "Ha!" in a rousing way, but then, shocked at Lewis's pallor, he said hesitantly, compassionately, "Dear Lewis. How *are* you? Better, I do hope." Slowly he unbuckled the belt of his epauleted old trench coat, pulled it off, and went to hang it with careful fussy love on the clothes tree behind the door.

Now, in response to Rupert's concern about his health, Lewis, looking pale as putty and feeling faintly dizzy, there in his tiny perfect hall with the gilt French mirror upon rubbed and exquisitely faded old French paper, felt a great urge to cry out to

Rupert that he was weak, that he had a pain in his chest that frightened him, that he was frantically depressed. But at the same time he wanted more than anything–was it because of the puppy-dog act, which he despised–to maintain a reserve with Rupert. With a kind of stubborn honesty, he did not want to use as a confessor a man whom he so constantly needed to pick apart.

"Old phouff," he thought. And for a moment he felt he cared very little for Rupert Knight. Lewis was this way about people–sensitive, touchy, without basic loyalty. He had few friends. Those he had had he had tended to banish when he felt they had betrayed him.

Now he felt this irritation with Rupert, and at the same time a kind of panic–might he be going to make the mistake of banishing Rupert Knight? Brushing aside the subject of his health as though it were inconsequential, even detestable, he said brusquely, "Uh, better. Better, thanks." He parted his lips, tautening them across his teeth. This looked like a smile, and Lewis meant it to be a smile, but there was no light behind his smiles, ever. His green eyes at this moment were kindly and a little teary, but could be sharp, or bleak, or even peacefully contemplative. There were lines of bitterness around his sensual mouth, grooved there by the conditions of his existence.

Lewis Cavanagh Lewis was the only son of a widowed mother, now dead, who had given an adored child a distinguished name, and, as well, the limitations of herself. He in turn had adored his mother, and continued tenaciously to keep alive in himself and in his way of life all that she had endowed him with, including his name, which sounded distinguishedly lineal, and to a certain extent was, and in which he had always taken a snobbish delight. His mother, Syra's mother's sister ("those Cavanagh sisters!"), an individualist too, but unlike her sister, addicted to luxury and to a decorative existence–there was monogrammed crepe de chine in her bureau drawers, a moleskin rug and a cut-glass vase with a single rose in her chauffeur-driven vintage Packard–this fastidious, iron-willed, shrewd, beautiful, confidently moral mother had given her son, her only child (born in her forty-second year, oh, never again that disfigurement, that agony), the most distinguished name she could think of, one that no one else was likely to have, that would look well on a calling card and that, when spoken, would command attention. Lewis had never stopped being grateful to her for gilding him with this name. In his business, it was invaluable.

His business was antiques, simply because it had been his mother's business, and in part his, for after graduation from Cornell and during his postgraduate years at Oxford, then the Beaux Arts, then the University of Ravenna, scouting for antiques for his mother's business became a plausible reason for choosing to continue his education in Europe. The pursuit of antiques actually grew to be more interesting to him than the study at Oxford of comparative literature, at the Beaux Arts of eighteenth century French architecture, or at the University of Ravenna of the history of art. Excel, excel–Lewis's existence was a flat plain with no horizon in sight, an open-ended waste land with excellence its only goal: "an insatiable scene," as he himself called it. But when his mother was gone–she had died when he was thirty-five–the impetus for striving for excellence was gone, too. And Lewis was left without motivation, and though filled to the brim with learning, with no incentive to put it to any use. As he became involved in the management of his mother's estate–he had perforce been drawn into the little business of "Meubles et Objets d'Art" (pronounced with unaffected perfection by her, and of course by him as "Meubla aye Aubjays Dar") which thrived in the basement of their house on East 68th Street in New York–he saw that he might just as well go on with it. What else? There was all this marvelous furniture. It was easy. With his left hand he could do it. But not in this city! A need had come over him for the country.

He had found the house on Deer Valley Road soon after his mother's death, and there, ever since, he had lived and moved and had his being, *and* business, as he liked to say. He had named the shop Fool's Paradise impulsively, and in a moment, perhaps, of heightened self-appraisal, self-loathing, and flippancy, for wasn't it an accurate description not only of the Road, this illusion of rurality in a rapidly suburbanizing countryside, but also a fairly apt description of the illusory nature of antique shops in general, and in particular of himself as an antique-shop owner? He loved antiques, or at least a part of him did, but the part of him that didn't believed that they took people into the attics of their minds, there to rummage purposelessly. Was that bad? He supposed it was, because of the way it made him feel.

After six years of living on the Road he felt himself as much of an old-timer as its sovereign, Mrs. Alexander. The women on the Road liked him more than the men did, except for Rupert Knight, who could see, beneath the surface of Lewis's fussiness and passion and moroseness and gaiety and nastiness and radiant warmth, what was real about him.

There was speculation on the Road as to whether Lewis was homosexual–the antique shop, the fastidiousness, the flower arrangements, the elegant clothes, the faultlessly furnished house, the famous food. The women of the Road said that he wasn't, they knew it in their blood, and anyway look at his many and heavy love affairs with women. The men of the Road countered by pointing out that he could be bisexual. Mrs. Alexander knew he wasn't "gay," (that word she loathed), and she indignantly reprimanded whoever insinuated it, though few people wanted to or even dared to talk to Mrs. Alexander about a subject they knew would so profoundly embarrass her. And

Lewis, who had gotten wind of the gossip, of course knew that he wasn't gay, loathing the word every bit as much as Mrs. Alexander did. At the same time he knew that everything about him pointed to the scourge–he thought of it as that–because in his business he was constantly having to rebuff the overtures of the homosexuals he had to deal with. It was distasteful to a man of Lewis's almost excessive heterosexual virility and crying need for acceptance, and the standards of "good taste" he set such store by, to be thus labeled. It was not only distasteful, it was dreadful. But he was not going to give up any of the accessories to the supposed fact in order to begin anew a life of so-called normality.

Furthermore, it was an inescapable need for him to live his life in the midst of chairs and tables and highboys and consoles and tapestries and bric-a-brac–for "Meubles et Objets d'Art" were the omnipresence to him of his mother. No gossip in the world, no stigma, were going to make Lewis other than Lewis Cavanagh Lewis, and everything his mother had intended the name should connote.

Still, he loved nature sincerely–forests and fields, small wild animals and birds; spring rains; winter snows. And above all he had grown to love the Road. He worked hard at trying to keep it the beautiful old way it was, and had from the beginning assumed a relentless responsibility for the preservation of this paradise. The Road's chief upholder of community solidarity, its militant spokesman in town meetings about any infringement of its rights, he organized watchdog committees, was himself a watchdog committee of one, ready to pounce on anyone who let down the standards of the Road. He had made more than one enemy by interfering where he had no right. In fact he was no longer on speaking terms with the Moores because of reprimanding them for letting the field beside their house become a honeysuckle-choked jungle.

He knew he was a scold but could do nothing to stop himself, nor did he want to. Yet he knew that enmity was a great effort and a monumental waste of time. What else, though, to do with his time? He was always in an uproar about something, and saw to it that he was. While telling himself that Syra's way, her mother's way, was an easier way to live–they let things go, they let live and therefore lived–he also knew, or perhaps had learned in his brief period of psychoanalysis, that there could be no such ease of existence for himself.

Contrary to Mrs. Alexander's conviction that Lewis scorned psychotherapy, he not only did have respect for it (although publicly he debunked it) but had even had some analysis himself, for a brief time after Syra married Georges. The analyst, a gentle gray-haired woman named Clara Tallent, whom Lewis had loved and clung to instantly, had died during his tenth month of analysis, and he had decided then, with convenient equivocation, that it was all a never-ending self-indulgence anyway, and that there were better ways to spend his money. "She *died* on me," he would cry to himself with an anguish no less real for being mocked.

Much of what Lewis had gained in his psychoanalysis was a knowledge of Syra, though not about himself in relation to Syra. He described to Clara so rhapsodically and so repeatedly that eventually even he was sick of it the summer of their "childish, idyllic love." He also repeatedly described the picnic on Syra's thirteenth birthday, and the blissful fearful arousal he labeled calf love, soon to be outgrown. "That was in April. In June Mother took a house in St. Jean de Luz for a month, and on the boat going over I met a cute girl I proceeded to lay–on the top deck in the white moonlight. It was my first copulation, my first, Clara. And. It. Was. Great! That fifteen-year-old chick was no novice, believe it or not. Then in St. Jean I had a fisherman's daughter for a playmate, a dark-eyed Basquaise. Ah, what a playmate! Her hair smelled like a mermaid's. By the end of the month I was as clever in the art of amour as any Frenchman, I do believe. The young learn easy. And I *was* young. fourteen. Oh yes, on that European trip, I outgrew calf love for Syra–those first adolescent stirrings–and in the arms of first one, then another little succubus, I became a man.

"Anyway, in the long run Syra and I were actually more like a deeply attached brother and sister." He described their mutual dependence as children, as teenagers, as young adults: "'Ausec,'" he cried to Clara Tallent with his green eyes tearful, his mouth soft and yearning. "'Ausec,' that wonderful, what shall I call it, life-saver? Anne Knight would call it a support system. Christ, yes." He described with total recall every detail of Syra's wedding–her ballet slippers, new for the occasion, and white, not black, her new cotton shift, her bouquet of daisies and buttercups. He told Clara about giving Syra away, about the seriousness and solemnity he had felt as he had taken her down the aisle on his arm; he elaborated on how almost weak with relief he had been when the ring was safely on her finger and the ceremony concluded.

"I gave her away, Clara."

"Indeed you did."

"What's that tone of voice in aid of?"

"It is for simply agreeing with you that you did give Syra away."

"There's something in your tone of voice that implies more than meets the ear, Clara."

"Is there? Well, then, if there is, tell me about it."

"There's nothing to tell, beyond that. Except my immense, powerful relief at seeing Syra settled. Married. I'm her only close relative. I'm next of kin! I am responsible for her in a way; or rather, was–Georges is now. She hasn't two pennies to rub together. She's a wage earner teaching guitar, and pittance wages they are. She's never wanted to take money from me. But on the other hand, well, my God, she's entirely self-sufficient, isn't she, so what am I saying? But sufficient for what? She's so wackily unworldly. Anyway, I've always felt responsible for her, perhaps because she's so alone. I mean, generally speaking, people are suspicious of Syra, they don't *get* her and so they don't like her. She's different, and so they're afraid of her. She doesn't give what they expect to receive, and she doesn't accept what they need to give. If politeness is called for and she doesn't really feel it, forget it. She can't utter it. *Can't*, doesn't know how to. She's really like an honest child. Most of the manners, the formalities that people support each other with and console each other with in this artificial world are out of the question for Syra. All this, as I've told you, Clara, she was taught by her mother. Of course, it's innate in Syra, it has to be, but still she was shaped by that amazing woman. Poor, darling Syracuse (that name!) is, I think, discovering all the time that the world at large is not the secure paradise of Cazenovia, that safe little town she grew up in and where, up there in the cupola on the roof, her mother taught her, drummed into her, that simplicity and independence that makes her tick, and that to me is so incredibly, soothingly wonderful."

"You make Syra very clear to me, Lewis. Very. And the individualistic mother who named two daughters after upstate New York towns. Pretty names, I think, Syracuse and Geneva. But Lewis, I wish you would tell me now more about your *feelings* for Syra. Will you?"

"Gladly. She is the best thing that ever happened to me, and I could talk about her endlessly, except that I've already told you everything about her, endlessly."

"Yes. But not about how you feel about her. How *do* you feel about her, Lewis?"

"I love her. I've told you again and again that I love her."

"In what way?"

"Well, for one thing, I love her because she loves me, as I've told you endlessly, Clara. She is the only person alive, except you, who makes me sometimes feel good about myself, or if not good about myself, then not always abysmally bad about myself. Also I love her because what comes out of her mouth is so daft and bewitching and childishly wise. She's such marvelous *fun!* Also, she's a person who doesn't latch on. She can love me without moving in. She has no desire to reach out to have and to hold me, and of course it doesn't occur to her to want to influence me. Oh, I'm a shit, I know that, but Syra never criticizes me, or judges me. She lets me be, she doesn't tell me how to be.

"Of course if you want to be critical of Syra, you could say that in one way she's not a participant in life, because she's not in there, fighting, uninvolved I believe is the *mot.* She doesn't *take on* your problems, my problems, world problems. She just does not! Never mind. Let Anne Knight do all that, she's so good at it. No, what's important is that from Syra I even understand, in a part of myself that you and I, Clara, know is as different from my behavioral self as night is from day, that the yes-no consciousness obfuscates, it fucks everything up. Well. Syra hasn't got a yes-no consciousness, basically."

"I wonder, Lewis, if I can interpret what you are saying as meaning that you sense Syra doesn't need to *impress* you with the fact that she loves you; that if Syra did need to *demonstrate* love, she would be overloading you with herself, superimposing her emotions on yours, diluting you with herself, so that you yourself would not be there for her."

"Clara, I get you! You mean, what would be there instead would be an unmanageable blend of Syra and me? Is that what you mean? That by Syra's not forcing love on me, *I know* that what she sees is me? Not some need of her own, but only me, unshadowed by her? Fantastic! If that's what you're saying?"

"Yes, Lewis. You know, sometimes you amaze me. You've paraphrased me exactly. It seems to me that Syra has a way of seeing that is not filtered by self, that loses self in the seeing."

"My good God, woman, that's a nice summary."

"Also, Lewis, I liked your saying quite simply that Syra doesn't judge you. Perhaps that's all one needs to say. That simple word, judgment."

"Oh, yes. Judgment. That word again."

"It's an important word not to forget, Lewis. I hope you never do."

"Oh, I won't, I won't, my Fairy Fay. Not so long as Syra is around. But now don't go lecturing me. That's not what I'm here for. I'm here to say just what I feel like saying, the way Syra's mother taught *her* to do. Actually about her mother, you know, Clara, if anything, Syra is of course a bit too strong on her mother. She's always talking about her–'Mother said this, Mother said that,' spookily, as though her mother were still alive. A bit obsessional about her mother, wouldn't you say?"

"Both you and Syra were strong on your mothers."

"Yes."

"How about your mother and judgment?"

"Well, for Christ's sake, Mother was different. She was conventional, for Christ's sake."

"Conventional?"

"Yes. *Conventional.* I've told you again and again about Mother. I thought we were talking about Syra."

"We were. We are. We were talking about your giving Syra away, to Georges."

"Anne sends her love," Rupert was saying, moving into the living room after Lewis with the book on Vietnam in his hand, "and she says to tell you you *must* read this. We both feel it's very well worth reading." Rupert loved this room, in which everything was faultlessly beautiful. Sun was pouring in the windows whose pitted and uneven old lavender panes, which Lewis had installed, rendered the outdoors disconcertingly indistinct. There were antique wing chairs on either side of the fireplace and above it, always stunning to Rupert, a large painting of an ancient sailing vessel tossing on a turquoise-gray and wildly white-capped sea. The fire was fragrant applewood, snapping gaily, for Lewis had just put on a large log. "Oh, *thisss* is nice. *Thisss* is nice!" Rupert said, looking around him reverently.

Lewis went over to the fireside and dropped into one of the wing chairs. "I'm not going to be a good host and offer you coffee, Rupert," he said apologetically. "I don't have any made and I'm weak as a kitten. But there's sherry. C'm on, how about a sherry?"

"No, thank you, Lewis. Nothing. I'll only stay but a minute, Anne warned me not to tire you." He sat down in the chair opposite Lewis and beside the pleasure of the lively fire, putting the book down on the coffee table. He thought he'd better wait a decent interval before bringing out the agent's letter; Lewis, of course, came first.

"You're not working this morning, Rupert. I thought you were a stickler for the nine-to-twelve bit."

"Well," Rupert beamed, then he dropped his mouth open, and his eyes grew distant, luminous, "well, to tell you the truth, I–" but he couldn't bring himself to say that he'd come here especially to see Lewis when he knew he'd come mostly to show the letter, and he had no lies in his mouth. So he shut it.

At that moment a massive thrumming arose outside–hundreds of redwings rising as one from the lawn. With a rushing twittering upsweep, together they rose black against the sky, then turned and were silver in the sun's glare, then wheeled, black again, and dropped like stones to the field beyond the fence. Lewis and Rupert sat up alertly, both their faces keen, then soft, watching the miraculous contraction and expansion and sweep of it.

"What in life," Rupert cried with stern passion, "tell me what in life is more marvelous, marvelous, than those birds arriving in the spring!"

Lewis, who thought this too but didn't feel just now like letting himself be drawn into Rupert's drama, made a poker face and said nothing. He put his elbows on the arms of his chair, slowly brought all ten trembling fingertips together and pressed them into steadiness, then let his eyes dwell challengingly and coolly on Rupert. Old Phouff, he thought again, coldly, sadly, guiltily.

Rupert made a slight uncomfortable noise, part laugh, refusing to let himself be put out. But then compassion for Lewis took over, and he asked, though he didn't want to know the answer, "How does it go, Lewis, really?"

"Uh, better," tersely. He would not confide in Rupert Knight. He would preserve his self-respect by not blurting everything out to Rupert Knight. "I get tired easily, but I'm sure that's par for the course. Uh, one or two little quirks. Nothing serious, I'm sure."

"The doctor feels everything's all right?"

"Rupert, look, I didn't see the doctor. I called his office and canceled the appointment. You know how I feel about doctors. Anne was kind to think of it, but I don't have any faith in doctors. None of them know anything. I never go to 'em. I know Anne meant well, Rupert, but she did go behind my back, y'know. I didn't ask her to call the doctor, she did it without my knowledge, and then presented me with the fait accompli. But I'm grateful for the thought, the warmth, for her true concern." He was. "Anyway, uh, I'm certainly better. Fever gone, et cetera, et cetera. Only one or two little quirks now."

"Quirks Lewis? Such as?"

"Uh, little pains here and there." And even as he warned himself not to, he heard himself beginning to spill out to

Rupert. "Sometimes not so little." A bright, savage smile flashed on, then off, leaving his face slack. "Oh, look, this pain's from concern, I know it is. And I don't want to go on about it. Don't let me." Though in the next breath he burst out, "The thing is I'm so depressed." He turned his whole body suddenly to take a cigarette out of a little pewter chest on the table at his elbow, thinking with a stab of fear that this was his fifth today. He lit it with unsteady hands, then sank back into the chair, collapsed back, the cigarette wobbling in his fingers, while above a bravado smile, his eyes begged. "It's probably just being weakened, but I can't get out of it."

Rupert cleared his throat uncomfortably, wishing Lewis hadn't spoken this way. He did not want to get into a discussion of illness, either physical or mental. He knew Lewis was calling for help, he could feel the appeal vibrantly, but he did not want to get into this at all, and would not, particularly on this day that was so gloriously *his*. He would not, *would not* have the joy of this day diminished!

He wanted to change the subject, but helplessly, not a thought came into his head. To have no words, to be soundless in the presence of another, was disturbingly unfamiliar to Rupert. He felt vulnerable, as though naked in a dream.

At length he said decently, gently, "Dear Lewis, I'm no expert, don't you know that? It seems to me it's a doctor you should be talking to. Or Anne." He brightened. "Yes. Anne would, I know, love to help you, if she could. Anne's *professional*," he cried on an upsweep of confidence.

But help from Rupert was what Lewis wanted. Let him be weak, and let Rupert be self-contained, he suddenly needed a confessor above all else, needed rescue. And not, God forbid, from Anne. He wanted Rupert to reassure him, to dispel his fears, to tell him it was all nonsense, to tell him that he had no real reason for being depressed, that everything passes, that tomorrow he'd wake up and find this whole miasma of fear and concern gone. That was what he wanted from Rupert, and he could have swallowed it, he could have been instantly and greatly cheered had Rupert only chosen to say all this to him.

There was a long, pounding silence, which Rupert brought to an end by cautiously clearing his throat.

Oh, fuck off, Lewis thought, and he drew a quivering sigh, sucked long and avidly on his cigarette, and tried to pull himself together. So there was to be no help, anywhere. Well, of course. How childish to expect rescue from without.

"Well, well," he said briskly, "enough of this." He reached for the book on the table, turned it over and glanced impatiently at the back of the jacket and then set it down, almost slapped it down, onto the table. "Another book about Vietnam," he said tersely. He felt a flush of irritation. And he said to Rupert in a voice without conviction, thin and even timid, "Well, thank Anne for it. I don't know when I'll get to it, mysteries are all I feel up to these days, light reading. Uh, really I think you'd better take it back. But thank her for it. I know about his work, he's very good, Bernard Fall is. Very good."

"Well, you do like his work," Rupert said. "Then keep it, keep it. We're through with it." He waved a hand in a slow, grand way that seemed to Lewis both impressive and irritatingly arrogant.

"I really *can't*, Rupert," Lewis burst out sharply. "I have just finished explaining to you that I *can't*! It'll bother my conscience if it's there on my table day after day, unread. Listen, *I* know the world needs to be reformed, too," he cried combatively, "but *I* don't feel a perpetual obligation to reform it, the way Anne does. Anne's a *reformer*."

Rupert sniffed and compressed his lips. His brown eyes had dulled to a flatness, evasiveness. He felt uncomfortably unable to stand up for Anne, though he thought he should. He cleared

42

his throat, embarrassed. "I wouldn't say that, Lewis," he said carefully, while thinking that because of Lewis's unpleasantness, of course he could not now show him the letter. And he should go, obviously. "I wouldn't say that at *all*," he said again in a fair, reasoning way that further irritated Lewis.

But he didn't want to rise to leave too abruptly, reminding himself that Lewis was a "handful" these days, and feeling keenly the rawness of the man's misery. He would leave in a leisurely, dignified way; he had no wish to return rudeness for rudeness.

Silence. The fire pranced with a loud, cheerful insensitivity. Neither man looked at the other. Rupert studied his fingernails, debating how he could say, considerately and not too abruptly, that he must leave. Lewis pursed his lips in defiance and shame, wondering what he could say to redeem himself.

But he could think of nothing to say. And really he was damned if he wanted to, anyway. Let there be silence, he thought. There's nothing the matter with silence.

He let everything go for a moment. He let any kind of effort go. And into the space of his mind, suddenly as though it had only been waiting for a cleared stage, there flashed the whole scene of Syra's birthday party by the sea. It had seized him in the middle of last night, this memory revisited, revitalized, and had been in him vividly on and off all morning, growing, expanding, aching, so that he had sat trancelike for hours, completely taken over by it. He had forgotten those dark areas in himself, and that they had once ached fully; he was amazed, curious, even frightened, that even now they could ache dimly. A discovery, he thought, that's what had seized him in the middle of the night, a discovery. All morning he had been wanting to come back to what there was about it that was a discovery.

Rupert was looking at him curiously.

Ha' pas' kissing time, Lewis thought. He should say something to Rupert, who was staring. Kissing time, how accurate,

Syra and Georges kissing behind some dune. A birthday present for Syra. He felt suddenly furious with both of them.

For a moment he thought he knew that this was the discovery. But then he said to himself, no. Ridiculous. Then he said to himself that the discovery had to do with being alone, that is, being without sexual fidelity. And he assured himself that this was of course so. He was alone, he had no woman. He had never felt aloneness as clearly as he had that day. None of them, that day by the sea, had really had anyone, most of all himself. Heloise had been shown to be an illusion as far as fidelity to himself was concerned, and fidelity to Syra was an illusion, for Heloise had made it clear that she was tempting Georges, and Georges had made it clear that he was tempted. Which left Syra alone, didn't it? All of them alone.

He saw now that he desperately needed Syra to be safely, respectably married. He had given her away in marriage, delivered her over to the safety of marriage. The thought that it mightn't be safe made him anxious in a new, compelling way. And this felt like an idea leading to the discovery, coming close to the discovery.

Ha' pas' kissing time...Yes, take it or leave it, that was the discovery, that silly sentence. Why the hell?

Fury rose uncontrollably in him. Syra and Georges making love behind the dunes, flaunting sexuality that way, right in front of everyone, in front of the children, in front of him!

He looked at Rupert. He must say something. "Excuse me, Rupert," he said coolly, "I lapsed. I was thinking about Syra's birthday."

"Oh?"

"Yes," he said forcefully, giving Rupert a cold stare back, "next week's her birthday, her thirty-eighth."

"Oh, *indeed?*"

44

A knock on the porch door was the sound of rescue to them both. They rose with a haste they both found absurd and embarrassing, looking eagerly toward the hall, as they heard the door open, heard quick steps. And then here was Mrs. Alexander, striding into the room.

"Well, look who's here," she cried. "How nice. Lewis, good morning. And Rupert." She held out her hand, smiling and saying, "Hello, there," to Rupert, who took it in both of his as though it were a gift and pressed it with warmth.

"I just stopped by on my way to the village to see if there's anything you need," she said to Lewis, going over to him and touching his arm. Her jaunty voice was the voice of a ministering angel, flooding the room, Lewis thought. He perked up, still eager for rescue though now he darkly disbelieved in the possibility of it. He would have liked to put his arms around her marvelous little person, and hold onto her, knowing he would feel both the bedrock of her strong small muscular frame and the senescence of her cloth-enclosed loose skin. But he loved that. His tiny mother, when he hugged her, had been weightless and dry as old ashes, and fragrant.

"Well, Rupert, what d'you think of our boy? He looks better, don't you think? He's the limit, though," she said with dry vivacity. "Know what I found him doing yesterday? Defrosting the icebox. You're just terrible," she said to Lewis, and patted him.

Rupert loved her. And in the tension of the moment, he loved her particularly. He looked at her small face, which was almost square, plain, but with so much self-assurance evident in the set of the head, in the unhesitating mannerisms of the mouth, in the strong, amused, even arrogant penetration of the fine eyes, that he had never once thought of her as plain, had never even bothered to define her as either plain or pretty.

"How are you liking your new pedometer, Mrs. A?" he asked suddenly. "Anne and I can't get over your buying a *pedometer!*"

Mrs. Alexander crimped her mouth into a smile that delighted in and just barely apologized for audacity. "Oh I threw it the hell away," she said.

"You *did?*" Rupert burst into an explosion of laughter, Lewis too.

"I did indeed. It kept bashing against my hip and I couldn't get my mind off it. Spoiled everything. Silly. Anyway, I don't need to know how far I walk. I've gotten along all these years without knowing how far I walk in a day. I was finally just curious, that's why I fell for one," she said, smoothing her hands down her corseted neat front. She had on a citified navy blue wool dress with a jacket, the type of thing she always wore, country clothes being alien to her. Tweeds and sweaters, a country look versus a city look, had been unknown to Mrs. Alexander's country-bred mother, and to Mrs. Alexander as a girl and a woman. Even now, she thought of "country clothes" as costumes. It always amused her that the minute city people moved to the country they peeled off their finery and put on the worst old things. "You should hear her on the subject," Lewis would tell people delightedly.

Her navy blue oxfords were polished, and there was nothing indeterminate about the two small feet so securely planted on the wonderful colors of the old hooked rug. Her stance, Rupert thought, told almost everything there was to know about her. There she stood (and he could take comfort in the sight), with her granite self-assurance, with her energy disproportionate to her size, and with a simmering enthusiasm for life and an expectant eye that hoped for, he thought, and usually found, amusement in it somewhere.

"I haven't seen that Anne of yours in ages," she said to Rupert, who charmed her, squeezing his sleeve and running her freckled dry hand up and down it until with a final series of pats she took it away. "And isn't this a day?" she said. "No, I'm not even going to sit down, no, no, really," as Lewis began to pull another chair toward the fire. "I've endless errands. And Bernice needs flour. Within an hour. Rupert, there, that's a poem, my dear. I give you leave to use it in one of your columns. So, my dear," turning to Lewis, "what do you need? And sit *down*," she ordered. "I'm going to quickly do your breakfast dishes, but sit *down*, Lewis, truly."

Lewis sank back into his wing chair, looking happily helpless, and jabbed his hands out, palms upward, fingers stiff and tremblingly widespread. "See how she bosses me around. She came in here and drove me out of the kitchen yesterday, she marched up to make my bed, only it was already made." He grinned impishly. "You should have known it would be, Mrs. A., I'd make my bed if I had to do it with my teeth. I can't stand unmade beds."

"Well, neither can I. But do tell me now, though, what you need in the village before I go out to the kitchen so's I can check your icebox. I'm going to the drugstore, and the A&P, and the cobbler, and I'm even going, believe it or not, to that new, vast, milling discount place to buy a transistor radio to take out to the garden while I'm doing the weeding. I know it'll drown out the birds, and that appalls you both, but truthfully, I'd rather listen to the ball game. I know you'll say I have no imagination. And I guess I haven't, come to think of it."

Lewis reached out a tender hand and put it on her shoulder. "You don't need it."

"Gracious. I don't know about that."

"I do."

"They say it enriches you."

"I'd rather be without it. I'd rather be like you."

"Don't say that, my dear boy. You are as you are. I like your imagination. Look at this perfectly beautiful room. Look at the way you've fixed those flowers on that mantlepiece."

"I like his imagination, too," said Rupert. "It gives me great pleasure. And Anne."

"Oh God," said Lewis.

"Why, oh God?"

"Just, oh God, period."

There was a strained silence. Then Mrs. Alexander said vigorously, "I must be going. First, I'll just pop out and do your breakfast dishes."

"No, no, I'll do them," Lewis cried, jumping up.

"You most certainly will not. It'll take all of three minutes."

"But I'm not that weak," Lewis protested. And he wasn't. Yet how good to be coddled.

"I must be going, too," Rupert said. "Lewis, I'm glad I can go back and report to Anne that you're looking better." He smiled kindly. Mrs. Alexander had saved the day and the little squall was already banished from his mind, hadn't happened. He just felt compassion for Lewis, and understanding. And since he was itching to, he thought he *would* show the letter after all, or perhaps better not *show* it. But he'd tell!

He cleared his throat once, cleared it several times. Then he said grandly, "I've some news I feel quite sure you both may be pleased to hear." He threw Lewis, then Mrs. Alexander, a sly, radiant look. "Pangrove Press wants to make a book out of my columns! They've *approached* me."

"Why, Rupert, that's just marvelous," Lewis burst out incredulously.

"My work has begun to improve, you know," Rupert said in a confiding calm way. "The editor of Pangrove likened my work to E. B. White. First Thoreau—my agent tells me I'm like Thoreau—and now E. B. White! I am very reassured, very," he said with a complacent strong pride that appeared, Lewis thought, to be in agreement with both plaudits.

In spite of his contempt for such boasting, Lewis couldn't help but say, "I know your work's getting super, Rupert. It certainly deserves being brought together in a book. My very, very sincere and very heartfelt congratulations."

"Oh," said Rupert with a great smile of pleasure, "well, well, I'm so *pleased*, so *pleased*," while Mrs. Alexander chimed in, looking polite. "Pangrove! My! I think it's wonderful, and I'm just delighted for you." She was, though she had preferred Rupert's weekly gardening columns in the *Deer Valley Gazette* to the essays he had supplanted them with. She knew about his longing for recognition, though she hadn't much patience with it, couldn't understand it, to be exact. "I hope I'll get an autographed copy," she said airily, and with this remark, which Rupert thought frivolously inadequate, she turned and went off to the kitchen.

"The letter was most flattering," Rupert said to Lewis quietly, but then he swaggered a little to cover a certain embarrassment, and tipped his head to one side in a pose of bashful modesty. "The advance will be quite princely. At least to me it seems so."

"Well, money's always nice," Lewis said flippantly, because he did dislike that roguish pose, and, come to think of it, that vanity, that vanity.

Rupert shrugged. "Yes, money's always nice." He put his hand on Lewis's shoulder. "Lewwwisss. Lewwwisss. Take care of yourself now. Get rest. Rest a lot. Let me help with the heavy work. I'd be glad to. Don't overdo it." He gave Lewis's shoulder a warming squeeze, but his eyes were secretive, and he did not smile.

From the kitchen, from out of the clatter of dishes, came the lively voice of Mrs. Alexander. "That's right. You talk turkey to him, because that's what he needs. He needs to be talked turkey to."

They both smiled at this. And suddenly Lewis couldn't bear to have Rupert leave with questions and regrets about this visit. He wanted peace. He was ashamed. He wanted the perpetual warm neighborliness of the Knights. And the friendship of this man. He put out a hand, touched Rupert's arm, thinking to be companionable, to make amends. "If I were you I'd be delighted at the flattery," he said, overflowingly. "I don't know anyone who deserves it more." He cocked his head to one side and looked pert and sagacious. "Anyway," he intoned, and the quote poured out like some sudden uncontrolled excretion, "anyway, 'pampered vanity is a better thing perhaps than starved pride.'"

This struck Rupert as outrageous. He turned without a word, massively. And Lewis at once knew his own spitefulness. How, and why, in God's name, had that come out of him? Feebly, apologetically, he followed Rupert into the hall, finding nothing to say. What could he say?

Rupert hunched himself into his coat and without looking at Lewis called out a controlled goodbye to Mrs. Alexander, and left.

And Mrs. Alexander came striding out of the kitchen, smiling, talking, wriggling widespread fingers that were not quite dry. "I do wish they wouldn't *perfume* dishwashing liquid. I often ask myself what Mother would think. Mother had a scorn of folderol."

"Did she?" Lewis asked. "I'm sure she did. You have too, haven't you, Mrs. A.? *I* have too," he said, tragically, but with a sort of smirk, making failure seem appealing rather than despicable. "I have too, but no one will ever know it."

❧ IV ❧

THE desk faced the window, and on it were islands of neatly stacked and weighted papers in conscious design to please the imitatively aesthetic eye and the organized personality of Anne Knight, whose room this was and who sat there now writing a letter, her sturdy legs wide apart and her feet in old embroidered mules braced upon the floor in a determined way. Her narrow face had a healthy, clear-skinned pallor in which her light gray eyes blazed with fierce purpose. She was seething with concentration, her body held so still as to appear scarcely breathing. Only her hand moved, the pencil occasionally slashing across the yellow pad.

An hour had passed when suddenly she was finished. She flipped the pages back to the beginning and with difficulty read what she had written–sections of it were crossed out, reworked, bracketed–holding her hand with pencil immobile high above the pad, as though by some command, moving her lips in a little biting anxious way as she scanned it back and forth, back and forth, hating those words which didn't seem to relate to her, sickening words. She both hated them and couldn't believe them. She slumped back, sighing with a kind of impatient anger. Then she flung the letter onto the desk, fed up with it, and not sure of it, either. She turned her head to the window and looked out again upon her world, twilit, and April, and full of a number of things that she had been fool enough to neglect for the past hour.

"Magnificent," she whispered energetically. She heard the robin, who had all along been filling the twilight with his trilling tremble of song. Deep in the woods, beyond the gray and black of old stone walls, sere grasses and leaf floor, tall bare trees and their long strict shadows, beyond what was visible, a woodpecker rattled. And giving the sound of it her complete attention she felt an almost lifelike relationship, suddenly, between it and the pencil in her fingers, insistent and sharp-pointed and instrumentlike and disruptive of the cool spring peace.

She thrust the pencil impatiently into a mug full of them, to rid her fingers, herself, of the scourge of mentality. The machinelike thing she was momentarily sickened her, and she softened and yearned toward an amorphous something out there, or in her perhaps, a secession from living in the mind, something free, fluid as the robin's song, belonging, as its song did, to the joy of spring.

And now I will stop thinking about death, she said to herself, suddenly and impatiently. She leaned forward against the desk and crossed one arm over the other in preparedness for concentration, and began to read what she had written.

Friday, April 9th
For Rupert, a letter to you in case I should die before you:
Rupo dear,
If I were to begin with "Beloved Rupert" I would be acting in accordance with the horrible convention of obituaries the sense of which I am setting out to eliminate from my own. That sounds pompous and portentous, and I mean it to be. I must admit that I was tempted to begin this obituary of mine with that corny salutation just for the fun of it. The light touch seems to be insisting that I make its little voice heard, probably to cheer me up for the task at hand.

Yesterday we signed our separate wills. (And how many yesterdays have elapsed since then, I wonder?) Yesterday was the 8th of April. And what is today's date, I mean the date of the day you are reading this? I wouldn't know, being as I am, dead.

The facing of my will was an act of more significance than I would have expected. I didn't relish that substitute-for-reality interchange of questions and answers, of signatures, of perfect manners. I signed a paper whereon were words I had conceded: "And, if I should predecease my husband..." Those words struck me like knives, I'll tell you the reason in a minute. But in spite of the unpleasantness I felt at conceding those words, still, I felt I was lying, knowing consciously that I do not mean to die, even though unconsciously I have accepted the fact that I cannot live forever. I suppose there is no paradox here. For even though I have at last, about to turn fifty, assimilated the knowledge of my own mortality, I still "rage, rage against the dying of the light." Yes, I have acknowledged my mortality with both practicality and rage. But contradictorily, like billions of other poor humans, I at least *know*, and yet I don't *believe*, that someday I will die.

Anyway, yesterday, just as we were coming out of that office building, the idea came to me, I suppose because of our discussion of wanting to be cremated and Mr. Holdsum's suggesting we both write letters to that effect to be left with our wills, the idea that I would leave a letter of instruction with you about the kind of memorial service I want for myself. Knowing your tendencies toward church services and music, which isn't my kind of thing at all, I guess I do want to tell you how important it is to me that I be assured I won't have that sort of dramatic memorial service. I so passionately believe that eulogizing wipes out the real person, is the final burial, the final fraud.

So, here is my proposal, bequest, you might say. I call it my legacy of truth. I would like to have a memorial gathering held for me in my own living room long enough after my death for you to be up to it. I would like to have everything eliminated from it that smacks of that word "beloved," which only has meaning when it is meant. I would like it to be devoid of any funereal element—no music, no flowers, no hushed voices—just an informal gathering of a few friends who will sit down in comfortable chairs, maybe with drinks or tea, and "pay their respects" to me (I mean that literally) in a spontaneous and honest way, that is, talk about me not with obituarylike hypocrisy, but with naturalness. I consider that to be respect for the dead.

I ask people gathered together for this memorial, then, insofar as they possibly can, to speak about what they truly feel about me, so that hopefully a sense of the real me will be felt, rather than that of some unreal, idealized woman. I ask them please not to just pick out the good parts of me to talk about, because that won't be the whole truth of me, and will have no more meaning than the funeral oration by the clergyman who, more often than not, never even knew the deceased and whose eulogies are only based on what the grieving, sometimes guilty bereaved have told him. I would wish that each person will try to express as honestly as possible what he or she feels about me. At least then they'll all know that the service has been about me, not about someone else, and so will you, and I feel that for the duration of this memorial gathering, at least, I will be remembered as I truly was. (God, how I hate that past tense!) I want the dignity of this kind of a memorial service.

As for who should be invited to the gathering, well, close friends—Lewis, Mrs. Alexander, the Metcalfs, my "adopted daughters" of course—Ava and Susan and Eunice, and a few neighbors and such, only the closest, those who will give you the most solace by their presence. I only wish

I didn't have to miss it! (Maybe I don't mean that. Maybe it will be hard even for you.) Anyway I hope that what results won't be too hard on you, dear.

I must force myself, now, to write what I have to tell you. It's the sickening news from Dr. Lovelace (what a name for a gynecologist!). Six months ago I went for my yearly checkup, and also because my periods were getting longer and alarmingly extreme. He said he hoped it could be controlled by medication, but to come back to him in three months' time if the pills didn't work.

Well, they didn't. So I went back, just three months ago, in January. It was then he told me that we should give it another three months' try, with another kind of medication, but if that didn't work, I'd have to have a hysterectomy!

Well, my dearest, the fact is, these pills aren't working either. And I seem to know, in my bones, that they won't. And that I'll have to...Oh no, I can't even say it again, much less write it down. The intensity of my reactions is really beyond my grasp. But there you are, or I mean there they are. Between menstruations, I've managed to bury the whole thing. Almost. Sometimes during the night I think about it.

I didn't tell you, Rupo dear, deliberately. Telling you would have exhumed the faint alarm over it. And I wanted to ignore it.

But apparently this whole *Will* thing, along with the likelihood of that operation, has brought about some kind of crisis in myself. And what I'm having to face, Rupo, as I'm about to turn fifty, what's suddenly so difficult for me to deal with, is that I've deprived us both of the child I could have borne. That's what this miserable situation has precipitated in me, brought to the surface, I mean has revealed to me. What am I trying to say? What I'm trying to say, and will say, is that you've always wanted a child so terribly. Lovely, gentle man, what a father you would have made. Did I want a child? I don't *feel* as though I did back then. I had you. And work has always been, aside from loving you, my basic need and satisfaction. I know I couldn't have worked and had a child, too. Many women do, but not me. A child would have taken all of me, I know this absolutely.

We talked it all over, as you know, even before we were married. You said you wanted children. I wasn't sure I did, though I love children. Then, after we were married, I was just starting my business. I couldn't have had a baby then. And when the business was going well, by that time I was almost forty, and we'd begun to save up for a country house, and we couldn't afford a baby then, either. And we both agreed it was too late to have a child.

But I think it was at that point that I was beginning to be divided about wanting a child. Sort of. Yet I couldn't, in myself, decide *for* it. I couldn't. Oh, Rupo, my love, why? Why couldn't I? And why, Rupo, come to think of it, didn't you press for it? Why did you always go along with me? Was it *my* voice that decided this sterility for us? Somehow I always felt that you agreed with me, even though I knew how much you longed for a child. I know, too, that you would have had to stop writing, and go to work, and that that was a major consideration in our never having a child.

It was the major consideration in what I am now going to have to tell you. Looking back on the difficulty of that decision, I know that I was right, agonizing though it was. And yet the sorrow, and the guilt, yes, guilt, have never left me. I was, I see, both right and wrong, even though such a statement may seem to make no sense.

So here goes. You will be shocked. You will be, perhaps, outraged. You may hate me. But I am going to tell you nevertheless. Seven years ago this August I missed a period. At first I didn't believe what it was. Then, all of a sudden, a panic of both fear and wild joy hit me, both dread and hope. I had the rabbit test, scoffing but hoping, hoping with an incredible joy. The result came. *Positive!*

Suddenly I was someone else. I was a woman going to have a baby. My whole world shifted. My body became a different body–woman's body functioning in its primary way. Can you imagine, yes, you can, how I longed to rush to you and tell you that you and I were going to have a baby? I will never get over what I missed by not seeing the look on your face when you heard that you would be a father. Yes, my first, wonderful impulse was to rush to you and tell you. But then something just as powerful drowned out my heart and body longing, something more powerful, you see, for I did not rush to tell you. Instead, I waited. I waited one week. I waited two weeks.

A third week went by, and I still hadn't brought myself to tell you. I didn't know what was holding me back, and so I waited. Then, one day, sitting in my office, I suddenly realized I wouldn't tell you. I knew, with a feeling, I have to admit, of great, of poisonous relief, that, though part of you wanted a child, yet a greater part of you powerfully did not, and that you had never pressed for it because that was so. Yes. I saw, clearly, terribly, that neither you nor I could live that way. I sat there, in my career-making office, and saw that if we had a baby, you would lose your writing, having to go out to work while I stayed at home. At least for a few years. Which would be enough to absolutely crush your way of being. I saw us both losing our work, losing–ourselves. It was too strong, this long habit of the building up and the development of our work–career making, not child making. And I knew if I told you I was pregnant, you would want to keep the child. I know this absolutely. You wouldn't have permitted an abortion–not because you're antiabortion, but simply because you are you.

Anyway, then and there I simply needed to get that child out of me, and to get us back to normal. So after much desperate furtive research I gave myself an abortion with a drug that is supposed to cause uterine bleeding and in my case did. Dr. Lovelace told me later that I would probably have aborted naturally anyway, at my age and with my tendency to hemorrhage that was already beginning to develop. There was a moment of relief in knowing that, which didn't last long. For after all, I *had* decided against it, and I *hadn't* told you, and I *had* tried to destroy it–him/her. Oh, God! Him, her! And I knew the monumental unfairness of that. For I do believe that you, as my husband, have rights to my womb. I remember asking myself whether a womb was solely its owner's, or there to be jointly owned. And my answer, positively and passionately, was that it was there to be jointly owned. A womb cannot perform its function without a man's impregnation of it, so therefore, if a man and a woman intend to put her womb to use for the creation of their child, then that womb is in part his. (I should have been a lawyer, yes? no?) Therefore, I am biologically *and* spiritually bound to consult my husband if the occupant of that womb, put there by him, is to be destroyed. A splendid concept, yes? Which I believed, but did not adhere to. And so here I sit, ashamed of myself, knowing that nothing will ever alter my conviction that I had no right to destroy your child without consulting you.

Have I lost you, Rupo? Are you sitting there, looking at these words, and hating me? That's all I can think of these days, plus the operation. And the fear and panic about that, which comes and goes, I *hate*.

I didn't plan on telling you this, when I first thought of my memorial service letter. It somehow flowed out of me today as I started to write. However, in a certain sense it's been good to get it all down on paper. Oh, dearest Rupo, how I love you. And if there is anything in you that can accept that I made the decision to destroy our child primarily for your sake, perhaps you can forgive me.

Your Anne

She put the pad down. She felt a certain bravado, and a certain bedrock relief. But she also felt a strange, unfamiliar unsureness, along with a fear she couldn't understand. And because she could not understand it, fear increased, setting her heart to pounding.

What had she done? Why had she wallowed in a confession? Yes, wallowed was the word. Hadn't she done something, well, weak, something perversely unlike herself? It was only, looking at it clinically, a self-indulgence, wasn't it? Getting it off her chest, in order to rest in peace? Confession–that most enfeebling of all human impulses! Anne, how could you have lapsed so unprofessionally? she scolded herself. She despised the thought of any confession, but a *posthumous* confession! What cowardice. If she was going to confess to Rupert, she should do it now, face to face.

Ordinarily she was self-confident, even aggressively so. She knew the reality of standing on her own two feet, of working to earn her and Rupert's living, and because she faced the world and knew she could deal with it, she was determined never to let inner questions, fears, slow her down or pit the granite of the solid self she had sculptured. Even as a child she had had to let the fire and pluck that were native to her decide her behavior and her direction. She learned to fight coolly, with her mind. And usually won. Grew vivaciously and cleverly bossy. Uncompromising. Needed to lead, and led.

Yet now she sat here helpless with uncertainty.

Suddenly she snatched up the pad and began to read the letter again, sighing now and then impatiently, for the words had become a force to plow through, like a strong incoming tide, something against her. At the end of it she caught her lip under her teeth and held it there and closed her eyes.

She heard Rupert in the kitchen, walking slowly back and forth, opening the refrigerator door, closing it. She heard the clatter of ice. Oh, how I want a drink, she thought furiously.

She opened her eyes wide. Then with no hesitation and with a sigh of relief, as though she had saved herself from a blunder of unimaginable consequences, she set to work to remove from the pad the whole section of the letter dealing with her confession.

When this was accomplished, she smacked paper and carbon into her typewriter and set brusquely to work to type the memorial service letter—let's get the thing out of the *way*! When she had finished the last page, she ripped it out of the typewriter and read it through swiftly and appraisingly. "Okaaaay," she said aloud.

Then she picked up the handwritten sheaf of yellow pages that was the confession and held it up in front of her, looking at it and consulting it in such a thoughtful and inquisitive way that it developed its own authority and seemed to be the controlling factor here now. The question was, should she keep it, and if so, why? Something had come out of her, something that felt like a part of herself, organic really, something that was alive in her, like an organ, or an artery. Or, a fetus? She couldn't destroy it.

She held it uncertainly, respectfully. Finally she took a paper clip from a tray in front of her and secured the copy of the typed letter to the face of the confession. And then with a decisive movement she opened a leather folder at the back of the desk, thrust the papers into it, and flapped it closed.

She signed the typewritten letter and folded it in three. Taking an envelope from the drawer, she addressed it to Mr. Holdsum and put the letter into it, and thence into her briefcase. She would sent it to Mr. Holdsum in due course, and there it would be, a part of herself to be handed to Rupert after her death. A voice from the grave. But nevertheless a voice, she told herself jocularly.

"And now I really will stop thinking about death," she said emphatically. She picked up a pencil lying on the desk and put it carefully back into the mug. She saw pencils and concentrated on pencils, trying to obliterate a fresh flood of alarm that was making her breath come short and her hand shake. For a moment she didn't know what to do, where to turn in order to deny all this.

On impulse, though she had planned to do this sometime during the evening, she picked up the telephone and dialed Mrs. Alexander's number, and then sat back in her chair, listening to the ringing, which meant that the line wasn't busy and that in seconds Bernice would be answering. She began to select her opening words, and her hand, whose shaking had appalled her and that she saw as milk white in the dusk, gradually steadied as she concentrated on it, and on those words forming in her head, so that this pale light hand of hers and these words of hers became to her dominant and strengthening.

❧ V ❧

IN her upstairs sitting room, Mrs. Alexander, her white head alert and still as a deer's, supper tray on her lap, was watching the evening news, with Walter Cronkite. An electric heater throbbed and whirred near enough to fan its dusty warmth upon her as she ate the last of her lamb chop, casting her eyes down now and then to its growing coldness to pick fussily and hurriedly with knife and fork at the morsel of meat between the sheathes of fat, then with relief looking back to the television screen, where not duty, but interest, lay. Her purée of lima beans was eaten, and her mashed potatoes, for those she could eat without looking down, simply by stabbing her fork into what felt soft on the plate.

Bernice appeared in the semidarkness and ambled in to take the tray, bringing a saucer of fruit jello.

"Ugh," said Mrs. Alexander, casting a quick glance at it.

"The doctor says you've gotta," grumbled Bernice, who had bossed Mrs. Alexander for thirty-five years.

"I know it," snapped Mrs. Alexander. Then she said jauntily, thrusting a quivering hand that held her bunched-up napkin toward the screen, "I've got a crush on him."

"Likewise," said Bernice musingly. She sat comfortably down without invitation in the little rose velvet fireside chair, which creaked, swayed under her weight, and holding the tray on her wide lap, concentrated her sour old creased face upon the screen.

"They pronounce it Cron-kite, not Cronk-ite the way you'd think they would," said Mrs. Alexander, but to herself and only for the sound, the bond, which talking made, for this was not the kind of topic Bernice could get into. "He's just so *nice*."

"I wonder is he married."

"Oh, I should think so. Lucky woman."

"Ayah."

Their companionableness, in the theatrical dusk and the crackle of video noise, was easy and time mellowed. Bernice burped. Her large bosom jumped, as did the tray, clattering, on her lap. Mrs. Alexander dipped unwatching into the smoothness of fruit jello, for this she could contend with too without looking at it. "How old would you say he is?" she asked through a nicely managed mouthful of jello, as the commercial for Kent cigarettes came on.

Bernice laid her arms across her stomach and began to knead the dough of her elbows with ruminative fingers. "Well," she said finally, "my guess is about middle fifty. The way he gets around. And plenty of hair still."

"Yes. And his *mind's* so active. I can't get over all he knows about space and blast-offs and capsules, all of which utterly mystifies me."

"Ayah."

The telephone rang. It was not spry Mrs. Alexander who got up to answer it, but Bernice, for this was the order of things. Sighing, she put the tray on the stool and rose hippopotamously. Arthritis she had, too, as well as excess flesh, which made going doubly, ponderously slow. "For you," she said, holding out the receiver. "Mrs. Knight," she muttered. Then, sighing again, she took the tray and went, for this was the order of things too—no lingering to overhear Mrs. Alexander's telephone conversations.

On her desk beside the silver-framed Bachrach photograph of her long dead husband Billy, Mrs. Alexander put down the saucer, and picked up the receiver.

"My dear, how are you?" With a blue-veined hand Mrs. Alexander reached impatiently for the cord to pull the old faded chintz curtains across the window behind her.

"Hi!" Anne's eager, light, pouncing voice. "Look, am I interrupting your dinner?"

"Not at all. How are you both?"

"We're okaaay," rather shrilly. "How are you?"

"In love with Walter Cron-kite." Mrs. Alexander scooped a mite of jello into her spoon, brought it to her mouth, sucked it in and smiled wickedly.

Anne, unable to be amused, paused before saying "Oh," in an uncomprehending way. Then she gave a gossamer tardy laugh, paused again, politely, and launched, because these preliminaries chafed her and let's get on with it, into the reason for her call.

"Look," she said with great, significant emphasis, "I'm very concerned about Lewis. And to come straight to the point, what I feel, Mrs. A., is that we've got to think of some way to get him to a therapist. This I feel very strongly. I was wondering, do you know whether he knows anyone he likes and trusts? I know several excellent people, one woman in particular who'd be very good for him, who has the delicacy I think Lewis would react favorably to. I myself favor a woman because he's more comfortable with women. But then of course that's his problem. I was wondering." Anne slowed down to an ingratiating, calmer pace. "What is your thinking about Lewis? And would it be possible for *you* to suggest therapy to him, do you think? I feel we can't ignore what's going on there. Lewis needs help. Be under no illusions, Lewis is a sick man. Look, I know one has to want therapy, and I understand the danger of interference. Perhaps it won't work. But I feel we must try."

"Wait a sec while I turn off the sound," said Mrs. Alexander. Then, "Sorry," breathlessly, "that thing was making such a racket." But she had left the picture on, to watch when Anne did the talking, which Anne was apt to do interminably, she knew.

"Oh," said Anne. Another light laugh. Then seriousness again. "What is your thinking?"

"Goodness me. Why, gracious, I don't know. I don't know a thing about therapy except what I read now and then, articles in magazines. I don't know a soul, I mean any therapists. Oh, but what you asked me was whether Lewis knew anyone. Why, Anne, not so far as I know. We've talked about psychoanalysis sometimes, I don't mean for him, I mean about the subject of it, but I think he has a kind of scorn for it. You know our boy." Mrs. Alexander leaned over and turned the electric heater so that it beamed upon her legs. Then she said firmly, "My dear, I think Lewis'd be furious if anyone suggested it to him. I do agree with you, though, that Lewis is awfully tense. Picky. I was there this morning and he was being awfully picky. I don't know what manic-depressive means, to tell you the truth. That's the kind of thing you psychological people know and I don't. *However,* Lewis *is* tense. Though don't you think maybe it's just this flu thing he's had and it's been such a long winter, here in the country alone? Though I know he adores it. Don't you think it's just that, just this flu thing and being cooped up with it? Poor boy, he's really awfully alone in that house by himself. I often think for a young man like Lewis, a city's better."

Anne paused, gathering her forces to deal with ignorance. Then she said confidently, "I think I'll go down in the morning and have a talk with him. I'll be careful."

"Anne, please don't do this," said Mrs. Alexander, sternly and unexpectedly.

"You think it's unwise?" Anne could back down faster than anyone would suppose.

"Yes, I do. I feel he does need something, my dear. Maybe just a regular doctor. But there's only one person can get to that man, and that's his cousin Syra Gachet."

"Do you think we should contact her?" The genuine part of Anne's concern made her suddenly warm, hesitant.

"She's on vacation in Nassau. But gracious, I think it would be a disservice to Lewis to *write* to her. This would seem awfully alarmist to me. I don't think this is a situation for going behind Lewis's back. No, I think that would be out of the question." She yawned, pushed up her glasses and rubbed at one eye, then let the glasses drop back into place. "I don't think there's anything to *do*, my dear, except what we've been doing. Going in and seeing him, and doing whatever errands he needs." She looked at Billy and blew him a little kiss with her forefinger.

"Perhaps." Anne was uncertain, unconvinced, but respectful of Mrs. Alexander, whose clearance, after all, she had felt the need of. "Well," after a long pause, "Okaaay." The word drawn out and skeptically acquiescent.

"Nice to talk to you, Anne," said Mrs. Alexander briskly. Good-bys were exchanged. She put the receiver down, perplexed to the point of exasperation, but too good-natured to dwell on it. What did manic-depressive mean? Anne, or what she really thought of as Anne's "type," was a stranger to her, and she had the effect on Mrs. Alexander of making her feel, as she would put it, like some old has-been who knew nothing about anything that mattered.

Walter Cronkite, she saw, was pushing the papers about on his desk, which meant that the evening news was ending. "Drat," she said aloud, watching her idol's lips say soundlessly, "And that's the way it is," words that echoed so exactly her own tolerant acceptance of this world.

"And thaaaat's the way it is," she lilted, picking up the saucer and spooning the last of the quivering jello into her unrejoiced mouth.

And Anne? She had turned on the lamp and filled her room with cheering light. And she had acted, moved out of her own plight into someone else's. And tomorrow, Mrs. A. not-with-standing, she would most certainly go down to help Lewis.

PART THREE

❧ I ❧

THE plane was steady as a line embedded in the sky, the sound of the motors rich and full-bodied and flawless. Earth, which had raced life-size away from the rushing plane, now was far below, fixed and toylike, a spread-out dream. Then almost at once, there was the flatness and the shock of open ocean.

Syra unbuckled her seat belt and pushed her shoulders up to her ears, then, luxuriously, let them drop. And with a loosening and a lightening of everything in her, she looked down at what she was leaving and for a moment she had a smooth sense that in being herself, here, alone, doing what she was doing, there was something absolute and inviolable.

With the unbuckling of seat belts there had come a quick release of voices and of activity. The unseen pilot broadcast an announcement of flight plans in an everyday voice. A steward took a position at the foot of the aisle and said into a microphone, "May I have your attention please. In the event of an emergency landing..." and then commenced his bland demonstration of how to put on and blow up the life jacket, his unworried young college face with cheeks puffed Triton-fat, making incredible any such disaster.

Another steward and a stewardess had begun to guide a beverage cart down the aisle. When they get to me, I will have a martini, Syra told herself. She drew a pleased breath and regarded the rows of seats down the length of the aisle, where the tops of heads were showing, smoke beginning to curl up from cigarettes now that the no-smoking sign was off. I will, in fact, have a double martini. Or no, shall I play a pretendy game with myself and have one now, one later, like a double treat?

The sea was no longer visible, shut off from view by clouds soft and fog-gray and steaming and dense. She thought of Georges, down there in the sun below this cloud cover-up, and felt a sort of quiet in being buffered from him like this. The clouds suddenly felt to her like an ally, helping to blot out what was down there.

Syra in the sky had then, suddenly, a strange new sense of Georges on the earth. She felt him, saw him, as separate. He on the difference of earth, sitting in the patio of the hotel, did not have any relation to her in the difference of the sky; he on the earth was sitting at that table in the patio as though she in the sky did not exist. "I would like a double vodka martini, please, half dry vermouth and half vodka, on the rocks. Thank you very much," she said to the stewardess who was bending over her.

A sudden tipping of the plane, a rushing by of vaporous cloud, sent her hands flying to clutch the arms of her seat. The seat-belt sign came on, and Syra, taking her bag from her lap and tossing it onto the empty seat next to her, fumbled to buckle the belt and to lower the tray on the back of the seat in front of her in readiness for her drink.

Her hands were shaking a little as she received her glass with its golden promise of oblivion, and took a long, fiery swallow of it. I shrink into a fig of fright on planes… She licked her stinging lips and shrugged, and settled back to enjoy all this and to forget about being afraid; and to begin to think up a plausible explanation, an ironclad lie, for the moment she would walk in on Lewis, unexpectedly, on indeed yes, she thought, and closed her eyes, for she was remembering looking through the keyhole and then barging in on the frightened little boy, and the boil. What had happened then? It was strange not to be able to remember.

She opened her eyes and took several long swallows of her drink. The seat-belt light went out, and she unbuckled the belt and laughed at it. I am already drunk… She set the glass down onto the tray, thoughtfully, her face vacant, dreaming. I believed Lewy was born with that part of him all wrong because it was small. I felt sorry for him because it wasn't big, like Father's was that Sunday afternoon and because he was all bald, no hair like Father's. I wondered whether it was because he was only a little boy and Father a man that accounted for the difference in size of that foolish-looking thing. But then I sensed no, that wasn't it, because I associated bigness there, a big finger, with a male's happiness, and smallness—poor Lewy had only a little boy's finger, and some little swellings as well—I associated that imperfect-looking small thing, like the boil, with my sense of a male being in danger.

The plane was above the clouds now. The sky was clear. Sun, shining through the tiny window, was warm on Syra's bare arm. The sun is stroking me through the window… The motors ground surely and thrillingly, just the right full-throated sound, she thought, of there being nothing wrong with any of them.

She looked out at the sky that had no beginning and no end. Her sight blurred. A peaceful smile touched her lips. How often she had smiled at the memory of that demoniac helpless ecstacy on her father's face that Sunday afternoon. And on her mother's

71

face, too–an inhuman look of ecstacy like no other expression of happiness she'd ever seen.

She let herself be pulled back into memory, easily, longingly, because it was there she wanted to be now, and that way she wanted to be again. It was essential to be back in that place where her flesh expanded like flowers opening, as it should, as it was meant to, as it did in Nassau and did not at home. She was desirously alive, back there under the perfume of the locust trees.

Summer. Sundayness, the day without end. Time stretches out because no one is watching it, or doing things by it. Lunch will never end. Mother and Father let her have a little wine in her glass of water. And they drank all the rest of the bottle, glass after glass. They laughed a lot, too. Laughed and laughed. Mother's face was shiny pink and bunched up with laughing, as she reached for her package of little cigars and said to Father, "Since its al fresco, may I have your permission to smoke, kind sir?"

Who was Al Fresco, Syra wondered.

Father fed Mother pieces of chicken salad on the end of his fork. "Now, oooopen up, thaaat's right, wiiiide open." Why did they laugh so hard at this, Mother flopping back in her chair, pretending to fan herself with her napkin. What was so funny?

"Send her packing, Cleo," Father said.

"Pet, would you want to go play in your pine grove house while Father and I take a nap?"

"Can't I take a nap with you?" She'd eaten chicken salad with them, drunk wine with them. She was a member of this Sunday lunch.

"No," Father said strongly. He widened his eyes slightly, looking at Mother. "That's a very unusual request for a child who hates to take naps."

"But I do want to, now," she whined. "I don't *want* to play alone. I want us to be three."

"I'll find you a picture book, daughter. Come along, Cleo."

She sat on at the lunch table, refusing to open the picture book, plotting, nibbling at a lace cookie, watching them climb the porch stairs and go into the house. She felt like taking a nap with them, and she would. She finished her cookie. But she was a little afraid of Father, and so decided to eat another cookie and think about whether to take a nap with them or to look at the picture book.

It was very still. Underneath the honey-sweet locusts, which made small dark moving intricate lace patterns on the white tablecloth, the empty plates, the emptied wineglasses, she sat and wondered and schemed and crunched the sweet, brittle cookie between her teeth, seeing that it was a piece of lace like the locust shadows, but round and small.

Suddenly she knew she would do what she felt like doing, as Mother had taught her to. She licked the crumbs from her fingers, and went into the house and up the stairs, and down the hall to Mother and Father's bedroom.

The door was closed. She put her hand on the knob, and turned it, and pushed at the door, but it wouldn't open. They had bolted that door. Only once before had that door been bolted, when Father was in there with a sick heart and he had had to be kept very quiet, with just the nurse there. She started to call out to them to unbolt it. But at that very second she heard them laugh. So, they weren't napping, they were laughing some more. Were they drinking more wine, instead of napping?

They had deceived her. She couldn't believe that Mother had actually deceived her. Unsure, she was suddenly suspicious. And–curious. A small new body-knowledge stirred in her. Her seven-year-old female heart began to beat with illicit excitement. She kneeled down and put an eye to the big keyhole.

There was the four-poster bed, most of it rewardingly visible, and Mother and Father on it. They didn't have any clothes on;

and that was intensely, disturbingly puzzling. It was exciting to spy. She sensed in it some daring, some promising advantage. It was like going to the movies.

But they were awake, they weren't taking any nap, because Father was kneeling over Mother. And out of a lot of hair—hair, there?—unconsciously puzzled, her hand went up to touch her own hair—out of all that black hair was a large finger, like a giant's finger! *Father* had a *finger, there? Another* finger, besides the fingers on his hand? Shocked, she looked down at her own hand, and spread out her small fingers, and counted them. Then she pulled up her dress, and looked down at herself, where there was of course no other finger. She was bewildered and suddenly felt a little sick from the wine and the cookies. Mother had black hair there, too. Was that what they were laughing about? It certainly was funny. She felt that she ought to be laughing with them.

Then Father came down onto Mother, and the finger went away, and their arms were all the way around each other, and Mother's face was loose and wild looking, and they were kissing each other, kissing, kissing. They were certainly happy. She had never seen Mother's face, or Father's, happy like that. She wished she could be playing that game, so that she could be happy like that. Then they both made loud, funny noises, cow sounds, and suddenly both grew still. Then Mother brought a hand up and stroked Father's cheek, softly. And Father closed his eyes.

She got up from her knees, stealthily, so as not to be heard, for she knew intuitively that what she had just seen she was not supposed to have seen, had been barred from seeing. She went off on tiptoe, down the hall to her room and closed the door softly. There she flung herself onto the bed and burst into awful sobs.

Created thoroughly in her mother's image she was; but without that hair, which felt to her unjust. Unjust, too, that Father had an extra finger. And she had also been deceived. And left out. Frightened, betrayed, she poured her tears into the soft pillow.

Geneva's conception, Syra thought, and smiled sadly.

All at once she was uncomfortably aware of the existence of Georges. She realized that Georges felt like a *thin* fact. The tropics was a newly-arrived-at *fat* fact, Georges was an always-there *thin* fact. The sense she had of him was just that. And for a second it was not Georges alone down there on the difference of earth, and she alone up here in the difference of sky, but she and Georges together on this plane as they had been coming down, both of them thin facts sitting side by side. She felt suddenly, distressingly crowded in upon herself, thick inside, as though she had overeaten. She had a second of sharp alarm. She looked about as though wondering how to get away from it, where to go. Was there any place to go?

Yes. Back to memory. Geneva's conception. She sighed with relief. Unlocked herself, expanded again. Ah, this is safe, this is me. How happy Mother and Father were, making Geneva, that little life that didn't last...

She had forgotten Georges. He was not here, for she was not here. She had drifted back to another summer, another time, a time that was wholly simple and sweet—summer days bound to this plane by nothing but the sound of the motors droning steady and solid in space. There is an oasis in herself that is a very bright light, demanding memory to fill it. And, as though it were always there in that oasis, a feeling appears without effort, a feeling drowned in light that flows into images, scenes—summer again, the summer before the perfume of the locusts and the wine and the nap that was not a nap. She is six and Lewis is seven, walking with arms across each other's waists in hot gold summer light. Two children move like a simple song through the summer, a ribbon weaving in and out of those days, together as naturally as birds, from the time they get up in the morning until they go to bed at night, strolling along the lake shore, or through the waist-high fields, or into the hushed woods, or down the village streets. Lewy constantly kissing her cheek, she constantly kissing Lewy's cheek, kissing from an inexhaustible well of tenderness, forever kissing. They send messages that swear eternal love, pulleyed back and forth in a tin can dangling from a rope between their bedroom windows, they crawl into their secret hideaway in a clearing in the pine grove behind the barn, where they sit and play house, and talk, and kiss, drenched in aromatic warm sunshine filtered down through shading branches. In gentle separateness from everyone else, they are safe as they will never be again. In perfect innocence, they are never apart. They play with no one else. They are a couple in love, set apart from the other children, and strangely not mocked by them.

There was nobody she could tell this to, there never had been. She would like to bring it all back, give *then* the shape and the blessing of *now* by putting it into words, by explaining to some interested, sympathetic person about the love of two little children that had been of a simplicity and sweetness and bigness perhaps rare on this earth–a pure fire of devotion burning as straight as a candle flame in a place where there is no wind. "A perfect *dream* of innocent love," Aunty Sally called it, and Mother had called it "the idyllic love of those two infants." And they *were* infants–only six and seven. Aunt Sally, who liked to say smart and funny things, said that they were "at sixes and sevens." They were a little boy and a little girl who were actually magnetized to each other, or truly, yes, made for each other. And it was all utterly nonsexy. Utterly. Two unfledged cherubs. It was their hearts and their heads and whatever else, but not their genitals, from which that summer's love sprang. Father and Mother and Aunt Sally and Uncle Edmond were enchanted by it, even though sometimes they looked worried and talked about "inbreeding"—a scary-sounding word she and Lewis of course didn't understand then, but heard and internalized and understood when they were old enough to.

And she would like to speak about the underside of it, cutting into her now with its tiny troubling pain. It was never to be like that again, she is saying to someone she suddenly longs for, some presence that listens and gives the listening back to her deepened by understanding. Never again, she tells that presence, because the next summer I was seven and Lewy was eight, and I saw Mother and Father taking a nap that was not a nap, and *it* had been born in my body and in Lewy's body, the *thing* that spoiled the innocence. She wished there were a person to whom she could talk about the way everything, in just one year, had stopped being a shining straight line of ribbon and had begun to be a twisted one. More twisted and more twisted always. Moreover, it felt as though she and Georges had been caught in that twisting. Caught and held. Like animals caught in a twisted wire and stopped from running.

The stewardess had begun a purposeful, maternal roaming of the aisle, bending, bending. The plane was again in the clouds and was beginning to shake a little.

Suddenly the plane did something powerfully lumpy, then something powerfully up-and-down hard in a lurching way, then at once became again a safely straight long quiet mighty line.

Syra shrugged nervously. But it must be all right, the stewardess looked unconcerned, thrusting her swan neck down over this seat, that seat, protective, murmurous.

She took up her glass in both unsteady hands, and drank a little from it. Her hands tingled. Looking down at them, thinking about this tingling, there in her palm she saw the yellow light of a buttercup's reflection.

"Hey, Siry. Look." She saw Lewis's little-boy hand pressing

her fingers up to make a cup.

The cup blurred, and she saw upon this chalice a montage of Lewis framed in the keyhole, and then blending into this blur, Aunt Sally's beautiful wasted face, her gray hair tied up in a black velvet bow, and her mother, smoking, talking, both of them rocking in porch chairs. "Well, they've outgrown it, Sally, thank the heavens."

She was entirely owned for a moment by these images, and then by the memory of herself and Lewis walking along the road, two strangers, no more idyllic love, no more love letters, no more kissing, no more arms across each other's backs. Awkward. Shy.

"Hey, Siry."

A spread of yellow buttercups, and a little bone-white house. Yellow and white and a lake breeze and an intense purpose in her, beneath her starched lavender dress with purple smocking, where her heart banged with a great and fearing purpose, reckless.

"Hey, Siry, this is magic." A strong wet breeze came from the lake. They were knee deep in buttercups. Lewis had one in his hand. "Lookit this." With his other hand he grabbed one of hers, pressed her fingers up into a cup and brought the buttercup down into the darkness of this warm tingling cup. And yes, there was a little glow, a faint yellow reflection.

"This is scientific. Hey. Do it to me."

Across the field, beyond the yellow lake of buttercups, on a little rise, was the schoolhouse, closed now in summer. And behind it the little outhouse, weathered sides bone white. Inside sulphur white. A place that drew her.

She had decided that morning, even before their walk took them past it, that the outhouse would be the place.

Sulphur white, the whiteness of seat-wood polished from long use, the tense nostril experience of sulphur coming up from the dark now deadened depths of those two holes. This was the place for it to happen.

"Lewy."

They were on the road, below the schoolhouse. Up there on the hill, behind the schoolhouse, the little temple was bone white in the sun. Inside, hot, still, secret.

"Lewy. Let's go into the outhouse."

The sudden curiosity in his green eyes. Startled. Then faintly—was it dread and excitement that made his voice come out so faint—"What for?"

"Oh. For fun."

Incredulity wiped his face of expression. Amazed green eyes. Then gradually his pink full child's lips parted with interest, while his eyes began to flicker with fear. Curiosity and temptation and fear fought there in his widened eyes. Suddenly he said, but weakly, with no conviction, "That's dirty."

"*Dirty?*"

He turned with a suddenness that violated her. She watched him walking down the road, his shoulders pushed up, the back of his head stiff, flailing at the buttercups with cutting sweeps of his hand. Then he began to run.

"Lewy called me dirty."

Mock orange smelled heavily sweet. Everywhere was the sharp strong friendly smell of tobacco, and the large perfumed mock orange air. Mother was sitting on the back steps smoking her little cigar. Father hated the smell of it and so Mother always smoked outdoors. Mother had on her white cotton Japanese kimona with great jagged dark-blue birds flying all across it. On her feet were her little black ballet slippers. One foot was tapping the porch steps as though to music inside her. The inevitable book was next to her on the steps.

"Lewy called me dirty."

"He called you dirty? Where are you dirty, Pet? You look

clean as a whistle to me. Let me see your hands."

Palms up, she held out to Mother her spread hands, wherein only a while ago there had been the reflection of a buttercup. "Because I asked him to go into the outhouse with me he said I was dirty and he ran away from me. He's mad at me." She began to cry terribly, and put her head down onto the bluebirds of Mother's lap.

Mother said nothing at first, only stroked her hair. Then abruptly she stamped out the little cigar and began to part the tangled strands of hair in order to pull out a burr.

"Ouch!" She pulled away accusingly and stopped her crying. How could Mother *hurt* her, *more*?

Mother's face was like a cat's—triangular, with wide cheekbones sloping down to the sharp V of chin; and her eyes, above those high cheekbones, were black, and old, and soft as night. She drew the tangled curls to her shoulder and began again to stroke them. "Why did you want to go into the outhouse with Lewy, Pet?"

She couldn't say it.

"Why, Pet?" with quiet, calm insistence. "Why did you want Lewis to go in there with you?"

Finally she could say it. "To take down our panties."

"Oh. I see."

"Lewy said it was dirty." She began to sob again, horribly.

"Now listen to Mother, Pet. I do not believe at all that it was dirty. It was quite natural. You were only wanting what every child wants, and does. Look here, look up at Mother." She poked up the wet chin and gazed at the streaming eyes. "It is *not* dirty to be curious about a boy's body. I am telling you that it is *just the opposite*. It is *clean*. What is natural is clean. Now, then, stop crying. You are crying because in a way Lewy has gone now. Isn't that so? And because he has made *you feel* dirty. Isn't that so?"

"Yes, Mother."

"So now, something upsetting has happened between you and your best friend Lewy. But you'll both get over it. And do try to forgive Lewy. He couldn't help what he did. Aunt Sally won't understand, of course. But forgive her, too, for that. No one is perfect. And you are not dirty."

Syra looked down into her drink, struck gold with a slant of sun. And there in the transparency of liquid and the light of sun was Lewis, dressed elegantly for the funeral in a dark blue suit, and with a black necktie, his face genuine and open as a child's with misery, all the lines of bitterness and cynicism gone away, leaving a flat surface upon which there was only the pure drained vacancy of desolation. She walked straight over to him where he stood abandoned, and they stretched out their arms to each other without even thinking, simply put out their arms as though that was what arms were for. And then they stood holding each other for such a long time, with the strongest feeling of absoluteness that was perfectly calm and so deep there was no bottom to it. For that minute there was no dead Aunt Sally lying in her shiny black silver-handled coffin.

But then they stopped holding each other, and suddenly and badly it got back to being the funeral. It would begin in a few minutes. Shortly, they would get into long gloomy limousines, and drive to the strange difference of a dark church with the unwanted, unnatural light of red and yellow and blue stained glass windows making blotches of color they would have to sit down on, and which would then be on their laps and on their hands.

Syra set her glass down and brought her hands together, and brushed at their backs, brushing away the stain of those deceiving colors. And this sharp image began now to be clouded with an intolerable, a hopeless color—the schoolroom in which she taught, her pupil William playing the Villa Lobos Prelude with wrong notes and with no feeling, Georges in the gym, blowing his whistle while his cheeks bulged out and his eyes bulged out.

Georges is only an athletic director and a teacher of the French language, she said to herself factually. And she realized that she was thinking "only," because it was Georges's view of himself, which she had absorbed. And she saw that it diminished him, or rather, she saw that he felt himself to be a diminished man, a meaningless man.

She heard her mother. "That's my girl." With a panic of love and loss she hadn't felt in months, Syra felt her mother, who came to her now, and calmed her, holding out her hand to her, leading her back. Leading her forward. "That's my girl."

She woke up thinking that she had not been really deep asleep but only nodding, and opened her eyes in a slow dazed way.

She knew at once she felt transformed. She felt soft and loose and soaring, with a black-and-white difference, as though the person before sleep had been black—black for darkness, and the waking up person was white—white for light.

The plane rose straight up, suddenly, then dropped back again, a bottomless moment. But this was as pleasantly sensational as a roller-coaster ride in childhood, for it now did not matter to Syra what the plane did. She sat up and looked around her and stretched, relaxed and benign. She turned to the window. The shock of purple and orange clouds met her—streak of fire-orange through intensifying blue—the beginnings of the sunset that would be, she thought, a royal-purple sunset. She felt, with a sense of the miraculous, that she was way up here on a level with the sun, far, far from the earth—straight line of plane, straight line of molten orange, two parallel lines.

The plane was drenched in a deep, winey light, faces roseate from it. The crackle of the loudspeaker came on, then the pilot's everyday voice, announcing the beginning of the descent into New York. Syra got up and made her way down the aisle to the rest room. She locked the little metal door and put her bag on the counter, taking out of it her comb. When she looked into the mirror she was surprised. She felt as though she had never seen her face thoroughly, not so much my face, she thought, as me, the me behind the skin and bones, and what the skin and bones reflect of me. It was no use to keep on looking at her face because it changed as she studied it and stopped being interesting, but she kept the feeling of pleasant surprise as she washed her hands and combed her hair.

When she got back to her seat and sat down in it, and looked with a throbbing regard into the tranquil blazing royal sky out there above the earth she was descending to, she felt a sudden passion of excitement. In no time at all now, she thought, I will be in a taxi turning onto Deer Valley Road, then climbing Ogilvie Hill and going past Mrs. Alexander's house and the Knights', then descending into the valley and passing the woods, and the swamps. Then the church.

And then–Lewis.

She was as unfit for the sudden transition from southern beach to northern metropolis as though prodded out of deep sleep by an alarm. After the assault that New York had been, after the bedlam of the airport, then the torrent of boulevard traffic in which she felt helplessly borne along as in raging floodwaters, then Grand Central Station and its six o'clock muted roar and swarm; after the rattling, slippery-seated train (how tired she really was), and the depressing sights it presented to her bewildered eyes–slums and wasteland and factories and prisonlike housing developments and teeming highways, beyond which the endless, free blue sea could only be wistfully imagined—after all this, Syra, descending that Friday evening to the clear-aired quiet of a country station, sank into a taxi with a long, long sigh, as though only now exhaling a deep breath she had drawn six hours before, and had held for all that time.

"Deer Valley Road, please," she told the driver, only a boy. The cab stank of the smoke of the cigarettes that had dyed his nail-bitten fingers sepia, and Syra with her small square tanned hand lost not a moment in wheeling down the window, though it was cool here, even cold. The stores across the quiet street were closed now—seven o'clock had emptied the town of its commerce. As the boy crashed his gears into action and cowboy-careened out of the empty station yard, above this violence Syra heard a massive muted twitter, a migrating flock of birds swarming and then settling into a tree. As though the bare tree is in sudden leaf, she thought.

"Oh, this is better," she said aloud, "this is happy making," though she was only speaking to herself. And, beginning to be here, she sighed again, with huge relief, as though rescued, hugging the treasure of her tropical lassitude. In a new, determined way, she felt embattled about losing it.

She was familiar with the route to Deer Valley Road, having visited Lewis often during the six years he had lived here. She realized with an exuberant pleasure that it was not smoke she was seeing in the valley but the silver blur of swamp maples and the rosy smudge of their beginning buds. Cold air poured into the cab and swirled her hair about her head, across her face, into her eyes and mouth, but she didn't care and even liked it, needing to have fresh air blow away the death smell of New York.

Picking a strand of hair from her lips, with an awareness that was at once tactile (moist lips, clinging hair) and mental (the thought stood new and untroubled in her mind), both tactile and mental experiences so reinforcing each other that the clarity of the decision was never to be forgotten, then and there she knew she would move to the south. Soon. And, first things first, with or without Georges in constant residence, since her life depended on it.

She saw him high-stepping and dancing in the surf, discovering his reservoirs of joy. But he seemed far away. Naked in the surf. She shivered in the cold air. The boy turned his radio on, rock and roll burst forth, and Syra began to tap her foot to its rhythm. The half-smile that was often there grew into a full smile, lighting her young calm face. This was now, new, wonderful...

And here was the turn into Deer Valley Road, and now the descent into the valley, and now the long curve, the rise to the lookout of Ogilvie Hill, and now Mrs. Alexander's white house, lights on in the dusk, set back in the darkness of lawns and the deeper darkness of tall maples, sentinel maples they'd be called, thought Syra, and they're right to guard her. And now across the road a swarm of migrating birds appeared for a blackening moment above the Knights' old barn, which was silver-sided in the last of the sunset, smoke from two chimneys curling straight up in the windless evening. Soon Lewis's house. "I cannot wait, I cannot wait, I have cymbals on my heels," she whispered, and her spirits lifted, the taxi flew, curving, racing. Arriving!

A fragrant darkness of woods rushed by, the sound of a stream. And there was Lewis's sign, Lewis's great maples, and under them, the house, its dark red almost black in the dusk, with four glowing squares of lighted windows. The taxi lunged into the drive, and stopped. Syra put money into the boy's cold hand. Her heart was beating harder in a suddenly sobered body. Because what was she going to say?

The sudden, strident attack of the reality of this moment of arrival upon only the imagining of it struck Syra so that she drew her hand back from the cab door she was about to open.

But then her hand, hesitating for no more than a few seconds, returned, grasped the handle, resolution having taken place this swiftly–she would of course walk into Lewis's house and into his arms as she had always done, and of course she would tell him truthfully her reason for coming. "Lewy," she rehearsed, "I came because..." But peculiarly, dismayingly, she did not know how to finish the sentence. Instead, her mother's voice was here, in the dusk beneath the darkly moving great trees. "When something feels unnatural to you, Syra, get out of it by doing what feels natural."

❧ II ❧

LEWIS was in the front hall leafing through the disappointing pile of junk mail when he heard a car crunching into his driveway. Too exhausted for company, yet eager for it, he dropped the mail with alarm, turned to look out of the window, and saw a taxi slowing down.

Baffled, curious, yet hopeful, and with a show of false hospitableness, he unlocked the door and grudgingly opened it.

Walking towards him in the path of light was Syra.

He was blankly perplexed, or was he dreaming? Struck numb with perplexity, even with dismay, he did not move.

In a second he knew of course that this was real, but still he could not move and could not speak. I'm sick, he thought implausibly and wildly, fighting against Syra coming toward him, to enter his house, to enter him. To disrupt.

"Lewy, love," she called out. Then her arms were around him, she was kissing him full on his aghast mouth, she was drawing away and looking up at him and smiling nervously. "Oh Lewy, I guess I should have let you know, not barged in like this. But your letter worried me, love, so I came, I did."

Horrified at not being able to appear joyous, at not being able to cry out ringingly and sincerely with joy as he surely should, at last he found his voice. "Oh no! Well, frankly, I'm so flabbergasted, I don't know what to say. I just can't believe this."

"Well, I guess this does seem very pell-mell of me, but I came because I thought you needed me, my very dearest. I had the feeling. It was in the letter. You did say 'ausec' in it, you did."

"Oh. In the letter. Oh yes." He smiled his glassy smile, actually shaking as with an unwilling show of hospitality he closed the outside door and picked up the guitar and her old suitcase, and then suddenly felt such defenselessness, such terror, that he could not have said anything unrelated to that terror.

The grandfather clock in the dining room, off in that dark polished room where his mother's portrait hung over the Hepplewhite sideboard, struck seven, slowly, resonantly. A welcome of sorts, this familiar voice of their childhood, giving Syra, even Lewis reassurance.

She smiled almost shyly up at him and then said with a firmness that was beginning to return to her, "Dearest Lewy, I have missed you most terribly, and here we are, together again. And I am no longer feeling such a tired traveler drifting over the face of the earth. And guess what? I'm thirsty, cousin." It had just occurred to her, her spirits rising, that any moment now she would be offered a drink. "And I'm a mess from travel. First thing I do, I want to clean up. And then I would like a drink to soar me." She looked up at him cheerfully but also uncertainly.

"Siry, my God," Lewis managed out of his agitation, "you left Georges, you left Nassau. Why?" But he knew why. And relief began to spread through him like anesthesia. *Syra* was here! The hall grew lighter, warmer, his body, numbed and stiffened for weeks, became suddenly his own natural-feeling body, he was aware of the Jacobean chest, stately, bearing the silver card tray he loved, the cards of his trade. Syra was here, in his hall.

In the silence he heard the living room fire snapping. And he was suddenly hungry, thirsty. At ease. Come to life. He drew a great sigh. "Oh, for goodness' sakes," he said unsteadily, shaking his head, "cousin, cousin." Though in his return to aliveness, a trace of terror still remained.

"Bliss, a fire," Syra exclaimed as they came into the living room. She went across and held her small cold hands out to its blaze, not just to warm them but to reach out toward something alive and comforting, looking up gratefully at the painting over the mantlepiece, welcomed by the familiar ship—poor ship, she thought, pitching on that wild sea, forever pitching, never any safe harbor, always this storm, forever this storm. And on either end of the mantle, sure enough, there were two of Lewis's perfect flower arrangements, small, exquisite, in two little china bowls, which were undoubtedly rare. Forever there, she thought, uncomfortably. She put up a finger and touched a daffodil, stretched up to put her nose to it. Yes, a faint green smell of spring. She found herself wishing, for Lewis's sake, that he had left it in his garden. Nosegays for Aunt Sally, she thought, and turned away from them.

Lewis stood foolishly in the middle of the room, tongue-tied, still holding her suitcase, hoping she would speak again so that he could manage to. He put her suitcase down, the scarred old thing on his beautiful old hooked rug suited him perfectly. And suddenly he felt marvelous, no aches, no pains, no depression, no shakiness. "You want a drink," he cried in a burst of feeling, "of course you want a drink, but first, oh cousin," and he crossed to pull her into a great hug, "cousin, what a gift! You'd go to the ends of the earth for me, wouldn't you?" He kissed her hair, which smelled of fresh air, and let her go.

"Probably," she said without expression. And added, a half-smile twitching, "what a nice trip that would be."

He laughed. And he felt so exultant all at once that he rose on his toes, flung his arms straight out and twirled once, joyously, on the points of his polished English shoes.

"The men in my life seem to be dancers." She watched him, smiling quietly, loving him for his gaiety. He seemed to be all right. A little pale. But himself. Then why had she come?

She watched him hurry out of the room, exuberant, his shoulders raised with excited purpose.

She felt a little strange all at once. And suddenly very tired. What a long day it had been. She went over to her suitcase, picked up the battered, somehow comforting old thing, and climbed the steep little stairway to the guest room under the eaves, where a fireplace and an immaculate tiny bathroom and a big four-poster bed were hospitably waiting to soothe her, she knew, for she had used them often.

She found herself wondering how many of Lewis's girls (Heloise?) used them too. As a regular thing. Used the fireplace and the bathroom, that is. For the bed they would use was across the hall, in Lewis's room. Such a thought had never occurred to Syra in full force before this minute, climbing her cousin's steep little dark stairway, with the prints of old Paris on the walls and the faint musty wood smell of an ancient house captured in its tunnel. She came to the top of the stairs, and averted her head from his open doorway as she passed it.

It was as though she had been here forever.

"Another drink," Lewis murmured–this was to be their third, not asking, stating, unfolding his long length to get up and reach for his glass, and hers. "Gimme, gimme," he said softly, taking the glass out of her willing hand. "Your hand's cold."

"Only from the glass. My back's far from cold, though, cousin.

My back's marrr-velously hot."

She was sitting on the old brass velvet-upholstered firebench
Lewis had put there because he loved firebenches nostalgical-
ly–there had been one in Syra's home in Cazenovia. "I love to
perch and be toasted," Syra had said to Lewis long ago in her
mother's living room, and then when he had bought this
firebench, she had sat upon it for the first time, and had said
again, "I love to perch and be toasted," not realizing she had
said exactly the same words once before to Lewis.

But he remembered. His bald head was rosy in the firelight as
he bent over her, and smelling the fragrance of soap (she had
showered, and changed into a short amber silk kimona that
doubled as dress and dressing gown), sensuously aware of the
amber of her silk upon the red of the velvet with the shine of
the fire all around her, Lewis said, as tenderly as a lover, "You
love to perch and be toasted."

Syra felt happily at home, hearing Lewis say this. And she
knew that the breath she drew, and all the flesh and bone of this
body of hers that sat here on this firebench, belonged to his
remembering her saying that.

She felt miraculously at home, here in this room, and also in
herself. Yup! I'm happy, she told herself, as though this was the
first time in her life she had *known*, in feeling and in her mind,
what it was to be happy. She felt strange to have captured and
given a name to what was going on in her. So this was happiness, she thought. It feels like being something round and perfect, like the moon, or a pearl. I was a balloon this morning, so I
won't be a balloon now. Anyway, happiness doesn't feel like a
balloon, because balloons are unvaluable.

And then she had the sudden curious realization that being
with Lewis this time, surprisingly but oh so naturally, was like
going back to being the way she was before she married
Georges. She felt in possession again of an entity that was famil-

iar, and though she hadn't the words for it, but only the feeling, she knew thoroughly at this moment that the entity had been lost, or at least diluted, by marriage, and by the world she had been taken into by marriage.

She felt impelled to tell this to Lewis. "I'm having a funny feeling, Lewy. Different from yesterday, and all the other yesterdays. You know, this April has chased me around. Oh it's been the most running-away-from-me-month. But here, suddenly, I think it possible that I've stopped running. What's going on feels so unusual to me, like magic, I have to tell you. I don't understand it," she said quietly, "I just don't understand it. I feel so easy and simple here. I do, I do. There's something so familiar. I feel way down inside myself, like in a place where a little door just opened up and I was in that perfect place that made me wonder why I'd left it. As though all other places were wrong. I think that's the way I felt when I was a little girl. It must have been uncomplicated to be a little girl. Remember how excited and scared we were the night we went to our first party together? You were visiting us at Christmas, remember? I was fourteen, you were fifteen. I can even remember my dress, pink iridescent taffeta appliqued with silver ribbon in a sort of sawtooth pattern around the bottom of the skirt. And my armpits stung because I'd shaved them, and then put deodorant on. Agony! We waited, remember, on our firebench, which is why I'm remembering, for the Newells to come and pick us up? Mother gave us each a 'thimbleful' she called it, of sherry, to buck us up. This firebench brings it all back, and being with you, and all. Why? It's so strange. Here I am. Feeling like me. For the first time in a lot of years. For the very first time in my–uh, oh, Lewy, sentence unfinished! Gods might be listening and grow annoyed at a mortal being so cocksure.

"It isn't that I want to be a little girl again," she went on, looking up at him, "but I do want to be the way it felt before I started becoming an adult and being pulled to and fro by the moon. Oh, you know me and the moon, Lewy! But I do wish that when it wanes, I didn't feel so uneasy and unhappy when dark comes. But on the other hand, it gives me the most peaceful feeling to have the moon be responsible, for it's just a case of waiting for the new moon to dawn me also. Why am I rattling on and on about the moon? Maybe instead I can blame the Welsh in me for black moods. It's always good to be able to blame something."

"Amen, baby," he murmured. "What would we do if we couldn't?" Holding their glasses, shaking the ice around in them nervously, looking down at the top of her head and at the touchingness of a few gray hairs among the brown and to the quiet that rose solidly from her like a pillar, filled suddenly with a complete sense of the happiness she was feeling at being here, Lewis reminded himself now that she had come all the way from the Bahamas to comfort him. She had left Georges and cut her vacation short to come to him. She was here, and she was elated to be here, and she was looking up into his eyes with a steady and luminous attention. Those truthful eyes (oh how he loved the truth in those eyes) made him feel very happy all at once. The tension in his face cleared. He drew a deep sigh that expressed both an exaggerated relief and a kind of euphoric hopelessness. "I'm a lousy bartender. I do want to say, though, and it's high time, that your coming has made all the difference." And when Syra said nothing, only continued her intent looking, he said, rousingly, "Well, we need another drink. Don't we."

She watched him loosely and gracefully stride off to the kitchen, and she thought how much she liked his elegance. It had a flavor, what was it, of worldliness? She could see him, she thought, striding down a London street in his perfectly cut tweeds, swinging a furled umbrella; oh, his style, the loose and swift and beautiful way he moved, women turning to look at him. Even his bald head had a kind of distinction. Better than all hair.

She was smiling at her fantasy as she called out matter-of-factly, "Cousin dear, I like your bald head. It's better than all hair."

"Come *on*, Siry," the refrigerator door slamming, ice rattling. "What the hell are you talking about?"

"About you."

"I love to talk about me."

She jerked her hair away from her neck. It was so hot by the fire. And all this liquor, she thought helplessly, happily. She leaned forward, ran a hand down her leg slowly, grasped her ankle, studied the slouched old ballet slipper on her foot. "Oh my." She sighed, she did not know why.

Suddenly, vividly, she saw Georges. She felt herself to be sitting at the table in the patio in Nassau, sitting there with him in a kind of...what? Unaliveness? Noncontact? A kind of blur? What was it? Oh why don't I know, she implored herself, why, why don't I know?...

She heard the cheerful glug of liquor being poured from a bottle, and then Lewis appeared in the doorway with their glasses in his hands, grinning, his green eyes sparkling. He came over and handed her a glass, put his on the table beside his chair, and sat down, sighing blissfully. "Oh this is wonderful, wonderful. Little did I know this morning in the – " he was about to say "in the depths of gloom" but shied away from the memory of fear, from speaking about it and making it real again. At the moment he couldn't even remember what it had all felt like. "Little did I know this morning that tonight you and I'd be sitting here in front of the fire together. Siry!" He raised his glass to her.

"Lewy! I thank God every time I think of you, which is often, so maybe He is wearying of my gratitude. That sounds like a pagan's remark, which I am not entirely." She raised her glass to him. A look passed between them, an old fond deep connecting look.

He raised his glass to her, and put it to his lips, tilting it way back with a clatter of ice. Then he blurted out, "I may as well tell you, Siry. I mean to say," heavily, "I *want* to tell you. I'm glad you came. I was depressed. Christ, was I depressed. I didn't know how to get out of it. I even spilled over to Rupert this morning. In fact, without meaning to, I really insulted him. Maybe I did mean to, I don't know. But I regret it. Christ, he's such a combination of vanity and saintliness. It really gets to me. But then again he's such a sweet man. Incredibly, it appears that someone may publish a book of his essays. Maybe that's really legitimately what he needs, who knows. Anyway, depressed I've been. I've been worried about my body, and I've been worried about my thoughts, and then, being sick, I've been so damn lonely. The middle of the nights have been the worst." A sensation of heaviness would begin it, would gather slowly in his chest, where his heart supposedly was, so that the word *heavyhearted* would occur to him, then this sensation would increase until it was a hard, remorseless throbbing, while through his body despair would spread like a poisonous drenching, hopelessness driven through his whole body as though hopelessness were a liquid. Then this liquid would drain swiftly out of his body, and he would be left with the most absolute emptiness, and sweat suddenly all over him. Panic, that's what happened in the middle of the nights. "It's hard to describe to you how low I actually get. Oh, well, as Confucius say, 'our greatest glory is not in never failing, but in rising every time we fail.' Ha, ha. That's what *Confucius* say!"

"Oh, those ancient Chinese—all they did was sip tea, wave fans, and fish and come up with magnificent catch of thought."

"Well, not me. I am a pecheur sans catches, eternally."

Syra put her glass down on the table, drew a quiet sigh, and said, out of the blue, Lewis thought, "what about you and Heloise?"

"How did you know?"

"You wrote it in your letter, darling goose."

"Oh yes. So I did." He shrugged. "Very sad, very sad. Or perhaps not so sad."

"Well, it's too bad it's sad, Lewy," Syra murmured tonelessly, and looked at her hands, feeling relief.

"I really knew it wasn't going to work, that day last spring."

"What day, cousin?"

"The day of your thirty-seventh birthday. The beach party." He paused. Then he said importantly, shrugging his shoulders a little and looking wistful, "That sad day."

"Sad?" She was instantly alert with concern. "Sad, Lewy? I hadn't realized it was sad for you. It wasn't for us. That's too bad." It had been a wonderful day for her, fun and happiness all day, and late in the afternoon she and Georges had walked away down the beach and had had an awkward, quick, sandy lovemaking behind the dunes. She remembered the sea gulls overhead, watching. "I'm sorry to know it was sad for you."

Sad? Yes indeed it had been sad, sad in the worst way. "Sad I was," he said quietly. And mad, he said to himself. Sad and mad... And in spite of a euphoric desire to feel otherwise, he felt a sharp thrust of anger as those taunting words "ha' pa' kissing time" echoed again in his head. The words were like black teletype riding across his forehead. He had to make a great effort to erase them, and to suppress the anger that had turned them on.

Then here it is again, that whole day by the sea. It slides into his mind, and in a moment out of it, in one brilliant detailed flash, as it had in the middle of last night. It is not in his mind for more than a few minutes, yet it is all there, from beginning to end, with one central glaring truth, "ha' pas' kissing time,"

lacing in and out of a myriad tensed wires of interaction, staccato against the sound of the sea and the miles of lonely beach.

That vast beach. Its evening loneliness made it feel absolutely deserted, although the children, Georges's niece and her
boyfriend, were still dashing and shouting, and far away he
could see Syra and Georges coming back along the water's edge.
Bitterly, he thought they had been making love behind some
dune. A birthday present for Syra. The peace of evening gave
everything a luminous quality, so that, though the children
shouted and raced, their voices and their movements seemed
like dreams, seemed captured and held in that golden light forever. It was all beautiful. It was all melancholy. Beaches at
evening were always melancholy.

He had long since had everything neatly packed and stowed
in the cars, and had left that area of the beach upon which they
had picnicked as clean as they had found it, even cleaner. Then,
tiring of idleness, finally he had taken to brushing out the inside
of his precious vintage Pierce Arrow. A scratch on its fender had
plunged him into a fussy panic from which he had been unable
to recover, and he knew he wouldn't recover from it until the
scratch was repaired, or even that he would be left with a residue
of anxiety over the inevitability of the next scratch. Heloise had
fallen asleep hugged into her coat, her head tipped onto her
shoulder. Occasionally the wind ruffled her hair but she didn't
know it. He already sensed that she wasn't anything but today's
fascination, just another cunt, so to speak, but she was direct and
intelligent and somehow she stirred him.

He felt restless, angry too at Syra and Georges, and at Heloise
whom he wasn't going to have and perhaps basically didn't want
now that he had seen her make such a play for Georges. Poor
Georges. He had been like a little boy about it, braggadocian
and frightened and excited. And Syra seemed not to have
noticed at all.

He felt tender sitting there on the cold sand watching Heloise's hair blow across her cheek. His life, he thought, was like this day, unresolved and fraught with too much emotion. Such a waste. Soon *he* would have a birthday, his thirty-ninth. And forty the next one. Surely forty should be some kind of a marker in life. Surely one should be able to regard forty with some sense of accomplishment. Oh why, why when he so clearly saw the pluses of Syra's being, why in his observance and thus his knowledge of such life-giving attitudes, couldn't he learn from her to alter the minuses of his own being? Why? Oh, Jesus Christ. Complexly, hopelessly he knew why. Because Clara Tallent had died, that's why. Unfinished business. And so, alas, the most he could do was to bask, when he was with Syra, in the calm she spread around him, and to savor, for those moments anyway, the possibilities of calm.

The crash of the slick sea had become a lonely, thunderous repetition and it seemed to him that it was for no one to hear except the sea birds, and would go on this way into eternity, crash, then evening silence, hollow and mighty on the empty beaches of the earth. Way down by the water the children played, and their long-drawn-out evening cries came up to him where he sat, cold, fuming. They were untiringly doing things, constant movement. It had been going on all day, and would go on forever, he thought, sounds and movements drawn out through eternity. Geraldine stood still down there now, her skirt and her hair blowing sideways. Both of them, Geraldine, and her boyfriend Frank, even the dog racing around like a mechanical toy, were sharply clear in the evening light, and outlined in bright silver. "More happy love," he said aloud, to himself but wishing for someone to share it, "more happy, happy love! Forever warm and still to be enjoyed, forever parting and forever young." But Heloise had not waked up at the sound of his voice.

Four fifteen. Four thirty. Five. Five fifteen. And now the world was graying, the orange sun slipping down into the sea leaving an afterglow of silvery colorlessness and a sudden emptying out of hope for him. The water had a cold look, but still each mounting breaker was a brilliant silver cylinder in that momentary queer intense light. In the next moment the beach was darkened, a place to leave to itself.

The strange compelling light, the dying away of the day, felt pensively like something in him. He called the children—he would corral them and get them organized so that they could all pile into the cars the minute Syra and Georges got back. He called them again. Stood up and bellowed. But they were wild from the long day and didn't want to hear him. He had to plow down to them, across the sloping stretch of beach, be firm with them. "Oh no, oh Lewis, pleeese. Pleeese, plus, plooze, plums and apples, well at least can't we wait till Syra and Uncle Georges get back?" They were tired and unmanageable. They were contrary; elusive to the point of defiance. They were even rude. Blast all children! But gradually he herded them up the dunes, where Heloise, who had waked up, sat combing her hair. "The old baboon, by the light of the moon, sat combing her auburn hair," pealed Geraldine, and Frank joined deliriously in, "sat combing her auburn hair, her hair, sat combing her auburn hair."

And here at last were the culprits, Syra and Georges, Georges with a guilty face, calling, "We didn't realize it was so late. Sorry, people. Really sorry," seeing at once that everything had been done that they should have done—the rebuke in it. "Well, boy, I see you've got us all organized."

"Do you know what time it is?" Lewis snapped, curving his wristwatch arm in an important accusing way up level with his eyes.

"It's half past kissing time, time to kiss again," shouted that silly Geraldine. "It's ha' pas' kissing time," shrilled a similarly silly Frank, doing a drunken little dance and flopping down into the sand, "ha' pas' kissing time, and you give me a pain."

Syra was looking at him intently. He should say something. "Ha' pas' kissing time," he almost said aloud, as though to face Syra with it, as though to draw her into this with him. Fear flared in his stomach like steam, followed by a sudden hot jet of pain that plowed down his arm and then was gone.

He reached for a cigarette in the pewter box of them, took one out and lit it, and waved out the match violently, all with his head turned stiffly away from Syra. And then he found his voice. "What a long shot, to come all this way," he said, turning to face her. "What did Georges think? He must have hated my guts. He must have thought you were daft. Oh no, because he knows you're not. But what a long shot. Just because I was agitated, and so forth, just on the strength of intuition. Or maybe more. Maybe I spelled it out more than I knew. Yeah, I did say 'ausec,' didn't I?" He looked at her pleadingly, his heart sinking.

He tossed his cigarette into the fire. And then suddenly he slid to the edge of his chair and reached out and seized both her hands in his. He held them tightly for a moment, pressed them hard, and then, uneasily, let them drop.

Syra made a light, self-conscious sound in her throat. Then she shrugged and let a faint smile move one corner of her mouth, and looked at Lewis. "Two little birds, sitting in a tree, one is you and one is me. Why did I say that? I made it up."

Lewis smiled and nibbled at his drink. They both fell silent. The fire snapped in the silent room. Syra shifted her position on the bench, then cozily settled the elbow of the arm that held her glass into the support of the other hand. She twirled the ice around in the glass, watching it. "Lewy, coming here on the plane, I started finding memories, and the past was a wave. I felt that all of me was filled with space, and I'd better hang onto the plane seat in order not to float away. And after slugging down a double vodka martini I didn't feel anything but bliss, which was incompetent, but which made everything fine. Wassa matter with me? Do you suppose that maybe once the left side of my brain, the smart side, got unhinged in some accident? Or else the connecting wires between the hemispheres got ripped apart or something. I wish I knew more about brains. Is one side the everyday living, planning brain, and the other the intuitive? A wild guess because until Georges, who is hipped on these hemispheres, started lecturing me about it, I hadn't realized it was halved. I wish I knew more about brains. Oh, God, what am I saying? Of course I don't wish that."

Lewis looked severe. "Oh don't go questioning that wonderful brew up there in your skull, kiddo. Don't for Christ's sake start that again. You ought to be thanking God for quirkery, not be blasting away at him for it."

"Okay, love. Drunkenly I agree. What a relief. You know, I just thought. One of the reasons I love to be with you, only it's such a tiny reason compared to all the bigger ones, is because you approve of me. And more blessings on you to have you never tell me what to do. I think you are one of the few people who approve. Lots of people, most people, don't, at all. And there are those with disapproval carefully hidden, too, blast them. I think that is perhaps even less nice."

Candor flickered away from Syra's clear eyes, and they darkened, concentrated with a question that needled her, had the power to undermine, but which she was always dealing with, had dealt with so far—the attentive intelligence of her eyes showed that.

"Probably that's so, cousin. That has to be so."

"I'm so happy here," she said, looking down into her glass, "and I'm not really thinking about Georges, because I'm so happy here. I had no idea I'd feel so happy here. Or did I? I should really have my head explored, but shudder to think of the findings."

"It was a pretty drastic thing to do, to leave him."

"No it wasn't drastic."

"Well, let's put it this way. I can sympathize with old Georges."

"Dear old Georges, occasionally I gloomed at him in Nassau." Her face was quiet as a calm lake, but her cool eyes flashed. "Don't you have any olives or potato chips or something?" She smiled. "To buffer the drinks, like Georges did in Nassau. He squirreled vast amounts of peanuts when he had a drink. I'm being mean about Georges, aren't I?" She shrugged uncomfortably. Here was meanness again. And toward Georges. Always and only toward Georges. Oh dear. And yet there was a certain relief in going *against* Georges, as though the fact of herself and Georges needed to be gone against.

She shrugged helplessly. "I guess I'm being really mean."

"Yes, why? It's so unlike you." Lewis was sitting straight up and forward in the big velvet chair that invited relaxation, his full mouth parted in rapt interest. If ever there was a person controlled by *true* considerateness, it was Syra. Well did he remember, visiting that schoolroom in Cazenovia, her mother's injunction to her pupils about the purpose, and the need, of true, not false, considerateness, for one must only be considerate, she would say, if one really, truly, felt like it. Otherwise it was not true considerateness, but simply meaningless manners.

And now for a keen moment Lewis saw that schoolroom in the attic, and the cupola on the flat Victorian roof, a sun-blazed square of glass—"The Lighthouse," they had all called it. He loved that room, and loved the occasional times he had sat there and been exposed to the amazing exciting differences of his Aunt Cleo's teachings. Syra, he knew, was the product of an upbringing based on and guided by a philosophy; not the typical child guidance, child rearing programs of one's generation, oh no, nothing like that. For his Aunt Cleo's teachings were based on her unshakable belief that everything one needed to know about life was in Shakespeare, in Chekhov, in Jung, in Tolstoi and the Bhagavad Gita and Confucius, and of course the Bible. In his Aunt Cleo the written word spoke to a free heart, he knew. And it was from *her* mother, the minister, that Cleo had imbibed much of her evangelistic conviction and fervor. Everything is really simple, Lewis thought, and these women knew it. Syra knows it. And yet, in spite of her evangelical background, Syra's behavior showed none of the evidences of a didactic upbringing. She was as natural as a summer breeze. To a greater extent than anyone he had ever known, she lived not only spontaneously, but consciously as well, by the rules for behavior and for being that her mother had taught her. In fact, he had always been fascinated by the extent to which Syra seemed to be in close and constant touch with the voice of her mother. Or her own voice? Whatever. A prompter, he knew, was continually at work in Syra, guiding her and supporting her.

But for the moment, he worried, the prompter seemed to have been silenced. Syra was being mean. "I can't for the life of me see why you want to be mean about a thoroughly decent, kind man like Georges," he said rather petulantly. "I admire a kind man. Which I'm not."

"I don't know. But Lewy, my dearest cousin, listen. So you aren't kind. Period. But you enchant me. Absolutely enchant me. You ring all my bells." She lifted one kimona-ed arm, held it bent for a moment, stretched it way up, then shuddered happily as she dropped it. "I love to be enchanted. I'd rather be enchanted than bekinded." She began to laugh, they both began to laugh, and Lewis flopped back in his chair, laughing, his face puzzled, his face eager, holding his glass up stiffly so that the drink wouldn't spill over, and then, because it did, putting it down on the table beside his elbow, bringing out his handkerchief to mop the arm of the chair.

There was a silence now, in which Syra looked down into her glass, and swirled the liquid in it round and round thoughtfully, while Lewis watched her, his eyes staring and wistful. Then he sighed heavily.

"Play me something, Siry, I'm right in the mood for it. Would you? Would you mind stopping drinking long enough to play me something?"

"Oh but I'd love to play something."

Lewis sprang up, holding a hand palm out toward her like a traffic policeman. "I'll get it, I'll get it, don't you move!"

She began to laugh. "I wasn't going to." She was still shaking with soft private laughter when Lewis came back with the guitar case and put it down beside her. He stood rather sheepishly above her. Then he returned to his chair, picked up his drink, smiled into it foolishly, happily–he knew he was her slave–and said, "Play my favorite. Play the Third Villa Lobos."

She lifted her guitar out of its case and brought it up to her lap. Her eyes grew attentive and remote, as raising the instrument into readiness on the knee she had crossed, she dragged a loose-wristed hand across its strings, once, and then studiously began to tune it. Lewis closed his eyes, and lay back against the velvet of his chair.

She stopped. She waited. She gave her head a little flounce back and held it, chin raised, for a moment, then she bent to her instrument. With a dulcet buzz that was both stirring and tender, the preparatory chords mounted once, as though mounting gradually a broadness, worn and marble and ancient, like Roman steps; then, the peak reached, they descended, plaintively, inquiringly, uncertainly; came down to a long-plucked, serene chord; waited; then mounted the same steps again, in the same, slow, aspiring way, to the top, to what? What goal, what aspiration? Twice this ascent occurred humbly but majestically and then, arrived this final time, it paused before beginning the single-voiced melody for which it had been preparing.

Lewis held his breath, waiting. This was a pause at the end of a day's mounting struggle, he thought, the pause before...

Like drops of clear water the single singing notes began their descent—a pure, hesitant overstitch downward, to be resolved, after a suspenseful second of waiting, in one gentle, unassuming chord of the utmost serene finality.

Then again, a short upward surge, the box of the guitar humming with deep sweetness, and the peak reached, the breath held.

And as the pure single descent began again, Lewis felt himself, as always, cleansed, purified. The purity of this one note singing, stitching downward, a simple song that a child might hum, told him of all peace, of all simplicity.

And then the descent was completed. Syra raised her head as she waited before plucking the last note, one quiet note that was the ending.

Syra sat stilled in its spell, and Lewis lay back in his chair with closed eyes. Their ancestral clock, somehow of the same one-noted simplicity, was the only sound besides the soft stirring and collapsing of the faithful fire.

At last Lewis opened his eyes. "Thank you." His voice was as peaceful as the Prelude. "You can't know how that untangles me."

Syra nodded, and bent over to put the guitar back in the case. "Nothing can really come after that. I always play that either alone, or the last thing."

"Or just for me. The Prelude is you. It is you, giving to me, Syra simplifying Lewis."

Syra closed the guitar case and picked up her waiting glass. She tilted her head to get the last of her drink. The slipping ice made the only sound.

In the far darkness of a corner window, beyond, out in the night, she saw the new moon. So calm did it make her feel that she thought she had never really seen a new moon in a night sky until now. She was seeing it without any interference in herself, as though vision had become unclouded.

Syra simplifying Syra... This was what she achieved with her music. One of the things it was for. Music opened the possibilities of her being. She found her answers in music, never by exclusive means of her mind, and never in words. It was always as if her frame, her skeleton, was a musical instrument through which sound resonated, and as though this sound became a language within this frame. It was the frame that spoke, in echo of the sound, and her circulation pulsed with this sound language. Once this happened, there was no more conflict about whatever she had been in conflict about. The answer to what she wanted or should do was in her organism. Stretched out into sound was knowledge, then resolution.

And so now, the single note of the Villa Lobos echoed in her, kept echoing; echoed finally into a mound of visceral knowledge that sounded, and then took shape, and became idea.

And so she knew that something was plucking at the peace of being here, disturbing it in a way that she must now pay attention to. A concern, she saw, was growing in her about Lewis–and hadn't she known it from the letter?–so that it was impossible even for her, with her unwillingness, even her inability, to come to analytical conclusion, not to hear basically what Lewis was telling her, not to relate this concern to something and not to search for the source of it. Oh, what can I know, what can I do? she worried. My mind will of course fail because the halves aren't cooperating. Hell. There are moments when it would be handy to be an intellectual.

But then, quite clearly, it occurred to her that right here in this room she saw what she thought of as little clues to his unhappiness, like the daffodil arrangements on the mantle-piece, for instance, like the wing chairs, like almost everything else about this place. It was becoming impossible not to begin to see right here in this room—the slow, subliminal process of com-prehension visible at last through the Villa Lobos—why she had always had a sense of Lewis being in danger. She was beginning to sense that, confronted with shouting clues to a misery that was alarming, she was going to be called upon for more than passivity. And though she was suspicious of diagnoses, of final answers, she found that a knowledge of Lewis had risen finally to the level of her consciousness, that she was dredging up from herself a truth that was realistically right here in the open now, and which she must somehow deal with.

This sort of thinking bolstered her. She felt awed, she felt enlarged, adult. These knowings come from way down, she told herself proudly.

She looked at Lewis candidly, and it was the wing chair that bothered her. Wing chairs spoke to her of a period, of muse-ums—Williamsburg was full of them—and it made her uncomfort-able and frustrated to see Lewis sitting there in his, as though he belonged in it. She knew he loved those chairs. He had told her about them breathlessly when he had bought them, they were circa some very early and significant date. But those chairs, this room, everything in it, everything in the house for that matter, was, she now saw, just simply no more alive than a picture in a magazine. She felt a sudden strong sense of hating to have Lewis be a slave to this pretendy thing. Because nothing in this place of his is alive, she thought, nothing is breathing. And so maybe Lewy isn't, either. It is all very bad on his spirit, this place is. And then she said to herself surprisingly that Aunt Sally was behind all this. She wasn't astonished to realize this, because clarity often does not astonish, clarity often in its simplicity feels uneventful. But she knew, feeling it like a loud voice inside her, that Aunt Sally was behind all this.

For a tight moment she shrank from Lewis's mother who had raised him in this useless way. She saw the whole thing, not in words, but in images–shells, stones from the beach, ferns, buttercups, nosegays. "Nosegays for Aunt Sally." The text behind these images was vivid in her, too, and she could tell herself, though not in so many words, that from Lewis's earliest days he had learned to know what his mother thought beautiful, although *beautiful* was not a word he used then. A fern in the woods, for instance, was something for him to stoop over and to study wonderingly–the repetitious perfection of each frond. But then he would pick it carefully, his eyes glowing, and take it home to his mother, who would rave over its beauty and put it in a little vase on a little table next to her bed.

She remembered how, when his mother called attention to something beautiful, Lewis was drawn into her thralldom because he loved the dramatic way she seemed to expand and to glow. But though his mother's showy wonder over a fern, for instance, could enter lewis and fill *him* with wonder, still he wasn't associating the feeling with the fern. No. His mother's so-called reverence for the fern was obviously to Lewis only a way he should behave when observing certain things that were fascinatingly observable.

Thinking all this, Syra was touched, she was appalled. And she could now say to herself, and believe the words she had found to say it, that Lewy had learned to go into the fields not for himself, but for his mother, to bring back odd and naturally lovely bouquets–nosegays, Aunt Sally called them–that she would go into raptures over. "He has such a sense of beauty," she remembered his mother saying to her mother, "and that makes two of us."

And then, when he grew up, Syra thought, the nosegays he

brought to his mother were the honors he won at school and college. Aunt Sally was always there—at Exeter, at Cornell—for every tennis match Lewis played in, for every choral concert he sang in, for every honor bestowed on him, and of course for his graduations. Always, there was Aunt Sally in the front row, tearful with pride. And after college, in the place of the silver cups and the diplomas, the nosegays Lewis brought to his mother were rare antiques from all over the world. "Oh, he has such a nose for a gem," Aunt Sally would cry. "There's nothing he's ever picked up that hasn't made my *fortune!*"

Oh poor Lewy, oh, this arrows me, Syra thought passionately. What would your life have been like if the picking of a fern had been for yourself and not for your mother? Her heart began to knock against her ribs, as though it were doing this for some reason, like a fist knocking hard on a door that ought to be opened.

And then, briefly and searingly, beneath the banging of her heart, there they were, she and Lewy, in the back seat of the car on her thirteenth birthday—that sudden bottomless looking and then that incredible bursting into flame, at first up above and then *down there.*

We were so young, she thought, trying to erase the rapturous, the breathless discomfort, and she tried to sigh commiseratingly as though over something sweet and faded and long gone. Except that there was in her a ringing and singing, pushing upward, as though her body could float up like a bit of ash from the flame of the fire at her back.

Beyond the circle of the fire and Lewis and herself, Syra had the sense of an insufferable arbitrariness—nosegays for Aunt Sally, she thought frantically, as though the man was controlled by the pursuit, the never-ending insatiable pursuit of the chairs and the tables and the rugs and the lavender old windows, and then by the rules for arranging all these things together, as though there were an unbreakable rule about how one object must perform in relation to another object. Oh damn these antiques to hell, she cried to herself. My stomach churns.

He's mechanical, she thought, and she felt the wing chairs and the good tweeds and the flower arrangements on the mantlepiece all, all having nothing to do with the essence of this man. "I've always known I was someone else," he had once told her. He is like a wound-up tin toy, she thought, a tin toy scurrying around in senseless circles, bashing into a wall, backing away and swirling around and then bashing into another wall, circling and bashing and backing and circling.

And then she had a still moment of saying to herself, "But someday the toy will run down."

Lewis was opening the pewter box on the table beside the chair, taking another cigarette from it in his large, very long fingers, which shook slightly. She looked at him in a thorough, searching way she was unused to, seeing the lines of bitterness around his loose and beautiful lips as he put the cigarette carefully in the center of them and then lighted a match that shone briefly in his eyes, then shook it out with what seemed like sudden fury. And she saw him trapped in his period-piece wing chair, frozen there, as though the chair had cast a magic spell over him that would make him unable ever to get up out of it. She looked at the languid body in tweeds, glass of whiskey in one hand and a cigarette in the other—forever there in that chair, forever holding a drink in one hand, a cigarette in the other, forever an unresolved mixture of hope and helplessness. She had an oppressive sense of Lewis being trapped in that chair, and she cared terribly that he shouldn't be.

So, then, the question was—and hell's bells, how new, how difficult, how unnatural it was to know this, how unwilling she was to know it—the question was: What was a person to do about it? Was it up to her to *do* something?

But no! She could not, could *not* bring herself to want to interfere with Lewis. Though wasn't "ausec" just that? And "looking after Lewis"? That's what she had said to Georges in Nassau. "I look after Lewis." Must I *do* something? Oh damn, I come close and then the mist closes in....

Then. No, she said to herself with sudden energy, and with resolve, and with a relieving restoration of balance. No. I will not *do anything*. For I cannot. I *cannot*. I will just cross my fingers and put up magic. Or I will ask God please to give me some wisdom, and then I will simply sit back and wait.

She took several little sips of her drink in quick succession, looking at Lewis with now quite penetrating eyes. She felt lost, as though she were drifting away with Lewis into some unknown territory, and apprehensive, because now she knew she had no answer in her bones, no satisfactory answer to why she had come, or to what ought to be done. Oh, I wish my left brain could work all the time, not just in little spurts now and then, she thought despairingly.

"You need another drink, Siry."

She came abruptly out of her mind, gratefully. "I don't *need* one. Not a fourth drink. But I want one. How about you? Aren't you getting hungry? I'm starved. What are we going to eat? Eggs, maybe?" She would have liked a little golden squab to be brought to her this minute on a tray with a white napkin, a hot roll, and a glass of wine.

"Hungry?" Was he hungry?... He was startled to be reminded that there was food in the world and that one ate. No, he wasn't hungry, not in the least. And the thought of the kitchen, intrusive, practical, breaking the spell, dismayed him. But Syra should eat. And he supposed he should eat. "But listen," he cried, feeling the balm of a solution, "we'll got out, we'll dine out! How about it?"

"Lewy, that's an inspiration. No work!" The little golden squab would become a reality. She burst out laughing, knowing that she had had too much to drink. "Where will we go, cousin?"

Where will we go, she asks, not, Should you go out in your condition? She doesn't think about my health at all, Lewis thought, she hasn't asked once about it. But I feel fine, he realized. I haven't felt the pain at all, for hours. I'm cured. It was all psychosomatic. And he felt such a rush of elation that he leapt up from his chair (he's broken the spell, Syra thought amusedly) and flung out his arms, holding them spread-eagle over her, and beamed down on her, without his phony smile and with his eyes glowing. "Oh marvelous, marvelous. Know what? I'm happy."

"Are you?"

"Happy as a clam. Good God, do you realize what it means to be happy as a clam? Clams live in shells, buried in the sand. I'm a clam, cousin," said he a little drunkenly. "Feel my hand. Does it feel clammy?" He began to laugh, rather inordinately, putting his hand on her neck.

"Actually it does." She shivered.

"It's cold from holding my glass."

"Oh sure." She smiled a clean wide sudden smile, looking up at him with love. "But tell me where we're going, my wonderful and such fun cousin."

"To the Oak Tree Inn. Away we go to the Oak Tree Inn. You've never seen it for the simple reason it's new. Old. New. Both. It's an old barn done over, under the shade of mighty oaks. Old beams, candlelight, fires, red-checked tablecloths." Oh how surprisingly wonderful, he thought, picturing himself getting into the car and driving on a spring evening with Syra beside him to a cozy, welcoming little country inn, where there would be a fire burning brightly, and a candlelit table with a basket of hot bread and a bottle of wine.

"Let's skip the drink here, then, and have another one there. Would that suit you? Another one here, another one there, and I'll be drunk." She rose to her feet, unsteadily. She grinned up at Lewis. "Okay? Because I always love to have one when I get there, don't you? It seems only right." She burst out laughing again. Fun, fun, fun... "I'm a little drunk now," she said slowly. Then she flung her arms out, and they went into each other's arms, laughing, hugging, standing teetering together in a hug that didn't lessen, didn't want to lessen. She tingled against this man, not Cousin Lewis, surprised, puzzled, curiously elated.

She felt tiny and solid in Lewis's arms. He had never held her for so long, nor had he ever held her as a woman. She was such a certain little thing, so unquestioning. He felt his arms around permanence. Her breasts were two little hard mounds, somehow unquestioning too. These two small promontories thrust into his ribs—how could he not notice them? There they were for the first time. Although they were cousinly, weren't they? But it was she, wasn't it, who was making this different, and uncousinly, she who was doing the long holding on?...

Troubled, he gave her a last cousinly hug, laughed placatingly, and stepped away.

❧ III ❧

DINING out with Syra at a country inn had failed to live up to Lewis's expectation of it, though every aspect of its candlelit coziness, which he had pictured with such vividness, was there. Sitting down and unfurling his napkin, he had exhaled a great

"Aaahhh," of satisfaction, "aaahhh, isn't this nice!"—called for the waiter, ordered their drinks, asked for the wine list, lit a cigarette, exhaled another contented "aaahhh," and then sat back, beaming across at Syra, who had suspended concern about Lewis in favor of agreeable sensations.

But Lewis, who kept waiting for his faint disappointment to be cleared up, waiting for the moment beyond the present one, sat across from her, not really feeling her here as he had at home, looking about him with furtive anxious little glances now and then to see where the fulfillment of anticipation might be hiding. Was it in the drinks, perchance? because here they were, being borne in on a pewter tray. Was it in the food, was it to be the food and wine that would bring everything into focus? Occasionally, during the meal, he had the uneasy sensation of being in the midst of a familiar dream. "I keep wanting to pinch myself," he said to Syra. "I can't believe we're sitting here, sitting across from each other."

But Syra could believe it. She very much knew that she was here, with Lewis, and she was enjoying herself placidly. Hungry, she said very little, applying herself to her little golden crusty squab with interest and absorption. Her fingers glistening, she bit around a tiny leg for its every shred of flesh, her eyes smiling quietly across at Lewis.

Lewis, however, had lost the source of his gaiety and was searching hard and unnaturally for topics of conversation. The promising little loaf of hot bread on a cutting board had proved soggy, though he ate nearly all of it, wolfishly. The restaurant was crowded, it was hectic, it was dark—ridiculously dark, Lewis though contemptuously, a passion pit. True, their table was in an alcove, beside the fire, but right next to them was a table of twelve celebrating women, all wearing corsages, all dressed in sleeveless bright-colored dresses and very high heels, all hugely "hair-styled" in beauty parlors only minutes, Lewis was sure, before coming here. Their celebrating was sporadic—moments of shrieking group laughter, moments of awkward silence. They would, Lewis hoped, eventually drink a little too much, and have a better time. There would be a birthday cake, he was certain.

He realized he was exhausted. A group of men at the neon-lit bar were beginning to drape arms bibulously across shoulders, to weave determinedly and frequently to the "Messieurs," as it was called here, their faces blurred and dogged on this solitary urgent excursion. The sight of this human helplessness disturbed Lewis. He wanted to leave in the worst way.

And when, after he had paid the bill and they were sipping the last of their coffee, he said, "Now! Home!" his voice, his spirits roused once more in anticipation, only then did he feel anything like the elation he had felt before getting here.

Walking across the parking lot to the car, the air so cool, even cold, so marvelously fresh and clear after the stuffiness of the smoke-filled restaurant, he felt a surge of joy again, and, staggering a little, he reached and pulled Syra to him, holding her around the waist and tight against him. "Oh, cousin, isn't this a night!"

And when they got home, and were walking, arm and arm, unsteadily over the crunching gravel toward the house, in the silence of the country night, a million stars in the sky, suddenly Syra cried, "The peepers! Listen, Lewy, the peepers," and then to herself, softly, "Oh there are so many heavens, all the doors opening."

They stopped walking to make the silence complete, and stood listening to the shrill driving whistling chorus coming from the swamp in the woods behind Lewis's house. He said nothing, only stopped and stood to listen and to give himself totally to this vast clamorous announcement of spring. Finally, having experienced it enough, mutually they began to move toward the house.

"It's the first time I've heard them this year," Lewis murmured.

"How come?" Syra asked. "It's already April. Don't they begin in early April? Or even late March?"

"I think they do. But I've been sick." Plaintively. "This is the first time I've been out at night for three weeks or more. I haven't even stuck my head out at night. I've only heard them through layers of house, 'as through a glass, darkly'."

"There is a new moon Lewy, look." And then she said, quietly, "You are a sort of new moon to me, Lewy."

"Which means that I shall have to moon over you, does it not?"

"Uh huh! Oh that was nice, Lewy," Syra said, meaning the dinner, while Lewis groped for his door key in pocket after pocket. "Nice, nice, nice." He couldn't find the key, and, alarmed, tried the door, which was unlocked. "Good God, I went off and left the place unlocked, and the keys, you can be sure, on the nail in the kitchen." He began to laugh. "Good old meticulous me. You let me drink too much."

"You did the same thing to me."

"Are we drunk?"

"Soused."

"Goody."

Lewis bustled to rebuild the fire, which was now only ash and a few glowing coals. "You're not ready for bed yet, I hope," he said, looking at Syra, who stood tentatively beside a table, turning over the pages of a magazine with her coat still on.

She felt so strange suddenly, coming into this still room, alone with Lewis in his house and bedtime the next thing. She felt shy. She felt timidly unlike herself, her composure seemed gone. She did not want to look at Lewis. Studious over the magazine she said, "Oh no, not yet," stiffly, staring down at pages she didn't see. She felt lost, drifting into some unfamiliar place where there seemed to be no cues for what to do and what to say, and how to be normal about putting down the magazine and taking off her coat, and looking at Lewis. "No, I'm not sleepy yet."

But then she was struck, stunned. And a pleasurable shudder went from her shoulders on down throughout her whole body to her toes, then backwashed up again, leaving her with a sudden involuntary smile over which she seemed to have no control. That smile felt wonderful as it widened and opened and loosened whatever needed to be loosened, and took command, it told her that it was her acknowledgement, her permission to herself, her open encouragement. The rest of her might be helpless, but that open, blissful, goading smile was leading her right ahead. Having smiled like this, there was no turning back.

"Great! I'll get us a nightcap," Lewis cried. Then he stopped behind her and said impulsively, "I don't want to go to bed just yet. You know I can't bear to have anything end. I'm like a child, screaming when I'm told it's time to go to bed. I've never been able to bear the end of anything. The play ends, the curtain comes down. The lights go on in the theater. Dreary, unacceptable reality, that's what it is." He put his hand on her shoulder, she quivered from it, and, not waiting for her answer to this outburst, went off to the kitchen to fix their drinks.

When he was gone, she brought her hands halfway up to her face, palms upward, as though they would tell her something. They were pink, that was all. But it was nice that they were pink—very alive, pink palms. She felt perfectly helpless. Alarmed. Blissful. Yes, this was the way she felt, and there was nothing in her that wanted to fight it. She was sexual, gloriously so, and that was all she was. The blossom of her visit to Lewis. To comfort Lewis.

She smiled, swayed, gripped the table. She laughed, and as she was laughing, holding onto the table, Lewis came back with their two drinks. Those inevitable drinks, she thought, turning around to look at him. Now she saw his loved face as innocent, as safe in its innocence, and only then felt a pang of compunction, a question in the midst of her massing sexuality. What about *him*? How did *he* feel? What am I thinking of, she rebuked herself, and felt steadier, cooler.

The fire was taking quickly, and all at once the fireplace was full of a thundering, beating sheet of upward flame.

That was very silly, she thought calmly now, taking the glass Lewis held out to her. I'm a sexpot, she thought, with a certain deep regard for being this, with a respectful, grateful recognition of it, you might say. I'm out of my mind, she thought expectantly. Out of my mind, and in my body. And I should say good night to Lewis, now, without drinking that drink, and go straight up to bed, my bed, like a proper person.

Lewis, whose spirits had been continuously on the rise ever since leaving the restaurant, whistling, jaunty, put his glass carefully on the firebench and leaned over to poke the fire, which was behaving excessively. Men's legs, their rears, are good, Syra thought, looking with appreciation at his tiny rump under tight stretched pants at the top of his long, gracefully kneeling legs. Without any premeditation she put down her glass and reached to the little radio on the table and turned it on. Jazz burst into the quiet room.

Lewis got up from the fire with a slow look of pleasure. And Syra, gazing straight across at him, smiling faintly, peeled off her coat and let it drop to the floor, kicked off her ballet slippers and felt looser, surer on bare feet. Striptease, how joyous, how soaring, she thought, smiling more fully, and with a feeling of supreme ease, and a mischievous freedom she knew she'd been waiting to feel for all the years she'd suppressed it.

Lewis grinned, reached down for a quick sip of his drink, kicked off his shoes, too. Then slowly, like a heron rising for flight, he raised himself up onto his toes, poised, his arms spread like the heron's wings, waiting for what Syra would do.

Syra was going to kick over the traces. And the compact, severe readiness of her body, along with the shining drive of her eyes, proclaimed this. She furled one arm up, then the other, making a slow voluptuous S of her body from the bottom up, like smoke curling up from a fire, and then she flung her hair back and began to slither across the room with a quiet smile of concentration until she came right up under the spread of Lewis's arms. She swayed there, her body inches from his, smiling up into his face, moving just a little bit all over, as though she were loosening, pleasurably, every joint, one at a time.

Lewis drew a great breath from his toes, which stretched him taller, as though this would be the moment of flight. His face was serious now and riveted on her. Then he began to move his hips from side to side, stepping away from her, and around her, circling around her, lowering his arms and reaching them out toward her in an undulating scooping motion, his eyes intense, as though to suggest gathering her up into himself, but tantalizingly sheering away each time.

Their dance, to the hypnotic slow pound of the jazz, became the exploratory graceful circling of two wrestlers at the outset of a contest. Syra moved under the shimmering amber silk of her kimona with a suggestive ripple, and with a growing smile of wanton delight, for wantonness she was feeling at last, complete abandonment of reason, and there was such total joy in having this be the only dictate that she felt she never wanted to feel any other way. The cornet felt to her like a limpid pure shaft of musical sound, piped, like a rod of sweet amber oil, from the pouting lips of the cornetist straight into the center of her body.

Lewis was feeling Syra's abandonment, but not seriously relating it to himself. His dancing, drunk and euphoric as he was, was abandoned too, and wanton, for wantonness came easily to

Lewis. But the wantonness wasn't directed at Syra, or if it was, he didn't know it or admit it—there was no invitation in his, as there was in hers. The dance felt to him like all the others they'd had together when they'd both gone happily berserk, pretending in a clowning sort of way to be wildly aroused. He circled her, and hovered over her with outspread arms like a great predatory bird getting ready to pounce, but the gleeful sparkle of his green eyes told that this was all only fun.

The music stopped, the announcer's voice came on. They stopped, too. And for a moment, in the room full of suddenly stopped activity—the practical radio voice telling of alien, needless necessities, and the snap of the busy fire, and away off, the solid, sane monotonous ticking of the ancestral clock telling them of responsibility—for a moment, until the music started again, they panted heavily, not hearing any of these noises. Standing still, they both occasionally lurched from want of sober balance. Then Syra, without moving, reached down and snapped off the radio.

As she did so she had a sudden sure sensation that the deliberateness and the finality of the turning off of this button was a symbol of the power within her to manipulate a conclusion. Nothing could stop her now, she had turned off the music and the time had come. All the niceties and adaptations and taboos of her life were being deliriously and royally scuttled, and now she would be what she was.

She turned to face Lewis. Looked at him. Then she walked straight across to him and put herself delicately against him while with an almost inch-by-inch provocative melting into him, she slid her arms up his chest and wound her hands together behind his neck.

Surprise was Lewis's first, unemotional reaction. He was simply surprised. He even thought that this was just another part of the game of the dance.

Then in seconds he was bewildered.

Then he knew. He was so incredulous for a moment that he had no sensation at all. Then there was a slow invasion of feeling. It was horror. But her body. She was sealing it against him, he was catching fire from it. Helplessly he felt an impossible loosening and firing of his body. Just as powerfully, he was scandalized. "No," he whispered, begged, prayed. But with a strange gasp he put his arms around her, too.

They clung together, lurching, whimpering, and then, finally, as though they had searched together for years for only one thing and had finally found it, cautiously, they began to kiss.

It was total for both of them, hearts organs minds, a complete congruity of devout delicate racing lust, with robustness promised. They kissed for a long time, sweetened and fired beyond any belief. It was the simple answer of their lives, it had arrived, and it was just as Syra had always known it would be except that she hadn't imagined the extent of it, the never-ending feeling of saturation, as though unique saturation had arrived but was still arriving and would keep on arriving forever.

For a moment Lewis stopped their kissing. "Siry, love, no. No," he groaned, pleaded. "No, love, no. No." But his kisses returned at once, desperate, such a hunger not assuagable.

Finally Syra pulled her lips gently away, and looked at him. He saw the radiance of her face; in her clear eyes he saw a well of life for him, deep, bottomless. "Come," she said evenly, "come upstairs."

The word that was right there, all powerful, this word that was in command, shot out of him: "*No.*" And, astonished, appalled at himself, he began to feel this *no* in his mind forcing itself into and throughout his body. It made his arms drop away from Syra and he stepped back from her, while he felt, gradually, with panic but with a shrill mounting righteousness, all the loose full flow of his longing begin to freeze. Slowly, he began to look at this face below his, not with love and longing, but with a hateful-feeling, righteous-feeling repudiation. It was an incestuous face, the dark eyes were Circe eyes, pink Syra lips were adulteress lips.

He stepped farther away from her, trembling terribly. He stood furious, aghast, sickened. She was sinful. He was sinful. He was filled with bitter shame, for himself and for her.

He had a sudden pain in his chest that took his breath away.

Feeling hatred for her, he turned his back on her. How could she have done this disastrous thing? They'd had everything, and then, in seconds, nothing. What would they be together now?

Nothing, he told himself, picking up his glass shakily and draining its contents with the ice clattering in the silence, his back rebuking her while through his whole tormented being scandalized parents' eyes swarmed, punishing fingers pointed. Gradually he could feel, and with a loathsome, longing familiarity and relief, the powerful encasement of the *no*, hard and impregnable as stone, protecting him like the walls of a fortress from the soft infectious thing at his back.

Syra, wanting him unbearably, stood timidly behind him. Her head whirled, then began to spin. She lurched down hard onto a chair. Outside, the wind had risen, raving softly through the boughs of the maples over the roof. A gust came down the chimney, billowing the smoke out into the room. Bitter smoke, bitter silence.

Still with his back to her like a closed door, Lewis put his hands on the mantle to steady himself, for he felt dizzy. And he sensed himself hard as stone, restructured, a stiff unfeeling stone structure of a man full of horror and nothing. A faint visceral desolation, and a sick jerky panic in his lungs that was his breathing, were as nothing in the power of all this unyielding stone. He was back in it and he had to live in it, returned to it from a terrifying soft running-away thing that had no power over stone. He was back in it for good. Perfectly alone.

He put his hot forehead down onto cold hands. Well, he was safe now. There was a certain bleak comfort, a kind of justification of helplessness and alienation, in admitting the inevitability and invincibility of the stone that was the center of himself, though victory was in failure. And there was almost peace in being Lewis at last one hundred percent alone.

"But don't you see?" Syra was saying to his back, in a flat, slurred voice, "can't you see that it's—that it's—*here?*" But this was all that would come out. So frustrating. The knowledge was there. But there was too much drink in her mind and it kept the knowledge from being put into proper words, making them come out in such meaningless little broken-off threads. Maddening. But why try anyway? Of what use was persuasion against such indomitable refusal?

What wreckage, she thought, as she got up and turned and walked carefully, with a staggering kind of dignity, across to the stairs.

PART FOUR

ON Saturday morning Anne, sitting with Rupert at the kitchen table having an early breakfast, announced to him that she would like to do the weekend shopping if he didn't mind, since she wanted anyway to do lots of little personal errands, "which you couldn't possibly do for me, dear. Shall I slice you some more bread, dear?"

"No bread, dear."

It was a misty gray morning, seeming to Anne, in this warm kitchen where lights were necessary, to be a chill world out there that would offer no spring thrills and would be a rain-gear kind of effort to go out into. The whole idea of going out into it tired her. But I'm being negative, she told herself severely, feeling a sudden sickening faint flush of dismay that remained like something undigested in her stomach. There's no need, she once more told herself, to be negative—yet. And she ran a hand, seeking something, some panacea, along the deep softness of her gray cashmere sweater.

She looked hungrily at her husband, at his bountiful and wiry gray hair shining bright silver in the light from the over-head lamp, at his eyes which, over the rim of his coffee cup stared at nothing, brilliant and detached. She was having one of her frequent moments of seeing him thoroughly, and, looking at his rough large hands that chopped wood and washed dishes and scrubbed floors and wrote essays and made love to her, looking at this willing and tender hand lying inertly alongside his saucer, she felt moved and softened and pained by the sight of it.

"How about trying some of this new lemon marmalade?" she asked him anxiously, prettily.

"No, Anne. No," he said kindly.

He was in his detached mood of weighty and impregnable quiet, Anne saw, and she really knew better than to chatter to him. Yet she dared another attempt. "Bernice made it," she declared importantly.

Rupert only shook his head slightly, and this irritated her, slightly. But she steeled herself to say nothing more, and clamped her mouth shut. And she looked at his dark-skinned, weathered face with its lustrous orientally brown eyes secretive now, and wondered again why he was so unusually quiet. Strange for him. And yesterday after getting the letter he had been stunned, reverent with happiness. She worried about this, for much as, increasingly these days, she found herself disparaging Rupert's childish, explosive vanity, she was nevertheless uneasy to see him without it.

She felt quiet, too. Uncomfortably wordless. She was still so nonplussed by the letter's news that she couldn't feel anything she knew she should be feeling, couldn't even today summon the proper loving enthusiasm. It was simply incomprehensible to her that Rupert was going to have a book published. And she saw, she now admitted to herself, that with all the lip service she'd paid to the encouragement of such an accomplishment, she'd never truly believed it could happen.

They sat without words for a while. In the kitchen silence the Regulator clock on the wall ticked with a frenzied exactness. There was the occasional sound of one of their cups striking one of their saucers as it was taken away from silent lips and set down.

Their favorite room was this kitchen, but they loved all of the lofty-ceilinged old barn house, Rupert as much as Anne. Contrary to convention it was more his than hers, for it was a thorough expression of artistic Rupert, Anne's own personality showing nowhere, except in unsuccessful imitation of him. Worshipful and derivative, she had schooled herself to believe in only one look–Rupert's–and she tried with zeal to achieve this look in every room, whether in a calculatedly haphazard arrangement of books and magazines on the living room table, an arty display of vegetables in a wooden bowl on the kitchen counter, a seashell here, a rock there, a single graceful branch in a vase, two fat golden loaves of her own bread to give dimension, meaning, to the kitchen's look.

The kitchen seemed wholly Rupert's room. Here, in this uncluttered light-filled square, was old wood he had sanded and waxed, copper pots he kept polished, a big round table he had made himself, and, as of yesterday, an old glass milk bottle in the center of it holding a slender branch with perfect round tiny buds that shone in the lamplight like green seed pearls.

Even the floor could be called his. It was poplar, scrubbed to the satiny white of old bones. Scrubbed, on his hands and knees, by Rupert. A chore he enjoyed. Sometimes, since no one was ever around when he scrubbed floors, he made himself into a bear, growling and swaying his hanging head; or into a cat, arching his back way up, then collapsing it, spitting, meowing, clawing. Playing animal made the chore gay, made *him* gay. He loved to smell the wet wood, and then to see the cleanliness emerge as the floor dried.

Anne could not continue to have there be no sound between them. Experimentally, she parted her healthy amber-pink lips. And then at last, uneasily, she said, "Do you mind if it's me that does the shopping today, dear? I mean, were you planning to for any reason? I've the errands to do and also," she said quickly in order to give it the sound of no importance, "I'd like to drop in on Lewis briefly, to leave him a book I hope he'll read. So I'll do the shopping. Yes? That is, if you don't mind my usurping your... 'role.'"

To her surprise he spoke. "Not at all. Not at all." A pause. "It'll give me a chance to split some wood." Then explosively, "To get some exercise!" He smiled at the relief of this idea, pushed out his chest in an expansive sigh, stretched his great arms wide and then let them collapse. Then he looked full at her. He studied her a moment, curiosity in his soft brown eyes. "How did it go yesterday? The paper you were doing?"

"Oh, fine. No problem. How about you? How did work go with you?"

"Slowly. Slowly."

"Well, that's always the way, isn't it. Ho! That's Mrs. A.'s great line."

"Yes, that's her *philosophy*."

"Uh-huh. Except that she wouldn't think of it as a philosophy."

"She wouldn't. No. Dear soul."

"She *is* that."

An old man was coming for dinner tomorrow night, an artist friend who lived in New York, and they began to discuss what Anne would cook for his complicated diet.

"Poor Aldrich, there's the no-salt problem, isn't there," Rupert said compassionately, "and the no-fat problem."

"And the no-roughage problem!" Anne cried, and began to

laugh immoderately. "And *he* doesn't pay attention to any of it," she gasped, "so why should we? But we do, don't we? We daren't not. If he should drop dead the next day, think how we'd blame ourselves." And she laughed again, callously, Rupert thought. He was shocked.

"Don't be shocked, dear. I'm only joking."

"I don't think you should joke about it." Severely. "It's a deeply sad thing, really, Aldrich's increasing limitations. Such deterioration. Above all with that spirit, with that spirit. *That* doesn't deteriorate. One must respect Aldrich *supremely.*"

"I think you've got a very good point there, dear," Anne conceded, torn between pique and worship. "You're right. You usually are."

They continued to chat for a while about this and that in a long habit of companionable discourse worn hollow and smooth as the old wooden treads of a staircase. Rupert told her about Mrs. Alexander's saying that she'd thrown her pedometer the hell away, and Anne told him about hearing a bird song yesterday that sounded like drops of honey, then asked if Lewis had liked getting the book she'd sent over to him. She asked, again, after Lewis. There was something about Rupert's uncommunicativeness after getting back from there yesterday, that lay undefined at the back of her mind. "Is he better?" she chirped.

Rupert's mouth opened slowly, his eyes grew wide and staring. Thinking, he waited to speak. "Well, I'm concerned," he said finally. He tilted his head back and let his chocolate eyes rove across the ceiling.

"Dear, I have been too." Her clear eyes searched him. Did she see a question in those eyes she knew so well? "So *you* see it. I myself think Lewis needs therapy. Actually, last night I called Mrs. A. and sounded her out about it. Why, what did he do that made you feel that way?"

"Nothing particularly. Nothing particularly. But I feel he's so frantic, so unpredictable, so, so…well, never mind. He's pleased, though, about the acceptance of my book." Rupert flashed her a confiding smile, then said soberly, "He *can* be so decent, so absolutely sincere. He spoke about my work with such *genuine* appreciation."

"He's sensitive, very. But, I've thought many times recently, almost manic-depressive." Something now about Rupert made her give him a swift, shrewd look. He was disturbed, heavy with disturbance, no question of it. And the day before yesterday, he'd been so wildly happy when the letter had arrived. Something had happened at Lewis's. Yes, of course, because he had come back from Lewis's so much sooner than usual. Poor lamb, she thought envelopingly. And said, in a bright, coaxing voice, "Dear, I'm going to have more coffee. How about you? Yes? No?"

She's trying to change the subject, Rupert thought with an irritation that surprised him, and with the kind of resentful resignation he had been feeling lately. He was suddenly confused, having the familiar, solid knowledge of Anne's being everything to him mixed with a sharp, impotent feeling that in certain ways, and up to a certain point, he was manipulated.

Why must she always be so brisk, he fretted, so bright and brisk? Why must she always say, "Yes? No?" He felt himself set into turmoil by her briskness. For a moment he was agitated in a faint sad way. But he could not feel comfortable criticizing her. This made him feel agitated in a faint sad way, too. He made now a great effort to feel all of her, her briskness only a part of so much he thought wonderful.

His face softened. He reached out a self-conscious hand to touch one of the tiny smooth buds on the branch–a gesture he wanted to have noticed, and that Anne did notice, with a derision that surprised her. Then his eyes roved, and he cleared his throat unsurely. There was no single dependable mood in him this morning. Euphoria came and went in golden flashes, but the spaces in between were dark.

"Rupo, did something happen yesterday at Lewis's? I think something did."

After a silence Rupert said, "Noooo. Why? What do you mean? Why do you ask?"

"Well, you seem sad. Are you sad?"

"Noooo." With his eyes wide and staring at nothing, slowly he shook his head. "No. What I was thinking about was the other day, signing our wills in that *place*, that businesslike *place*. So unreal, so unreal. Having nothing to do with life as I know it. Or with death either. As I see it," deliberately, "as I see it." The making of wills underlay his mood like a bottomless lake.

"But Rupo, look at it this way—incidentally, I happen to agree with you about the inhuman quality of that place, but look at it this way." Her voice in its vigor grew insistent. "Look. It had to be done. Yes? It's good it's done. If anything, you've gotten over a hurdle. Wills bring something out into the open we don't want to face. But we did it! Now just be glad it's over."

Rupert sat wearily, listening because it wasn't in him not to listen, partly affected, partly bored, torn, but wishing mutinously that she didn't always so optimistically and so unalterably and so blindly feel that she must and could convince him, convince anyone.

"It's over and done with. Now you can forget it. And soon you will, I assure you!" For a second the letter of confession flashed into Anne's mind, and she felt a new, stronger flood of alarm in her stomach. "You're in a mood now, but it will pass. Everything passes!" she concluded with a flourish of trumpets, though in her voice there was a note of pleading.

"Dear, with you *everything* is going to be better tomorrow."

She sank back with a little hesitant guilty smile of appeal, suddenly deflated, "I know. But anyway, dear, as I said, everything passes," she murmured, calling him back to her, reaching out a hand to stabilize him, because she saw doubt in his face, and an alarm he was trying to disregard.

Rupert opened his eyes wide and cleared his throat importantly and did not look at her, indicating that he would ignore what she had said, indicating that he would acquiesce in none of her suspicions and surmises. He sniffed.

"Dear," Anne said in a soft little voice, her eyes sharp, "I think you will soon get back your perspective. That's all I meant." Then she gave a short laugh. "The trouble with us is, we're unwilling. Laugh, dear, that's funny." She got up abruptly and went over to the stove. "Sure you won't have just half a cup? C'm on. Keep me company," she said brightly, sweetly, standing half-turned to him, her old gray tweed skirt pulled tight over energetic big hips, holding out the coffeepot expectantly. When it came to Rupert, this forceful woman liked to be docile as a lamb. His slave. Even her voice took on a tiny, piping quality as she waited on him with sweet eagerness.

From almost the very beginning they had played this little game, or more specifically, since that winter night in New York when it had been agreed upon, in what they now laughingly referred to as "the taxi incident," that she *and* he both wanted him, needed him, to be lord and master, or at least to pretend to be. That night, coming out of the theater and anxious for a taxi, they had both (it wasn't the first time this had happened) dashed out into the traffic to try to flag one. Characteristically, it had been Anne who had succeeded in getting one, and when they were breathlessly in it–Anne triumphantly and Rupert silently–he had said to her after a moment, very quietly and very deliberately and very icily, "Now let's get something straight. From here on either you are going to get the taxis. Or I am going to get the taxis. Both of us are not going to try to get the taxis. We will decide right now. Shall it be you? Or shall it be me? That was an absurd performance. So which shall it be? You? Or me?"

A moment of shock and incredulity. Next, a wave of admiration. And then, cowering into herself, she had said in her tiny voice, "It will be you, Rupo."

From that moment on, his role of lord and master was really more her doing than his. She worshipped. He, kingly, swaggered with droit-de-seigneur importance, though it was partly an act in which he remained semiconvinced. But cock of the walk he was, though he had always had this tendency, since certain women had invariably been inclined to worship him. Yet he was at the same time the most decent of men, and had not been made impossible by being deified.

He had fallen in love with Anne the day he met her. It had been the fearlessness of this thirty-four year old Valkyrie—a calm maternal bravery that simply bowled him over—that had first stirred him that day to the thought that he might love her. If he had one memory that was persistently vivid it was the sight of Anne's smooth stocky brown legs mounting, as unhesitatingly as though it were any safe indoor stairway, the old wooden extension ladder leaning shakily against that mighty elm, there in his Vermont woods, while he, below, gripping with all his force, tried to hold it braced. He could still see the one long shaft of sun, in which millions of motes glittered, crossing the ladder at the level of his eyes; he could see her pleated skirt swaying, an elegant motion there in the beauty of the tree tops, and startling white in the density of green, as she moved swiftly up the ladder, firm on the rungs, going slower now as the ladder swayed, for she was near the top, (twenty feet above *him*, poor sweating earthbound sod) and reaching up for the crouching cat. It came to her after one moment's appraisal of her, as she took both hands off the ladder and grabbed. He could still remember the dizziness and the awe he had felt as she took both hands off the ladder, twenty feet up in the air, and calmly snatched the creature, his creature, his own cat whom he could not have rescued. He couldn't bear heights, had never been able to climb a ladder without terror and vertigo. Dear God, how beautifully, coolly, spectacularly courageous, he thought as he watched her descend, with the aid of only one hand now, for with the other she was sheltering the clawing cat against her shoulder.

They had known each other a day–a friend had brought her to the little red cottage he was living in that year, while writing the first of his unwanted novels. He had been immediately stimulated by Anne's vigor, and by her beauty, which he thought striking–fine boned, pure, staccato, not limpid, not passive, not a beauty that spoke of softnesses, of all the yielding, vulnerable sweetnesses of a feminine female, but rather of force and fire–fine skin drawn over exquisite bones, cool gray eyes. She had no lines in her face at all, it was smooth as a wax candle never burned, no muddle in it, because the passion and perplexity seething within her were kept in proper balance and not allowed to rage and ravage unchecked.

Rupert had been waked up, enlivened, by all of her, by her beauty, by her mind, by her drive. He had been delighted by the brisk bright way she went about washing up the dishes in the sink while he made coffee. After she left he had thought about her on and off, all day and into the evening. And he had gone to fetch her and had brought her back alone to his house the next morning. Listened to her. Argued with her. Her mind stirred his to new thought, though at that time of his life he was timid in expression, inarticulate. Articulateness, for him, was always a matter of confidence. But because she seemed to find him exciting, he began to feel so.

It was during lunch that his cat, which had been tucked up and dozing on the porch rail, was chased off by the farmer's dogs from down the road. And it was as Anne was climbing the ladder to the rescue, as her brown smooth legs with white pleats swaying against them climbed up and up, that he wanted her with a sudden boiling up of all that had been simmering in him since the day before, and wanted her, too, with tears of gratitude in his eyes. Anne liked to tell how she had decided the minute she saw "tall, black-eyed devastating Rupert Knight," that *she* wanted *him* and meant to have him. They were both tired of love affairs; Anne was then thirty-four and Rupert forty-four, and longing for something they called love, which they found in each other. They had both waited a long time for the perfect mate, and they regarded their meeting as the greatest event of their lives.

It was a year before they were married, a year of joyous ups and miserable downs, a year of what they called "adjustment"–"If adjustment," Rupert liked to say with puckish complacency, "can be defined as a campaign which concludes with a capitulation of both forts."

They were both living in New York that year, in the Village. Anne was just launching her own business as a career counselor for women, and Rupert was finishing a novel and beginning to toy with a play.

He had always been a writer, "even as a child," he would tell you. Writing was natural and necessary for him. "I have to write," he would say sincerely though a little grandly, "I've never had any choice in the matter." Until recently he had been for the most part unsuccessful, having sold, in forty years of writing, only a handful of short stories and articles. None of the three long, turgid novels he had written had been published, "and rightly, rightly," he would say now, looking back on them with a detached scorn. Of the body of his work, "All those years of effort, all those stacks of typewriter paper," he once said to Anne, chagrined and defeated, "all that I truly *am*, buried in a closet."

After ten years of city dwelling, they had moved to the Road. And there, in his mid-fifties and persisting anguishedly at what looked now to be a failed career, Rupert finally found–a break-through–that he was above all an essayist.

With the essays, he had begun to be published in little magazines, and gradually to have a certain succès d'éstime. With lesser involvement he had, for several years now, been writing in a Thoreauesque way a gardening column for the *Deer Valley Gazette*. And just a year ago, because of the popularity of his column, the paper had given him the option of writing about whatever he chose.

At the same time, driven by some nagging need to get outside of himself, he had taken, because he loved children so hungrily and with such reverence, a part-time volunteer job teaching creative writing in a local school program for underachievers, a job to which he became committed and which did much for his self-esteem, since he was successful in drawing out of these children the most amazing creations. The truthfulness of their writing often made him weep.

He worked hard at his writing in a thorough, relentless way; besides which, he kept house. The conventions of marriage were reversed in this household, giving it a zip, Anne liked to say, it might not otherwise have had, for Rupert stayed home to mind the house and she went out to earn their living.

She loved her work. Except for Rupert, it came first, she had told Mrs. Alexander. Perhaps, though, fundamentally, it came even before Rupert. She was good at it, expert in fact. She knew brilliantly the technique, or what she thought of as the art, of interviewing and counseling. But really she knew that her success was due to her sincere concern for the women who came to her for help. She advised, they prospered, she in turn was fulfilled by this development that had been her doing, and so it went, a continual interflow. She had had flourishing friendships with many of these women, over the years. A few of those she was fondest of had even become her "adopted daughters," as she called them. But she cared for all her clients, she lavished on them a concerned heartfelt caring. And besides all this, of course, she earned a substantial amount of money, enough for two she would think, proudly, though she had never said as much to Rupert.

Rupert did contribute a little something, too, though very little, to their income, from a small inheritance that yielded small dividends and that he had managed to live on before he met Anne. And in addition he now earned pennies from his essays infrequently published in quarterlies, from his columns, and from occasional local lectures, having become something of a small town celebrity. How he loved to lecture! But he had always been ashamed of the inequality of their incomes.

And now they had been married, blissfully, they would both have said, for fourteen years. Only a few months ago Anne had come home one day from the office to tell Rupert that, having made a study of the marriages of her clients, she would rate hers and Rupert's in the 8 range on a scale of 1 to 10. "No one should dare to hope for anything better than that," she had proclaimed in her usual convinced way, but with an exaggerated fervor.

Rupert sat in silence, debating whether to have more coffee. He sighed noisily, longing for the glorious elation about his book to return as absolutely as it had vanished, longing for Lewis's meanness never to have happened.

He was still stunned because fury had hit him all of a piece, like a fist. He hadn't known he had this much of it in him. He was almost as much concerned now about this unexpected disclosure of reservoirs of unappeasable fury in himself as he was by Lewis's insolence.

But the kitchen was warm, the table flooded with cheerful lamplight. And now, with the sight of Anne taking the coffee from the stove, with the reassurance of his home around him,

Rupert began to feel a faint glow of the elation returning. Anne restored him. Ah yes, she could restore him...

He got up with a sly look, pushed back his chair, cleared his throat preparatorily, and sauntered over to her. "Put the coffee down."

With rather nervous surprise, Anne turned and clattered the coffeepot down onto the stove. Before she could turn Rupert's arms closed around her from behind. He pulled her against him, locking his arms across her stomach. Then he bent and buried his face in the warmth of her neck and kissed it. She melted back against him and put her two hands over his, and turned her face and put her cheek against his chest.

They stayed thus contentedly in the silence, the coffee on the stove simmering faintly. Anne closed her eyes. But then she turned suddenly and clung to him, giving him a full-lipped soft long kiss.

He opened his eyes wide. "Why, dearest!"

She smiled at him, unsurely, a little sadly. Yet eagerly, too.

"Shall we continue?" he said.

Grateful, she moved softly and heavily against him, experimenting. She found nothing there, nothing to go on. She gave him a big, spasmodic hug, and stepped away. "Well, I guess no."

"I guess no, too."

"It would be fun on the kitchen floor, no?"

"On the kitchen *floor!*" he exploded.

She burst into gusts of laughter, rather hysterically. "Oh Rupo, dearest man, dearest man, why *not*, for heaven's sake, on the kitchen floor?"

He cleared his throat. "It's not what the kitchen's *for*," he said thinly, and did a little something sheepish with his mouth and sidled over and slumped down into his chair.

Anne smiled, broadly and resignedly. Shrugged a little. She turned to get the coffee. "This is what the kitchen's for. Yes?"

She came and stood and poured coffee into his cup, and he slid a hand across her sturdy behind, tentatively, a little sadly, then took it slowly away and picked up the steaming cup, sipping coffee he had taught her to make better than anyone else. "What a day. What a lovely, misty spring day," he said, almost sadly, as though of something lost, turning to the window and looking far off through the mist, to the woods blurred with beginning leaves.

❧ II ❧

IN her gray raincoat and boots and with the shopping list and shoes to be repaired and library books to be returned and Erich Fromm's *Escape from Freedom* for Lewis in her plastic tote bag, Anne opened the kitchen door determinedly. A rush of damp field fragrances and bird calls struck her, coming from the mystery of the mist—a lively, pulsing world, drenching wet.

"Why it's exquisite, Rupert!" she called back lavishly. "Who would have thought?"

"Well good, dear."

She walked briskly to the garage, her head lifted to the sky and rotating slowly, as though she were rubbing her face against palpable air, while on one finger she spun the car keys round and round.

In the garage she put herself smartly and effortlessly into her little dust-encrusted red Volkswagen, and after settling her bag upon the neighboring seat she backed out of the garage and turned and was off—all in only seconds. And the little red car hustling off down the driveway in the gray morning told the pert story of the two of them, Anne Knight and the car, purposeful, efficient, bent on getting where they were going and then returning, all with no nonsense and with no time wasted.

Before she had come to the end of the drive, she had decided that instead of going first to the village, she would go to Lewis's. She didn't know how long she would be with him, but she thought it could be for quite some time. She had already warned herself that she would have to ease her way into the subject of therapy, since one always did have to, and that if Lewis were edgy this morning she might not be able to broach it at all. In any case, edgy or not, he would probably taunt her about "shrinks."

And now, at this moment of going to rescue Lewis, suddenly she reminded herself, with fear quickening her breath, that she had vowed never to mix business with friendship, to have city office and country home be as separate as two worlds. Yet here she was on her way to offer unsolicited counseling to a friend and neighbor, and on a lovely spring morning that surely called for something other than this.

"Oh, this is nonsense," she said aloud, angrily. "Perfect, absolute nonsense. Stop it! This isn't work. This is friendship!" And she forced herself to think about Lewis, and what she was going to say to him.

But instead she said to herself unexpectedly and disturbingly that for all the five years she'd known Lewis, right from the very beginning, she'd been entangled with him in some continually goading and fascinating way. Not as woman to man—not sexually at all, she assured herself, and knew that this was so—but as complex person to complex person. Yes, that was it. And she saw, too, that she and Rupert and Lewis, as a threesome, had always been vitally and intriguingly and combustibly responsive each one to the others. Actually fascinated by one another.

Reassured in the purpose of her mission by this discovery, she dispensed with all doubts. The little red car sped and bounded along the tree-canopied, drenched road, taking the corners and the dips like some cheerful swift insect. Anne's lips were slightly, eagerly parted, her ice-gray eyes intent. She was on her way to succor Lewis, to rescue him, and now her whole being was coalesced into a throbbing ambition, a nurturing intention, as milk swells a mother's breasts.

In moments she had arrived at Lewis's drive, where the ancient seeming sign, "Fool's Paradise, Antiques, Lewis Cavanagh Lewis," hung motionless in the still, damp air. Three robins, russet breasts intense in the gray morning light, hopped about on the smooth immaculately kept green lawn that surrounded the perfection of the old maroon-painted house, the swept driveway, the ivy-filled urns.

She drove the car out to the back parking space, alongside Lewis's, shut off the ignition, took *Escape from Freedom* purposefully out of her tote bag, and opened the door.

The grayness, the misty stillness in spite of birds–or was it her own sudden temerity about the visit–made her hesitate there, one leg out of the car. But then she sprang out, and strode, head up, toward the house.

On the porch, a smile ready on her hesitant face, she rapped on the door, hearing the bright knuckle-on-wood *tat, tat, tat,* loud in the drenched morning. Of course Lewis was up. He was up every morning at six. She rapped again, smile expectant, scoffing at her doubts.

Now it seemed that she had waited a long time. Perhaps water was running in the kitchen so that Lewis couldn't hear. Perhaps he was round back in the shop. She put her hand on the dew-beaded doorknob and turned it. The door was unlocked, which meant of course that he was up.

She opened the door and stepped into the quiet of the elegant little hall, silent and polished and smelling faintly and fragrantly of beeswax. Again timidity struck her, even delicacy. She did not really like entering someone else's house without invitation. It was like taking unfair advantage of Lewis, like coming upon something extremely personal that she had a right to see only if he wanted her to see it. She had a strong feeling that she should turn and leave. Or at least go outside and try the shop door.

But she banished this instinct with derision. Why should she not walk into a friend's house—a close friend's house? she emphasized. It was the country way, or should be.

The house was utterly still, except for the clock ticking in the dining room. As she stood uncertainly beside the Jacobean chest, her watchful profile reflected in the gilt mirror above it, the clock struck ten, regally and with tantalizing spacing. It seemed to her like a human voice assuring her that all was normalcy here, all was as usual.

He must, she was sure, be in the shop. But first, in as loud a voice as she thought fit, in case he was somewhere upstairs, she called out to him, "Lewis, *yoo hoo*." The silence that followed seemed more intense than before, and now the ticking clock sounded to her like a voice rebuking her for intrusion. He's in the shop, she said to herself reassuringly, and strode into the living room, from which a passage led to the back hall and a private door to the shop.

But she stopped abruptly. On the living room floor, in a little sprawled heap, lay a woman's coat and black ballet slippers. And more, there on the table above it was a woman's handbag beside an overflowing ashtray and a glass of stale liquor.

Anne stood transfixed for a second in horrified embarrassment over having called out, her hand pressed over the mouth that had made such a gaffe. Her sense of intrusion came over her again with humiliating force, along with a flicker of irritation with Lewis, whom she had thought sick and in need of succoring. She had a muddle of feelings—she felt cheated, deflated, she felt terribly curious, she felt envious, she felt happy for

Lewis, she felt unnecessary. Mostly, she felt an utter fool. She turned to get out as fast as she could.

And saw Lewis.

He was sprawling half in half out of a wing chair by the fireplace, one floppy puppet arm cast across an arm of the chair, the other flung like a sandbag arm across his chest. His glass eyes stared. His bald, monk-tonsured head gleamed like white china. His mouth, a shocking cavern, was wide open, as though screaming without sound.

For a moment Anne could only think, he's a puppet man flung there, flung like a big soft doll and then stiffened, stiffened. She made a strange croaking sound. She had begun to shake.

But she was obliged to make sure. Though she was horrified, she had not lived all forty-nine years of her zealous life in order to fall apart at the sight of... So, with great effort, as though bent into strong wind, she walked slowly over to Lewis, leaned down over him, and put her fingers to his pulse. The icy hardness of his wrist told her she would feel no pulse on her fingertips. But still, responsibly, though she was beginning to feel sick, she kneeled quickly and put her ear against his chest, against the smooth cold cotton of his shirt, pushing apart the prickly tweed of his jacket. Hard and still as rock.

It occurred to her that she must try mouth to mouth resuscitation. She was so repelled by this command that for a second she was sure it was not within her power. But then she drew a long, stabilizing breath, set her jaw grimly, and, using every particle of her splendid determination, did what she knew she must do. It was a terrible experience. And of course, as she had known, it changed nothing. Lewis was clearly dead.

She stood up. For a moment she felt faint, and she staggered. Then she swung around with a great movement and dove for the telephone. Dialed her own number.

Rupert answered at once. "Oh thank God!" she cried.

"Hello." His velvet courteous voice, blessedly unconcerned.

"Rupert! My God, my God. Lewis. He's dead. I found him *dead*! Rupert! Did you hear me? I walked in and here is Lewis lying in... Lewis... lying..."

At last, in a thin closed voice, stiff with incredulity, "Dead?"

"Oh my God yes. Oh Rupert this is perfectly awful. Call Dr. Vose right away. And then come. Come. Hurry!"

She put down the receiver and walked shakily across to the firebench. "Oh my God," she whispered, sinking weakly down onto it. She closed her eyes, rejecting everything. She thought she should call someone else, do something. Take command. Accomplish. Clear this all up, settle it. Arrangements. Yes, she of all people was the best one to have found him, oh God yes. *Her* shoulders bore the world's burdens. *Her* hands did the world's work. How diabolically appropriate, she thought, for me to be the one to walk in here. But her knees were weak, and she did not want to move a muscle. She wanted to sit with her eyes closed, forgetting where she was. Just a minute, just give me one minute, she reassured herself, then I'll function.

She sat for some time with closed eyes, shaking. At last she told herself to open her eyes, and to look at him, "to look the lion in the mouth," as she had forced herself to look at the great seas of that sail from Cuttyhunk to Block Island—"Why don't you sit on the low side, and not keep watching what's coming?" she could hear Rupert saying. "Why look the lion in the mouth?" She could never forget that remark and how appropriate it had been, and how Rupert had managed so aptly to hit the nail on the head. Yes, she must always look the lion in the mouth, that was her way. Not to evade, but to cope, that was her way. And ought to be everyone's way...

"He is dead," she whispered to herself, as though the sound of her voice saying those words would make the awesome mountains of water more bearable. "This is death," she whispered, "face it." Like being in a small sailboat in the open ocean in a storm and trying to accept the reality of it.

She opened her eyes and forced her attention upon this thing that wasn't Lewis. Face it, she said to herself. She stared at the unfamiliar fixed arched face, oval like a white egg. Face it, she urged, begged herself. But instead she put one hand into the other against her breast, and leaned forward compassionately. Oh, Lewis...

But now she felt rage rising up in her, and she wanted to strike Lewis for his total, terminal silence, for this total accomplishment of his that kept the secret sealed. She looked at the grotesque sprawled figure that maddeningly kept the secret; or was it that the cessation of alive Lewis had in some way diminished *her*, taken a part of her and silenced and sealed it forever? Yes. She knew intuitively that this was it, that now Lewis would never tell her about herself. What Lewis had known about her, she would never know. There had always been some sort of struggle between them, and now they could never set it straight.

She was enraged by this. She flung up an arm, wanting furiously to strike him for his failure to live and to make what he knew about her known to herself. This is what the dead did. They took away with them all the mistakes you had made with them, and buried them forever. They absconded with *you*. They died, and thus caused that irreplaceable part of you that had interacted with them to die too. Oh, I hate this, she cried in herself, get me away. She drew a strangling breath, lowering her arm to wipe moisture from her forehead with a distracted gesture. But she was tied to the firebench. Couldn't move away.

Suddenly she stood up, as though the firebench had finally released her and ordered her to rise. She took a few slow steps away from it, out into the middle of the room. She stood there. Tears burned her eyes. She stepped impulsively across to Lewis and went down on her knees beside the chair and gathered the clumsy, angled, stone-heavy thing into her arms, against the soft warmth of her large bosom. She was not going to let him be alone in this. Tears flooded her fierce eyes and spilled down her cheeks. She was softened now, alive, functioning from the center of her being. The horror had gone, and the inadmission, and all the rage. She held death in her living, warm arms.

She was crooning something wordless, rocking on her knees, pouring into Lewis an agony of compassion, when she was forced to turn her head because of a sound, a strangeness.

A girl in a short kimona was standing on the stairs, one bare foot stopped, waiting to take the next step. Both hands held on to both rails, hard, the knuckles showing white in the dark tunnel of the steep stairwell.

In the appalling stillness, small sounds were suddenly very loud—the unperturbed, ceaseless life of the clock in the dining room, in the kitchen a distant whirr, then a jolt, then a deliberately purposeful and continuing hum—the old refrigerator starting up. Sounds in an empty house. Bird songs could now be heard, too, outside; the long, brazen whistle of the cardinal, the swelling cluck of the cowbird; and other birds, so many of them, their trills coming through the still mist with intensified clarity. The old house seemed to shift, to settle, every tiny sound of ancient nail seemed, in this suspension of all human sound, at long last to have the satisfaction of being listened to.

Finally the girl's foot moved, reached down to the next stair. Then she came slowly down the last few stairs, and stopped at the foot of them, her face incredulous. For a second she pressed three fingers to her forehead and closed her eyes and winced, swallowing quietly. Then she opened her eyes again, uncritical, very decent, but still tentatively, unpresumptuously incredulous.

In the great strangeness of this moment Anne was unable to move or to speak. She wouldn't release her armful of burden suddenly, she would want to do that tenderly and slowly; and she couldn't speak, there was nothing in the world to say in a crazy moment like this. Then she realized all in one flash of recognition that the girl was really a young woman and that, of course, the coat and slippers and bag were hers, and that she was Lewis's cousin, Syra Gachet.

Syra had now advanced on noiseless bare feet to the middle of the room, staring steadily at Anne with a peculiar gravity and still with that polite, concentrated incredulity, though now the corners of her mouth twitched with anger, and her round dark eyes were cold. Anne took her arms carefully away from Lewis, and rose, stepping away from him, so that Syra Gachet could see. For she hadn't seen. This was quite clear.

For seconds the shock of these two women was the manifest thing here, not the presence of death. "I found him…I dropped in." Anne spoke in a toneless whisper. "And he was…he was…so alone."

Syra stopped. Nothing stirred here in this room, though the outside world of birds swirled musically around its vacuum of silence. The room was a waxworks stage, set with all the clues—the ashes of a burnt-out fire, glasses of stale liquor, overflowing ashtrays, a tumbled coat on the floor, slippers, a handbag on the table, museum-piece furniture correctly arranged, a dead male mannequin sprawled in a chair, two female mannequins with artificial shock on their frozen faces.

Syra was looking down at Lewis, her face sharpened with surprise. She opened her mouth to speak. She looked at Lewis uncomprehendingly. Then at Anne uncomprehendingly, and accusingly. She closed her eyes for a moment, lowering her head and touching her forehead with fingertips, but then she opened startled eyes right away, and continued her stunned looking. There was no recognition of anything in her face, only stupefaction.

"Oh my dear," Anne whispered, unheard.

❧ III ❧

LEWIS had been taken away.

The day was still overcast and soft and quiet, no wind had arisen, no rain had fallen, no sun had broken through the violet clouds. It was late afternoon, the clock had struck four in this quiet house that was used to the quiet of Lewis's solitary life, and that seemed not to be altered in any way by the fact of his having left it for good.

Anne was in Lewis's happy old kitchen, where everything was up to date but charming, tidying up, washing the lunch dishes, thinking, planning, bustling about, exhausted but determined. Rupert had driven to New York to pick up Georges at the airport. Mrs. Alexander, grim, shattered, but the most comprehending of all of them, had finally gone home to lie down.

And Syra was upstairs, stretched out on the four-poster bed in the guest room, smoking, a thing she never did. Her kimona hung on the back of a chair, and she lay in her rumpled slip, covered by a hand-knitted mauve afghan with mauve satin ribbon binding which Lewis had kept across the foot of the bed. She stroked its ribbed softness from time to time with the hand that didn't hold the repetition of cigarettes, and sometimes slid her chin against the soothing satin. Comfort came from the soft bed, the soft wool, the soft satin, and from the cigarettes. She raised her hand to give the live cigarette an appraising congratulatory look. She had taken endless aspirins, and now her stupefying headache was gone. The relief of having it gone was a step forward.

The day was a dream, and her hangover state had made it more so. Everything had come to her through cottony thicknesses, her mind was numbed and was more than ever unable to think. She had seen, but she hadn't been able to add up. Anne Knight kneeling beside the wing chair with her coat on, and making love to Lewis and Lewis not making love back.

She smote her forehead with the back of her hand and moaned. Like me... Agony shot through her, making the moment electrifyingly alive, unbearable. For a second she was rigid with pain and awareness. Lewis was dead, was gone, and she had killed him. Heart, the doctor had said. "Has anything unduly stressful happened that you know of?" Standing slowly up from bending over Lewis he had looked at *her*. Oh that awful moment of saying nothing, like a criminal...

The late sun broke through the clouds with sudden benevolent concentrated glory, pouring through the dormer windows in two golden paths, bathing in rich light the floor, and the lavender damask of the bench at the foot of the bed, and the foot of the bed itself.

Syra put the cigarette between her pale lips and sucked on it. The thought of Georges floated into her, lower down, not high up and sharply near her heart where it hurt so unbelievably, but low down, a sinking heavy dread that she didn't want to deal with. And now, as she had done on and off all day, she warned herself that he was coming, that he was on his way, that he would be here soon. But there wouldn't be any comfort in seeing him, she knew. She didn't want to see him and she didn't want to have to be with him, she felt a great fear-suspended blank in imagining what it would be like when he walked into the house. No comfort, from him or from anyone else, ever, since she would never be able to tell anyone.

"Has anything unduly stressful happened that you know of?" That question again. All day, all day... She moved her whole body slightly, as though to extricate herself from it, but at the same time she told herself that it was something she couldn't shake off, it had a hold on her, it owned her now, it had become an incurable part of her, like some physical disability, like something you have to learn to live with. But there *must* be some escape, some choice! There must be something in herself that could alter it, or see it in another way.

An agony of incomprehension and pain stabbed her again. She reared up on a helpless, furious elbow and ground the cigarette out. Then she turned her head and looked at the impossible reality of a room, of a house around it, of a person downstairs, and more people coming, and doctors, and Georges, and Lewis off somewhere in some cold awful white morgue, and herself, above all, herself–she looked at this incomprehensible world, which she was going to have to deal with. And there was an unfamiliar, difficult desolateness about it that for a moment terrified her.

Suddenly she had a little clear new inkling of something. A way out. And now lucidly in her head were other things the doctor had said, other things beside that one stunning question. Of course! Yes! He had asked Anne, who had been answering all the questions having to do with who Lewis's physician was, and when he had last seen him and so forth, whether Lewis had ever mentioned heart problems–"cardiac complications," he had said.

Now, excitedly, she remembered that Lewis had had some little phase of heart trouble as a child–the result of their bicycling together around half of the lake on that hot summer day so many years ago. And my God, she realized, my God, of course! Father and Uncle Edmond. Both dying of their congenital heart disease, and in their thirties! My God, she thought, how could I have failed to remember that, to tell the doctor that?

And so it means that it wasn't necessarily my fault, she cried to herself with wild relief. That means that it might have happened anyway, or at any time. And his illness, couldn't that have hastened the final attack?

But then she shook her head slowly, hopelessly on the hot pillow, accepting the ugly knowledge that this somehow made it all the worse. She had known before she came that Lewis was ill and depressed. That's why she had come. And knowing this, what had she done?

There was Lewis, lying in the chair, so cold. She would never in her life forget that coldness. But neither would she forget that desire, that warmth, which had killed him. It was uncontaminated, it was still in her, intact. No, of course she didn't feel desire now, but she remembered feeling desire, and she was remembering something good, bona fide, true as the sun that lay along the windowsills, and she knew this, clung to it.

But hadn't she always had it?

Yes, she had always had it. She saw now that this was so, it had begun a long long time ago, and she had known when it began that it was the best feeling in the world. And she still knew this. It had always been in her.

It began to pour back into her now in a warm drowning flood, and she lay softly under the mauve afghan, beginning to be wrapped in lulling memory, beginning to float away from misery and to be gradually isolated from it. She remembered sounds of traffic, hot sun, smells, voices, she was in her mother's car, beside Lewy, on the way to the Falls...

"Happy birthday, Siry."

"Sing it!" Cruel, because his voice would crack.

Fleshy smell of sun-baked hot car leather. A hot stab shocked her thigh touching Lewy's. The feeling sprang into the pit of her stomach and wafted up through her, lightly as rolls of mist, making her breath come faster. A never-before feeling. And it was then that she decided. It was the best feeling, the best, she'd ever hope to have in this world.

His brand-new flashy sports shirt printed all over with pink and orange tropical fish. "Lewy, that's spiffy!" Shiningly scrubbed, close to her he smelled of Pear's Soap.

"Aw, it's crazy."

"Come, thou goose. It's a fun shirt."

Both long gangly arms lying along up-jutting long legs, big feet pressed together, obviously so as not to risk contact with her sneaker, big-knuckled hands lying limp over his knees, his body touching hers but neither of them could help it, jammed together in the back seat surrounded by picnic gear–folding chairs, umbrella to keep the sun off Aunt Sally, old blankets, the cat curled dozing on top of the hamper.

"You sure got a day for your birthday, *I'll* say," his voice cracking open, popping out in the funniest squeak. "I'll bet you feel lucky getting a day like this for your thirteenth birthday when it could've been anything, it could've snowed."

"Oh, Lewis, it's too lovely." Her mother was driving, Aunt Sally in the seat beside her. "It's never once failed to be a possible day for Syra's birthday outing. She's a lucky girl, my girl is."

"That's really something!" bubbling in helpless excitement. "Gee, last night I was listening to the radio just by accident and they said it was gonna be in the seventies. Boy, look at this traffic, I'll bet everyone's going somewhere today! Look at that fellow with his top down, well why not? Say, that's a Veloce!"

"A what, dear?" Aunt Sally's voice, indulgent, proud.

"A Veloce, you pronounce it Vee-low-chee, that's an Italian car, an Alpha Romeo. They have a Giullietta Spider, and then this model, it's a hot car, a racing car, boy is that a beauty! It has Weber carburetors."

Vee-low-chee... Syra smiled now, letting herself be happily back in everything there was about that word, about that cracking fourteen-year-old voice. And Weber carburetors. How he'd gone on and on and on about Weber carburetors, whatever *they* were.

She felt the slight sickening approach of now, and closed her eyes to shut it out, to shut out the room, the horror edging back in. And then how easily memory lapped over her again, her heart opening to view, to sound, to feeling.

There they were, trapped in the moving car, she couldn't manage a sound, not a word, since there was everything in the world to say, but not here. And perhaps not at the Falls, either. Perhaps not. And the Falls was twenty minutes away. To have to sit like this for twenty minutes. How awful. Yet the feel of Lewy's thigh lying against her own; was there anything else in the world but this feeling, the sudden terrifying, real warmth of his thigh? She felt she must look at him. But to turn and look at him—how could she do this? She didn't want him to *know*, or anyone in this stifled car to know. Even her breathing made too much of a sound, and did her quick breathing give anything away?

She sat feeling stiff as a statue, trying to breathe naturally, wishing that she weren't here, that she were back home, that she need be taken no farther than this. She leaned forward suddenly and began to tuck up strands of Aunt Sally's hair, making a great concentrated loving fuss about untying the black velvet bow and taking out all the pins and pulling all the loose strands neatly together. She fussed over that hair until she'd done every possible thing there was to do to it.

Then she thought she'd dare to look at Lewy. "I noticed that car too, Lewy. I'll bet you get a sports car when Aunt Sally'll let you."

"You can say that again."

So, thus, their eyes met. And instantly she knew that she would never want to stop this bottomless looking, this burning of their bodies up and into each other's eyes. Detached from matter, no seat beneath them, no earth, only the sky above them toward which their bodies raced up light and strong as flames. They were the only people in a world that had stopped. She felt that this molten looking could do everything it was said their bodies needed to do, that this did it all. It could go on forever.

But then Lewy let his hand slide off his knee and down into the folds of her skirt, and her hand slid furtively to meet it, and touching hidden there, the hands burst into a loud flame which sent fire darting down into...into...*there*, so that they had to take their eyes quickly from each other, for this was something else, this was more than looking, and different from looking, to be held secretly and fearfully inside her, since it told her that they had not had it all. And what fearful, fiery thing could the rest of it be?

Syra brought her cold hand up and put it over her mouth, and opened her astonished eyes wide, very wide. She lay there for a moment, transfixed, absolutely transfixed in the certainty, which the horror couldn't touch, that everything else might be gone, but she could still know, not only *feel* but *know* something, and this something was that her desire last night, and for all the years before that, was unalterable and was natural as breathing and was herself, and perfectly all right, not wrong. Yet it had killed Lewis. These were two facts: What had been happening in her as a little girl, as a bigger girl, and yes, as a woman too, though she'd buried it then, was as natural as breathing and was herself. But it had killed Lewis.

She drew a great wretching, ugly sound up from her gut, which exploded into a flood of tears. She cried with her whole body, violently. She had never cried like this in her life, nor had she seen her mother so vividly since her death, her tears allowing the revelation of long-suppressed pain, of loneliness, and the living presence in that pain and loneliness of her own, her darling, her loved mother.

Tears streamed down her face, down her neck, over her chest, while with a furious gesture of helplessness she tried to wipe the slick wetness away. Between strangling hiccups she whispered, "Mother, Mother." How instantly, vividly she was seeing her mother–the white kimona, the jagged dark-blue birds. Time had sharpened the scene. Colors were of a hallucinatory clarity and distinctness, forms were immobilized, defined in some strange, informative, insistent way, as though the passage of years had purified and stilled whatever had gone on there and was now giving the summation, the brilliant essence of it all. Syra's head back there in her mother's lap was Syra's head now, thrashing in agony upon Lewis's drenched pillowcase. The same head then, the same head now. And her mother alive–then, and now. The same life-giving warm hand on her hair–then, and now. The smell of tobacco, its pressing, acrid over-all-ness, its impregnation of the sweet warm cotton of that lap, then, and now, its nostril-offending stench coming from the overflowing ashtray on the night table.

Her mother was here, and Syra spoke to her, as her sobs began to subside. "It was all right, Mother, wasn't it? It wasn't dirty?" Was she actually speaking, or was she thinking the words? She didn't know.

"You have to do what you feel like, Pet. That's all you really have to know." Was she herself saying this, or thinking it, or was she actually hearing the sound of her mother's voice?

"But that was fatal, it was fatal to do what I felt like. It killed him. You were wrong. Go away, Mother. You lied."

"It was not dirty. It was natural."

The shuddering sounds grew quieter, then quiveringly stopped. "No you didn't lie, Mother. Don't go away, Mother. But what is so wrong? Were you wrong, Mother? I know you didn't mean to be wrong, but were you?"

White kimona. Dark-blue birds. Whiteness and blueness a piercing sharpness that hurt the eyes. And above it, her mother's face with its imperishable sameness, the black eyes fixed with everlasting honesty upon the object of their love and their tutelage.

Oh no. How could she, the daughter who had learned non-judgment from that face, now judge it? No. Judgment, thanks to that face, was not in Syra. What her mother had known and taught, she had believed, Syra was now certain of that. And this thorough sense-knowledge quieted her, was like a sudden presence beneath her of solid ground.

In the living room, tidying up for the fourth time today, Anne picked up the ashtray Syra had left on the firebench and tossed its fetid heap of ash and cigarette stubs and twisted matches reproachfully into the gray maw of the fireplace. Her finely carved nostrils widened with distaste even as her eyes yearned with pity.

She thought she would sit down now for a minute or two. On the firebench. To try out how it was to sit there now. To try, perhaps, to feel again what she had felt sitting there this morning.

Her eyes flashed with purpose. She sat down, emphatically. Since this morning she had been in contact only once with the mindless, visceral panic of her own predicament, and only then to look at it head on and say to herself, with a burst of candor, jocularly, "I may have to lose my uterus, but I'm not going to lose my reason." And forthwith, with reason and with energetic purpose, she had gone about what had to be done, oblivious to her own troubles in the face of those that were in this house.

But as she sat there on the firebench, her eyes sought distraction. Things around her began to present themselves to her, urgently, for her recognition. Lewis's things, witnesses to Lewis's life; and the only witnesses, she thought, to the last moment of Lewis's life.

Had Lewis been aware of any thing or things as he died? she wondered. Had he looked around him for help? Had any thing he happened to see, if he had, done anything to him, there in those last minutes? Or had that last minute of looking told him anything, one way or another, about himself?

And then she thought, do you look at *things*, during those last minutes, or do you look beyond, to that ceasing to breathe, that total blackness, that nonexistence? Or do you see everything, clearly, as it is said you review your whole life in seconds? And does that mean that all the tangents and complexities of your life have in fact been only one single simple pulse, that core of your own unique soul, and that all of the seemingly complex experiences of years reviewed so swiftly and clearly in a matter of moments were really always only the one single simple heart you so brilliantly, and too late, see?

A sudden compassion galvanized Anne. Poor lonely, fastidious, object-surrounded Lewis. All this ancient elegance. To die amid this, she thought sadly, to have this be the sum of one's greatest efforts. Oh my God, Anne wondered, did he know this as he died?

Suddenly she saw, with awful vividness, Lewis flung across his wing chair, like something discarded. Tears blurred her eyes. There it was, the terrible sad foolish puzzle and failure of living and dying. What could you do? There it was, a little futile ending, one of a billion such endings. It was overpowering and simple, a piteous little fact. There wasn't an answer, there was no philosophy, it was just this, a simple empty little ending, without even the beauty of an autumn leaf fallen. This was what the hope of Lewis's birth had come to. There had been the greatness of his birth (all birth is great), and then immediately the long hard passage downward to the littleness of his death, to this unimpressive petering out. That's the way it is, as Mrs. Alexander was always saying. So why did she, did Rupert, everyone, search for philosophies about death, for ways to make it heroic, and beautiful as autumn's fallen leaves; for meanings, justifications? Why search for all these fictions when that's precisely what they were, fictions, when there it was, just a sad little tumbling end, another fly swatted? Inevitable. Why try to dress inevitability up in palatable disguise? Why not accept inevitability, have it be a part of one's living since it was going to have to be a part of one's dying? Yes, why not?...

But she knew why not, or felt why not, as she sat there with this procession of thoughts in her amazed mind. Inevitability, she sensed, was too loose and too uprooted and too anonymous; you had to let go of something powerfully central to you, to want to let inevitability take over. If she were to accept inevitability, where would be the fun of striving, of having something shining always ahead of her, all the time, feeling the excitement of herself in forward motion, loud and strong?

And yet she could remember how she had almost felt relief as she held Lewis, as she let herself go down, down into the warm receiving anonymity of inevitability. It was as though she had been brought down from something high and shrill and lonely to a sort of level, a quiet place that held no fear but was alive, in which her power felt different to her, pure and as it should be.

She sat for some time with her eyes closed, while a sense of the depth of her fatigue began to steal over her. She wanted to be home. Lying on her bed. Away from all this.

But I must get up, she adjured herself with brisk mind if not brisk body, I must get going, feed the birds, leave a note for the milkman, try to tempt Syra with some food.

Sighing wearily, she pressed her palms on the velvet of the firebench and pushed herself up, reluctant to leave what could happen here. And she thought with sudden amused interest that the firebench was like Lourdes–drag your ailing self there, touch the altar, and rise up healed; or if not healed, at least enlightened, she thought, shaking her head wonderingly over the strangeness, the unusualness of the way she'd been thinking.

The sunlight had retreated from the foot of the bed, and now all of the bedpost was in shadow. Downstairs a faucet shuddered and vibrated as it was turned on, then off. There were quick footsteps across the kitchen and into the pantry, the sound of a cupboard door being opened, a rattle of plates, the small hollow smack of its door being closed, then the determined footsteps going back into the kitchen again.

Syra began to pass a finger over her lips, slowly, thoughtfully, while her eyes grew studious. Something clear was rising up through her derangement, some idea, some memory, some promise, having to do with Anne Knight down there in the kitchen, taking care of everything.

She sat up and turned sharply toward the box of cigarettes on the bedside table. But as she reached toward it she said to herself, no, that's enough of that. She flung her hair away from her neck. A comforting feeling, her own hair brushing her neck.

It occurred to her that a bath might help her in some way. She lay down again and closed her eyes, pulling the soft mauve blanket up under her chin, to think for a few minutes about the prospect of taking a bath, and about the prospect of enduring.

She looked at the lower, sun-reddened half of a carved post of this bed, the post rounded and grooved and tapering up and out of the sun and into shadow to end in a small pineapple, and she was obliged to concentrate on this long-enduring, inanimate and yet characterful object that had seen and served so many generations, but had nevertheless remained so gracefully separate and intact. I do think this noble bed is trying to impart something to me, she thought.

The smell of bread toasting was introducing itself throughout the house, coming faintly, warmly up the stairwell and into Syra's room as though to assure her that, buttered and perhaps sprinkled with sugar and cinnamon, it meant soon to be tasted. And she knew, as surely as she knew her own name, that downstairs in the kitchen Anne Knight was getting tea ready right now, and that presently there would be the clink of china on a tray and footsteps on the stairs. And then there Anne would be in the doorway, smiling and holding the comforting tray. Like someone's mother. Overflowing with kindness, like someone's mother. Strange woman, hard and flashing as a diamond, but so soft somewhere in her, too. Lewis had always had mixed feelings about her.

Lewis! His letter!...

This was the clear small suggestion that was struggling up through her. Lewis's letter! Anne and Mrs. Alexander taking care of Lewis!... She flung back the afghan and scrambled down off the high bed and crossed to get her bag from the dressing table and brought it back up onto the bed, digging into it until she felt the rectangle of folded crisp paper that was Lewis's letter.

She opened it avidly, but as soon as she saw Lewis's handwriting she was split open with such agony that she folded the letter blindly and thrust it back into the bag. Innocent Lewis, and I came and ruined his innocence, his expectant cousin child love, I contaminated him. But with hot life blood wanting him, which felt like the right answer at last to everything. Insane!...

There was the tinkle of china, and careful footsteps on the stairs. Anne stood in the doorway, holding the tray, though she wasn't smiling. Compassion, and a kind of hesitant delicacy about walking in on grief, allowed the shape of her fine-boned face its natural purity and seriousness.

"You've brought tea," Syra said flatly. "I smelled the toast and hoped it was for me. Thanks." She sat back against the pillows and crossed her bare legs and tucked them under her, pushing the afghan aside. "You could put it here. Thanks. This helps a person."

"Well, I thought, I'm so glad," said Anne brightly but gently, and in a little moment of awkwardness and silence she leaned across Syra and put the tray at her feet. "There." Now she smiled, hesitantly. "You haven't eaten a thing and you should. Here, shall I pour? Bed's a rather shaky foundation for a tray."

"But aren't you going to have some? I see there's only one cup. I wish you'd sit down and have tea with me." Suddenly she was glad not to be alone.

"Oh, I've had so many cups of tea I'm afloat." Anne smiled. "Thank you, Syra. No. But may I sit?" She went over to the small tufted mauve velvet slipper chair beside the window, and sank down into it with a faint sound of enormous relief. "Just listen to those robins. They're doing their best to remind us that it's spring, and that life goes on."

Golden early evening, steeped in quiet, all the day's activity stopped except for the birds at Lewis's feeder below, tiny constant sounds of feathers, whirs, soft cluckings, tappings, flutters; and occasionally the redwing blackbird's triumphant call, *conkereeee, conkereeee*; it all soothed Anne, told her of other ways, of alternatives vague and undefined, of soul's ease.

Quiet lay in the room like the evening light. Both women, constrained, unable to be anything but strangers to each other, were nevertheless pressed down by the quietude, by the truth of a spring evening hushing the room with dusk and death, pervading it with all the spring greenness of life but with the heavy darkness of death, too, which because of the spring seemed not to be an ending, not to be final. Anne felt something taken out of her hands.

But she shivered in the sudden cool of the evening air. "The sun finally came out," she said with forced liveliness, "thank goodness." She settled more deeply into the chair, as though for warmth, and hugged herself with crossed arms.

"It finally won out," Syra said flatly and swallowed some tea.

"Yes. I didn't think it was going to. It helps. Sun somehow always helps."

Syra began wolfishly to eat the toast, this first food of the day. "This tastes so good. Yum." She pressed a forefinger carefully down upon a crumb that had fallen onto the tray, and brought it up to her waiting tongue.

Anne was surprised at the "yum" which had a slangy sound, incompatible, she felt, with grief. She couldn't imagine herself, under the same circumstances, saying anything of the sort. However, tastefully, diversionally, sparkingly, she cried, "Look, can't I get you some more toast? It will take only a little minute. Yes? No?"

"No, Anne. Thank you. I'll eat dinner later."

"Oh, I'm so pleased to hear that," cried Anne, her face lighting up eagerly. "I'd thought, I'd hoped, really, that you might want to come up to our house tonight, when Rupert gets back with your husband. Mary Moore did the marketing for me, bless her, and I can whip up something in no time. Look, would you feel up to that, do you think? If not I can so easily fix up something for you here, if you'd rather stay quiet here, you and your husband, which I could so well imagine."

"Oh no, the very best thing I can think of is what you said first, coming to your house." Syra was enlivened by this unexpected break, which meant that she wouldn't have to be alone, at first anyway, with Georges. "But you must be so tired. Must you cook? Couldn't we just have sandwiches?"

"Look, don't concern yourself about that, Syra. We'll have something very simple. The important thing is for you to keep up your strength."

"Oh, I can almost always eat, I'm almost always hungry," Syra said in a spiritless voice. "I'm hungry now, finally."

"Well good, my dear." She looked at Syra, who was bending over the tray, her hair hanging forward along her cheeks, holding the teacup in one unsteady hand and staring down into it with apparent concentration, though concentration it probably was not, Anne thought. She was given this opportunity, though, to study Syra. So far she had had no chance to really take her in, nor had she had any need or inclination to do so, the horror and distraction of the day being what it was. There was something about Syra, though, that disturbed Anne. She looked at the wearied blue eyelids lowered in a kind of patient misery Anne thought admirable, at the bare shoulders that were surprisingly wide for so short a body and somehow giving the impression of capability, at the small square shaking hand that nevertheless seemed sure.

There was a certain power, Anne felt, in this young woman's unassuming manner, and why was that? Could this amount of modest potency be the result of an unimpeded self-assurance? She was puzzled and fascinated. This little quiet person, so shattered and mute all day long, sitting, endlessly just sitting in one spot on the firebench the whole day with her hands folded across her lap, and her plump Botticelli fingers white as wax, and runs in both stockings, somehow so insensitive–at a time like this it seemed all wrong not to be neat, without flaw–and trembling constantly, and staring at nothing, and smoking interminably, and turning away and then turning back, but rooted to that one spot–how could she have conveyed strength and self-assurance so forcefully? Anne wondered. She was puzzled, she was fascinated, even awed.

She was obliged to think about it. Was it, perhaps, because of the way Syra looked at one, that clear, steady, penetrating gaze? Yes, she had to admit that Syra's gaze had the undissimulating clearness and curiosity of a child's. Or was it the quality of her face, which was strong and open and yet hadn't those characteristics that Anne thought of as character? Was it sophistication that gave her face such command? It was empty of those qualities that made a face soft and loving. And yet why look for those qualities in that face? Absurd.

Anne raised her lovely chin. She didn't like the feeling of being on the low side. She didn't like to feel her own ongoing force immobilized, confused.

And yet, at a moment like this, she could wonder about the peculiar, uneasy sensation of slowing down, of being immobilized by another personality. She even had a grudging respect for this moment of slowing down, of watching, of feeling a void that she was not filling with her own force and that she was permitting someone else's force to fill.

Now she wondered about Syra's body, and she had a summarized sense of reproductive organs and breasts. They were small breasts, Anne saw, with large tight nipples that made the silk of the slip protrude. In this fleeting summarized digest, Anne let herself disparage this body. It was not, she concluded smugly, a body made for motherhood, as her own was. She saw a lithe teenager body that looked indifferent to conceiving and nurturing life in its womb. Oh yes, the whole sense of this small, curveless body was incompatible with pregnancy, Anne assured herself. She was certain of this, and she felt relief as she thought it, she felt a relieved falling away from competition, she felt high and dry. No, I just can't see her pregnant or ever wanting to be, she thought with irresolute triumph.

Syra pressed a finger to another crumb, brought it up to her waiting tongue, looking away from Anne, whose attentiveness she was uncomfortably feeling. A wave of disgust and despair came over her because of people, because of herself. This was new country. Scary. For a moment there was nothing that was bearable.

But then, saving her, something sprang into her head that had held a ray of promise a while ago, some small suggestion—Anne, and Mrs. Alexander, and taking care of Lewis, and Lewis's letter. She closed her eyes, trying to remember.

She remembered. She opened her eyes and she said, her voice cool and unnaturally driving, "I've been wondering, Anne. My mind is slightly unbuttoning itself, and I'm just now remembering things the doctor said. He said that Lewis might have had a heart condition, didn't he say that? Wasn't that your impression? Wasn't that what he implied?" She picked up her cup and drank some tea, gazing steadily over its rim at Anne.

"Oh yes, that's certainly what he suspected; otherwise–it makes sense even to me, who knows very little about the human body–otherwise how would you explain it? But we'll know, after the autopsy." She thought that this was a time for silence, and so she said no more.

The clock downstairs, perpetual heartbeat behind closed doors, lonely and dogged and filling the silence with its steady tocking, told of hearts that stop beating. And Syra came back easily to the raw awfulness. She sat her cup down on the tray, noisily. "Why," she cried, bringing two hard fists down onto the soundless bed, which quivered all over with the force of the punch, "why didn't anyone know that? You must have known something was wrong, because in Lewis's letter to me he said you wanted him to see a doctor. And Mrs. Alexander must have realized he needed a doctor. Her husband was a doctor, she should have known. How could I know," she cried hardly and wildly, "I wasn't *here*. But really I think it was up to all of you to see that he had a doctor."

Anne was nonplussed. She sat up straight in her chair gathering her forces, her face accusing Syra, pleading with her. But then she relaxed. It was clear. She knew survivor guilt when she saw it.

"Look," she said, clear-eyed and therapeutic, leaning impulsively toward Syra with her large-breasted love and her science–the overflowing heart and the driving mind, smooth-functioning team–"look, my dear," she said vividly, "you mustn't blame yourself, there's no one of us, you must know that, who could have prevented this. Above all, you mustn't blame yourself. You mustn't let guilt enter into your feelings. Oh, I can imagine how terribly you feel, we all know what he meant to you and you to him, but you mustn't, mustn't allow yourself to dwell with guilt." She sank back in her chair, and smiled a little, apologetically.

"Guilt?"

The word hung in the air. It had left Syra's mouth, separated itself from her, and hung alone up above the bed, almost visible, certainly audible. Syra could hear its palpitation up there, could hear it beating its loud wings, meaning to stay right there, getting louder. How could Anne know?... "Guilt?" she asked in a strong, cold voice, echoing the sound up there.

"My dear Syra–look, there isn't a soul alive who doesn't feel guilt when a loved one dies. It's a classic reaction. We are all guilty of all kinds of failures, some overt, some subtle, toward those we love in meaningful relationships. More than anything, too, I think, we are guilty over being the one to stay alive. There's even a textbook name for it–survivor guilt. Guilt has innumerable sources, innumerable manifestations. Look, if you can only realize that, it might help, though I know it's little use for me to try to convey this to you. We have to come to these things ourselves. I *did* try to get Lewis to see a doctor. I feel I want you to know this, but you know how he is about doctors. Of course I realize now that I should have persisted, and that my worry was legitimate. But *you* couldn't possibly have prevented this. How could *you* have known Lewis had a heart condition, if, as we're almost certainly sure, he did have? Really now, how could you have known, and even if you had known, *how* could you have prevented it, unless you had happened to be there when it happened and had called the doctor immediately, but who knows even then? Perhaps Lewis died instantly. Look, you simply mustn't blame yourself," she begged.

Syra pushed the tray away sharply and swung off the bed, standing there small and isolated and alert in her rumpled slip, which was pulled at the seam, Anne noticed. She felt a crazy desire to call it to Syra's attention and to offer to mend it for her, but the impulse felt so mechanical and so crazy that she was flooded with anger, felt blood rising from her toes, flooding up through her body to pound hotly in her cheeks. Enough is enough, she scolded herself savagely. Oh, she hated this whole situation at last, had had enough of it, wanted to be out of it.

"You've been very kind," Syra said in a stiff, conclusive way, searching around for a familiar kind of dignity, or poise, which had left her. "I think I'll now take a bath and see what that will do." She looked Anne in the eye, steadily, coolly, demonstrating to her that though guilt might be the classic reaction to death, here was one person who was not a classic reactor.

Anne jerked her head back in surprise, and her eyes widened. But then she collapsed, docile, and said cheerfully, "Okaaay," drawing the word out in a sprightly, glossing-over way that would sound unoffended. "You should have half an hour or so before they get here." She went across to pick up the tray.

"I won't be that long. In fact, I'll only shower. Then could we go to your house? We could leave a note."

"Oh?" Anne stopped, with the tray in her hands, the silver gleaming against the soft gray cashmere billow of her breast. "You'd rather do that, and not wait for them here?"

"Yes. I do think yes. If you don't mind."

"Of course, my dear," she said consolingly. The bereaved were unpredictable, and one should humor their every whim. "I'll wash these while you're showering. Then we'll pop into my car and go up home. A fire –" she smiled brilliantly "– won't a fire be lovely? don't you think a fire *helps?*"

Syra's face warmed and she smiled a little, couldn't help it. "Oh, I do."

167

...You like to perch and be toasted... A bewildering pain caught Syra. She turned away from Anne and walked to the window. "Oh," she said to herself, "this is awful." She leaned against the window, looking out at nothing, and knew that she was in a place of terror and unanswerable accusation, and that there was no escape from it. Oh the peril of not knowing how to think about it, of having nothing reliable like that in control!

As she stood there by the window, she saw Rupert's car turn into the driveway. For a moment it was simply that she was seeing Rupert's car, Rupert Knight had driven up as he had on and off all day, and would get out, and come in. But then, like a blow, she remembered, saw at the same time, that Georges was with him.

Anne, standing with the tray, worried, unable to pry herself away, heard the scrunch of gravel, then the car stopping. She sighed. "Oh dear, someone's coming. I'd better get on down."

"It's them," Syra said faintly. "It's your husband with Georges."

"They're here! So soon!"

Syra's heart had begun a solid fast pounding. She watched the car doors open, watched both men climb out, saw the scene of strained amiability, polite smiles as Georges's suitcase and top-coat and folded newspaper were taken out of the back seat, as some little joke passed between them that made Georges smile sweetly with quick sliding eyes, in spite of the seriousness and tiredness of his face.

She felt the impulse to run away, to hide, to postpone walking toward Georges with heavy dread.

Then she saw that Georges was a stranger. Standing beside Rupert Knight, Georges, her husband, was as much of a stranger as Rupert was. Two strangers. She was stunned by such clear recognition. It was as though a person other than herself was standing here beside her, seeing and knowing this fact.

Watching the pantomime of the men, whose voices she could hear though she couldn't make out what they were saying and wasn't thinking of that anyway, she saw that Georges was a man she didn't know. She was embarrassed. She had a sudden embarrassing intimate picture of what was in the suitcase he was holding, seeing each object she had watched him unpack–the Pycopay Extra Hard Two-Row Natural Bristle toothbrush, the drip-dry pajamas, the rubber drawstring bag with all six little plastic bottles of pills, four new shirts with the price tags on, a paperback of *War and Peace* and another of *The Autobiography of Malcolm X*, new bathing trunks with the price tag on, brand-new white suede loafers, worn once around the house to break them in.

She burned with shame over knowing about these things so intimately, feeling she should never have known them, as though she had agreed to them, been an unwilling part owner of them, by knowing them. She felt shamefully altered by having been married to them. Why had she ever agreed to buy, per Georges's specifications, that bossy, self-righteous sounding toothbrush? In the same embarrassed way she thought of his Hi-Protein cereal and his warm ritual coffee-kiss and their setting out for school together in the morning and his being gone then as though he had never existed for her, being totally absent from her mind until they were together again in the evening. And as she had this sudden sense of what it was they shared, she felt a futile boredom and humiliation, a helplessness, and then a flurry of panic.

She looked sharply away from him, toward the woods, which were melancholy majestic black against the last faint orange rim of the sunset. She was alone. The solitude of those woods, and of herself in the world, was the same thing. She was alone. Georges was a stranger. This was a clear relief, though terrifying.

I am somewhere new, she thought. I am trying to think and I am lost.

PART FIVE

❧ I ❧

T HE church, on this afternoon of Lewis's funeral, was
flooded with warm sun. A soft breeze bore April fragrance through the open windows, for the day was
unusually warm. Beyond the windows, bird song caracoled unfu-
nereally, the trilliop of robins in particular seeming inappropri-
ately and insensitively cheerful. And inside, the old organ played
hymns, softly. The sucking sound of the doors opening and shut-
ting with increasing frequency spoke to Anne and to Rupert,
who were so grateful, of the church filling up behind them.

Quietened now, for the first time in these hectic three days,
they sat close and stoically together, their bodies touching for
comfort, in a kind of pensive jubilation over being alive and
together, warmed by the sun that poured in over them. It was
Rupert who had insisted obstinately, against Anne's scandalized
protests, upon the church service. It was Rupert, too, with Syra
in agreement, who had known that Lewis would want the old
hymns, and who had spent hours with Mrs. Alexander, she at
the piano, going through her hymnal.

Syra, wooden and mute, had agreed passively to everything, as though having no wishes, and, as Anne had acidly observed to Rupert, was no help whatsoever. Nor was Georges, who had spent most of his time shut away with Syra, trying lovingly, patiently, and at last even irritably, to probe her stony uncommunicativeness. Mrs. Alexander, shattered, had for the first two days taken to long afternoon naps beneath her afghan, her sleeping face drained and sad. So that the Knights had had to do everything.

But they wanted to! A kind of purposeful executive energy had fired them. They had surmounted, or buried, the initial horror, and as pivotal figures in the crisis functioned efficiently and considerately, were its organizers, leaders. Their house was headquarters, and there, busily, they throbbed with purpose, with caring, Anne with constant vivid compassion, Rupert with slower, sterner attentions.

Anne had come to the church today in a kind of euphoric windup of frenetic purpose. Rupert, too, had reached a peak of something, a kind of melancholy rapture upon entering the sunfilled old church. And now the solemn moment had come at last, the service had commenced.

From the balcony, where the organ was, came the careful emergence of another hymn, swelling tenderly, sibilantly into the sunlight, encircling celestial white walls, God-fearing red plush; throbbing around bowed heads, heads tilted to whisper, heads held in stiff, unseeing meditation; setting atremble the great brass eighteenth century chandelier, which the man whose funeral this was had given to the church. "Abide with me, fast falls the eventide..."

The numbers of the hymns to be sung were posted on the wall beside the pulpit, and because Syra, in this public churchly situation and as its central figure, uncharacteristically felt a need to seem to be participating, a need to behave decorously, she looked down at the hymnal open on her knees and spoke the words to herself, soundlessly, moving her pale lips upon which she had deliberately not put lipstick, "paying lip service" to propriety, she had thought with a flash of sardonic humor. She wore a black chiffon scarf over her head and tied tight under her chin, which, seized with this new need for decorum, she had asked Anne to buy in the village.

"The darkness deepens, Lord with me abide. /When other helpers fail, and comforts flee, / Help of the helpless, oh abide with me." She choked on the word *helpless*. And then she gave a great, hiccoughing sob. Georges reached for her hand, but she tugged it away from his compassionate pressure. The bravado hurt of his face deepened. Nevertheless, he put an arm across her shoulders, and there was no loss of understanding in his melancholy eyes.

The hymn ended. There was a moment of no music, of creaking pews, hushed voices, coughs, rustling paper. Then another hymn crept forth, which Syra followed with quivering lips, as though compelled to–a dutiful child in Sunday School. "My faith looks up to thee, thou lamb of Calvary / Savior divine: / Now hear me while I pray, / Take all my guilt away / O let me from this day / Be wholly thine!" When it was over she fell to sobbing again, louder now, recklessly.

Mrs. Alexander, who was stony, heard the sobbing with relief. She was knocked all of a heap by this shocking thing, and her perennial gaiety was simply nonexistent. Lewis had been her constant companion, her best friend. Bleakly sad, she had at first been helpless as no one had ever seen her. Though gradually her balance was being restored, and her forces were gathering themselves to transcend her own shock and pay attention to Syra's. For here, she saw, was an immense and perhaps even unbalanced grief.

Beside Mrs. Alexander sat Bernice all dressed up, here out of excitement and morbid curiosity and mild regrets about Lewis, whose affectionate teasing she had grudgingly delighted in, and more, out of an unspoken attention to Mrs. Alexander, whom she seemed to be guarding with her great body, though she was finding pleasurable the whole conspiratorial air of mourning that pervaded the church.

The warm air that blew softly in through the open windows smelled of the freshly cut green grass of the churchyard and faintly, damply, of the woods beyond it. The heterogeneous gathering of mourners sprinkled throughout the church sat watchfully, alert and appalled. Because of the calamitous nature of this risky life, they were here without having expected two days ago to have to be present at anything of the sort, here with surprise, with dread, with resignation, and with a strange obedient shocked expectancy, for drama is the very stuff of funerals.

In his vestments the Reverend Merton, lounging watchfully behind the lectern in the high-backed rococo red plush Victorian chair that Lewis had bought and placed there, waited with a composed and compassionate countenance for the last arrivals. Being the minister of the Presbyterian church in town, he had known Lewis only slightly and so had spent part of Sunday afternoon with Rupert and Anne and Mrs. Alexander, boning up on the deceased. Thus his short funeral oration would be, as Anne disdainfully knew, impersonal and second hand, and she had nothing but contempt for such hypocrisy.

Again the syrup-sweet breathy tentacles of organ music began to weave through the controlled silence of the sun-flooded old church, the rustlings, the coughs, the nose blowings. The last hymn was commencing. It was the one of them all that Rupert loved most, though he would never have chosen it had he known what it would say to Syra.

"Dear Lord and Father of mankind, forgive our foolish ways," she murmured, mechanically, pressing her hands together between her knees, as though to warm them. "Let sense be dumb, let flesh retire..." She began to sob loudly and horribly. And Georges, quickly, made a sort of tent of himself over her, trying to quiet her. "Hush, dear, hush," enclosing her in his arms. There was quite a stir throughout the church, and the Reverend Merton shifted in his chair so that he could see around the lectern, and stared down upon Syra with furious sympathy.

Rupert, his face gaunt and watchful, was terrified of her keening. And yet not. He had a moment of knowing that Syra's keening was natural, in a way in which *he* had never experienced naturalness. Terrible but natural. She had been to him just a plain little wooden doll during these past two days. Yet now he wondered about her. He felt released by her keening, and was in a strange way comforted by it.

The hymn ended, and abruptly so did Syra's sobs. And the organist now began the opening, soaring bars of "Jesu, Joy of Man's Desiring," a favorite of Lewis's, as Anne and Rupert had known. The music built up, welled up into the sunlit loftiness of the old church, affirming, with a gentle rejoicing, all that was life, sun, joy. And the minister, for this was his cue, stood up. When the last note had echoed away, and after a moment of pregnant silence, he began, with a paced, exultant solemnity, "I am the resurrection and the life..."

The short oration and the prayer that followed were, in spite of the sincere efforts of this clergyman, without inspiration. What little he had seen of Lewis, frankly, he had not been drawn to. Syra didn't care; she sensed the hollowness of it immediately and didn't listen to a word of it. Rupert was fatalistic about the inadequacy of it, knowing that circumstances couldn't have fostered anything other than this cautious eulogy.

But Anne was outraged. She felt her temporizing of the service, her "weakening" as she saw it, toward justification of it, as a moment of utter delusion, and she rejected all endorsement of it and all connection with it. Here was exactly what she was opposed to, what she had written her memorial service letter for. Who would ever *know* Lewis from what this man was saying of him? Yet at the same time her emotions were confusedly aroused. She felt used, manipulated, felt something being done to her against all her own reason and control.

When the Reverend Merton had brought the service to an end with a benediction, when Purcell's *Coronation Music* pealed forth like a release, when Syra had been led from the church by Georges, when Anne and Rupert stood up and turned around to face the assemblage and to make their slow way out of the pew, Anne then said to Rupert, "Thank God that's over," so violently that he shrank within himself, knowing that this explosion was a forewarning of bombardment to come. Used to this, but nevertheless feeling now that it was an invasion of *him*, of his own private sense and experience of this service which she had no right to violate so soon, he did not reply, but, huffy and muted, moved off down the aisle a little ahead of her.

But it was the time, anyway, for their zealous teamwork to begin to collapse from the weight of its own excess. In a moment they were both going their own ways, Rupert was talking quietly to the Moores, who were red-eyed, and Anne chatting constrainedly with Mrs. Alexander, who, for the first time in these three days, seemed to be moving with some of her usual compact energy.

The throng of people flowing out of the church on the flood tide of the organ broke up into groups on the freshly mown grass, and stood about in the deepening sun, talking, departing. The heavy presence of gasoline fumes hung in the warm windless April air as car after car started up and slowly drove away.

Syra stood, small and quiet, with her husband and friends protectively around her, all of them concerned about her. Georges, brooding, exhausted, worried, looked pale beneath the tan that made his blue eyes even bluer. Syra's eyes were swollen from weeping. She looked at the ground. She hadn't spoken.

A wooden doll, thought Rupert, looking curiously at Syra. That lifeless. But those sobs! There must be something to this pallid little automaton. He wore a handsome navy blue corduroy suit and a navy blue silk shirt, in the open neck of which a foulard ascot gave discreet color. His hair was a bright silver against the darkness of his clothes and against the gaunt beauty of his dark-skinned face. The balminess of the day was making his spirits soar–the fragrance of the nearby woods, the daffodils among the graves, the newly cut grass. Oh to be alive! And in the spring! What a reprieve after the last few days!

Mrs. Alexander (without the vigilant bulk of Bernice, who had been driven home by the Moores) stood facing Syra, the same small height as Syra, her arms folded purposefully down across each other, her feet once more energetic on the ground, legs tensed, as though ready at any moment to stride off somewhere. The old familiar authority of her face was restored as she looked penetratingly at Syra. "Well," she said with quiet geniality to the group in general. "What a perfectly beautiful afternoon this is. What a blessing to have a day like this." It was evident that she meant to get on with life again. And yet there was no sparkle in her face, which looked older, paler, but strong and calm. It was teatime, and Lewis would not be coming.

What Rupert had missed in her face, anxiously, was the old good-humored fatalism, the acceptance, "and that's the way it is." He needed her to have it, to assure him that both death *and* life could be borne. While she was without it, he was uneasy. So he saw the gradual return of her spirit with an almost childish eagerness. "Beautiful," he echoed Mrs. Alexander, raising his face to the sun and loving its warmth, "utterly beautiful." Then he said softly, still with his face lifted to the sky, "Just for Lewis. And for *us*," he added strongly, "for us!"

There was a silence, filled rather awkwardly with the pulsations of Rupert's rapture. Anne coughed into her hand. Georges thumped his hat against his knee. Mrs. Alexander fixed a tolerant gaze on Rupert and smiled a little. No one spoke.

"But look," Anne said suddenly, energetically, "why don't you all come back to our house for tea, or drinks, or whatever. Yes? No? Wouldn't it be nice? We'll have a fire as the sun goes down. Oh do!"

No plans had been made for after the funeral, out of deference to Syra's evident wish to be left alone, and so this outburst was followed by a puzzled silence.

Then, "Marvelous," Mrs. Alexander said almost excessively. "What a nice idea, Anne." And Rupert with expansive dramatic relieved cheer cried, "Great! Do come. What's more, I'm going to have a drink. Those who want tea can have tea, but I"m going to have a *drink*." And Georges, looking tentatively at Syra, said, "I'd like to, but how about you, dear?" How he longed for normalcy, longed to be free of all things funerary, hated the thought of going back to Lewis's house alone with Syra. "It would be nice, dear, don't you think?"

"Yes, I do think so. Thank you, Anne." Syra had spoken so seldom in the past three days, or rather, so little of herself had come from her lips, that they were all surprised, as though a new person had appeared in their midst.

"Well c'm on, then," said Rupert rousingly, taking Anne's arm. But she was looking brightly beyond him. "Why, there's Heloise," she exclaimed. She began to wave.

"Oh, now, isn't that nice," Mrs. Alexander turned, searching.

"She must have been sitting way back. I didn't see her come." Anne had a new look, watchful.

Rupert, happening to glance at Syra, saw her mouth, half opened to speak, close slowly. He took note of this, thought about it. He turned and watched Heloise, who had detached herself from the one group left in the churchyard and was approaching. Then he turned back and looked elaborately around, in order inconspicuously to catch a glimpse of Syra's face again. She had composed it now, he saw, but the light that had been in the process of livening it had gone.

And then here, among them, somehow importantly, was Heloise, a short, elegant young woman with a cap of swinging, shining auburn hair and a nicely outstretched hand with the sound of bracelets rattling. They all greeted her as though eager for the interest of someone new in their mourning monotonous midst, and self-possessed, she shook hands gravely with Mrs. Alexander, who was delighted to see her because she liked her, with Anne, who was cordial but wary; with Rupert, with Georges. She turned finally to Syra and said nothing, only pressed her hand and let it drop.

"Well," said Rupert in his gently lordly way, "we're glad indeed to see you here, Heloise."

"Heavens," said Heloise, "of course. Words can't express..." Somehow she was reducing everyone to silence. They were all overwhelmingly aware of expensive perfume, silenced by it. Then, too, her elegance was of the sort that reduces less elegant women to wordlessness.

But Anne was not going to let this paralysis continue, not for another moment. She smiled brightly at Heloise. "We're all coming back to our house for tea," she cried with shining cordiality. "Of course you'll come too?"

"How nice of you. I'd like to very much."

Anne's vivacity had broken the spell. And now they all began to talk at once, to make tentative and then decided movements of departure. But Syra stood silent, her hands rammed down into the pockets of her old raincoat.

Rupert found his heart aching for her, he felt instinctively that she needed to have something done about her. Needed something. Hesitant, compassionate, he turned to her, his head tilted in youthful shyness. "I was thinking that you might like to walk back," he said to her quietly so that no one but she need hear him, "in this lovely afternoon. Would you like to do that? Anne will have to get the tea organized, so we won't be holding anything up. I'd *like* a walk, myself. Would you join me?"

Syra looked at him. Attention seemed to be stirring in her, rising up in her and bringing life to her frozen face, so that it changed faintly, even some slight color warming it. Then suddenly she smiled, her wide fresh smile, and Rupert was nonplussed to find standing before him a young woman he had never seen.

"All right," she said, in her direct way, so directly and so simply that Rupert felt increased, both increased and eased.

"Good," he said softly, "I'm glad. So *glad.*" He put his hand under her elbow, then flung the other arm eloquently toward the sky, and cried, "We're walking!" But because he didn't want Georges, or Heloise, or Mrs. Alexander, to join them, since he knew that his sense of things had been right and that Syra should be taken out of this group for a while, and because he was emboldened to pretend to echo her directness, he didn't suggest to any of them that they come along, as ordinarily, courteously, he would have. "We're walking," he cried again, with a radiant, challenging smile for everyone. "See you all back at the house."

ぞ II ぞ

THEY walked slowly along the road in the declining sun. The air was sweet and woods scented and still, rippling with bird song. Rupert strolled majestically along, looking continuously, solicitously down at this silent young woman who walked so heavily along beside him, as though weighted.

Because she hadn't said a word since they had left the church-yard, Rupert was talking, talking. "I'm sorry you and Georges wouldn't come and stay with us, as we would have liked," he was saying deferentially. "It would have been better for you not to stay in Lewis's house. I think." He could begin to say things now that had been on his mind for days. Because of that direct "all right." The "all right" had taken him into another world, where the constant, trying push of his own pressures seemed muted.

Syra reached up suddenly and tore the black chiffon scarf from her head. She opened her hand so that the scarf could float away, be gone, then shook her head, freeing her hair. She drew a deep breath and slowly let it out, which allowed her shoulders to relax. The dread she had become reconciled to as a permanent condition for a moment seemed to recede. She grew aware of breathing, of air coming into her lungs.

In the woods bordering the road, brown swampland glittered and whispered with springs and threadlike streams; and the new chunky claws of skunk cabbage, obscenely speckled as with dis-ease, could be seen everywhere in it, some of it taller than oth-ers, even beginning to turn into the lovely green it would even-tually be.

"Just look at that poisonous-looking skunk cabbage, begin-ning to grow such a beautiful color," Rupert said softly, sweeping an arm toward the woods.

Syra looked. And in a moment she smiled faintly, "Baby birds are ugly too. And toads turn into princes."

"Oh, my dear young woman. Yes. Yes. The miracle of change. On a sad day like this, there it is, declaring itself."

A little breeze flurried around them, bringing the scent of woods. It stirred Syra's hair, lifting a strand of it and laying it across her cheek, and she reached a hooked finger to pluck it away. The whole movement seemed to Rupert slow and sweet. Then he said to her, boldly, he felt, "May I say again that Anne and I have been concerned about your staying in Lewis's house. We've said so often we wished you were with us. Or with Mrs. Alexander, bless her." He waited, quiet, seeing almost with surprise an answer gathering in her.

"It was the only thing to do,"she said at last, and so surely that he felt in complete agreement. "And that's where I'm going to stay now, for a while. In my cousin's house."

"Oh?" Startled. "You're not flying back tonight with Georges?"

"Oh no," she said, feeling a bursting release at this unexpected, this astonishing idea. "No." And then left it. She raised her face to the sky and the sun, and over it stole a softening, as though words, decisions, be damned. She began to listen, as she strode along, to the ringing whistle of the peepers coming from the swamp.

And then suddenly, overwhelmingly, she was with Lewis crossing the driveway to his house in the silence of the country night, under a million stars.

The joy of that moment softened into her. The joy of the sound and the memory rang in her.

But instantly, brutally, it was struck down by the rest of everything. And then there were those two conflicting voices again, one side of her head talking to the other side of her head, repeating and repeating and getting nowhere, that what had been the fullness of joy to her had been something that had killed Lewis.

So where does that leave me, what kind of a person does that make me? she had catechized herself, again and again. She had never had to wonder about, or ask herself in any deep way, what kind of a person she was, except in terms of what she considered the imbecility of her mind, although she had been troubled in a surface way all her life by the critical view people had of her independent behavior. But other forces in herself, encouraged by her mother, had been too strong to allow any powerful doubts about herself to control her. Until now. Until this awful, this terrifying now–again and again, hour after hour, day after day and night after night, no end to this inquisition. It was like being on the rack, pulled two ways in perfect agony–she had loved Lewis, she had desired him. She had killed him–killed him with what felt right to her.

Fearfully, she felt that there was no longer any credulity in the spontaneous feeling and behavior she had lived by. Belief in the proud independence of her existence was nowhere to be found. Her confidence was gone. For the first time in her life, consciously and believably, she doubted herself. What she innately was, and what her mother had fostered in her, had turned out to be something that could kill. The end result of the freedom her mother had instilled in her had been destruction, had been murder of the person she loved best in all the world. All the sure persistent sense of herself was dispersed, smashed to bits, and she simply did not know how to behave, how to be, under such circumstances. It was like knowing nothing, seeing nothing, feeling nothing. It was like being no one. It was, she sensed, like death.

She walked heavily along, falling a little behind Rupert now, looking down and watching, in a mesmerized way, one black ballet slipper stepping, and then the other slipper stepping, again and again. Everything is repetition, she thought wearily, like this foot and then that foot and then this foot and then that foot, again and again and again. And my mind rattles harder and harder, like dice. She pressed her teeth together, so that the muscles of her jaws tightened and quivered. And she lifted her head suddenly and turned toward the only sense of help she'd had so far. Turned to Rupert, who was watching her.

Rupert was quite interested. This little person had said almost nothing so far, yet he found himself engrossed. For one thing, he was puzzled, had been from the beginning, he now realized, by the intensity of her grief. He, like many of the people in the church, had wondered more than once *why* such grieving for a cousin, and he and Anne had discussed it at length and often.

More than that, though, it was a new experience for him to be with someone who made no curtsyings of conversation. And what he already sensed as her total lack of obligatory politeness was only increasing his nervous need of it.

"You're a guitarist, I believe. And I understand a very accomplished one," he said with a formal, courtly kindness. "Lewis told me you've begun to perform for audiences."

"Yes."

"Where, may I ask?"

"Sure, ask. I like to tell. Most recently, and most importantly, too—the other recitals weren't that important—at Kilbourne Hall at the Eastman Theater in Rochester."

"You performed solo?"

"Yes. As well as being guest artist with a chamber music group, the same concert. It was utterly lovely, all the young creatures, and so clean and nice and gifted. I'm scheduled for a reappearance with the same chamber music group next spring, in Cambridge—Sanders Theatre. So. Yes, I've begun to perform outside my own little puddle. Right now my creative life is nil, which of course makes a person not whole."

"Oh my dear, naturally. Quite naturally. But I am indeed impressed about your performances. As an artist of sorts myself—I'm a writer—may I aspire to express appreciation and understanding of what that means?"

She looked at him–he noticed the roundness of her smooth young chin, the roundness of her high cheekbones, and of her ingenuous eyes–but from her parted pleasant lips no words came, though he felt, gratefully, that her eyes spoke.

They walked on in silence. And though Rupert was chafing to break what to him was the discomfort of silence, he did realize, even in the force of his own unease, that he was intrigued by the force of her ease. He fell to thinking about the chocolate cake he hoped Anne would take out of the freezer for tea, which he would have, he decided, before he had a drink.

"I know Lewis's house so well," Syra said at last. "I know my way around in it, is what I mean. I know where everything is. That's why I'll be staying on there. It's like home to a person." I will explain this very carefully to Georges, she would have liked to say aloud, but did not.

Rupert cleared his throat, a long, exploratory careful rasping. Then he spoke. "Just the same, I should think you really ought to get away from here. From all of this. If I were your husband, I'd hate to leave you here all alone." Somberly he looked down at her, his velvet eyes compassionate.

Husband?

Syra knew suddenly that she didn't have a husband.

I will not stay married to Georges, she thought with unperturbed clearness. And she saw that she'd known this ever since looking out of the window and seeing Georges get out of the car, a stranger. Or else she'd known it always.

Yes, she'd known it always. Or felt it always. But just now it had sprung into her forehead like a beam of light and had become acknowledged, clear fact.

I am sure of this, she said to herself, and she turned the triumph of her eyes away from Rupert, toward the woods. I am sure of something, she exulted. At last I *know*, in my *mind*, about Georges and me.

She turned an open, faintly flushed face to Rupert. "I *will* stay here, though. Until I've gotten used to all this. This is the best place to get used to it. In Lewis's house, in Lewis's world. If I leave now, I'm afraid, I'm afraid of not understanding. Because I am so totally, totally, totally without understanding. I am simply unstuck with being without a feeling of understanding. I do not in any way understand this dying." Her eyes gazed on Rupert with the round puzzlement of a child's–unguarded, pained.

Rupert was amazed by the suddenness, the candor of this confidence, which left him almost embarrassed, and yet mildly elated. He had never, with an adult, had the experience of such childlike directness. It was finding its way into him like a stimulant. And he said floridly, casting down upon her wiser eyes than hers, "I don't think, you know, that you can achieve what you want that way, I mean by staying in Lewis's house. No. No." He shook his silver mane, raising his head to the sky, strolling in his imperial way. But there was a brooding goodness about his face. "No. You see, if I may be so bold, understanding cannot be forced. Understanding will come in its own way, in its own time. And, I venture to say, will come more fully if you have the perspective one can only have away from something. You must know what it's like to go away from home, and see it with new eyes when you come back. Anne and I went to Italy two years ago, and when we got back, why–" he flung up an arm "–all this was pristine. Pristine! *I* had been so refreshed that this was refreshed."

Syra said nothing, though she turned to him with a sudden, trusting interest.

In his ease with her, in the naturalness she was infecting him with, Rupert wondered whether he should presume to speak to her about the service, and then decided that it felt right and so he would. "I'm afraid the service was hard on you." he said gently. "One goes ahead, sometimes blindly. Anne was against it. I felt the need of it, because I believe in ceremony. Though it went deep with you. So I'd like to know whether you are glad or sorry we had the service. I'm damnably sorry I forced it. I felt so responsible, somehow, for your tears."

"Well," said Syra practically, "don't worry about it. I don't know whether I'm glad or sorry. My mind has not been exactly working." They walked in silence. Then she said, "It was all right, I guess. Though not real. Perhaps that was the first time all the awfulness was sublimated, or glamorized." *Heavens, I didn't know I knew such words!...* "Perhaps it was a helpful transition." *There I go again!...* "So it was a good thing, not a bad thing. So don't worry. Be glad. And it's just what Lewis would have wanted, in that pretty church of his. But as for me, well," she said, "church really isn't a grownup thing, I mean, it's awfully make-believe."

"My dear young woman, how wonderfully well put, even though those aren't entirely my sentiments. With all the words I search for, all the sentences I chisel and polish, here *you* are hitting the nail right on the head without any effort whatsoever. Even though I myself feel church has its beauty and its function, and I rather like the drama of it, nevertheless I do also believe it is, as has always been said, a narcotic. Anyway, I will remember your definition of churches–every simple, stunning word of it."

But suddenly he felt a fool. Talk, talk, talk. I, I, I. And then he realized something of such importance to him that he was never to forget this moment. And he said to himself–she doesn't need to make conversation, and she doesn't need *me* to *make* conversation, and as a result I don't need to. She makes it perfectly possible, perfectly acceptable, not to make conversation. Vistas of the possibility of not making conversation opened before him like some promised land.

His head went way over to one side, coyly, with embarrassment, and he said more quietly and in an altered voice, "Of course. Goodness me. Forgive me for going on and on.

Sometimes I don't know when to stop. You'll be staying, then. Well, do let us see something of you. If you want."

"Oh, sure," said Syra. "I'd like that." She sauntered along in her steady way, wondering about Rupert, taken out of herself in a sudden enjoyment of him. She liked him, and she felt warmed, supported, because he had said that understanding comes in its own way, in its own time, as though it were a very common thing, or even a good thing, not to be in conscious contact with whatever it was that controlled one.

She glanced curiously at him and saw that he was looking off into the woods, his face rapt. She began to observe him. And at the same moment that she noticed the fine thin bones of his nose and the freshness of his well-shaped mouth, she realized that he reminded her of Ezio Pinza. If he should burst into song, she thought, it would be very suitable.

"Do you sing?"

He looked quickly down to her. "Yes, as a matter of fact, I do. I love to sing. I haven't much of a voice," he said, not meaning it, "but I love to use it."

"I wonder if you'd want to sing? Right here and now on this country road, along with the birds? Would you? Then I won't keep hearing hymns."

He would. He sang "Who Is Sylvia," quietly and naturally in a harsh yet sweet voice, enjoying the sound unrestrainedly. "Who is Sylvia, what is she, that all her swains ad-o-o-o-o-re her..." When reluctantly he had finished the last long-drawn-out harsh-sweet note, he threw her a searching look, and then smiled shyly.

She smiled back. "How I liked that," she said. Then she made a little sound that might have been a laugh. "it even washed-those-hymns-right out of my hair," she sang.

Rupert threw back his head and roared with laughter. "Marvelous, marvelous!"

She continued to smile faintly, and they walked along together for a while without speaking, Rupert smiling and nodding his head from side to side and humming the *South Pacific* tune she'd sung, so that she thought it uncanny how much he really was like Ezio Pinza. Finally he subsided into occasional soft chuckles, occasional snatches of song.

"Outdoors is so normal," Syra said. They had begun to climb Moores' hill, panting a little, slowing down. "Spring feels so fresh and clean. Spring is one of the four nicest seasons of the year."

"Ha!" Rupert cried. "Exactly, exactly." And then suddenly everything seemed fresh and clean to him, too; and new. Fresh, and clean and new, like this April day. And again, as last week after he had had the letter from his agent and was walking down to Lewis's, he experienced a tidal sense of the potential and promise of himself. Once again he was an accepted writer of books and thus another person, a person new to himself. And here was this stimulating young woman! The two elations merged and swelled into the kind of energetic optimism and excitement and unshakable confidence in himself that he remembered feeling in his youth. And at that moment the rippling, pebbly explosion of a redwing came jubilantly from somewhere to echo this excitement.

They walked up the hill slowly, heads bent with the effort. Alongside the road a thread of stream, perpetual and small voiced, slipped downhill through sluices and little basins with sandy, pebbly bottoms, sometimes leaf matted. "Stop and listen," Rupert commanded, reaching for Syra's elbow. They stood and listened to the tiny liquid voice, infinitely quiet and occupied and soothing, and not quite soundlessly coloratura. They stood and felt the peace of it for a long time. Then Rupert moved to go, and they began to climb again.

"Well, I guess this is us," he said in a moment, reluctantly turning into his drive. "That was such a nice walk," he said, "such a nice walk. We'll do this again." He tipped his head way to one side and looked at her with kind, shy brown eyes.

There was something Syra wanted him to know. She gazed up at him. Then she looked away, looked toward the house and saw parked there the two cars that had brought Georges and Anne and Mrs. Alexander and Heloise (Heloise!) back from the church.

She drew a deep breath, the nightmare had begun to sift into her again. In there was Georges, and she would say to him, "Georges, I am not going home with you."

She and Rupert were now, in silence together, almost at the house. She thrust up a proud chin. She stopped. Rupert stopped, too, considerately. She had nothing to say, but she turned to look at him. She wished she could tell him something, something in the nature of gratitude for his helping to revive her, or perhaps even something else, some groping sense of their recognition of each other.

She looked at him. And Rupert was struck wordless by the depth of her child's cool stare. He stood quietly, free of words, and free of any sensation except an invigorating, expanding peace.

❧ III ❧

"Well here we all are, and with the nice, unexpected addition of Heloise." Anne was determined to make this thing go, smiling fiercely at the chocolate cake that she was cutting across into small squares. "There! Now who will have a piece of cake? Mrs. A.?"

Mrs. Alexander and Rupert sat at either end of the red velvet couch, across the room from the fireplace and facing it. Behind them, beyond the glass wall of windows, was the great field sloping down to the woods, and the evening sky.

Heloise sat with Georges on one of the two red velvet love seats at right angles to the fireplace, and Syra sat across from them alone on the other one. The coffee table, presided over by informally low-seated hostess Anne, was a large circle between the two love seats, and all the action, all the sound of the large quiet room, of the subdued people in it, seemed to be centered here upon its polished surface where the firelight danced, the teacups rattled cheerfully, the hostess's determined hands darted about pouring tea, cutting cake, handing cups, her chatter in its forced cheer rendering everyone else mute.

But now Mrs. Alexander's voice, deciding to break up this stalemate, came across the room with sudden strength, a new force. "I never refuse chocolate cake, as no one in their right mind would, though I've been told I should. But Billy always told me I decided my own 'shoulds,' and I do." For cheer, her own and everyone else's, and as a sort of party touch, she had tucked a pink silk scarf into the neck of her navy blue dress, on her brief return to home. It was a surprising feminine softening around her corded neck, a frivolous pink billow beneath her industrious face in which her blue eyes were casual, experienced, bleak. "I'll come get it. No, no—" to Rupert who was lumbering to rise, "—you sit still."

But Georges was quicker than she, or Rupert. And his action seemed to release the others, so that there was much sudden pent-up talk—a chatter as energetic as the busy fire: Heloise to Anne, "I've been sitting here admiring this fabulous room," and Georges to Mrs. Alexander, "Here, dear lady, is your 'should,'" and she to him, "How charming you are, you nice man," and

Rupert to everyone in a loud rich voice, as rich as his velvet emotional eyes, "It *is* nice to have the addition of Heloise. We needed you, my dear. We've been a closed, sad little circle," and Heloise to Rupert, "Well, heavens, I'm so terribly pleased to be included in it. Really."

Anne was grateful for all this suddenly released cheerful chatter, grateful now, really, to be released from the hostess role. Her intense face was luminous as she sat quietly beside her tea tray, content to rejoice in the sound of people pouring out toward one another. She stared into the firelight, hot-eyed, mesmerized, sipping her tea, listening to Heloise's low, slow words, to the single chirrup of a robin out on the lawn, to Rupert talking extravagantly to Mrs. Alexander.

Hers, his voice was hers. Like the warm light of the fire, his voice glowed over there behind her back, was her need, and her sustenance, and the beloved habit of her existence. His voice, in his body, was her voice in her body, they were two, but one. She closed her eyes over tears, because of the gain of something, and the gratitude for life and Rupert, which had occurred since Lewis's death. How rich she was, inhabited and expanded by Rupert. She could even acknowledge for a moment the deterioration of her womb, and admit dispassionately that it would probably have to come out, and that this could really be endured.

She picked up her cup to gratify herself with a sip of tea, to add something to something, let's drink to happiness. She drank elation from the cup. She set it down. She ran a finger around its rim. She felt elation draining away. Then she became frantic and groped for its fading light. Now it was gone. What had it felt like?... But it will come back, she assured herself.

She sensed a slowing down of conversation between Heloise and Georges, and glanced up from her thoughts to find Heloise looking searchingly at her. In her melting mood, this pleased her, she forgot for a moment to be wary of this woman whose skillful attractiveness, and youth—still young enough to have a child, undoubtedly—had put her off so disturbingly when she'd first met her at Lewis's only last month.

Seeing responsiveness in Anne's face, Heloise pounced. "Tell me, Anne Knight," she said in her deep lazy flattering voice, "*who* is responsible for this perfectly marvelous house? There isn't a thing I look at that doesn't make me wild with jealousy. I'm a decorator, you may or may not know. But I sometimes have to concede that there *are* other talents besides mine." Her eyes enlarged and glittered—humor, perhaps, though there was no evidence of it in her face. "Honestly, you know you can't replace natural talent. There's nothing like it. And I'd say its *your* talent that's responsible for all this gorgeousness. Now c'm on. Admit it."

Anne felt a sudden flareup of impatience. She detested flattery. She drew herself up and declared summarily, "The house is all my husband's doing, entirely Rupert's doing," and then, "more cake anyone?" she cried, looking brightly around. "More tea anyone? Mrs. A., more tea?"

Heloise crossed one elegant skinny knee over the other. She didn't care. Swallowing affront was the story of her business life. She thought that Anne was a dragon and a naive one at that, and she let it all go, calmly. She supposed that she'd sensed Anne's aloofness from the beginning, or she wouldn't have wanted to butter her up.

"Well, it's time for a drink!" Rupert stood up. He had been talking about his asparagus bed and Mrs. Alexander's asparagus bed, and though he loved Mrs. Alexander he now wanted to get away from her, toward a drink, toward—Syra. "What will you have, Mrs. A.?" He bent courteously down to her, overflowing toward her now that he was released from her and was about to have his drink. "What will it be? Your usual?"

"Yes, but could you possibly go easy on the Scotch? *I* know *you.* And a whole lot of ice. Thank you, my dear."

"Drinks over here? Ladies, Syra, would you care for a drink? What can I fix you?"

"Thank you, I feel awful and might as well. Do you have any rum?" said Syra, licking chocolate frosting from her fork.

"I'll be darned. No one ever asks for rum. But yes, I do have it. With tonic, I assume?" She had on an amber silk kimona-type dress that glowed in the firelight. All that honeyed light on that dark red velvet. And her short legs so primly together, like a child's. He lingered over her a moment. And then, still smiling, he went around taking the other drink orders. "Dear," to Anne, "can I make yours for you?"

"No, because I'm going to bring out the tea things. I'll make my own. Thank you, dear."

"Aaaahhh..." And then again, louder, more attention-demanding, "Aaaahhh!" Rupert tilted his head, reached both hands down with demonstrable affection and placed them upon his wife's shoulders, which he began to knead possessively, she wondering why he always did this only in public, never when they were alone. "What could be nicer than this?" He beamed around at his friends assembled by his fireside, while Mrs. Alexander rose spryly, released too, to come over to the empty space on the love seat beside Syra.

"We've all been through something together," Rupert said, suddenly grave. "I feel it's brought us all together in a certain precious way. We value our own lives more now, I think. Life seems very precious indeed, doesn't it?" He cleared his throat, took his hands away from his wife's uncompliant shoulders and placed one upon the other before his chest.

The letter came back into him now with fresh glory, and all the excitement of it which he had lost during the past three days suffused him again. "Mrs. Alexander knows about it–" he looked down at her with an accomplice's smile, "–but I don't believe that Syra does, or Georges, or Heloise. I think you might all be interested in knowing. I feel I'd like to talk about it at this time, because it feels to me so much a part of what we may all be experiencing now, it feels like new life.

"What I'm driving at–" he smiled happily, "–is this: Just the day before Lewis died, I had gotten a letter from my agent telling me that Pangrove Press wants to bring out my book of essays. I can't begin to tell you what it meant to me. It was like a rebirth. I don't believe I've ever known such joy, such joy. But it went away, it simply evaporated, with Lewis's death. Quite naturally. There was no room for joy, that day or the next or the next. But I think we're all coming out of it a little." He searched hopefully the faces looking up at him, Anne's, which was twisted around and staring up. "I feel that Syra did, on our walk,"–he gave her a shy, luminous glance. "I know *I* did. It was spring, the redwings were singing. I began to feel the beauty and the joy of being alive, almost in a new way. And you helped me," he said, looking at Syra. "Then I came back to my home which I love. A fire's burning happily in my fireplace. My beloved wife has fixed an excellent tea. My dear friends are here. We are all alive. And so much lies ahead. It's all within our power. I'm talking about new life," he concluded. Then he swept out his hands, as though he would say more. Dignity and some pride remained, but frustration passed over his face, clouding it, and he shrugged, cleared his throat, said, "Well," lamely, almost apologetically. "I don't know that I've managed to convey anything."

"Well dear, you've managed to convey to everyone that you're going to have a book published," said Anne to her own astonishment, quietly and tartly. Everyone laughed too suddenly and too loudly, except Syra, who said to Rupert, "You conveyed something to me."

Rupert's face throbbed with sudden shame. Then slowly it

went blank, became a mask, as he raised martyred, perplexed eyes to the ceiling.

"Well, now," said Mrs. Alexander briskly, planting two little polished Red Cross shoes on the floor and rising, "let me help with these things, Anne." She was astonished at Anne Knight. Though she had no real fondness for her, she had always relished Anne's adoration of Rupert and her tact with him. She felt that Anne worshipped this man, and would protect him like a lioness–never a word of criticism from her, on the contrary, worship, worship, worship. "Let me do *something*," she said. "Here, let me take out the cake plate. And this teapot."

But Anne sprang up, all abustle and wanting to smooth over her rudeness to Rupert, her beloved Rupert. How could she have!..."Goodness no, Mrs. A. But thanks. Rupert can carry the tray, can't you dear?"

"Rupert can and will," sang out Rupert too rousingly, and tilted his head way over to his left shoulder, so that his long gray hair swept it. "Just watch the teamwork of this household." And in minutes these two efficient hosts had piled the tray high and safe with used saucers, cups, plates, spoons, and departed for the kitchen, strolling Rupert bearing the tray ceremoniously as though it were a crown on a velvet cushion, smiling with an effort and nodding his head slowly from side to side as though in time to some little inner tune that he would have everyone believe he was pleased with.

"Rupo, I'm sorry. Really sorry, darling. All I can say is, this has been such a strain and I'm not myself." Anne, with an apron over her dress-up gray flannel dress, was swiftly and nervously transferring the plates and the tea service from the tray to the counter.

She poured the cold tea into the sink with a great splash, put the teapot down on the marble counter rather too hard for the safety of the old china vessel, and then abruptly she turned around to Rupert. "Darling, I could bite my tongue off. Honestly."

Rupert, wordless at the bar counter, making a great deal of deliberate clatter with bottles and glasses and ice cubes, his back an ostentatious rebuke, said nothing.

Anne went over to him. "Rupo." Her voice begged. She snatched the tray of ice cubes out of his hand and set it on the counter. Then she took both cherished big hands in both of hers, and leaned down and put a penitent kiss first in one chilled palm, and then in the other. She looked up at him with pained eyes, and he saw tears there. "I'm really pretty much of a wreck, Rupo, after all of this, and because of, well, and because of all we've had to do. That's all. That's all it is, my love."

Heloise relaxed, and as she shifted more comfortably into her corner of the love seat, the perfume she wore was faintly released toward Georges. He was flung back against the cushions and was staring with melancholy intensity at Syra, who had kept her plate and was eating her third piece of cake as naturally and swiftly as a hungry dog.

The perfume and the small sound of one silk knee crossing the other caught Georges's attention. Yet across the way was Syra, his wife, the solidity and the heart, or else the investment, or else the habit, of his life. He saw the round high cheekbones, the rounded chin, the roundness of her whole face, its self-contained, biding sensual roundness. He felt the softness and the recklessness, really the immense sophistication of that face. He thoroughly respected this unusual woman he so unaccountably was wedded to, and so he had been obliged to respect her odd sorrow and even her aloofness.

And yet he was deeply wounded by the calm, cold way she had shut him out. And so now, as though he had been given sudden sanction to, had been released from the obligation of his

melancholy staring, as though Syra's detachment had commanded him to, he ceased abruptly to look at her, and turned to
Heloise with an exploratory look in which both shame and an
uncertain boldness grew.

Heloise drew out a cigarette and tapped it against her nail,
which was long and pointed and pink. She bent to light it, and
her russet hair swung in a heavy short sheet across her cheek.
Then she thrust up her chin and blew out a whistle of smoke.

All this, with new daring, Georges appraised. He saw that her
cheeks appeared sucked in beneath broad cheekbones, her skin
grainy and pale. He saw that her wrists were tenderly small and
fish-belly white with blue veins, emerging from the bulky sleeves
of her suit. He was aware of the fragrant and inviting combination
of cigarette smoke and perfume, and the clank of gold bracelets as
she stretched her arm to tap her cigarette against an ashtray.

Heloise turned to look full at him. "You look as though you'd
been south."

"Oh. Why, yes. We're just back from Nassau. Lucky in our
weather. Only one day of rain out of eleven. Half a day, to be
exact."

"You are *kidding*."

"No, I swear."

Syra was only partly listening to Mrs. Alexander, who was
talking worshipfully about Walter Cronkite, for at the same
time she was attempting to hear, curiously, what was going on
across the way, while trying to make some decision about how
and when to take Georges aside and tell him she was not going
back with him. When she caught the innuendos of intimacy in
those two voices, she turned for a second away from the safety
of Mrs. Alexander's kind chatter and looked across to Georges.

She saw his expression. And she felt something like relief.
Well, not all relief, some pique too. But much more relief than
pique. And faintly, she felt a kindly admiration for him. Could

Heloise be the sort of woman he was best with? She certainly, Syra thought, is much more Georges's type than she was Lewis's. Heloise had never been Lewis's type.

Lewis and Heloise... Syra saw the dark stairwell, the prints of old Paris like mounting steps, one above the other, on the walls, she smelled the faint musty smell of an old house, she was coming to the top of the stairs and passing Lewis's bedroom, and averting her eyes. She felt a swift sharp pain, and then panic.

"We'll have to be watching the time, honey." Georges looked across at Syra and then down to his wristwatch. He had the patient, uncertain expression of a parent trying to deal with a child who intimidates him. "We have to pack," he said, "and wait for a taxi. I'm not going to let Rupert drive us to the station—which he'll insist on but he's not going to get away with it. Mrs. Alexander, have you any idea of trains? We're getting a ten o'clock flight out of La Guardia. Which means..." he looked down at his watch again, calculating. "Which means that we should be in New York by eight-thirty or so. Now I don't know what trains there are, but I'm thinking we may have to think about getting a move on fairly soon. I hate to break this up."

"Well, my heavens, I'll drive you. I'll drive you to La Guardia," Heloise said. "It's hardly out of my way at all, since I live way up in the east nineties. I'm only minutes from the Triborough Bridge. Truly. I'd much rather not drive back alone anyway. You'll be doing me a favor."

Georges turned his whole body to her and smiled his sweet sudden smile, which startled and moved her. "That would be perfect, if you put it that way. I wouldn't want to say no." He laughed delightedly, his high, child's laugh, and looked tentatively across at Syra, who had said nothing. She looked golden in her kimona, and detached, loosened, remote in the dusk. "Honey, isn't this nice? Now we can relax and enjoy our drinks. It won't take either of us long to pack. Is there anything we have to do about the house?"

Syra drew a long breath, opened her eyes wide, opened her mouth to speak, but Mrs. Alexander was saying quickly, "Oh don't worry about the house, for mercy's sake. Bernice and I'll go down tomorrow and clean out the icebox, and whatever other cleaning up there is to do. Don't give the house a thought."

"Oh, but that's an imposition," Georges exclaimed.

"It's not in the least an imposition. I've no plans for tomorrow, and it's not Bernice's day to bake, that unshakable habit. And anyway, she'll be doing most of the work. Plus the fact that I would like to be in Lewis's house, and with my own two hands, set the place to rights." She touched the scarf at her throat and then the corners of her mouth with uncertain fingers that for the moment didn't know what to do with themselves—the only evidence of her distress, for her face was composed, reliable, and her fatalistic sharp eyes were stern and strong. "It's like a second home to me. I'd like to tuck in his treasured crewel bedspread just right. I'd like it to be perfect and neat, all the rooms, just the way he liked it. I'd like to wind up the grandfather clock. And keep it wound, every few days, so the ticking goes on. I don't mean that the place should be kept like a shrine, I don't mean that at all. What I mean is that I'd like to be custodian of that house, if you'll permit me, Syra, until it's lived in again. I'd like to keep it clean and alive, for Lewis."

There was a heavy silence, Lewis brought back to them, and they had been so free of the burden for the last hour. But Syra closed her eyes over a sudden stinging that might be tears. Then she stretched out a hand, placed it on Mrs. Alexander's knee, withdrew it in a moment, but not before Mrs. Alexander had put her own small warm hand briefly on top of it.

After waiting a proper interval of respectful silence Heloise cleared her throat and spoke in a lowered tone across to Syra. "How long will it take you to pack, do you think? We might do a little figuring now, before we all begin to drift away on the lovely tide of alcohol. Oh don't worry about me driving. I never drink much, particularly when I drive. Be assured."

In the silence, while all of them waited for Syra to speak, the fire collapsed suddenly and burst into new strong flame–the response that no one else had made. But then Syra spoke. "I've decided not to go back, Georges."

"But – What on earth!"

"I can't go back, that's all," she said. "I can't leave Lewis yet. Mrs. Alexander has just said far better than I ever could what I feel about Lewis. I mean about his house. I have to stay in it. I can't leave it yet. It would be very bad on my spirit to have to leave here." She said all this clearly, factually, not unkindly, and every word had a slow, rounded completion.

Both Mrs. Alexander and Heloise stiffened, waited. Heloise stopped the hand that held the cigarette she was bringing up to her lips and kept it in front of her mouth, waiting.

"But – What on earth," Georges said again, excitedly. "What about William's recital? What about your classes?" And what about me? he wanted to cry. And why are you springing this on me at the eleventh hour, here in front of these two women? It sounded fishy to him, it felt wrong, and in his heart he knew it was wrong.

But he was too proud and too polite to let an embarrassment grow and so he said at last, flatly, "So. You're staying here. I *see*." His eyes, flicking over at Syra, then away, were bewildered and humiliated. He lowered his head, spread his knees, and with his elbows on them, rammed his hands together, driving fingers between fingers, and then began to drum those agitated fingers upon the backs of his hands. But then he shrugged, clapped both hands down upon both knees, turned his head all the way around to Heloise, and smiled sweetly, more sweetly than bitterly, though there was bitterness in his eyes, "Sooo, I'll be driving in with you alone. If that's all right with you."

From a fascinated, embarrassed silence Heloise roused herself. She turned to Georges with abrupt compassion. "But of course," she said, too heartily, "of course it's all right with me." And to try to ease the strain with humor, with prattle, "Why on earth wouldn't it be all right with me? I'll tell you the story of my life. You may not think that's any sort of treat, but believe me, it is. It's a crazy story. Lewis always told me it was stranger than fiction. It's your typical soap opera, it has to be heard to be believed. Well anyway..." She turned to stare at the fire as though she'd said more than she'd wanted to, and put the cigarette between her lips in a slow deliberate way.

I *am* mean, Syra thought with shame, realizing at once that she could have and really should have spoken to Georges alone, feeling as though she were soiling some pure connection that bound her to her mother; feeling again the new, muddling presence of self-doubt, self-examination. Oh yes, I am mean, she thought, feeling shame.

But then something rose in her to contradict shame, because that, too, felt unusual, as unusual as meanness. And she had a sense that meanness was not natural for her, that she did not, at bottom, live and breathe a *wanting* to hurt with meanness. And so she understood, almost as an idea but mostly in her senses, that she had become this way because meanness presented itself as a safe delay, as marking time, in the accident of being a wife to Georges. Caught in the subtle crime of a wrong marriage, she had used meanness as a safe way to strike at it, to chink away at its edges, without actually destroying its center.

Okay. So I've been mean. Surprisingly, she could say this to herself without shame now. But I am not essentially, in a big way, mean. I have had to be this way, like a porcupine has to have bristles to protect himself. And I have been this way because I haven't *known* anything.

And so she felt sure, at this moment; she felt blankly, unthinkingly peaceful about what she had done—the clean relief of no more Georges, the perfect clear black-and-white conviction of that severance. For that's what it was, of course, severance. And besides, nothing seemed to matter much. She and Georges were strangers, their marriage was mediocre and a lie. It was almost a relief in the knowledge of this great mistake, to do something stark, offensive, to strike out against it.

I keep doing outrageous things, she said to herself with resignation.

And then for a moment, Syra was absolutely alone. She was without the other self of her mother. She was Syra unmothered, Syra outlined and informed by no one but Syra. She was empty of conflict, solid, absolutely alone. Beside her she felt Mrs. Alexander release her breath.

And then, like rescue, here came the clink of a laden tray and the rousing voice of Rupert, who, having gradually allowed himself to be kissed and apologized to and made much of by Anne, was once again euphoric. "Drinks, everyone! Here I come bearing drinks!"

Hurrying, Anne scraped the plates and stacked them in the sink. Clucking, though, and hostess-ship be damned for another little minute, she took the time to scoop the scattered tea leaves together in her fingers and dump them into the waste pail in the cupboard under the sink.

As she did this, she felt a sudden gush, and then a slow warm pouring on the inside of her thighs.

Her hands, about to close the cupboard door, froze there. She looked at her hands. They were wet. Brown tea leaves clung to them. She saw the tea leaves. One was a tiny brown stick.

The slow warm avalanche was moving down both legs now. Warm, sticky, ruby. She looked down. Three large drops, on the floor, spread. They were three enlarging little puddles, very red on the clean white floor. She watched them being joined by more red drops, *spat, spat.* Then—she felt the bigger blurting out—the flow down became a massive fast pouring, streaming down one leg and into her shoe and all over the floor. Wet red all over Rupert's floor.

She seized a kitchen towel in a wildly shaking hand and bent to mop at the floor but then instead, with an exasperated "Oh God," she pressed it to herself and dashed for her room.

In the bathroom, she stripped off the hated clinging sticky underwear and got quickly under a hot shower and stood there for a long time, letting the drumming water blot out everything.

When she felt the hemorrhage abating, she turned off the shower and then slowly she dried herself, finding that reason was beginning to press into her: This could be only a heavy menstruation, reason suggested to her, even though it was two months since her last one. Menopause was like that. On and off. The last hemorrhage had happened like this, like a sudden, tidal menstruation.

And then came a wave of wild happiness. It was still here, wonderful warm pouring blood.

But in the bedroom, taking stockings out of the old drawer that always stuck, she yanked so savagely that the drawer leapt out at her and almost fell to the floor. Catching it before it did, appalled at herself, she fitted it back with hands whose shaking she wanted to disown.

She took the stockings and went over to sit down on the bench at the foot of the bed, where she pulled them on over still-damp legs—shaky legs, she saw disgustedly. She drew a long breath, which was meant to convey to herself a return to stability. She stood up, crossed swiftly to her dressing table, and picked up a lipstick from the silver filigree tray, thrust her face toward the glass, saw terror in unrecognizable eyes, smeared the lipstick exactly over lips that didn't need it. "God, what next," she whispered, smearing.

She ran the comb, unnecessary too, though her hair. And then, with her head high, she strode over to the door and out of it.

The room was completely dark except for the glow of the fire. Rupert had not wanted to turn on the lights, thinking that the new strange mood of strain he had sensed in it when he came back might be dispelled more easily in the darkness.

He was the only active one, perpetually up and down, replenishing drinks, passing food, putting logs on the fire, Anne having seceded as hostess with strange abruptness, he thought. To his dismay she had come in with a tall very dark drink, something she never did, and after swiftly downing that she had gone out to the kitchen and returned with another one. Attributing this to penitence, Rupert felt, along with his concern, a certain complacency.

They had all, except Syra, begun to talk about Lewis. First they had begun to re-create the service, to glorify it, extracting those elements from it that could be complimented. "The sunlight!" Rupert mused. "And the birds, did you hear the *birds?*" "And the Purcell," Mrs. Alexander murmured. "Wouldn't Lewis have been pleased!"

From the service they had advanced, first one and then another, to the subject of Lewis himself, extracting from Lewis, too, those qualities that could be complimented. They had come to Lewis's quotations. "What a joy it was, that capacity of his to produce word for word the perfect quotation at the perfect time!" Rupert said, remembering with grudging recognition how accurate Lewis's cruel quotation had been the last time he had seen him. Seen him for the last time. Yes. Lewis had been right. I am the vainest of the vain...

Mrs. Alexander took a sip of the Scotch she so much liked; she always drank in little sips. "I remember well how he always said, 'Everything has its beauty but not everyone sees it.' Lewis could see beauty in a single leaf, in a cobweb. I know he had an awful struggle about destroying cobwebs, he loved their beauty but they didn't do, of course, inside the house. I remember one morning going in there and seeing him standing by the living-room window looking at a cobweb on the outside of the window; it was covered with tiny drops of dew and was sparkling in the sunshine—the loveliest thing, you have to admit—and there he was trying to persuade himself to let it stay."

"Did he?" Syra asked.

"No, he didn't. He went out and swept it off with a whisk broom."

"The one I always remember," said Anne, holding her glass toward the firelight and gazing into it, "is one of Lewis's favorites, he told me. And it's gotten to be one of mine. The first time he quoted it, I was profoundly impressed by it. And I think of it constantly, and quote it constantly." She paused. Then she began, dramatically, "'That which is for you will come of itself into your hands. But if you strive to overtake it, it will destroy that lovely flower of your peace that is so short of blooming.'" She continued to gaze raptly into her glass, then brought it to her lips with slow thoughtfulness. "Lewis couldn't remember the source. I've always meant to try to track it down. Now, did he say that it was from the dance of Shiva? I believe so. I was so impressed by it that I'm fuzzy about our discussion about the source."

She smiled and shrugged. "Maybe it's this drink that's making me fuzzy. Anyway, I feel it says so much about our culture, about the Puritan ethic, if you will, I mean I think it points the finger at it. Lewis always said, there's a message there for anyone who wants to get it. He always said that with utter despair. Well, there *is* a message, don't you agree? Yes? No? *I* know plenty of people who could very well profit from taking it seriously. I don't know how many hundreds of times I've quoted it to young women who come into me wanting number one money, number two fame, and it seems to me happiness and fulfillment not at all. Usually they don't react to the message, as you would expect. They think I'm out of my mind, me, a job counselor, suggesting that they not strive. It's that word *strive*, a question of semantics, I suppose. But then they don't really get the rest of the message either, which is *not* about what they think it's about. They don't get the message even slightly. But be under no illusions. That was one of Lewis's favorite quotations."

Rupert, restive at this monologue, cleared his throat, looked courteously at Anne, and said, "Yes," dismissingly, "yes indeed. I remember it." And before she could speak he went on, "I thought the Reverend Merton did well. Considering."

"Considering what?" Anne asked sharply.

"Why. Considering that he didn't know Lewis well at *all*."

Anne drew a deep, exasperated breath. And she thought: This mood is false. This is only firelight and liquor and euphoria over being alive, and sheep huddled together in a storm. What's more, I won't be shut up!

She took another long swallow of her drink, and then set her glass down on the marble table, hard, a sound that shocked. "Well, who *did* know Lewis?" she cried. "I mean, of course *you* did, Syra. And you, Mrs. A. But I didn't. And here I am grieving, and I wonder almost, who I'm grieving for. Look," she cried with sudden passion, turning to Rupert, "that service had nothing to do with Lewis. Nothing. The fact is, that service didn't give us anything of Lewis. It falsified and dramatized him. Perhaps that's all right, and that's what funerals are for, but I don't happen to think so. I think you only pay your respects to a person by showing him in the round."

She was hugging her large smooth bare arms under the gray flannel expanse of her bosom. Her eyes were on fire. "What sort of a memorial is it to pick out the so-called good parts of a person to talk about?" she cried ardently. "*This* ought to be Lewis's memorial service, right here. Now. With his closest friends together. That's the only way we can show meaningful respect and caring for Lewis! By re-creating the whole of Lewis! Erich Fromm explains that our word *respect* comes from the Latin *respicere*, to see. What Lewis deserves is for us to *see* him, and thus *respect* him!

"Look," she cried with a new burst of feeling, "I'm talking about the promise of clean relationships, of being lifted out of false mawkish muddle, out of fraud, up to a plane of cleansing honesty that can make not only Lewis known to us, but make all of us better known to each other. Oh, I ache for it. And I'm terrified, too, frankly, at the thought of how totally death, Lewis's, mine, everyone's, can extinguish, leave nothing. Lewis should be resurrected. Saved from extinction! That's what we all hope for, really, isn't it, after we die?"

In her fervor, the flash of her eyes, the opalescent pallor of her face and neck and bare arms, Anne was a white flame burning straight up. No one stared at the fire now, they all stared at Anne. She was breathing rapidly, her large bosom rising and falling. "Rupo, don't you think so? Don't you agree?"

All the fascinated or perplexed or skeptical eyes in the room now shifted, as though commanded, from Anne to Rupert.

Above lips that he pursed, Rupert's dark brooding eyes glowed, and he shook his head slowly from side to side, until at last he spoke. "If you're asking us to talk fully about Lewis, now, here, and I think you are, I'm afraid of it, for some reason, Anne," he said gently, thinking that she had drunk far too much. "I feel we must all think of ourselves now. We carry all of Lewis in our individual hearts. Must we crudely, perhaps ineptly, perhaps–" his eyes narrowed secretively "–even antagonistically, say *words* about Lewis that may do nothing to fasten a better memory of him in us, but may very well create real discord among ourselves? Or else reveal ourselves to each other in a way we'll later regret? No, I think we must accept that the traditional service has been here a long, long time, and has some important function. This is something I think we should respect. No, my dear, there's something about it I don't like at all. And after all, isn't a memorial service just for us, anyway, just for the living?"

With a flush of anger that she would have liked to suppress and to disown, Anne cried in a voice that surprised her by its stridency, "Well, *Rupert*, speak for your*self*, for heaven's sake. I don't feel it's *fair* to outline all *your* concerns, which may not be the concerns of others. What you fear of course *could* happen, but we ought to be able to risk all that. Nothing risk, nothing have," she cried, her eyes blazing.

But then she shrugged expressively, and, struggling to find some calm in herself, she smiled around ingratiatingly. "Let's hear some other reactions," she said in her "little" voice. And she gave a light laugh and looked charming, her keen eyes darting from face to face.

Heloise sat forward slowly, and looking straight at Anne she said carefully, cheerfully, "As far as Anne's idea is concerned, I think it's one thing if a person's great, or if there's enough good in him to offset the, well, not-so-good, so that if people discuss him as Anne suggests, then at least a large part of what they say will be about nice qualities, not un-nice ones. But–" she shrugged slightly, "–I really don't think the memory of most people could survive such an exposure. Most of us are far, far too, well, human is the kindest way to put it. For a Martin Luther King, yes. For most of the rest of us, no. That's the way I see it. I'm sorry. Perhaps that's why eulogies are in order at funerals, so that–"

"No!" Syra drew her shoulders up high, clenched her fists, and pounded the air with them. Her nostrils were widened in fury and her eyes flashed. "No! This is loony. Listen, Heloise! I think it's pretty empty for you and Lewis, that you were a good friend of his and didn't even begin to know that perfectly enchanting man. If you'd known him even slightly, you'd know he most certainly *could* survive such an exposure, as you put it. I can tell you plenty about the wonderful parts of Lewis, and without making him not real, as Anne seems to think we're doing. Honestly, I don't think you could really have known him in the least, Heloise!"

Passion made Heloise uncomfortable, and she was tired of being attacked. The others were stunned by such intensity from quiet Syra, Georges grievously so, for he had never been privileged to see her passionate in that way about him and this made his heart feel heavy and cold as a stone. "I think that's probably very true, Syra," said Heloise now, husky, tactful, faintly scornful, bracelets clanking as she sank her chin into her pink-nailed hand, the worldliness of her eyes as she looked at Syra telling that all this passion and foolishness was not going to touch her. "But then I think you were so much closer to Lewis than any of us."

"Well, I want you to know that Lewis was one of the dearest men alive," Mrs. Alexander said heatedly, fixing a cold and noble eye on Heloise. "I think he could easily survive being discussed. He had his faults, of course. But as far's I'm concerned, Lewis was a perfect darling, and was my mainstay. I think this is all wrong."

"And so do I," said Rupert in a slow grieved way.

"Oh, my God!" Fury with Rupert shook Anne, fury scalding and pure, erasing every other feeling she had for him. She suddenly saw him as pompous and childish and she felt she despised him, despised her blind worship of him, despised the self-applauding existence he led, the playacting way he and she lived together. She felt she absolutely could not stand this man who was a child and a peacock, and who lived a lie.

"My God, Rupert! All I'm asking is that for once you don't

give some long laudatory lecture which has nothing to do with Lewis but is only selling *yourself*, urging yourself upon the world." She brandished an arm. "That is not truth. Dramatizing is falsifying, it is *not* truth. And when I ask you to join in something as important to me as life itself, and I mean honesty, *honesty*, you say in your saintly, lecture-platform way, oh no, that won't do."

She was furious and unashamed, panting, her face strong with convinced rage. She knew what she had done and it didn't matter. Truth had come out and it was cleansing. She felt the precariousness of their marriage, it seemed unreal in the most muddled and obdurate way, and she really knew that *this* was the truth that was coming out. Who was he? Who was she? And who were these people?... "When I ask any of you, for that matter, to pay real respect to the dead–" she flailed an arm at the lot of them "–you won't do it, because this is the way people are, the way the world is."

During the terrible quiet that followed, in which, watching the shock and then the shuttered pain of Rupert's face, Mrs. Alexander and Heloise and Georges dared not move, dared not breathe, in this battle lull, Syra turned to Mrs. Alexander. "I'm wondering," she asked tonelessly, her face frightened and sad, "could I spend the night with you? Then tomorrow I'll go down to Lewis's. Begin at Lewis's. Tomorrow."

How did any of them get up, get moving, part, speak, Anne with her exalted triumphant frightened calm, Rupert impassive, his black eyes bullets, shattered and so uncertain in his movements that he was unable to carry out even the amenities of holding the ladies' coats, not a word out of his furious impassive face, which was already growing set and martyred. How could there be any word from anyone, though Mrs. Alexander with distaste and stoicism written all over her face had nevertheless been able to murmur to Syra that of course the guest room was empty and waiting for her. And what was there now for Georges and Syra to say to each other?

They all went out through the door that a Valkyrie Anne, defiant, her wax-white face fierce and convinced, held open for them, though proudly, with no word–Georges with Heloise, toward her car, Mrs. Alexander and Syra arm in arm toward the gate, silent figures moving away into the darkness. The host and hostess, hospitable to the last you would say, though doggedly, even deliberately so, stood waiting at the open door in the cool night air, postponing the closing of it as long as they could.

The car door slammed. The motor started up, the car backed, turned, accelerated. The door of the Knights' house closed, leaving blackness where a rectangle of light had been. The dark bulk of the car moved away down the drive, first its headlights, then its red taillights picking out by the side of the road the figures of the two small women it passed. No one waved.

PART SIX

❧ I ❧

EVERYTHING about this month of May should have been as it always had been–a joy that Anne and Rupert shared with all the enthusiasm of their natures. White lilacs banked the garage, blending their perfume with the lilies of the valley girdling the base of the old apple tree by the driveway, so that the two perfumes together wafted thickly toward the house. The asparagus bed, this third year of its life, was yielding a generous crop. Beside the silvery old barn house the blossoms of the dogwood were vivid white, intense as emotion. Redwing blackbirds settled in its branches. And, a new thing, bluebirds came, dozens of them, swarming into and out of the great maple over the front terrace.

"Anne, come here. Hurry. I've never seen this. Bluebirds. Hurry!" But Rupert's voice was thin, without timbre. Trying for naturalness and spontaneity, it only sounded strained and anxious.

Nothing was spontaneous between them any more. They lived together in overly polite watchfulness, in dread and in confusion, their voices sometimes sharp, their eyes not meeting except occasionally in sheepish challenge. All these usual May delights, the flowers, the birds, the asparagus, only intensified their alienation; they were a joyless couple in a joyous season.

But because of Syra, Rupert had his moments of savoring. He and she had almost at once established a ritual, except on Anne's weekend days at home, of taking long afternoon walks together. And so while dread and confusion was the breath Rupert drew at home, there were moments when the rarest sort of ecstasy pierced him, a new, pure joy, an anticipation. And because of his growing absorption with Syra, he could not, would not allow himself to try to meet Anne on the old grounds of love and trust, to forgive her or to understand her. His righteous withdrawal was convenient, though he wouldn't have put it that way. He was a man excoriated and scorned–he found it providential to employ this interpretation of Anne's outburst to bolster his real alienation from her as his attraction to Syra grew.

"I don't see what you see in your little friend." Anne had taken to calling Syra "your little friend." "What do you see in her?" she kept saying.

If he had been willing to, he could have said "She is passive in such a life-giving way," or "What she says interests and enchants me," or "She's that rare species, a person who doesn't *have* to make conversation." He could have said all of this and a lot more, the complexity and profundity of which he still had no notion of. But he was not going to be forced to put into words, for anyone, this experience he was having with Syra, least of all for Anne, whose snide questions he felt demanded of him the dignity of not answering. Syra was his treasure and, above all else, not something to be delivered into Anne's hands.

"I will never forgive you." He had told her this with a deadly calm that night, after he had closed the front door and before turning to mount the stairs to the guest room, where he would sleep alone.

He said the same thing to her again, the next morning. He walked into the kitchen slowly, heavily. He sat down at the table across from her. He cleared his throat (I hate that sound, she thought) and then he said, with a rehearsed perfection and with an enormous quiet that terrified her, "I will never forgive you, Anne. Never. Because there's no question in my mind, no question at all but that you believe everything you charged me with. You'll respect me to the extent of not pretending that that isn't so."

Anne put her trembling hands around the warmth of her coffee cup. "I did believe it when I said it. But it's more complex than that." She kept her fierce, evasive eyes on the coffee, whose comforting steam rose uselessly. She had not slept at all, and there was no resolution in her dazed mind. She felt naked, powerless, and without a plan. "What I said last night came out of me, yes, I admit, it felt violently, cleansingly truthful. There, you see, I'm not pretending." She darted him a little spiteful look, tightening her lips. "At least you should know I never pretend," she said, believing this.

"I would have said not. But until last night I would have said, too, that you respected me. I would also have said, up until last night, that you loved me. Now, Anne, you've left me nothing to believe in. What are we to do?"

"What do you mean, what are we to do?" she said in a weak, alarmed voice.

Rupert spread shaking fingers on the sun-bleached table, alongside his coffee cup, which was empty; he had had three cups of coffee and he would have no more. He had not slept, either. Exhaustion was rendering rage and fear unmanageable. And yet he felt a queer relief, even an interest in it all. "Since you are the one who has challenged our marriage, it seems to me that you are the one to answer that question."

"For God's sake, what are you saying? I love you, Rupert, for God's sake." She looked fully at him with torment and love–but not with a love which overrode everything, for now there was a new, disturbing, restraining edge of caution in her, and in her voice.

Rupert heard it. He felt himself sinking, as though there was nothing under him at all and he would go down, be lost. Her total unquestioning commitment to him, expressed in passionate fullness, had for fifteen years been a sound that wrapped him round.

For a moment he felt lightheaded. Then the strange relief came over him again, and dazed, he fingered the handle of his cup and lifted it slightly, put it down. He cleared his throat and she thought again, I hate that sound. He spoke. "I don't think you do love me," he said waveringly. "I think we very seriously have to consider that possibility."

"I certainly do love you Rupert, for God's sake." There was now a very strong, matter-of-fact conviction in her voice that unsettled him and was even unwelcome.

He sniffed. He rose importantly from the table. But all his elaborate composure could not conceal the turmoil beneath it, nor an incredulous pleading look that, like a mistreated animal's, both accused and begged some alleviation or denial of cruelty. "If, in front of other people," he began, unable to keep the quaver from his voice, "you can do what you did to me last night, I feel I've never known you, I feel everything's blown up, gone, that you've turned into a monster. But how could that *be*? I asked myself that the whole night long. How could that *be*?" For a moment his stony eyes showed agony. "Have you been nursing hatred for me all these years? I simply can't comprehend it. *You?*" He glared at her sickly, and yet he was full of the power and the righteousness of the persecuted and was not going to let that advantage go. "As I see it," he now said with awful, conclusive quiet, "if you can scream at me in a voice of pure hate in front of our friends, scream out monstrous accusations that I sell myself, that I dramatize myself, that I don't tell the truth—those were your very words you know, I haven't forgotten a one—'laudatory lecture,' 'urge yourself upon the world,' 'saintly lecture-platform way,' I have your exact words, Anne, stamped in me like brands and ineradicable, Anne, *in-e-radicable.* If you can speak such words about me, and in *public*, then you believe them. You'd better know what you've done. You've done me an injury I think I'll never recover from. Because if you can scream out insults at me, heartfelt insults—you should have heard your fishwife voice, Anne, shrill with hate and so heartfelt, so heartfelt—if you can say and feel what you charged me with last night, then I say, without a shadow of a doubt, that you don't love me. And you can imagine what it is for me to learn *that,* after fourteen supposedly happy years. Well, I've finally experienced what true shock is. But *why?*" he cried suddenly, turning to her in such helpless misery that Anne would have gone to him and flung her arms around him if she had not been glued to her chair by an unfamiliar resistance. "Why, why?"

"It's not the way you think," she said feebly. "I wasn't myself last night." The temptation to tell Rupert about her fear stood suddenly, imperatively in her mind. I haven't been myself for days, she would tell him. I haven't been myself for days, weeks, months, because I'm afraid. I'm afraid my uterus may have to come out, she would tell him.

But instead she said, whispering, "I had one of those hemorrhages out here in the kitchen last night. It frightened me. It needn't have, but it did. See those spots on the floor? I tried this morning but I couldn't get them all out. I'm afraid you'll have to sand them. I'm sorry."

She would tell him about Dr. Lovelace, about the months of worry and suspense, about the hemorrhages that came and came, in spite of all the medicines. I'm senselessly disturbed, I'm really bordering on a nervous wreck over it all, she would tell him.

But no! She would not tell him. The thought made her feel naked, impure, flimsy. She wanted no part of a reconciliation based on sympathy-begging. But more than that, her womb, and the ending of its function, were now separate from Rupert, she had taken the function of it out of the "we" of their life. It was *her* "empty bag," and she would ask no sympathy for it, no protection from *him* for its fate.

I'm left holding the bag, she thought, and was not bolstered by this humor. But she would not ask for sympathy. And so she only said with quiet pain, "I wasn't myself. But I know it was a terrible, terrible thing to do."

"Yes." His eyes were bleak as he turned away. And his voice was tired and drained. "It's beyond my comprehension. I don't know what either of us is going to do, now. I feel totally lost. Totally lost." His voice broke.

"Oh Rupo!" Compassion seized her again. But still she couldn't leap up from the table and go to him. Neither of them wanted this. There was a new barrier. She was in agony over having hurt him, and yet she was aware that he was feeling sorry for himself and was dramatizing his self-pity, and this recognition of weaknesses she shrank from revived for a moment some of the spirit of last night's rage. She made an exasperated sound and flung herself back against her chair. "Oh God," she whispered.

"Oh God indeed," he said wearily, and with a detachment that chilled her, before walking out of the room.

And that was the way their first and only discussion about her calamitous outburst had ended. Neither one had the will or the desire to bring it up again. Rupert continued to sleep in the upstairs guest room, grateful, increasingly, that a justified separation from Anne allowed him this privacy. The loss of her from his bed at night, though, was painful to him, like an amputation. And sometimes, as he flung an arm or a leg out across the smooth, cold, empty side of the wide bed, he thought that this cold emptiness was the feeling of death. Anne was not here. He was alone in a bed for two, where a large warm soft body should be, and was not. It was as though Anne had died and he was a widower, sleeping alone.

And yet at other times he felt, along with a constant, muted desolation, the freedom of being separate. And even as he was beginning to experience himself as a separate organism from Anne, he began on occasions to see her with a kind of merciless clarity in the midst of his angry prejudice. Still furiously wounded, but with his need of her diminished, and feeling separate, unwedded (although contradictorily he could still at times feel as though he were cemented to her), he began to see her as a person distinct from him, as though he had never known her intimately.

One moment he would see her dominance as a steamroller that was annihilating him, even if it were only her suggestion that he put a Band-Aid on a blistered finger. The next moment he would see her quick, warm intelligence, her energy, as strong and beautiful and admirable–the thrilling woman climbing a ladder to rescue his cat. He sensed that in this compartmentalizing of her he was serving some purpose of his own, which made him feel sterile, not himself, and he tried to remember how it had been when the whole of Anne had been in his vision, the whole Anne, whom he had always absorbed without inquiry. And at these times he would have the aching sense of the woman within, complex, secret, rich, whom he didn't know at all, had never made contact with. And he would turn to study her, covertly, feeling a hesitant tenderness toward her, though he didn't want to touch her.

And he could sense that she was making herself untouchable. But at the same time he could sense that she longed to break through to him. And yet there was something new in her, too, something withdrawn, cold, that supported his emancipation but increased his fright.

The contract for his book had come. He had walked back and forth on the freshly scrubbed kitchen floor with it in his hands, reading, marveling, exclaiming, while Anne, at the sink peeling potatoes, was pointedly wordless.

The check for the advance had come, and unable to keep his excitement and pride to himself, he had burst into her study with it, thrusting it toward her with a hand that shook, forgetting everything in the need to share this with her.

Outwardly calm, she had taken it in two hands, pleasantly. She had looked at it, her heart trembling, and managed to smile up at him impersonally. Then she had said gently, but coolly, "Well. That's quite a lump sum for you. It must be very gratifying." And handed it back to him.

After that his bitterness toward her was implacable. Yet he continued to be unsettled by their estrangement. What had loving her meant? *Had* he loved her? *Did* he love her?... These were tormenting and unanswerable questions in his present mood, particularly since some new young elated unknown Rupert was growing inside of him.

So it was. They went their separate ways, Rupert in stubborn refusal to allow any softening of attitude, Anne in baffled inability to break down either her own or Rupert's impregnability, held back too by some new attitude toward him, toward themselves, which prevented her old, unquestioning effusive worship.

One day, though, she thought of putting lilacs up in the guest room on his bedside table. She knew he wouldn't think to do it himself, since it was her role to pick and arrange flowers. Suddenly, poignantly, she wanted him to have the experience at least once this spring of waking during the night to a faint fragrance in the dark.

But she couldn't make herself go this far toward him. Soon the lilacs would be gone, and he would have missed the experience. Her sore heart ached when she realized this, but she was frozen in containment, all outpouring of herself was arrested. And so she knew that something drastic and irrevocable had happened, something that she could not explain away, but that Rupert would have to explore along with her. Yet she couldn't, daren't initiate the exploration. And each day it became less possible to do it.

It had also been impossible for her to make any attempt to reestablish herself with Mrs. Alexander. She wouldn't apologize, of course. She was too proud to do any such thing.

It had been Mrs. Alexander who had smoothed the way toward a resumption of easy neighborliness. She had asked Anne and Rupert and the Moores for drinks the week after the "scene," as Anne thought of it. Her April fire was lit. Bernice labored in with a plateful of wonderful hot cheese puffs. Syra played the guitar. And Judd Moore (who planted red geraniums in an old black coal scuttle, Anne remembered Lewis saying disparagingly) made a great deal of convivial and often humerous noise, banal as his coal scuttle, but with a pleasant loud rousing quality that managed somehow to gloss over the nervousness of the others, and to make the party go.

After that, communication between the two houses was more

or less as it had always been. And of course Rupert was over there every day, Anne knew. She rationalized that Rupert was turning toward Syra and away from her as a means of punishing her. But she also knew, furtively, that Rupert's interest in Syra was not this, was something very worrisome indeed, and that, unfortunately, she was in no position to say, or to do, anything about it. Actually, she had a rock-bottom belief that Rupert would always, in the long run, be hers, and so her jealousy of Syra was only intermittent and not profound. Nevertheless, Syra worried her.

One Saturday morning, while she was doing her marketing for the week, Anne met Syra at the A&P. She saw Syra, calm in the swarm and clatter of the crowded market, leaning over into a blue hyacinth plant on a counter, her face, slack with ecstacy, bent into the waxy blue spires.

Anne walked behind her without disturbing her, and set about selecting grapefruit from the nearby stand with a halfhearted methodology—they must be heavy with juice, their skin must be thin and tight, not thick and loose, their color must be yellow, not green, their shape must be perfectly globular, not lopsided. She worked automatically but without her usual fervor because she was distracted by Syra's oblivion and rapture, which she would glance at between the weighing and inspection of each grapefruit. "That's what I call religion," she thought, ripping a plastic bag from the roll above her head and tumbling the grapefruit into it.

Just then Syra came out of her trance and looked up. She saw Anne immediately. An expression of greeting altered the detachment of her face, which was nevertheless cautious, for she was wary of Anne. Unexpectedly face to face with her, she was rattled—the fragrance of the plant and the tension tightening her stomach were two contradictory sensations that further confused her—and she said almost inaudibly, "Oh, hello, oh. Well, I think I'm planning to buy this hyacinth for Mrs. A. I mean I'd given up the idea of buying it, because I only have five dollars and two dimes left, and they cost two ninety-five, but now maybe I can buy it if you would loan me the two ninety-five. Then I'll have enough for Bernice's groceries. This is lucky, meeting you. If you can do that without getting too low yourself. I'd love Mrs. A. to smell this. I don't think I'll be coming here again soon. I rarely come here because of all the dashing-around people."

"Oh yes, of course." Piqued at being viewed as no more than a savior supplying cash to Rupert's "little friend," Anne put the bag of grapefruit in her cart and lifted her purse out of it. "Here we are." She opened her wallet, giving Syra her "little" smile and her "little" voice–meekness disguising something altogether different. "So. Two ninety-five you said?" She handed over the change to Syra, who took it carefully. "Yes, Mrs. A. will love that," Anne went on, "although I myself find hyacinth over-poweringly sweet. A *thick* sweetness. Well, that's the A&P for you, you can buy anything here from soup to nuts, *plus* plants, *plus* kitchen utensils, *plus* lawn chairs, *plus* magazines. *Plus* tabloids that dream up freak happenings gullible people *eat up*. Like last week, standing at the checkout counter I saw a head-line in one of those wild tabloids–see if I can remember it exact-ly, yes–it said "Bride gives birth at the altar."

Syra laughed, a loud hoot, and then more little hoots that were torn up from her belly and exploded from her delighted mouth, the quivering plant in her hands exuding its perfume. "Oh I think that's funny, I do, I do," she said, as the hoots tapered off. "Do you think it really did happen?"

"Of course not. But I keep thinking about it, half-believing it, I suppose. Well, it *could* be. For instance, supposing the bride *went* to church even while having labor pains, and then was caught right there during the ceremony, and had to lie down on the floor and give birth?"

"Yes. Or even, suppose she *wanted* to give birth at the altar, like a kind of publicity stunt, and so she went to the church knowing full well what would happen, and simply lay down on the stone floor and out popped a little baby."

"Could be. But the timing seems rather improbable, wouldn't you say? A lot stranger than fiction. Anyway, there's a whole novel in that one sentence. I'd tell Rupert about it as a theme for him, except that of course Rupert doesn't write novels any more. And it's not the sort of thing he writes about anyway."

"No. I can see that," Syra said, bending her smiling face to her plant, then looking up unsmiling, as though the sweetness of the plant had disposed of the mirth.

"Have you read anything of Rupert's?" Anne asked, trying to keep her voice casual.

"Yes. Sometimes he brings notebooks along on our walks, and we find a place to sit down, finally, and he reads to me, and then I am in a state of marveling that he seems to have all those words, and other people have none."

"Oh." A long pause. Anne turned and put her hands firmly on the bar of her cart. "Well, I've got a big list, I'd better get going on it. By the way, how did you get here? Can I give you a lift home when I'm through?"

"I hitched. But I'd love a ride back. Don't hurry. I've the groceries to get, Bernice's list. Blast, she's written down something called 'capers,' I *think*. Can't read her handwriting. Do you know what on earth that is?"

"Follow me and I'll show you."

Capers were located, and explained. "Shall we meet at the checkout counter?" Anne asked with careful sweetness, tilting her head to indicate a studied politeness with which intonations of sweetness must not be confused. "It shouldn't take me more than another fifteen minutes or so to finish up. Or if you'd rather, wait for me in my car. It's unlocked. It's the red Volkswagen, identifiably beat up. You can't miss it."

"Oh, I'll meet you out in the car then, because now that I've got the capers, I've only butter and cottage cheese to get."

"Who eats the cottage cheese? I'm curious."

"Mrs. A. She hates it but is told to eat it by her doctor. And Bernice makes her."

Anne smiled in spite of herself. "Ah yes. Good old bossy Bernice." She turned and walked off pushing her cart with the grapefruit, waving a hand slightly above her shoulder without looking back.

They met in the car and started off. Syra sat tranquilly, her bag of groceries in her lap, the hyacinth pot on the floor safely immobilized between the clasp of her two ballet-slippered feet. She was uncomfortably aware of the tension and constraint between her and Anne, more intense here in the small space of hot, sun-stilled car than it had been in the crowded and noisy market. She tried to distract herself from discomfiture by thinking about Rupert, who was allied to this setup. But then she saw that he did not belong naturally here, and she found that a sure sense she had had of Rupert was gone away. Instead, here, he was no one, or no one's, he was jagged, pulled apart, he was pieces of Rupert, directionless pieces, magnetized neither to Anne nor to her, but just crazy floating-around jostling pieces. Yes, he was torn apart, here in this electric atmosphere that was discrediting him.

Anne drove rapidly, making vivacious conversation interspersed with bright laughter. Syra said almost nothing in reply, and Anne was gradually nervous about her silence, then embarrassed by it, but then, grudgingly, curious about it. Rupert had said of Syra, "She doesn't have to make conversation," and Anne understood that Rupert thought this admirable. But could it be that Syra didn't make conversation because she had nothing to say? Anne's eyes grew studious. She took her lower lip in her teeth for a second before saying, with cautious nonchalance, "You say Rupo reads you his stuff." It was "Rupo" now; he was hers, and would be declared so. "I do hope, for his sake, you like it."

"Some of it. The parts I understand. Some of it's poetry. Oh he is a poet, a poet, a poet."

"He is indeed." Proudly. "So you like poetry?"

For a moment Syra felt obligated to answer this–professional person, though she would have preferred not to, and was on the point of saying, "Yes, I like poetry." But then she shut her mouth softly, and said nothing.

In the pause that followed, Anne narrowed her eyes, cleared her throat. Then she said, "Rupo must be pleased you like his work."

"I guess he is. Yes. He says he is."

"He loves acclaim."

"Yes. And he deserves it."

"Indeed he does. But now, tell me, you're an artist, performing for audiences. Do you? Do you, I mean, like acclaim? Forgive me if that seems an intrusive question. It's just that I'm greatly interested in the subject of means and ends, of art for art's sake. If there is such a thing."

"Why yes of course," Syra replied strongly. "When I play for others, not just alone for myself, of course I want acclaim, if that's the word I'd use, I don't know. Why else would I be playing to people if I didn't want them to like it, if I didn't want them to get something good out of it? People's liking my music makes me feel as if a dove had brought me a branch of laurel. And it also means that there has been a reason to play to them. My music is two things. It's for myself. It's like polishing a person's spirit. But it's also for people." Like the filling-me-up satisfaction of having caused myself to flow across to Lewis, and receiving the baseline of him back, she thought.

"So acclaim doesn't feel just it," she said to Anne, "I mean I believe that liking acclaim means 'oh good I'm just great.' So that's not really the point of a, sort of, discourse, which is what my playing to people is, and feeling what they've gotten out of it coming back to me. You know though, it can't be put into a few words, music can't, or at least I can't put music into words, not really. My awareness only appears in rare moments of grace."

"Well," Anne said, and laughed shortly, "I think you've defined 'liking acclaim' very aptly. And that is just what I was driving at." *Oh good I'm just great*, she thought, was Rupert in a nutshell. So. Syra *did* have something to say, in her childlike way. But where did she stand on issues outside of herself?

At that moment Anne was forced to stop behind a school bus, its red lights flashing, children spilling down from high steps, then flying joyously off and away. They looked like freed balloons to Syra, and she smiled, feeling their release in herself. She would have liked to open this car door and spill out of it.

But the bus, to Anne, was suddenly a convenient pretext for sounding Syra out about how she felt on the subject of human rights. "What do you think about this busing situation in the South," she asked pleasantly, putting the car in motion as the bus started up.

"Oh my goodness, I seldom discuss deep subjects, if ever, so all I can say is, I only know what I've seen on television, with Mrs. A. and her adored Walter Cronkite. Why?"

"I just am interested in opinions about it. I'm curious. And then, too, I'm very distinctly upset about it. Tell me your thinking. I'm interested."

"I don't have any thinking about it. Or do I? Lewis told me I could understand if I put my mind to it, which usually I don't choose to do. But I don't think I have any thinking about the busing situation. Except that the mothers and fathers of the white children have mean faces. On television I see that the mothers and fathers of white children have mean faces." She repeated this in a strained way, an anxious way. "Like the very worst in these people is taking them over, it looks like. But then they get in the cars and drive their children home, and then they look just like every other nice mother and father. Looking at those mean faces destroys me for a day or two. But a person can be destroyed and not mind at times. But my thinking? Well. I don't like it that people can be so off."

Syra had the strangest experience then. In arriving at what felt to her like the adultness of taking a stand, of assessing people and then condemning them (and herself) for meanness, she had a deep, melancholy sense of loss, along with a strange new surface sense of rescue. Like climbing out of the lake onto a raft when she was a child. Safe, but having lost the lake.

"I agree about their faces. I'd go farther than calling them mean. I'd call them evil. But I am not concerned about *them*, as I am about the blacks. Those white children will grow up to have the same, as you say, mean faces as their parents when it comes to blacks. But the damage their own evil will do to *themselves* is nothing, nothing, compared to what it will do, is doing, has done, to blacks. There is no redemption for a black. A white can alter the misery of his *prejudice*, if he chooses to do so. There is therapy for that, religion, human growth. Whatever. But there is no foreseeable alteration of the misery of the black minority. There just isn't. I strive to make it so, I work for it, I hope and pray for it, but I'm not optimistic. Anyway, what I'm curious about, Syra, I mean actively concerned about—you know John Donne said, 'Every man's death diminishes me, because I am involved in mankind—' so what I'm curious about is, what can I, you, everyone do right now, to be involved in this busing horror, for instance?"

They were on Deer Valley Road now, climbing the hill to Ogilvie Lookout. Syra sighed. "I don't know," she said. "I don't think about that." She looked down at the blue spires of the hyacinth trembling between her clenched feet. "When I am with my black friends I don't think about that." She yawned. "Or even when I'm not with them. The only thing I think about and that bothers me, I wish they didn't want to be called black, because they're not. Each one has a special color–cinnamon, clove, eggplant, et cetera. I wish they would say beige, purple, or whatever they are. I loathe that coverall of black. Although I don't even think about *that* when I'm with them, really."

"Well," Anne said quietly, "I presume they like you for that."

She had come to Mrs. Alexander's driveway, and she slowed down and turned into it. She had no more to say as they sped along through the alley of maples. In the deepening sun, the shadows of straight tree trunks fell in swift succession–long dark bars one after the other–across the moving car, and across the two silent women sitting in it.

Anne lay in the wide double bed where Rupert wasn't, feeling the palpable accusation, the death of its loss of him. Sunlight struck across the floor, across the tumble of blankets–she had tossed and turned all night. She wondered how she was going to get up and get dressed and go to work.

She remembered then, with a sudden stab and yet resolutely, too, that day after tomorrow was her appointment with Dr. Lovelace. She had had another hemorrhage last week, and this time, with headlong panic, she had immediately picked up the telephone and called his office. And strangely, after facing it, she had begun to have a certain resignation, even relief. Inevitability, she had said more than once to herself, I am looking at inevitability...

An aching sadness overwhelmed her, so that tears welled up into her eyes and slid down along her temples.

And then all at once she knew that sadness had gone as far as it could go. She had had enough of sadness. The robin's cheer, out there in the sparkling morning, fortified her. And it was clear to her, easily and suddenly, that she would try to break through, that there was no hope of Rupert's moving from his unrelenting position, and that therefore it would have to be up to her. Everything was going to change, return to normal! It was up to her and she knew what she would do!

She flung back the covers, sprang out of bed, and crossed to the armoire to take out her embroidered gray silk Japanese kimona. But even before touching it she rejected it distastefully as coquetry, and hurried back to the bed for her old padded bathrobe, companion of many winters. Then she hurried across to the open glass door, almost running because she was afraid to slow down, to weaken her resolve.

The flower shears were hanging on a hook inside the garage door, and with these she began to cut the blooms from the great old lilac bush beside it, shaking from their firm cool white pyramids little showers of cold dew down her raised arms and onto her upturned face. What a delicate fragrance they had, in the early morning, in the thin cold sunlight! The easy tears welled up in her eyes again, because of all this gentle beauty that was being denied entrance into her, this springtime that was lost to her.

She did falter then, standing under the bush with the lilacs in her hand. But then she hurried back toward the house and into the kitchen, where she took down from a shelf the white iron-stone pitcher, filled it with water from the tap, and arranged the lilacs in it, nervously spreading them out, rearranging them, sensing the pure, cool fragrance, its calm, and the loud beating of her heart. Finally, impatient with postponement, she drew a deliberate, fortifying breath, crossed the sunny kitchen to the dim hall, and climbed the stairs to the second floor, feeling humiliated all at once, feeling a fool, then feeling angry with Rupert that she should be finding herself in this position. By the time she had reached the top of the stairs she had lost almost all of her positiveness and it was only stubbornness and desperation that kept her going forward toward the guest-room door, which was open, she saw regretfully. If it had been closed she might have been able to turn around and go back downstairs.

She tiptoed across the hall, her heart pounding. And feeling now quite unsold about this overture, but damn it, committed to it, she crept her head timidly around the door.

The bed was empty.

Her relief was so immense that she had to smile. He was up, and out walking, no doubt. But the bed was a mess—the covers had been dragged across it during Rupert's obviously restless night, and had come untucked at the bottom—a mess that struck Anne as symbolic, for it was Rupert, she thought, who had deepened and perpetuated the mess, though she had begun it. He's made his bed and he can lie in it, she thought, with anger but with compassion too.

Automatically she moved to straighten the bed up. But then she stopped. No. He had made his own bed up here every day since their separation, and what would it be saying to him if she were to do it today? She wanted to give no messages of that sort, no little behind-the-scenes, sneaky gestures of reconciliation. But weren't the lilacs just that? No, no. The lilacs were something from her heart to his heart. And yet she couldn't put them down beside that bed, now that she was actually here. She absolutely could not do it.

Her face hardened. She swung out of the room, hastened down the stairs, and went back into the bedroom, where beside their violated empty double bed, on her side of it, she set the pitcher of lilacs down upon the table. And I hope he sees them, she said to herself miserably. I hope he gets the significance of this lonely, terrible state of affairs when he sees that I brought lilacs in for myself, but not for him.

She began to dress for the city automatically—gray flannel suit, gray suede shoes. "Gray this, gray that," she thought wearily, "gray, gray, gray." And as she was putting her small gray leather notebook into her large gray handbag, suddenly she knew that somehow this would have to be the last day of stalemate.

And then without thought she went over to the pitcher of lilacs and leaned over and buried her face in the drenching fragrance. After a moment she withdrew her face, which had softened. And then she picked up the pitcher of cool white flowers and took it out to the kitchen and set it down in the middle of the table. Where it belonged, she thought, not for him alone upstairs, or for her alone downstairs, but for both of them, together, here.

❢ II ❢

"SUMMER!" Syra said this aloud, gloatingly. She lay in her soft bed, in dappled shifting sunshine, sensing for the first time, in the light that flickered over the pink blanket cover, the passage of time, the imminence of summer. Slowly she smiled a wide smile that felt happy, and she was peacefully excited to feel this sense of happiness duplicating itself on her lips, one of the first smiles of pure delight since Lewis's death, since Nassau, or, since when? Childhood?...

She loved Mrs. Alexander, had loved her immediately, and had stayed on with her, without plan or decision but in an evolutionary way, instead of moving into Lewis's house as she had thought she would. She liked Rupert, too, and their daily walks had been valuable in a way that, typically, she didn't understand; though even while feeling that she ought to, she knew she could not, and did not have to, understand.

This early morning in mid-May, five weeks after Lewis's death, she lay on in bed after waking up, as she usually did, fresh from the night's rest and with an initial ease and clearness that could easily, as it usually did, sharpen into a confusion of questions and no answers. But now, having just stretched and opened her eyes to a world that didn't like the kind of person she was–Bernice's ever-present scorn was a daily reminder of this, and at bottom unsettling–she began to sense, in a buoyant and deep way, that the whole world, the whole fullness of life, lay ahead of her, in spite of all the evidence to the contrary. This kind of ease–lying rested in a soft bed in the morning sun with happiness on her face–was an experience of her childhood, and this sense of an uncomplicated capacity for something total, something immense and easy, was a memory of childhood, too: Waking up in her narrow white bed with brass balls on top of the posts, with the sun dazzling those four little worlds, and lying there immense with the sense of the whole summer day, top and bottom, and as for that the whole world, being all open, and ready for her–all hers.

Her bedroom faced south and east, so that no matter how late she slept she always awoke to sun, if sun there was. It was a small pink room with a small brass bed, a few pieces of old but undistinguished furniture painted white, starched curtains at the two windows and a starched dust ruffle around the base of the bed. Starched was the feeling of the room, which was clean as all outdoors, and with a country oldness about it, an ancient musty smell in the drawers and closet. Everything in it had always been there. It had been Mrs. Alexander's room when she was a child, and for all the years of her growing up. There were cobwebby darns here and there in the old net curtains, and the pleated china silk of the bedside lamp shade was cracked, inclined to disintegrate at a touch.

Mrs. Alexander had discovered this, coming in one morning to rouse Syra since they were going into New York for lunch and Syra had overslept; she had seen it as she leaned down to give Syra a little awkward poke through the blanket, as much affection as it was natural for her to show. It was always a surprising joy to Mrs. Alexander to come in and find this young friend in the bed of her childhood. She had intricate and profound claims upon this bed, but it was a natural outcome of her growing love of Syra that it was easy to let the bed be Syra's in the same way that it had been hers.

She had forgotten that the lamp shade was disintegrating. She clucked at herself. "Well now will you look at that. Poor old thing. It's certainly had its day, and more. I'll never find another one like it, not these days. Do you know how many years that shade's been there?" She touched it affectionately, and smiled as a flake of silk broke off and floated down to the tabletop. "'The shades of night are falling fast, upadee, upadaa.' The ten-cent store has perfectly good paper shades. Or the discount store. My friend the discount store."

"Please don't change it for my sake." Syra liked the old shade, which spoke of Mrs. Alexander's past. "It happens to soar my spirits exceedingly. It belongs here, that's what. I don't see how you could possibly not let it stay here. It has to finish out its life here."

"All right." Pleased. "Shall do, as Anne Knight says. But come on now, Piglet, up with you. We've got to leave by eleven. I'll send Bernice up with coffee. I can see you slept well." She was glad to see the softness of Syra's flushed face just emerged from sleep and not ready yet for the pained perplexity that would deepen there as the day progressed.

"Oh I did. Just look at this sinshine, Mrs. A.," she said, yawning.

"It is pronounced *sunshine*."

"Didn't I say that, what did I say?"

"It sounded like *sinshine* to me."

Syra's mouth went wide and loose. "Oh how absolutely wonderfully funny. The yawn made it sound that way." How appropriate for me, she thought, and felt sadness stilling her.

But Mrs. Alexander burst out laughing. She sank down onto this starched bed of her childhood and leaned against the brass foot rail and laughed so naturally and so contagiously that Syra, suddenly feeling that sadness was silly, began to laugh, too. This was a room for female laughter. And the laughter of these two women seemed to Mrs. Alexander to bring the room back to where it had begun.

The room had been a powerful factor in Syra's gradual recovery, as had Mrs. Alexander herself. This room of a woman's childhood had given back to Syra, vividly at certain moments, and then with a gradual growing constancy, her own state of childhood. It had helped lead her back, as she had already haltingly begun to do on her own, to a feeling of what she had been as a little girl, and she was amazed at how clear and simply defined these recognitions were. She had said to Lewis that night, "I feel way down inside myself, like I'm in a place where a little door just opened up and there I was in that perfect place that made me wonder why I'd left it." And this was the way she felt now.

The confusion of questions and no answers that would begin to cloud her first peaceful waking usually had to do with the never-getting-anywhere back and forth in her head—like scissors in there, snipping everything into pieces—about the question of herself, her "identity," as she knew Anne Knight would put it, which had grown to be an unrelenting question, and as she would tell herself impatiently, so time consuming, so, basically, boring. Oh how hellishly tired she was of the cutting up of her mind. I cannot, I cannot just lie here and talk to myself all the time. Otherwise I'll scream the walls down—a female Joshua...

Omnipresent, of course, in this debate, was the presence of Lewis, and, though less frequently, of Georges. But often before the confusion would begin, she would lie for a long time in the soft bed remembering Lewis and their life together—little-boy lips on her cheek, fresh, smelling of wild strawberries. Waist deep in buttercups together and up there on the hill the outhouse, bone white, sulphur white. His thigh touching hers, that best feeling in the whole world, and that bottomless looking that told them both what they didn't dare to know. Memories of this intimacy came one after the other, and in the process, love for Lewis as a brother, as not-quite-a-brother, then as the closest of nonbrothers—always, she saw now, with the undercurrent of desire—love of Lewis came gradually and clearly into her consciousness. She could remember, in her eyes and her heart and her flesh, that deep connecting look of theirs, like a bridge of flesh between his body and her body. The look that had been love.

For in this room that had led her back to where she had begun she could at last feel and know that Lewis had loved her, too. They had always been like two sparks igniting each other. They had always loved. The tragedy was that they had not dared to know this. They had both been brought up to accept that marriage between cousins was, if not quite incest, the next thing to it; not really wrong in the sense that incest was thought to be, but nevertheless not really right, not even grudgingly right, and that because of their fathers' congenital heart disease, their marriage would be an inbreeding that could have tragic consequences for their children. But her mother and Aunt Sally had never said this in so many words. No one had ever said, "It looks as though you two are heading towards marriage, and that is, of course, absolutely out of the question." But somehow she'd gotten the message, and so had Lewis, she was sure. And when their fathers had died of the same heart dysfunction, both in their thirties, the message had become very loud, and entirely clear.

But, oh, she would mourn, if only Lewis had been able to follow his true nature, his true desires, if only he could have, they would have gone upstairs that night, and gotten into Lewis's bed, and made love like Mother and Father, oh yes, surely yes, it would have been that marvel of union. And afterward she could have stroked Lewis's cheek, softly, Lewis's cheek–rather concave beside his beautiful, sensual, slightly decadent mouth. It was around his mouth that he was most achingly attractive. Kissing it, and lying beneath him, and stroking his cheek softly with love, they would both have been happy at last. As a result of which, indelicate as it would have felt and been–and Lewis would have suffered over the impropriety of it, and of having to dispose of Georges–after that sad, bad happening, she would have divorced Georges instantly, and she and Lewis would then have married. No children of course, but that was a sacrifice that could have been made for the sake of the greater happiness of being fully together at last, as from the very beginning they were meant to be.

But. On the other hand, free at last of marriage, and brought back to her childhood simplicity, she now felt that she had gotten marriage out of her system, or, as she put it to herself, gotten its system out of her. And so she wondered whether, really, she would have wanted to *marry* Lewis. Would she have wanted a day-in, day-out alliance, upstairs-downstairs, with Aubjay Dars? Would she have wanted the four antique walls of that house, and the four elegantly enclosed walls of Lewis himself, day in day out? Didn't she need *no* walls, *no* closed windows? Didn't she need air, air upon which music lay like strands of sun?

She had no clear-cut answers. On the days that she was trapped in the squirrel cage of her mind she kept crying to herself, my mind isn't working, my mind isn't making anything stick. I'm still thinking, but am lost. Oh come on, woman, do a little left-hemisphere brain work up there!

But on the days that she escaped from her newly monitoring mind, she was directed by a natural strength not dominated by thinking processes, and on those lively and peaceful days she would shrug and say to herself, well, I can't have everything. I'll have to live a flow-along life. Have it your own way up there, you two hemispheres. I give up!

Yet she was no nearer to an understanding of what had happened with Lewis, and because of it, what had happened to her own self. And she was sure that her battle would never be over until she knew. And she didn't know how she was going to know. She would wander through Mrs. Alexander's garden, and through her back fields, unable not to feel glad a lot of the time, but more often than not stopping to drop her head into her hands, and to murmur over and over again, "I feel my insides shredded by this, shredded, shredded, shredded..." For there was still no doubt in her mind that she had killed Lewis. The autopsy had revealed heart failure due to valvular stenosis, the congenital disease of his father, and it had been further explained by the doctors that Lewis's chest pains during the weeks before his death had all been precursors of the final attack. Rationally, she knew that the attack could have come any time, anywhere, and was certainly getting ready to come soon.

But she knew, unequivocally, that his shock at her advances had been the cause of his heart attack. The cause of his death. She knew this. And nothing had made this knowledge bearable. She missed him terribly. Not only the Lewis she had desired that night, but the Lewis who had been her companion, the best friend she had ever had. Their word, *ausec*, was perpetually in her mind, sometimes it was black letters she saw when she closed her eyes. She sorrowed all the time for him, for the cutting off of his young life. There was an oppressive sore area in her chest that hadn't gone away, and this was the loss of Lewis—his loss of his life, and her loss of it—the sore open wound of loss.

Even her resolution to stay in Lewis's house, to abide with his memory, proved to have been an undependable emotion. For, as she had come to understand, she hadn't had to be in Lewis's house to be with Lewis. He was in *her*. And his house told her nothing new. In fact, being in that house felt morbid to her, with its wing chairs, its tapestry pillows, its grandfather clock ticking for no one. The house would be hers in a matter of months, and then she would sell it, and everything circa this and that in it.

In the meantime she was here, with all she needed except peace of mind—with Mrs. Alexander and Rupert and her guitar and the country and this room, this starched innocent pink-and-white haven of renewal and peace.

It was time to get up. She could smell bacon from the kitchen below, and coffee. She heard in the hall outside her room a frenzied little preliminary hum, and then the Dresden shepherd and shepherdess clock struck nine—nine spaced clear bells beyond her closed door. She smiled, thinking of the convoluted little china clock on the mahogany chest in a path of mote-filled sun.

She flung back the covers and got up, crossed to the open window and looked down into the tops of tall lilacs. The flowers were fading, browning, dropping, but the last of their fragrance rose to her. Beyond, the old tree-shaded lawn stretched down to the driveway. Syra watched a robin tugging at a worm. Beyond the robin was the bed of bleeding hearts along the path. Crazy exquisite little Valentines they seemed to her, a baroque bit of nature that looked unbelievably man-made.

The smell of the bacon and the coffee was more important here by the window. And the combination of all this bounty and beauty so overwhelmed her that she felt a rapture—there was no murdered Lewis, no Lewis at all, no Georges, no other person, no clamoring mind, only her refreshed healthy body, the breeze on her bare skin, the smell of lilacs and coffee, dew glittering on emerald green grass, a bird, and that miraculous achievement, a bleeding heart, and herself taken out of herself but rapturously in herself too, herself in all this and all this in herself.

Mrs. Alexander was in her upstairs sitting room eating breakfast from a tray. She was dressed for the day in a navy and white silk print, with a navy wool jacket over her shoulders, and reading *Time* magazine as she sipped her coffee. Crumbs from her muffin and a dulled marmalade-smeared silver butter knife with its embossed intertwining monogram, its repoussé garlands worn smooth, remained on the faded roses of the plate.

Sun flickered over the walls from the breeze-tossed branches outside, shadowing then brightening the faces, the attitudes, the puffed sleeves and the whiskers and the christening-robed infants in the photographs, framed ovally and squarely and roundly and rectangularly, in silver, in wood, in inlaid ebony, in gold leaf, in ivory, in floral painted papier maché. This was the clamor of Mrs. Alexander's past, and even her present, for here and there in their ranks were snapshots of Lewis–Lewis in front of his house beneath his swinging sign, Lewis draped in her wicker porch chair in his graceful puppet-flung way–and a heavily concentrating Rupert Knight studying a leaf.

Bernice sat on the chintz-cushioned window seat with her arms folded across the mound of her stomach, kneading the loose flesh of her elbows. She sat massively and grumpily in her soiled green uniform, waiting in her usual way until she had recuperated from the effort of getting one breakfast before setting about getting another. This was *her* window seat. And this was her "slow-down" time, as Mrs. Alexander put it. She would not budge until she was ready to. Furthermore, by staying here longer than usual, she could communicate how put-upon she was by having to wait on two people instead of one. Though her whole life was "tasks," and she wouldn't have known how to wish it otherwise, still she found herself greatly upset over having these tasks suddenly augmented, and by someone like Syra. She resented Syra, who made more work for her–breakfast at all hours, another room to clean–and whose presence disrupted the routine twosome of herself and Mrs. Alexander, which had come to be the benign habit of her existence.

Then, too, Syra was not Bernice's stereotype of a "lovely person." To Bernice, Syra's directness was impudence, even callousness; her lack of effusion, lack of manners; her cool, matter-of-fact voice, effrontery; her frequent oaths, coarse, unladylike language; her good appetite, sound sleep, calm, untormented face, lack of proper mourning for Mr. Lewis; her staying so long with Mrs. Alexander instead of going home to her husband, suspicious and unnatural, *and* sponging; her clear, probing eyes, bold.

"Good morning, Mrs. A. Good morning, Bernice."

"Piglet!" Mrs. Alexander looked up with delight. The surprise of this unexpected enriching of her life was always in her voice. "You look marvelous. I can see you slept well."

"I did, I did. Sweet summer sleep. And I found a music box way back on the shelf in your closet, and I made so much various tinkle-crinkle music on it last night it transported me, made me a child again." She went lazily over to the other sun-warmed window seat and sat down on it, pulling up her legs and tucking them under her. "And you, Bernice, did you sleep well?" Syra's eyes were bright and frank with interest as she regarded this great stolid old creature whose burning looks she would not take seriously.

Bernice shrugged and made a derogatory fluttering sound between her lips.

"Oh ho, I know, you bake all night long, like the seven dwarfs."

"Oh I do not," exclaimed Bernice.

Mrs. Alexander pushed up her chin and made a derisive mouth, though amusement and an exasperated affection softened her eyes. "You utterly humorless creature, you."

Bernice shrugged faintly, smiled faintly, indicating that this, like everything else Mrs. Alexander said, was the benign immutable law of her life. Then, "Do you want I should get your breakfast now?" she asked Syra, sufferingly.

"I'm in no hurry."

But Bernice sighed and rose to her feet. "I s'pose I might's well go get it." She lumbered to the door. "I s'pose you want bacon," she said self-pityingly, not looking at Syra, and without waiting for an answer, closed the door after her with restrained force.

Syra came over and sat down in the little rose velvet fireside chair, across from Mrs. Alexander. "I'm in a fearful quandary. Shall I wash my hair and look clean, or leave it unclean and thicker which it isn't? Maybe for a change I'll part it on the side and cut a piece of bangs there at that point so there's a little more bangs action there. That's a pretty plate. I haven't seen that before."

"Yes. Isn't it. It's Limoges. And I wouldn't at all like more bangs on you, Piglet. But now only one's left. Plate not bangs. Sometimes Bernice trots it out. She likes a change of china. Well, there's precious little change of china left. But Piglet, I somehow don't think of you as taking to china. I'm fascinated you notice china."

"I like it. I mean beautiful old china. I do so get enchanted by such. Mother and Grandmother had odds and ends of it, stray teacups without saucers, saucers without teacups, three-of-a-kind service plates, things like that. I always loved a certain pink lustre teacup of Grandmother's, and a Gaudy Welsh saucer Mother used as an ashtray."

"Ashtray? Your mother *smoked*, Syra? How astonishing. Nowadays, of course, but then? That was certainly daring, I should say."

"I guess it was. It didn't seem so to me, of course, because it was simply a part of Mother. And daring was what she was, everything she was. Oh what a benison thing. Come to think of it, no one else smoked then. Father didn't. He hated Mother's smoking. She only did it outdoors, he insisted on that. Mother smoked little cigars."

"Cigars. Good grief. Or 'Blow me down,' as Lewis would say."

"Wouldn't you like some of Lewis's old china? When it's mine?"

"Why yes Piglet, how wonderful, I'd love it thank you very much. I'd adore to have it. How lovely of you to think of that." But in a second she sighed, and smiled wistfully and a little hopelessly. "Oh, I don't know. Really I don't think so, Piglet. I'm getting uninterested in things. What would I do with a set of twelve Sèvres dinner plates, really? When *you're* here, it would be festive to trot it out, but I so seldom have people for dinner, because of Bernice of course, goodness, she does limit my life, doesn't she, but I don't really care all that much. I sometimes don't even care all that much, oh, a little but not greatly, if I don't have four of something, or six of something. But maybe I could use six good wineglasses. And six martini glasses. More, actually than china, I need them. Lewis had some good Baccarat, I know that."

"It's yours, Mrs. A."

"Well thank you my dear Piglet. I accept with pleasure. You and I can then sit down to some real élègance "–she pronounced it as the French do–"and toast the man responsible for them."

"That would be lovely." Syra's face was soft. But then the softness faded, and her eyes grew large and anxious, and she said abruptly, "I know this heaven can't go on." She searched Mrs. Alexander's shrewd bright face for an agreement that would bolster her new decisiveness which in its suddenness she was not yet entirely sure of. "You know I told you I wrote Georges almost three weeks ago about my decision not to go back to him. And I haven't heard, and am now frightened. Mail looks at me with dragon eyes. It's sort of eerie, not hearing. There's no sound out there. Thank heavens he hasn't called me up, anyway. I have suddenly taken a great fat burn about not hearing, and am very pleased with myself." Syra crossed her legs and studied the toe of her old black slipper, and then looked up again, searchingly, at the alarm in Mrs. Alexander's eyes. "But whether I hear from him or not, I'll have to start thinking about a direction. I woke up feeling that. At least I think that's what I woke up feeling, that the time has come to start something else. But it's no joke my leaving this infinite heaven, leaving you I mean."

Mrs. Alexander reached up for her glasses, deliberately, and removed them, deliberately, and took the sleeve of the jacket which was across her shoulders and began to polish the lenses with it, first blowing on one lens and then polishing it with the soft wool, then blowing on the other lens and polishing that one. Finally she thrust the pointlessly polished glasses back on, cleared her throat, and spoke. "My dear," she said quietly, "of course I've known this, deep down, though I haven't wanted to think about it. It's been so divine having you here, it's been a breath of fresh air, and frankly I'll be devastated when you leave." She fixed a strong stern eye on Syra. "However, that's utterly beside the point. You were not sent to brighten my old age. I do think you're right, Piglet, you'll have to plan a future, and if you're ready to think about it, more power to you. But what about Lewis's house?" she asked wistfully. "Does that seem a possibility to you? Piglet, I've never asked you why you're leaving Georges, he's such an awfully nice man, but perhaps dull I should think, and I don't want to know unless you ever want to tell me." This was not true, for Mrs. Alexander was consumed with curiosity about the rupture. "However, I know you know your own mind. And I know you're going to have enough money, so I don't worry about that. My only concern for you is that you've been too hasty. About Georges. And yet, I do believe in you, Piglet, I honestly do. I've always given you the benefit of the doubt about that nice man. But I do find myself wondering sometimes. However"–emphatically–"you've got to live and teach somewhere. Now where will that be, Piglet?"

"Well, not in Lewis's house, that I know. Because it would shred my insides to *feel* Lewis all the time. That house and everything in it–oh it was so against this ardent desire he had to set his spirit free. *That* would be there making sounds and shredding my insides; and all the happy sounds, the game we had of arguing and screeching like banshees, and talking with fond rudeness because it was such fun, such hilarious fun; and free, free as air, to say whatever we felt like saying. No, I won't live in that house. Because for another thing I couldn't stand that beautiful perfect house, and anyway I'd let it go to pot." A sudden wide smile. "You'd hate that too. I'm quite sure I'll want to sell that house, and everything in it. Offhand I'd say that I'd like to go to some southern spot, maybe an island, some place where there'd be people I could teach guitar, and settle down, and have time leisurely spread out, not divided into a patchwork quilt. And sometime soon I've got to face going home to Auburn and getting my things, such as they are, clothes and books and music and things belonging to Mother."

"I sense how much you loved your mother, Piglet. I loved my mother too, enormously. It's good to love one's mother."

"I guess so. Since I can't imagine *not* loving Mother, I can't imagine what not loving a mother would be like. I can't even remotely imagine what that would feel like."

"How old was she when she died, Piglet?"

"Sixty-six. She got pneumonia, shovelling snow after a blizzard, while still recovering from flu. There was no one else to shovel the front walk. By then she had almost no money left, so she had no one to do the chores but herself. My heart was broken, and I had to keep trying to grow a new one."

"This was in Cazenovia?"

"Oh yes, beautiful, happy Cazenovia. Infinite heaven. I mean, I did love that place. Still do. Of course the house is gone. Sold I mean. The people who bought it turned it into a bed and breakfast, quite nicely too, surprisingly. That soared my spirits a lot. But I hated, hated to leave wonderful Cazenovia, but I couldn't earn any sort of a living there for myself *and* Mother, so I had to go to the city for a teaching job, and leave Mother alone. Nothing else would work, to maintain the two of us. She after all had the house to live in. Oh, if only I could have stayed with her!" She paused. Then, "Do you know Cazenovia, Mrs. A.?"

"Do I know Cazenovia! My dear, Billy and I used to stay in the Lincklaen House every time we motored up to Buffalo. Billy was an upstate New Yorker, you know, born and raised in Buffalo. But Cazenovia, oh my yes, we loved that handsome little old lake valley town and that splendid old inn. Is it still there?"

"Yes. That will always be there. But the Cavanaghs won't, I'm sorry to say. I won't go back there, of course. But I'm sorry there's no more family there. My grandfather Cavanagh was born there, and Mother and Aunt Sally, and I. And the little person who didn't last–Geneva."

"Geneva?"

"A sister who lived for seventeen days."

"My *dear*."

"Yes. It was at first a big fist in our lives, and then it grew into a flat colorless sadness. And Father died soon after. So very young. And in months, Uncle Edmond died, Lewis's father."

"Oh my *dear* Piglet."

"For Mother it was simply, for a while, endurance, I think. But someone like Mother could never stay with colorless sadness. Anyway, where was I? How awful the way I rattle along to you. Where was I? Oh, we started talking about our loving our mothers. And my mother having no money. None of our family ever had enough money, because Father was a professor and Grandpa Cavanagh was a country lawyer whose clients a lot of them were poor, and never paid their bills, and Grandma Cavanagh was a minister, Congregational minister, and there was no inherited wealth on either side. It never seemed to matter much, though. Because life was the most benison kind of thing. Except for Mother having to do the chores when she was too old for them, and that is why she died."

Mrs. Alexander sighed, and fixed a bleak, compassionate eye on Syra. After a moment she said, "Lewis told me a lot about the school your mother started. I must say it's beyond me, Piglet my dear. I'm such a product of conventional education myself." She raised her chin. "And I have great faith in it," she said, with spirit and rather defensively. "Lewis used to try to talk me into unbending about progressive education, as he put it. But I'm a believer in discipline."

"Oh?" Syra said quietly. And then emphatically, and rather with defiance, "My forebears were some of them out of step with the times, and glad I am. That's where Mother's individuality and convictions about private, you might say, personalized, education, came from. Mother's mother was a Congregational minister, and she was also, I guess you'd say, one of the early feminists New York state was famous for, like Elizabeth Stanton Hardy, Annis Eastman, Antoinette B. Blackwell. And so forth. I wonder *why* New York state? And from little country towns, or cities, of New York state? Isn't that fascinating? Although I have chanted and chanted to people about that, I never thought of it before, but it's really fascinating, isn't it? So. Anyway, Grandmother Cavanagh was a person who thought her own thoughts, not other people's, and those thoughts were like the ground beneath her feet and the air she breathed and well, they led her. They really led all of us. 'Judge not and ye shall not be judged' wasn't exactly the way she saw things, or else, yes, she preached that. But in addition she preached, 'Judge and destroy, judge not and enjoy.' That was the title of a book she wrote, taken from one of her sermons. Anyway, these were two extraordinary women, Mother and Grandmother. Grandmother was a great beauty. She had wonderful black eyes, like Mother. She also, Grandmother I mean, had these incredibly beautiful hands. They were very slender and long, the fingers were very slender, and curved way backwards, so that when she was preaching, and oh that was always another peak, sometimes she seemed to me like a Balinese dancer, the way she would move those lovely slim hands bent all the way back from the wrists.

"Anyway, where was I? Oh yes, about Grandmother's non-judging slogan." She fell back in her chair. "Whew," she said. And she smiled timidly at Mrs. Alexander, not in apology, but in a small plea for recognition, for approval of this past which was, she knew, a treasure beyond all treasures, if only others could see it.

"Well, my dear, I don't quite get that, I must say," Mrs. Alexander said with spirit. "How can you live in this world and not judge? I'd be lost without judgment."

"My grandmother would have been lost *with* it," Syra said proudly. "I find it fascinating what she had to fill her sails with."

"Hitler! He certainly filled his sails—I love that expression—with great big winds. Do you just sit back and say 'Here am I. There is Hitler. Go ahead, Hitler, you fascinate me'?"

"Certainly not. Grandmother could get mad. She could get furious. Once when Grandfather at the dinner table called the new Episcopalian minister an effeminate counter-tenor, she got *furious* at him and told him with the most icy, outraged calm that turning a collar back side to didn't make a man a eunuch. In fact she was furious a lot of the time. She would pound the pulpit with her swan-neck hands. She told us that Jesus Christ was furious a lot of the time, too. And *I* can get mad, Mrs. A. I am amiable, but on the other hand I am quite fierce. If someone is really bad I know it."

"Well, it's an interesting point, I do see that. *However.*" Mrs. Alexander was beginning to be uncomfortable. She was being shown another world, another way, which without hesitation she disapproved of, but because it was lived and obviously enjoyed by a well-born, distinguished lot, it was not quite possible for her to brush it all aside entirely. And she was, in spite of herself, fascinated. She knew, too, that she trusted what Syra was, completely. And what Syra was was the result of this upbringing, evidently. Also, she sensed that Syra was opening up in an almost starved way, and she wanted to show gratitude for this, and to give Syra something in return. And so she said generously, "I'm fascinated. Now tell me more about this school."

"See, Mother started it because she said if I went to a regular school she couldn't raise me the way a child should be raised. So she taught us herself."

"'Us'? Who was 'us'?"

"Me, and two other girls and two boys, there were only five of us, in our third-floor schoolroom that had a big lovely cupola. They were children of friends of Mother and Father. Rather especially unlike most of the villagers. The parents were, I mean. Today you'd call them 'far-out.' There was quite a little group of far-out people, then, in Cazenovia, believe it or not.

Mother called it the Bloomsbury of the Finger Lakes."

"Amazing, and how did you begin the guitar? There?"

"No. My teacher was in Syracuse. Eva Ely. She was a solid joy. One of life's great experiences. Among other things she was an absurd, fairy-tale feminist. Plus she was so wise. See if I remember how she put it—well, the gist of it was, 'I don't use the words *right* and *wrong*, Syracuse.' (She called me by my full name.) 'The minute you think you've gotten to be right, you're wrong. There is always more to be learned, and to be felt, always. You'll stop dead in your tracks if you think you've got a passage *right*. You can always do it better. *How*ever.' She always emphasized the '*how*.' '*How*ever, what you should, what you can say to yourself is—that's as good as I can get it for now.' This soared Mother's spirits, she thought this was absolutely wonderful. After that she tried to teach us in our school not to think in terms of right and wrong. But it was tricky for a person. Even she admitted that it wasn't easy. And oh dear, I tend to forget, so often, because everyone, everywhere, I mean it's implicit in everything, right or wrong. It really, to be quite truthful, drives me up several walls."

"How perfectly amazing," Mrs. Alexander said sharply, almost querulously. "Why, my entire upbringing was *based* on right and wrong, and rightly so, I think. It's an essential ethical stance. That's my view of it." She was wholly out of her depth now, and if the truth be told, upset, and wanted to change the subject.

"I don't see your breakfast appearing with the speed of light," she said brightly, and looked straight at Syra with a stout pride, but with a faint uneasiness in her smile that attempted a sincerity and assurance she sensed was not succeeding.

Increasingly alert these days to tones of voice she interpreted as against her, and also somewhat defiant about intimations of censure, for a moment in Syra, some of the wholeness, the rosiness of this friendship in this house in this month of blossoming, promising May wavered, and she felt herself leaning more trustingly toward departure from it. And she said hurriedly, and a bit unhappily, "No, I see no breakfast being cheerfully, swiftly, willingly brought up to this intrusive guest. But to get back to what this conversation started with. I wonder *why* I haven't heard from Georges. I'm uneasy. I'm silently saying all the worst curses I know. I wish I'd hear from him. If I don't within a day or so, I believe I'll simply call him up. Just like that. Oh dear what a thing to have to do. Ouch. I don't want to do it that way, though. But I *must hear* from him."

"You don't care for Georges at all?" Inquisitively. "Oh I know it's none of my business. Is it *that* Piglet, real lack of love for him, and not something else that could be worked out between you? I must admit I do feel sorry for the poor man."

"It's lack of love." Syra gave Mrs. Alexander a long, level look, then tossed her hair away from her neck. "I've realized that I never loved him. I think I married him for several funny reasons, *idea* reasons, not *feeling* reasons. With all those wrong ingredients thrown in, no wonder the cake didn't rise! Oh God. How bad of me to do such a thing. I could dig a hole and bury myself. But Georges will not at all suffer, you know, without me. He takes better care of himself than I ever did. I don't think there's really any reason to feel sorry for Georges."

"Well dear I feel sorry for his losing you. That can't be any light thing."

"He'll be a lot better off for losing me, when he gets used to it. I am not the woman for him. I never was. I guess it is a case of luck, finding a person you love. You find whoever belongs to you in both sexes, like my finding, for instance, Eva Ely. And you. And Rupert. And if someone *doesn't* belong to you, it turns you evil. But to have one or a few to love, I think maybe is enough, and praise goes up for them. But Georges is very bad on my spirit. I have a feeling he's always known that, too."

"Well frankly I *can* see that. I've often wondered who you are the woman for?"

"Well I don't wonder about that. I don't think about it at all. In fact, I almost never think. I'm a feeble thinker. I'm sure Anne Knight has me set down as a feeble thinker."

"My dear Piglet, she has us *all* set down as feeble thinkers. But anyway, I can understand your not thinking about a man. Not yet anyway." Mrs. Alexander sighed and shifted in her cushioned chair, moving her small brown-spotted hands aimlessly about on its arms. She was silent a moment. Then she said firmly, "I know you've sensed what it's meant to me to have you here. We have such fun, don't we? Of course I'll miss you like blazes. It's been an amazingly easy and happy friendship, I think. And I feel you do too. I can't remember ever having such a feeling of ease in a friendship with a woman. I see I just sit and chatter, chatter, chatter unendingly to you. I get carried away. But I love it, my dear."

Suddenly she made a little pseudo-malicious mouth, her eyes twinkling. "Having you here has had one *disastrous* effect," she whispered, leaning toward Syra. "It's made me realize how boring it's been to have to live intimately year in, year out with Bernice, who *is* a dullard, truly."

"*I'm* sort of a dullard."

"You!" A hoot. "That's the last thing you are. You're different, but you're no dullard." She fell back in her chair and her face settled into seriousness again. "But every day you stay is a joy, so stay, stay, until you feel you have to leave. It won't be habit forming. I'm not a dependent person," she said proudly. And then very earnestly, "Furthermore, I'm utterly used to being alone. Of course I had Lewis, and now he's gone. There's no one to replace Lewis. But that's the way it is. One of the things I miss most about him is the fun we had. I love to have fun. Piglet," she said then, unexpectedly, with sudden seriousness, "I've never had so much fun with anyone as I had with Billy. There was always something to laugh about. We had a wonderful time together. Not having any children, I suppose we depended more on each other than people with children do. But honestly, Piglet, I don't think we really missed them. Isn't that a funny thing to say? At least I know Billy didn't. Perhaps because he was a doctor and he gave so much of himself to his patients.

"But not having children didn't make a hole in our lives. We were always on the go, and we adored that. We were great dancers. I never dance any more, and I know I'm not too old for it. I often think I'll start going to Arthur Murray's. Billy and I used to go in to the St. Regis about once a month, to the Iridium Room in winter and the Roof in the summer. Now there's no more Iridium Room. Gone." She waved a wrinkled hand, and in the sun her single diamond on its gold band sparkled. "Gone with the wind. Like everything else. Billy was an expert dancer and extremely light on his feet for a big man, though big men often are. We'd whirl and whirl. We had a step where he'd hold me off with one hand, and I'd do a sort of whirling dervish underneath it, once, I'd whirl once. We'd dance the entire evening. Neither of us could stay put, once that music started up. And we used to dance right here in this house, in the downstairs hall, to the victrola. Goodness, I've got all those old records down there still, it just occurs to me. We used to love the Fred Astaire musicals. He was always saying to me, 'Janest, I missed my calling, I'd like to be Fred Astaire.'"

"Janest, is that what he called you?"

"Yes, it was kind of an endearment."

"Oh you mean like dearest."

"Piglet, my dear, I love you for knowing that so instantly."

"It's nice. What else did this man like to do, besides dance?"

"He was a tennis maniac. He loved fruit farming. Once this

place was a thriving fruit farm. I kept up the fruit farm after he died, as long as I had the energy, actually. Oh and American history. Apparently the subject was endless. He loved American history. Maybe you've noticed the shelves and shelves of it in the library. I've never read a one. Can you believe that he took the two volumes of Dumas Malone's *Jefferson* with him on our wedding trip? I was young and silly and I was wounded. I thought he shouldn't be interested in all that ponderous stuff when we were on our wedding trip."

"Where was that?"

"Bermuda. At Pomander Gate. We stayed at Pomander Gate. Enchanting place, full of antiques, and they had lettuce all around the edges of the flower beds. It was terribly rough coming back and I didn't get seasick. I was proud as punch for not getting seasick. And Billy said, 'Janest, I knew I'd married a sturdy girl. Maybe I married you so I wouldn't have to doctor my wife!' Well, I've always been strong. Never sick. It was Billy who ..." her voice faltered.

Syra knew she was listening to love. She was greatly moved. She felt passionately grateful to Mrs. Alexander and Billy for affirming the existence of love. But it made her feel unformed, and outside.

Mrs. Alexander sighed. And then she said abruptly, "But gracious, here I sit, chatter, chatter, chatter. You ask what I have to do today, my child, you should just take a look at the list and you'd quail. Piglet, I've nothing up my sleeve for you today dear. Today I'm deserting you. I'm going to Mt. Kisco. I've my hospital board meeting this morning. Then lunch, we always lunch together afterward. Then I've my gynecological checkup, they never find anything, but he makes me go, so I obey, I'm a doctor's wife so I obey. Then after that since I'm all the way over there I'm going to do a whole host of little errands, such *as*, getting a wedding present for Franny's granddaughter. Well, I won't go on all down the list. You'll be walking with Rupert, I s'pose. I'm so glad you have that nice pastime. How does he seem these days?" This carefully casual question, which Mrs. Alexander occasionally asked, was her oblique effort to elicit from Syra some information about the state of affairs between Anne and Rupert, which she had been concerned about ever since the night of Anne's outburst, and about which she was perpetually curious. But not waiting for an answer, because she was suddenly embarrassed by her own tactics, she hurried on. "Shouldn't we have them over for drinks this weekend? And perhaps maybe the Moores? It went well the last time. Let's have a little quiet party." And then, irresistibly, "You *are* walking with him this afternoon, aren't you?"

"Yes, we'll be walking as usual. Bless his dreamer's ways. He is a solid joy."

"Well have fun, you two."

"Is there anything I could do for you around there this morning?"

"How terribly nice of you to offer, Piglet. Why yes, you could surreptitiously do the dusting upstairs here. It certainly needs it. *She* won't do it. Are you any good at dusting, Piglet?

Syra smiled. "You don't think of me as a housewife, do you?"

"Frankly, no. And you're not, what's more."

"True. But I can dust. After which I will lie in the sun and blot out my mind, or just sit mouse-quiet out on the front porch. I'll dust the little china clock, I will, I will. Lovingly. And your bedroom, and this room, and the two bathrooms. You don't need a person to go rambling forever though all the guest rooms, dusting, do you, angel?"

"Oh my goodness no. Just the four rooms, that would be a big help. Thank you dearest. Dust depresses me." She rose sturdily, with purpose and interest, brushed at her lap for crumbs, shifted her jacket over her shoulders. "Now I'll go down and have a little fruitless discussion about what Bernice's supposed to do today. We keep on playing the game. Everything I tell her, I preface with, 'If you get around to it.'" She smiled and shrugged helplessly. It was humor, as much as anything, that had always borne her along. Then she crossed to the door. Beside Syra, whose face was turned up to her, she stopped, and cupped a hand along her cheek. "Angel yourself," she murmured lightly, but with a thorough ferocious affection.

❧ III ❧

SHORTLY after arriving at her office and while she was having a comforting cup of coffee with the Danish pastry she ordinarily denied herself, Anne got a call from Brandeis University that decided her to fly to Boston that afternoon.

Frantic last-minute changes, it seemed, were needed in a paper on which she had collaborated with a researcher in the Department of Psychology there, dealing with yet another appraisal of the status of women. It had to be sent to the journal that would publish it no later than tomorrow. Could she, the researcher begged, spare a half-hour now to discuss it? Over the telephone, unfortunately, but what else was one to do?

"Look, why don't I come up?" said Anne brightly, surprisingly. She put down the telephone with a strange sense of anticipation and relief. Thus does the unexpected reveal the existence of new possibilities. She knew at once that she was glad not to be going home today. Going home at the end of each day, with no will to resolve the deadlock, now seemed masochistic, abject, like a dog that knows no other way. And going away, and staying away, was a suddenly revealed new weapon—might not Rupert begin to miss, or to need her, and to experience the reality of separation? And might not she, too, get a new perspective? Why hadn't she thought of this before?

A kind of dread was mixed with a febrile relief. She could not disregard this unexpected relief, which was something new. And her frightening feeling of promise assured her that she was going to take some kind of a new plunge, which would have consequences.

She opened a desk drawer and took from it the manuscript of the paper on the status of women—"Towards an Evaluative Synthesis of the Mutational Dynamics of the Status of Women in the American Metropolis." She read this title, and as usual, found that it said everything, and felt a flurry of pride over its being her wording, and not her distinguished collaborator's. She turned to the first page.

An exact forefinger, with a rounded white half-moon of a fingernail, immaculate, pounced onto the page, pinpointed a trouble spot, his, not hers. She reached for a pencil in a pottery mug on the blond wood desk. Neatly, authoritatively, she crossed out four words; neatly, authoritatively, she introduced two new words above them. The next page needed no changes, nor the next, nor the next.

The air-conditioner roared mutedly, and beyond it, in a muffled way, the violences of the city. She worked for an hour. Then she put her pencil back in its mug, and put the manuscript into her briefcase, and then she sat back in the revolving chair and looked at the telephone.

After a second she looked at the electric clock. Then back at the telephone. Finally, with resolve, she snatched up the receiver and dialed her home number, gave the office number to the operator in a voice that shook beneath its shrill cheer, then waited, waited, while the phone rang in an empty house. She let it ring seven times. Then, cautiously, as though Rupert could hear her and rebuke her for the relief she felt at not having to talk to him, she put the receiver back down in its cradle, and exhaled massively.

It was now ten-thirty. She would go out at twelve for lunch and some shopping—night clothes and a toothbrush for overnight in Boston—come back to the office before leaving for the terminal, but until then, until twelve, she would sit here and think about what lay behind her pounding heart, and her vast relief at not having to talk to Rupert. She would sit here and think things *through*. She would not call him again, she would leave instructions for Ava to do that.

She got up and went to the door of her frosted-glass enclosure of an office. Her secretary-receptionist, Ava Aranson, sat at her desk in the outer office, a cigarette in the exact center of pressed lips, the fingers of one hand thrust up through the hair springing from her forehead, the other hand scribbling furiously with pencil across shorthand pad.

"Ava dear."

"Yes'm." From around the cigarette.

"I thought you'd stopped smoking last week."

"I did."

Anne smiled faintly. "But you started in again. Yes?"

"Yes." Ava flung down her pencil, removed her fingers from her hair and the cigarette from her mouth, and gave Anne a mocking but adoring smile. "I was *dying!*"

Anne went over to her. She put one hand on the springy black hair, and with the other hand tilted Ava's young chin up to look at her. She gazed long and searchingly into those eyes. "You *can* do it, honey. Try once more, honey. Yes? No?"

A long sigh. Proud eyes, but slavish, looked up at Anne.

"What I can do, I'll try a new technique. I'll start smoking a half-hour later every day. Taper off."

"That's smart, Ava." Anne stroked the hair back, then patted Ava's shoulder, and started toward her office. "I'm taking the shuttle to Boston this afternoon to see Dr. Orientes about the paper," she said over her shoulder. "So will you cancel the afternoon appointments? There're only two. And then call the Copley Plaza there for a room, dear, will you? A quiet one. Say I'm a country woman."

When she got to the door of her office she turned. "I'll be back tomorrow morning," she said lightly. "Oh, and will you call Rupert this afternoon sometime. Probably after three. He always walks till about three. And tell him I've gone to Boston. Tell him I tried to reach him this morning but couldn't. Oh, and—" She drew up her bosom. Raised her chin. "Tell him I don't know just when I'll get home. Because of work. Because I'll be behind by going to Boston. Tell him I'll be staying on here for a bit with Eunice. At the Fifth Avenue Hotel."

"Will do." Ava picked up her cigarette, thrust up her chin, and placed the cigarette back between pouting lips that waited for it. "Don't forget your doctor's appointment day after tomorrow. Friday at eleven."

"No," said Anne, and then after a moment, "no. I won't forget."

She closed the door of her office and sat down in her swivel chair. What she would do, she thought, if between now and lunchtime she could think things through, would be to write a letter to Rupert, which he could chew over until she returned.

If she returned.

She was astounded to have said "if" to herself. Did she mean it? She didn't know, and was terrified over having said it.

She was beginning to think unfamiliar thoughts. Something was boiling up in her that had begun this morning, and that "if" was the key to it. She was extricating herself from the morass of the past five weeks (and of how much longer? she said to herself). At the same time, she saw her total blind commitment to Rupert bursting open at the seams; all of the power and sincerity she had for fourteen years believed it to have, now, suddenly, seemed weak and transparent and a long lie, leaving a vacuum. She was terrified that this could be. Why should the loss of this intensity leave her with such emptiness? Was this fourteen-year-old palaver over Rupert only a cover-up for something, a kind of deliberate obscurantism? But no, she loved Rupert. She adored him. There was no other man in the world for her but Rupert!

Suddenly, going to Boston seemed insane, seemed like an irreversible action.

She crossed her arms on the desk, and put her head down on them. In a moment she raised it. Her keen, pearly-white face was sharpening with purpose. She picked up her telephone, pressed a button on its base, and spoke to Ava. "Ava dear, I'm not taking any calls. Say I'm in conference." Then she opened the deep bottom drawer of the desk and took a little strongbox out of it, unlocked it with its combination, and lifted out of it her Letter. She closed the strongbox and put it back in the drawer, then reached for a yellow pad, and a new sharp pencil, and began to write to Rupert.

Dearest Rupert:

Five weeks ago, before everything blew up, or rather, before I blew everything up, I would have addressed a letter to dearest Rupo. I still feel the "dearest," because I love you. But I couldn't say "Rupo" and not be feeling us. "Rupo" is for closeness and we are far apart.

At last I find myself ready to break through the terrible stalemate of these past weeks. I've come to a certain point of not wanting to endure this deadness any longer, and now I'm able to speak up, at last.

I don't know yet why I suddenly fell apart. Or no. I

don't think of what I did as falling apart, so I correct myself, because something important happened. The knowledge is still in me that my eruption was cleansing for us both. An awful way to do it, though, I know, in front of people. So unlike me.

I think I erupted because it was unbearable for me to have you reject something so vital to me—honesty. It was as though in rejecting honesty, you were saying, in effect, that that vital part of me was either unknown to you, or trivial to you. And that you yourself had so little knowledge of this vital thing that you couldn't even begin to comprehend its significance to me.

I believe the reason I got so furious was because it was unbearable not to have you agree with my hopes. For a moment I saw you putting your seal on dishonesty, admitting and approving of dishonesty. Your rejection of my plea for honesty was the ultimate dishonesty, it was the dishonesty of you, of our marriage, of the world we live in. Oh I know you didn't know all that was going on in me, and so I was expecting far more at that moment than I should have. I was ready for the "test" moment, but why should you necessarily have been? Anyway, it was unbearable to me for us not to have the same vision and not to have agreement about it, and I know that somehow this issue was the essence of our marriage, the essence of you and me together.

Rupert, all those things I said about you that night are true. Do you know that? But it's not the whole truth of you. Because besides being what I said you were, I know what else you are, too—kind, alive, gentle, warm, good, charming, deep, intelligent, responsible, a pillar of a man, as well as fun, fun to be with. You know, I was as astonished as you were to have all that invective pour out. I didn't know I knew. It was good for me to know I knew. There's been too much worship and not enough real respect (I use respect in the sense that Erich Fromm uses it, respicere, to see). He says, and I know he's right, that one can only really love when one sees the whole person. I feel a sort of emancipation, a pristine quality, a promise, in knowing that I have more balance and perspective about you.

We could have talked all this out if you had not been so persistently remote. That's all been so unlike you. I've been unable to understand it, and deadened by it, too. I can only conclude that your hurt was too terrible. And yet, do you ask yourself whether there is any truth in what I charged you with? You would never read the two Erich Fromm books I so longed to have you read, but I wish now that you would, because I know you would gain some insight from them. (They are in my study, on the shelf, under the Fs, should you want to dip into them.)

I'm glad of this chance to go to Boston, to get away. I don't want to come home again until, or if, you are ready to talk this out. Ready and willing and eager. I am ready. I love you and I think you're wonderful. But oh Rupo (now I feel close, now that I'm talking to you and opening up to you), there has been something wrong. Can we change it? We have love as a foundation, that I'm certain of. That should make it possible for us to go forward to a sounder and more meaningful relationship. I think I know now that we can't stand still, can't remain in our fourteen-year-old pattern of blind devotion.

I'm enclosing this other letter for you to read, because I hope it will make me and my tirade against you clearer to you. I had it here in my desk planning to send it along to Mr. Holdsum, but I haven't gotten around to it, what with everything that's been happening in the past five weeks.

When, and if, you are ready for me to come home, will
you call me? I'll be coming back from Boston tomorrow,
and will be staying with Eunice at the Fifth Avenue Hotel.
In any event, somehow, sometime, we must talk.

Anne had written at fever pitch, barely pausing for thought.
And now, as the clock in the church across the street struck
twelve, appropriately, she thought, hearing it, she wrote the last
words–"Abiding love, Anne."

She put her pencil down and began to read the letter. Her
keen eyes, blinking rapidly, raced across the lines. Yes, oh yes,
her animated approving face said, this is good.

She drew a long sigh that had in it a great relief over having
come out into the open, and a sense of accomplishment, and
something unsatisfied, too. She hadn't begun to say what she
wanted to say, and she thought that perhaps she didn't know
what she wanted to say. The letter made her feel uneasy. And yet
she had spent an hour writing it, and it was a communication of
sorts and it made her feel close to Rupert again, thank God, and
she would send it. Imperfect as it was, she would send it.

Noon sun slanted dustily across the desk as she picked up the
thick brown envelope addressed to Mr. Holdsum. She had not
reread the Letter since finishing it five weeks ago, and she was
suddenly very curious about it.

She read it through, slowly. Then slowly, she put it down. She
felt foolish. She felt shaken. She threw a furtive look to the window, to the door, as though she did not want to be seen. She was
entirely disassociated from the drive behind the writing of this
letter. And though she was sure that the concept of the memorial service did stand up, and was bona fide, she could not imagine
now why she had had to make such a cause célèbre of it.

She snatched up the letter she had just written, and read

through it again. She put it down.

And now, furtively, she began to feel that she had left something out that was important, that there was something central she hadn't put her finger on.

This letter is only part of the truth, she said to herself. It's a lot of well-worded baloney.

She sat in tenuous uncertainty with her concepts and her directives and her falsehoods spread out on the desk in front of her. She felt so tired, so tired of living up to her own demands. For a second, she longed in the deepest recesses of her being to let it all go, to give herself up to something other than herself, to let something else take over.

In the outer office, Ava's typing–keys in dutiful motion responding to mind in dutiful motion–perpetual, employed, dedicated, sent a wave of abhorrence through Anne. She closed lavender-white eyelids. Her lovely mouth was slightly open and slack and unmuddled. She ran her tongue out over her lips, once, and in the dusty sunlight that was full on the thinking mask of her face the moisture remained on her lips, glistening.

Suddenly she opened her eyes which had come to blazing beneath the lids.

"Shit!" she said, in a loud voice.

She reached for her letter to Rupert and tore it quickly into small pieces, and dropped them with repugnance into the wastebasket at her feet. Next she picked up her memorial service letter, and ripped that pleasurably, victoriously into little sharp-edged shreds, and let them all flutter out of her fingertips and down into that conspiring wastebasket.

Now her desk was clear, there were no papers on it, no words. She felt lost, curiously empty, but relieved too in an uncertain way, as she rose and took her jacket and handbag from the clothes tree where they hung, and marched with no loss of her old vigor out into the noisy sunshine.

❧ IV ❧

AFTER Mrs. Alexander had left, Syra dressed, and then began a desultory dusting whose only satisfaction was an absorbed examination of everything she dusted. Her fascination grew as she discovered objects, memorabilia that she hadn't noticed before. She studied the photographs on the wall, delighted by Mrs. Alexander as a little girl, young woman, middle-aged woman, aging woman–always the same, always with that faint amusement in her capable face, as though she had been born knowing that life was marvelous but absurd. She studied Billy from young manhood to middle age, and knew she would have liked him. She loved this room and loved being in it alone, though finally she left it abruptly, having had enough of being lost in the past.

The big house was quiet, except for ticking clocks and familiar faint kitchen noises from below. She put the feather duster in the hall broom closet, and stood there a moment, irresolutely, and then went to the end of the hall and looked out of the window. She felt restless. Restlessness was unfamiliar to Syra, and it left her puzzled and nervous. She wondered whether it was the house that was aiding and abetting her restlessness. This house, the faces on the sitting-room walls–looking at them, Syra comprehended the triumph of Mrs. Alexander's life. Ogilvies and Alexanders had been solidly and safely rooted here for close to a century, and had been enabled, Syra sensed, by this solid safe rooting, to embrace the world beyond it with evident elegance, strength, humaneness, dash, and enjoyment. Instinctively, Syra knew that this house, and its custodian, were an expression of the very best of an old order. It was powerfully seductive to her to be enfolded in it, protected in it, accepted in it, to pretend for a while that she, too, was one of the ones the world wanted. Her own background had had this quality, for her mother's family, though not affluent, had been such a tribe, but with the additional strain of unconventionality.

She went downstairs with nothing in mind, a spring in her step. Lots of buoyancy with no place to go. At the foot of the stairs, in the sun-splashed long hall, her eyes, which had grown exploratory, lit on a row of record albums in the bookshelf along the wall. She went over to it and knelt on the blue-and-gold Chinese runner, kneeling in gold of sun on gold of rug, a pool of goldness warm to her bare knees, prickly and dusty in a familiar way—it was many years since her knees had encountered the reassuring, solid-based tickle of a worn Oriental rug. Sun warmed her back as she tilted her head to read the titles on the spines of the albums. Years and years since she and Lewis had put on records and danced on Oriental rugs... The thought gave her no pain, only the memory of young robust joy.

She found a Fred Astaire album and put it on, smiling at the thought of Dr. and Mrs. Alexander sliding and whirling on the floor of the Iridium Room.

Music was a remarkable surprise. She sprang as though the sprightly slick music had actually struck her, and then began to run leaping and twirling down the length of the hall. She escaped out onto the verandah and raced its length with her hair flying, then pranced back with high-stepping sinuousness and a wild smile, and finally pounced through the open door and back into the subduing hall, where she slowed down, to undulate and to ripple her arms, ready to temper her first outburst of energy, for she was panting, though she had no desire to stop.

Bernice stood in the pantry door, watching. At the first blast of music she had come with ponderous speed from her kitchen sink to the pantry door that opened into the dining room, and there she stood, fascinated, scandalized, baleful, her arms rolled into her damp apron and plunked across her stomach.

Whirling, Syra saw her, but being so much in herself and the music, gave her little thought. For a few moments more the avid and reproachful face hung moonlike in the dark of the doorway, and in the next whirl Syra saw that it had vanished, and that the door had closed.

But one record was enough. She was ready for the next thing. And perhaps, too, Bernice's silent condemnation had had an effect. Now there was the outdoors to go to, and that was the place to be, not indoors, where things and persons, past and present, bound veils (shrouds?) around her face and held the ends fast, so that she was something reined in, secured from forward motion of her own.

She went out onto the verandah and sat down on the steps, pleasantly spent from her purgative fling and no longer so restless. And yet she was still a shade restless, and at loose ends, with Mrs. Alexander so unaccustomedly away, and no focus to the morning.

Suddenly this place—the smooth green lawns, the ancient shading maples, the long verandah with its white-painted, chintz-cushioned wicker chairs—struck her as being uncannily like her old home in Cazenovia. She was amazed it had taken her so long to see this. The wraparound verandah was the same, and the spirea banking it, and the wicker chairs, and the front hall door wide open, and Mother sitting there. Yes. There Mother was, sitting in Mrs. A.'s favorite chair by the railing, her ashtray on it. Her little cigar was fixed in the center of pursed lips, while her hands kept the newspaper on her knees from flapping in the breeze.

Syra shrugged and tried to smile the vision away—they're

playing musical chairs, she joked, Mrs. A. sitting down in her chair, where Mother no longer is. Now it's Mother's chair again. Now Mrs. A.'s. Oh this is crazy...

She sensed a muddle in herself that felt almost physical; her stomach, her head, her self, felt crammed, dense. She felt that she had to empty herself, so that her body would be light feeling, and free again. Hindrances–she felt full of hindrances, and they were telling her that it was time to move on, into the dwelling of her own self, from which she could begin to live whatever life was waiting to be lived.

She knew this only dimly, most of all through her restlessness, and her mild repudiation of these heretofore benign surroundings. She could feel the dream ending, herself waking up. Have I perhaps come from under the cloud, she wondered? A little, maybe, except that I'm not yet too smart. She sat on the verandah steps, leaning against the sun-warmed railing, watching the endless industry of robins on the lawn. She closed her eyes. The air! It was the air of this spring morning, more than any sight, that was the thing.

At that moment she knew she must act. Leave.

She stood up slowly and stretched, straining her arms up toward limitlessness, freedom, toward whatever was up, and away, and skyward. She felt herself pressing and flowing up from the soles of her feet through her body and arms and fingers, so that all of her was an earth-rooted upward flowing. She had the feeling that this powerful upward flood might begin to pour out of the ends of her fingers, spurting like the jets of a fountain. She strained and shuddered upward, feeling that her body was stretching and growing taller, and that the growth would never stop. Her head hung back, her eyes were open, her face flattened toward the sky.

Finally she subsided, in a long expiration of held breath. And she was hungry. She went out to the kitchen, which was mercifully free of Bernice–down cellar ironing, Syra supposed. She was relieved not to encounter that frowning face, whose silent censure of her dancing had left a feeling of distaste, even of uneasiness. Hell's bells, she thought, spreading peanut butter on whole wheat bread and walking away from the crumbs, I can't be drawn into something like that. She ate her sandwich on the steps of the kitchen porch, washing it down with long swallows of cold milk, hurriedly, for in a moment the shepherd and shepherdess clock would strike one–her hour to meet Rupert by his mailbox.

He was waiting there as usual. In his eagerness, he always arrived first. "Beautiful day," he called out rapturously, and she called back with a spirited and expectant contentment, "Hello Rupert." He wore a carefully considered tan corduroy jacket with his black turtleneck sweater, and he swaggered just a little and hung his head toward his shoulder to try to mask the transparency of his eagerness, though his black eyes sparkled with it.

They set out toward the fields that sloped away from Rupert's house, quiet at first, and Rupert was in no hurry to talk, for quietness was something he thought he was learning, from Syra, to be comfortable with. Yet he was only biding his time until he could burst out with everything in him that was pushing to be expressed.

"My, you look tired Rupert."

"Ah. I am. I don't sleep."

"I wish you did," cheerfully.

"So do I. These are not easy days, you know, with the difficulties between Anne and me. I feel completely at sea. Completely at sea. Life!" He raised both fists and beat the air with vibrating arms. "Ha! All this rare beauty around me and there've been so many times in the past weeks I couldn't feel it. That to me is intolerable, intolerable. To have spring come and not to feel it. *In*-tolerable! I mean to say that it doesn't hit me like a strong light, as it usually does, but like pallid light, different in *me* from what it is out there. Nothing in myself to match it. I can't begin to express to you how I long to feel a joy in me that corresponds to the beauty around me. Do you know what I'm saying? Am I making myself clear? I'm saying that that's the way I function. The beauty of nature–that's what's there when all else is gone. Enduring. The only reliable nourishment." He blew out a long whistling breath. "The joy of my life has been the sight and sound and smell and experience of nature. I *live* for spring. I live all *year* for spring."

"What a thing to say. What a madly joyous, soaking-everything-up-and-going-loose-yourself thing to feel."

"Ah yes. How can you so uncannily sense and put into words the way I feel, Syra? Amazing. But dear me. I see that what I'm talking about is joy, and needing joy for survival. Now that's a childish expectation, Syra, wouldn't you say? I'll have to find something besides joy to sustain me, won't I. Ah well. I've had a fortunate life, a fortunate life, no real trouble in it until, well frankly, until now, this thing between Anne and me. You see I find it very hard not to have everything be all *right*. It's new to me to be in the midst of trouble. I just want to be happy!" he cried, mocking himself and pushing out his lower lip in imitation of a thwarted child.

Syra walked along, listening carefully, saying nothing. But Rupert was finding it impossible to restrain himself. He told her about finding white lilacs on the kitchen table this morning, and how moved he had been. "Say it with flowers," he murmured, and he smiled, sadly Syra thought. He told her about an idea he'd gotten for the jacket of his book–an abstraction both linear and spatterdash, the linear part suggesting the call of the red-wing, the spatterdash part a Jackson Pollock of condensed sound, suggesting the din of peepers. "Nobody but me would know what it's supposed to be, of course. So Pangrove probably won't agree.

Ah publishing! It's still a miracle to me that after twelve tries my agent found a publisher. An absolute miracle. They all said my book was too quiet, wouldn't sell, wasn't marketable–that word!"

"Oh Rupert, I am really shocked to know the interiors of some editors. Or maybe they bow to the interiors of the majority. Unliterature is poured out for the masses. No, that isn't true. Maybe the majority aren't that way. What percentage shall we decide upon?"

"We shall decide upon the malleability of the masses, twenty-five percent for them, and seventy-five percent for the sales-oriented mediocrity of most publishers. I doubt if this scene is reversible, unfortunately."

"Oh let's talk about something else. About your love of nature, for instance. It must make your heart soar like a swallow to feel that way. Swallows are the happiest fliers. It's very moving, what fills people's sails." Syra smiled faintly. "Take Bernice. What fills her sails, I guess, is adoration of Mrs. A."

"I would say yes, that's right. But what fills your sails, Syra?"

"Hummmm. Goodness. Let's see. What fills my sails?" She began to laugh. "Ice-cream cones," she cried.

"I won't take ice-cream cones for an answer."

"Oh you won't, won't you? But why not? Why not take ice cream cones for an answer?" Music is what fills my sails, she said to herself, my guitar. Yes, music fills my sails. And being me...when I'm *being* me. And ice-cream cones, because that's just an offshoot of being me. But she would not say this to anyone. Not to Rupert, not to anyone. And ice-cream cones wasn't so far off, anyway. Or Planter's punches. Or peanut butter, or bleeding hearts, or Mrs. A.'s old silk lamp shades, or Anne's battered Volkswagen, or hibiscus. Or sex. Oh yes. Sex. Above all, sex. And wasn't sex just another great big wonderful ice-cream cone? Music, but all of these things too, filled her sails. She began to laugh. "Rupert," she said, "you know you *should* take ice-cream cones for an answer. Because it's the truth."

"Possibly, but not the whole truth. I wish you felt you could tell me the whole truth."

Suddenly she thought it would be nice to tell Rupert the whole truth, or at least, part of it. Lewis wasn't here any more. "Music," she said quietly, "music fills my sails, Rupert. Mostly, that is. But if I told you all of what fills my sails," she smiled, "I think the wind might die down for me."

"Ah yes!" Rupert threw back his head, closed his eyes, and drew a long, expressive breath. "Ah yes, Syra," he said, his eyes closed. "Forgive me."

"That's okay." She was so relieved. "Oh look, here are the little fists of beginning daisies. My flower. Every time I've had an anesthetic—twice to be exact—I have been in a daisy field with the sun drawing me up, like water."

"Ah. Lovely. Lovely. Remember in *Amal and the Night Visitors*, one of the kings sings 'Lovely, lovely, lovely' in a spine-chilling, spiraling-upward tenor. Like this. Lovely, lovely *lovely*."

"Oooh! Do that again."

"No. It's not for my voice, it's decidedly for a tenor."

"All right. Once is enough anyway. One piece of candy is always enough. God, Rupert, remember last week, how I almost stepped on that black snake? God."

"They're beautiful things, those great black snakes. But awesome. Swift and harmless to humans, but indeed yes, oh but indeed yes, terrible if you step on one."

Abruptly then he said, "However, let's not dwell on *that*. *You* don't look tired, my good companion. You look as though everything underneath your smooth healthy skin is streamlined, unbunched up. You look ironed out, and that does my heart *good*." He threw her a timid glance, but eager. "Well, anyway. What's new?"

"Oh ho, yesterday after our walk I went into the garden rubber-booted to prune Mrs. A.'s roses. I always search for a little bud place and cut just above it, the way Mrs. A. taught me to do. But, well, the thing is, a flower bit me. Mrs. A. warned me not to pick anything from that bush while the sun was on it. Now I have a blistered thumb, see, and the shrub will be pulled up whenever, with no compunction in Mrs. A., pulled up not because it bit, but because it smelled like a cat pan into the bargain. It seems like a small murder."

"Well, that's certainly refreshingly new. And what else is new? Anything?

"I am." She lifted up onto the toes of one foot as she said it, almost skipped. "Oh, heavens, my awareness only appears in rare moments of grace, so I mean I *think* maybe I am. New, I mean. Oh I don't know. I say this with fingers crossed. It is not wise to make such statements."

"Oh but it is," he cried excitedly, "it is." He gave her a paternal, encouraging look. "What a beautiful thing to hear you say."

"Oh I didn't mean to spill it. I feel released and hope it will last, and I won't get fits of sullens when Bernice glares at me."

"Well goodness my dear. I'm so glad you did spill it. Strangely, you infect me with your newness. As you always do, of course, with your *usualness*." He searched her face. "It means a great deal to me that you're beginning to feel renewed. A great deal."

Syra said nothing and they walked along again in silence. They had come to the woods and to the brook, whose short waterfall in a small way roared softly as it slid over the flat rock that forded it, and sluiced down, cold and crystal clear and swift between other rocks, and rushed over and polished a great jutting rounded one looking smooth as ice. Skunk cabbage grew profuse and jade green here, wild iris were opening, and ferns were rising in lacy greenness–the beginnings of a summer jungle. Syra took off her slippers and stood for a while on the fording rock, so that the cold water could rush over her feet. Rupert leaned against a tree, watching her. At last he sat down on the bank, being careful not to crush a froth of rue anemones. Sighing contentedly then, at last he leaned back on both elbows, and for a while he simply stared at Syra, unseen by her, looking at her reddened little feet in the icy water, and then at her calm, exalted face, and then at the remarkable way she stood. Quiet as a tree, he thought. He took his eyes away from her and looked up through the web of branches to the blue sky.

Sip, sip, sip. A chickadee making tiny sounds flew over their heads. "Soon they'll be gone," Rupert said quietly, "little dears. When they leave, summer is really here."

"Mrs. A.'s at her hospital board." Syra had found some violets and was eating one.

"Mrs. Knight's at her office." Rupert grinned. "And *we're* just wandering, wandering through the woods, 'lonely as a cloud that floats on high o'er vales and hills.'" He spread an arm grandly across the sky, and Syra, about to put a violet into her waiting mouth, held it there in front of her lips, looking at him. She thought that right now he had an impressive beauty—his great frame, the black of his high-necked sweater, the silver of his long hair, his burning happy black eyes, his irresistible joy in everything around him. She thought his mouth particularly beautiful—soft, generous, healthy, an innocent *young* man's mouth. She wondered about kissing. Would she ever kiss a man's mouth again? The sense of kissing moved into her.

They were threading their way through the dense part of the woods that came now, Rupert in the lead and turning to hold back branches until Syra could reach to hold them off herself.

"But I'm not lonely as a cloud," Rupert cried once, exuberantly, as he turned. "Not when I'm with my little companion." And he began to sing, in his rust-sweet baritone,

278

"Who is Syra? What is she?
That all her swains commend her
Holy, fair, and wise is she;
That heavens such grace did lend her,
That she might admired be.

Is she kind as she is fair?
For beauty lives with kindness.
Love doth to her eyes repair,
To help him of his blindness;
And, being help'd, inhabits there.

Then to Syra, let us sing,
That Syra is excelling;
She excels each mortal thing
Upon the dull earth dwelling.
To her let us garlands bring. Garrr-lands brin-nng."

He drew the last words out until the harsh-sweet note had died away, and then he turned down to her and smiled.

"I loved that Rupert. But I'm not sure Shakespeare'd like what you just did, Rupert."

"What I just did? You mean how I sang it?"

"Oh, no, no. I mean your saying *Syra* instead of *Sylvia*."

"I did?" Rupert exploded. "I *did*? I said 'Who is Syra?' Waddya know!" And he began to laugh, helplessly and delightedly, swaying his whole body from side to side as he strolled.

"Yes, you did. And I loved it. From now on, it's 'Who is *Syra*' to me, Rupert. I'm telling you. And with no apologies to Shakespeare."

"My dear Syra, I am absolutely and completely delighted with myself. Truth will out, won't it. Imagine my not knowing I was saying Syra! But oh my dear, how truly each word does describe you."

"Even holy? Oh no. Come on. And wise I *ain't*. Nor kind, *nor* fair, as in pretty."

"Well in a way you're holy. Yes. I mean to say I do revere you, Syra. Yes. I do revere you."

"Goodness. That doesn't feel like what I know of me."

"But it feels like what *I* know of you. Reverence does."

"Well good."

"Yes indeed, good." His radiant face suddenly went sober. He opened his lips slightly And opened his eyes wider. In them was stupefaction. Disbelief. A blankness came into his mind.

"I loved that Rupert. I loved that. There was something about all of it, your voice, you, the words, and me there instead of Sylvia. You gave me a super concert."

Beneath her feet the moss was soft and springy. She felt the earth beneath her feet, supporting her, and felt herself melt down into that support, so that she was divested of the weight of her body and was light as air.

An old familiar sensation–the great pleasure of her body, of her self from head to toe–came over her. She was lubricated, spacious. A sudden great joy seized her. She was a balloon let go, floating upward fast, into a free, light space where there was no fearful association with Lewis and his death, where there was nothing but sky. Had she come free of "it," broken away from "it"? Could it be that she was alive, whole, free, a balloon floating in space? But how could it be? She had killed Lewis. *Killing Lewis*–there it was, a phrase lettered in her mind. Yet it was not attached to any emotion. The sense of it, the feeling of it, had left her, and was only lodged in black letters across the inside of her forehead.

"Syracuse," Rupert was saying, beginning to laugh. "I can't get over it. Did you like that name when you were a little girl?"

"For a while in our school, no. But since my mother saw nothing wrong with it, eventually, I didn't either. Hardly anyone except my grandfather and my guitar teacher ever called me that, anyway."

"Well, it's a very pretty name," gently. "Syracuse." He repeated it slowly, pleasurably, as though tasting it. The whole of last night's wakefulness came back into him now. He had lain in the pressing dark and then right away, though he thought he had developed techniques to avoid it, that black devil of a sentence—*Timor Mortis Conturbat Mē*, had come into his mind. Why always that *Latin* sentence he wondered, rueing the day he had come across it, and as usual, puzzled by its reiteration and its power.

But as he lay there he realized at last that the sentence had perpetual impact *because* it was in Latin, and dramatic, and therefore less real—a nimble trick of his mind to disguise a fear that had come to stay. He had lain thinking about that bold black sentence, with its impact as of great gongs menacingly beaten. And suddenly he had had a new recognition, a new admission: *It wasn't all going to be the way he'd like it to be, ad infinitum.*

His whole being had struggled to escape the sinking horror engendered by this admission, and, searching frantically for something else to think about in his now irreversible wakefulness, he had began to puzzle about Syra and Georges, and what was going on there, wondering from what he had come to know about Syra whether her silence about Georges meant lack of interest, or lack of love, or repudiated love, or what. And was Syra a loving sort of woman, as Anne was?...

Unable to answer this question, Rupert found that he couldn't associate his sense or experience of "loving," with Syra, and this troubled him. What was the nature of her caring? For it certainly wasn't demonstrative, not mothering. Not *smothering*, he said to himself, and smiled in the dark. No indeed. Not that. Was she affectionate, that was the thing? No, she was not. Sensual, yes. Affectionate, no. He was pleased to discover that he thought of her as sensual, but couldn't explain this to himself, because he knew she didn't exhibit sensuality, didn't even look sensual. Was she then only sensual, and not loving?... He had finally fallen asleep tormentedly believing that Syra was unloving and that Anne was loving, yet trying to understand why Syra's unlovingness was easier to be with than Anne's lovingness.

They came to the edge of the woods, where Moores' meadows began, finding there, by the old stone boundary wall, an ancient gnarled apple tree in full pale pink blossom.

Exclaiming over it, they emerged into the expanse of the meadow. And then it came to Rupert that he knew about Syra and "loving." She was free of it. And he knew this with approval, not with censure. She had no great expectations, he thought with relief. Man-and-woman love would never swamp Syra, she would never have her life in a man. Never. Whereas Anne's loving was a record: "I think about you, I'm concerned about you, I'm here to promote your welfare, I care about you, I love you," turned on full pitch, morning, noon, and night. Never a lull in the *sound*. And if she did let there be a lull in the sound, where would that leave her? What would silence say to Anne?...

Then he realized how strongly and basically he wanted to be let alone by all such demands as someone else's abundant driving relatedness made. Syra had showed him that love, Anne's kind anyway, created a continually eventful, really relentless and never restful experience, a perpetual obligation to "receive" and to try to give back in return. Anne whipped everything up to such a pitch, such a pitch! Anne isn't good for me, he thought irritably. She devours...

He glanced sideways at Syra, then quickly away. Of course she looked sensual. Of course she did... But not in the obvious way, he thought, perhaps because her sensuality was akin to a certain distinction, or bearing, or conviction of something, that the little pink-and-white queens in Flemish paintings had. Yet, without the straightforward recklessness of her face–was this her conviction of her own unconventionality?–without that grave recklessness, she wouldn't be sensual at all, he realized.

Yes, she is sensual, and in the most magnificent way, he thought. Thinking this, he felt his body stir. Fearfully, he thrust one hand into his trousers pocket as he walked along, and in a moment, when he felt that this astonishing arousal had subsided, he withdrew his hand and cleared his throat in loud embarrassment, and looked far off, into the sun-lanced darkness of the woods.

But he couldn't get his mind off her sensuality. He turned to look at her curiously. Yes indeed, it was in her round dark eyes–that searchlight gaze–in the vigor and calm of her walk, in the easy shoulders, in the swinging of her hips, in the toss of all that hair away from her head, and in her lips–in those full lips that he could imagine parting slightly, waiting for, inviting, the mouth of a man.

They had come across Moores' meadows to the far woods that edged them, and here, through lichened stone walls, an old wagon road entered the dim, sun-infiltrated silence of a birch grove. Moores' tractor had been over the road recently, leaving deep ruts that were full of water–underground springs kept this section of the old road perpetually soft and muddy. Only the narrow crown of the road was reasonably dry, so that Syra and Rupert were forced to walk on it, and chose to walk side by side rather than single file. This came about spontaneously. Their arms brushed against each other, their bodies touched. And even after they had reached the dry part of the road, they found themselves continuing this way.

It felt unnatural and wildly wonderful to Rupert, along with the forest silence, its deep shade, and its secret shafts of sun.

It felt easy and happy, to Syra, and she said, "People aren't supposed to talk in church." She tilted her head back to gaze upward. "It *is* churchlike. I mean like cathedrals. And Rupert, I don't want to talk much."

"Ah! I know. I know." But then he said suddenly, inquiringly and with a certain caution, not looking at her, "I do have to say just this, though. Have you sensed as I have that we have a special kind of companionship? I know you don't want to talk, and after this I'll stop. But I do want to say it. What I mean to say is that a new, 'meaningful' relationship, as Anne would say, is marvelously, marvelously invigorating, alive, full of interest. Rejuvenating. Finding a friend is a rare thing. Ah my dear Syra, these walks mean so much to me." He bent his head and dared to let the reservoir of gratitude he felt pour out of his radiant eyes, down over her.

"I know. Me too. And you're very special for me, too, Rupert." Then she said in a quiet, exploratory voice, "I've never felt exactly this way with a man."

Disassembled fragments of mind and emotion were magnetized all at once into a single idea, and Syra realized, with an emergence of clear thought, that Rupert had helped to give her back to herself. And that she had helped to give him something essential to him, too, whatever it was. Thus in their mutual transfusing, they had brought about something good.

She looked at him searchingly. "Yes, Rupert," she said. "It is, it is—" she groped for a large enough way to describe what they had. But then she simply said, "It's so possible."

Rupert could not speak for joy. He looked at her. She looked at him. "It's awfully good, Rupert," she said. "I'm glad you mentioned it, because it brought into my mind how I feel about you. I hadn't really thought about it, or put it into words."

"Yes. It's so possible. That's a wonderful way to put it."

"Rupert, this is a beautiful spring day, and you and I are good for each other." She said this so matter-of-factly, and with all the solidity and honesty of herself behind it, that Rupert felt relief to be taken down from joy to a kind of bedrock permeating peaceful reality. He smiled happily, even gaily, down at her, and he would leave it all at that, with relief at not having to chew it over; with simple satisfaction at just being themselves, two people together, free and happy, out for a walk on a beautiful spring day.

From the wagon road they climbed steplike rocks to a small plateau where there was a stand of pine, a clearing, wild azalea in pink perfumed bloom, and the shiny green of much budding mountain laurel preparing itself for flowering. In a moment they came to another clearing, a promontory overhanging a great swamp where towering trees rose from shallow black water. On this promontory, moss and wild lily of the valley were a delicate blanched green in the filtered sunlight. A fallen tree lay across it, an invitation to sit and lean back.

"All right my dear," he said happily, "no more talk. We'll sit here for a while and listen to the swamp."

"Oh yes, this is a haunting place of drowned trees and their shadows. Rupert, we must sit here wrapped in silence for this beginning of the world."

Syra sank down by the fallen tree and leaned back against it, while Rupert lowered himself slowly and adjusted himself against the tree, close to her, for closeness had become necessary and natural. He reached for a wild lily of the valley, picked it and brought the furry musky faint fragrance of the small white spike up to his nostrils. "Oh my, oh my, oh my," he murmured.

Syra turned to smile up at him, and he saw that a green flake of violet leaf was plastered against a white tooth. "You have a bit of green violet leaf on your very white lower middle tooth," he said tenderly.

She curled her lips back and opened her jaws wide, jutting her face up toward him, as though he were a dentist. "Where?"

Very tenderly. "Right there." He put out a gentle finger and tapped the tooth. "That tooth."

"Oh, that tooth that's mine! The next-door one isn't. Dentist insisted on having it out. Who is it, sharks or whales, who grow new teeth? Even so, I prefer not being them." Blinking her eyes in concentration, Syra felt around for the leaf with a finger. Then she spread her lips and glared her clenched teeth at him again, "Did I get it?"

He ached with tenderness. "No. Here. Let me." He advanced a finger, which met her soft wet lip, and flicked off the speck of leaf with his fingernail. "There." The moisture of her lip was still on his finger, like balm. He felt a powerful tenderness over having done a little something like this for her. He watched a bronze fly settle and buzz in the shine of her parted hair.

She kept on looking at him, gravely. Then she said with some emotion, "Rupert, I'm going pretty soon now. I'll miss you. I realize how deeply, deeply, I do mean deeply, I'll miss you. Each walk with you has been a section of a long road in a certain direction, forward; where I have to go, I realized this morning. I have to move on in more ways than one."

Rupert threw Syra an incredulous look. Then abruptly he took his eyes away from her and raised his chin and looked off into the treetops. In a moment, carefully, he cleared this throat and said, to the treetops, weakly, "You're going?" And then again, quietly, wildly, "You're going?"

"Yes."

"But I thought...it never occurred to me..." He stopped and looked down at the wild lily of the valley in his hand, and threw it violently away. "I didn't think. That's what I mean. I never wanted to think about your going away. But I had the feeling, too, that you *weren't* going to leave." Now he turned to look at her, his eyes gradually admitting shock. "Oh what are you telling me, Syra," he said softly. "What am I to do without you?"

Syra's eyes engaged with the anguish and admission in Rupert's eyes, and she looked penetratingly into them. "I'm not going back to Georges, if that's what you mean."

"You're not? Yes, that's what I'd been feeling. That you meant not to go back to Georges. I see now that that's what I've been feeling. And it's not a sad decision, I feel. That's the feeling I get. That it's right and that you're not shattered. Is that so?"

"Oh yes. I don't love Georges. I'm not shattered at all. Not by that."

"But by *what*, my dearest?"

"By the..." By the death of the man I loved, she had been about to say. But now here, the words, both sets of them, had lost the life of needing to be spoken. They were printed words now, not feeling words. There was nothing present here to validate them.

Her eyes had not moved from the black intense glow of Rupert's. This strong glow, a shaft of it, was striking from his eyes across into hers, kindling a glow there in her own eyes, this glow being drawn radiantly down to her toes and then up again through her body and into her eyes, to pour back across the shaft into Rupert's eyes. "I don't think I'm so very shattered," she murmured.

Longing for Syra broke into Rupert's mind like a sudden light. For seconds disbelief fought with the pounding assurance that her telling eyes were making this no mistake. But then he knew that he dared reach out and touch her, because of what was in her slow, full eyes. He put a hand on her shoulder and felt the small bones. And presently she put her hand up and closely, warmly covered his, as though she would keep that hand there, persuade it, imprison it.

Neither of them spoke. Rupert came to his knees, without breaking their gaze, and put his other hand on her other shoulder. They kissed. Then after the long fearful struggle of this kiss, they slumped down together, and for a moment lay looking at each other in tender breathless fierce agreement, almost delicately, as though their two caring, agreeing selves ought not to be lost in what was to come.

Earth as well as flesh was its essence, the endless, the basic satisfaction of earth, and throughout it Rupert was conscious of this, of himself and the moss and the sound of birds and the sun on his back and this small solid ingeniously passionate nymph he was joined to. Even at its completion, he could smell the cool mushroomy dampness of the ground underneath them, and the faint fragrance of crushed wild lilies of the valley.

He rolled onto his side, leaving her sprawled, disarranged, radiant. Then he flung himself on her again, and began to kiss her all over her face and neck and smiling mouth, again and again and again.

She lay limp, being kissed. "It was marvelous," she kept whispering, "marvelous, marvelous." She was empty, complete. Back in herself.

They usually parted at Rupert's mailbox, but they walked by it in a daze without seeing it, hand in hand, then turned in at Mrs. Alexander's drive and walked slowly toward the house. Mrs. Alexander's car was not beside the steps, or in the open garage, which meant that she wasn't back, and this reassurance must have been telegraphed to Rupert, for he continued to clasp Syra's hand in his, kneading it softly and sensuously, smoothing his thumb along her fingers and knuckles, and along the small bones of the back of her hand—a lovely thing she gave herself up to with passive blissful entirety, responding only with an occasional pressure. Once she thought of Lewis, but with peace, and without any guilt.

It was now late afternoon, and cooler, the sun lower, for they had slept, and made love again, and slept again, time out of mind. Under the canopy of maples lining the drive, they walked in the alternate bars of sun and shade cast by the trunks of the trees. They moved in a trance, unaware of the clamor of birds in the branches overhead. And perhaps the magic was about to change back to some unknown bareness, Rupert thought, fixing his mind tenaciously on the trance, though he felt it fading. It was unendurable to him, and impossible, to conceive of what lay beyond saying good-by to Syra.

At the porch steps they stopped and turned to face each other. He took her other hand, bending over her and looking down at her. Then he brought both her hands up to his mouth and kissed one after the other with a luscious sensuality that sent lightning through Syra. "Tomorrow, my darling, at the same time? By the mailbox?" He smiled. "Rain or shine," he said with a passionate confidence.

She looked up at him luminously and gratefully, a message without words of the recognition of their closeness and passion, and of her conviction that she certainly did, now, know right from wrong. And Rupert in the dream he never wanted to wake from saw confirmation of tomorrow's rapture, and tomorrow's and tomorrow's and tomorrow's. "Good-by then, my darling Syra." He put her hands gently back to her sides.

"Good-by Rupert." She smiled almost incredulously. How really wonderful this man's passion was, such depth, and quality, such worth, like himself. She knew, absolutely, that he had had a lifetime of the enjoyment of vigorous and imaginative and tender and accomplished and savored sensuality. "Lucky Anne," she thought.

She looked up at him, still with her wide astonished smile. "Good-by."

❧ V ❧

BERNICE, in the upstairs hall putting freshly ironed sheets and pillowcases into the linen closet, saw it all. And when Syra came up the stairs holding a letter in her hand, there was Bernice standing in front of the open linen closet with the pillowcases between terrible palms, waiting.

"Oh Bernice. Hello." Waving the letter. "How come the mail's here?"

"He drove in with it, with that registerated letter for you."

"Oh is this registered?" Syra looked at the envelope from Georges, which she had snatched up from the hall table with a furtive anxious repugnance. "So it is. Well, well." Registered. How like Georges to *make sure...* Her heart was beating with unpleasant force. She hated having the letter come now, breaking crudely into the safety of this day's happiness.

"I saw you." Magisterially, Bernice raised an exultant hand, then smacked it down onto the pile of pillowcases.

"You what?" Preoccupied with everything else, Syra paid little attention, wanting only to get into her room and close the door and be alone.

"I saw what you and him was doing."

Syra turned quiet. She knew everything in that instant—memories of the hearsay of evil gossip, of what the consequences of this kind of ignorant hostility could be, telegraphed through her, and left her shaken and repelled. But she looked at Bernice with cold, untroubled eyes. "Whatever do you mean, Bernice? What did you see?"

"I saw you and him...*necking*, that's what I saw and you know it. What's more, I been here for thirty-five years in this place where no shenanigans never went on, and it's my duty to tell Mrs. Alexander the kind of person you are which I just now observed, which she don't know." Bernice turned and thrust the pillowcases angrily onto a shelf, where clean and neatly folded they were bathed in late sweet sun. She closed the door with a snap. "I never was so rocked in all my life, believe me, from seeing what I seen down below there. Him a married man, and you a married woman and your cousin not even cold in his grave."

A faint smile. "He was cremated."

"Cremated, buried, it's one and the same."

"But what did you see, Bernice?"

"I seen him and you necking, I repeat."

Of course she had seen. Of course she had seen the aureole of that golden afternoon around both of them. Yet, "You saw an affectionate good-by between close friends, Bernice," lied Syra calmly, though her voice shook with disgust. "Mrs. Alexander will understand that, since she knows the difference between necking, and a good-by between friends who won't be seeing each other again." As she said this, Syra knew it was so. She would not be seeing Rupert again.

She looked penetratingly at Bernice, and Bernice's eyes fluttered evasively, for here was a superior anger which she sensed could lick her in the end. "You can tell Mrs. Alexander anything you like," Syra said, "it doesn't matter to me. Nor will it to her." She turned carelessly away, walking down the hall to her room, her heart pounding. Behind her, like the clear placatory voice of reason, like a reminder of the normalcy and dignity and cheer of decent households, came the tiny chimes of the shepherd and shepherdess clock striking six—a part of Bernice's life, too, though a perpetual tinkling grace that had never penetrated her at all. Behind her, Syra felt the obdurate flaccid massive force of ignorance, of jealousy, of a long and barely lived and never woman-fulfilled life, standing with a terrible power in the gentle evening sun and the echo of immaculate chimes. Oh my God, she groaned, oh no matter. Throw her away.

She turned into her room and closed the door and flung herself onto the white-flounced bed with a long, almost good-natured sigh of futility, fury, resignation. Then she drew another sigh, and flung the back of her hand across her forehead, and looked up at the ceiling, while comprehension and the practicality of acceptance eased into those wide, clear, staring eyes. She was seeing, and without effort understanding clearly, that here it all was—complex challenging marvelous terrible absurd contradictory life, Mrs. Alexander's *That's the way it is*: The muddle Bernice was making, but the guilt about Lewis amazingly gone, plus the next problem waiting in the unopened letter, and then the next problem of leaving Rupert, and then the next problem of facing a Mrs. Alexander informed of "shenanigans," and then the next problem of where to go.

But all around it, and within it, was the returned reliable ability of herself to accept and cope with this bizarre compound that was life. Amazing how clear everything suddenly was! Oh these knowings come from way down, they do... She was back in herself again, and happy to be there. And she could take on these kinds of vicissitudes because she had always been accustomed to them. The thing that mattered, the only thing, was that making love to Rupert had returned her, wholesomely and guiltlessly, to herself, so that she knew at last that she had not killed Lewis. It wasn't my desire that killed him, she could say to herself clearly and sadly, it was his own failure that killed him. Heart failure. Oh yes, that's what it was, his heart failed him, his heart *couldn't*. It stopped. But Rupert's heart *could*. And that's what Lewis's response could have been, should have been, because it was what he really wanted, I know. His "no" to *me*, she said to herself, amazed at the clarity of her thoughts, was a part of his lifelong "no" to himself, to what he really was. Poor beloved Lewis. What *I* was didn't kill Lewis, but what *he* was.

She stared dry-eyed at the ceiling, where a wasp clung and crawled industriously. She was anguished yet peaceful about her recognition, realizing that it both twisted her heart and lifted her spirit. This was really all that was mattering to her, now. The joy with Rupert was secondary to it, though it had been a treasure. Her sex contracted in memory, then swelled and began to glow. She smiled. She wished it could go on. Not here, but somewhere else. What would it lead to, though? This was the kind of question she should undoubtedly be asking herself. And did Rupert love her? Did she love Rupert? No, to both questions. What they had had wasn't love, not the kind she had had for Lewis. She knew this in her bones. Anyway, Rupert loved Anne. Obviously. And they had made a life for themselves. This was why it was important to leave right away, before everything got mixed up and tragic. "You can stand on your own two feet, Pet, not lean on angels." Her mother's voice was here in this room. Right next to her.

Her thoughts swung back to Bernice. Would Bernice tell Mrs. A.? And what would Mrs. A.'s reaction be? A heaviness came over Syra, so that the shine and ease went out of her as she thought of tattletale Bernice, and Mrs. Alexander's reaction—doubt, distaste, withdrawal of love, disbelief? If only it could be disbelief... I will lie about it, Syra decided. It is better. Mrs. A. knows Bernice's small, starved mind. She will believe me.

She sat up suddenly and took Georges's letter from the beside table. Her hand shook as she tore the letter open, saying in a bravura voice, "I am crossing my fingers and putting up magic, I am."

Dear Syra,
    There is no use going into recriminations, though I do feel you have been unfeeling and cruel in your sudden

even public severance of our marriage. You never considered me, only yourself. If I may use a colloquialism, "you kicked me out." That's a very bad feeling. But you have explained why, and that explanation I do understand. Yes, you are right, I think. Our marriage was without the depth and satisfaction one expects marriage to have. As you say, "we were always trying a little too hard for something that one should not have to try for at all." Though I don't believe I even knew this until you explained your version of it in your letter. I have always respected you.

Your letter, I must confess, helped to free me. For I myself have been growing deeply involved with a woman with whom my whole being seems to expand and to blossom, and who feels for me the same thing. That woman is Heloise Herrick.

Heloise and I plan to marry as soon as I can be divorced. I feel no compunction, Syra, about asking you to get the divorce, since you were the initial cause of it. Agreed? Heloise has a lawyer in New York I've been in contact with, who will want to get in touch with you as soon as I have had, I hope, a favorable reply to this letter. But I see no earthly reason why you shouldn't want to agree. Do let me add, though, that my future happiness depends upon your agreement, and having so cruelly hurt me once, I hope you will not see fit to want to cruelly hurt me again. Oh but I know you. I know you will agree.

In short, Syra, what you have done is right, and I am grateful to you for your understanding of things. It's the way you did it I find unforgivable. You owed me more than that.

But in spite of the hurt you have done me, I hope for your happiness. I know you are well able to earn a living with your music and will not need my support which anyway I would be in no position to give, and that you will be well provided for through your inheritance of Lewis's estate, and in any case your action puts me under no financial obligation to you, as you will agree, so I have no fears on the score of your needing money.

I want to say this, though. I don't consider our years to be a waste, even though I know *you* do. And you gave me much for which I will always be grateful.

Georges

Syra continued to stare down at the letter long after she had finished reading it, as though there were still something there to be considered. He is the way he is, she was thinking, and I am very touched and very appalled. He is someone alien in every way to me. There is not one tune we could sing together in harmony, knowing that the sound came from a unison of the heart of him and the heart of me. There is no music between us at all. There is no sound between us, and sound between me and a man *must* be music. The sound Rupert and I sing back and forth to each other is music shared, felt, completely understood. That's the way it has to be, for me.

And now Georges has found the kind of woman he should have had. How he'll love living chic-ly, and how happy Heloise will make him, because she's undoubtedly ready to settle for permanence.

And I'm free.

She smiled faintly with relief and abruptly pushed the letter back into its torn envelope. She sat for a moment against the pillows, her smile broadening incredulously, delightedly. She was at peace in her depths, and she knew it. "Good God, what sublime happenings," she whispered, looking up at the wasp on the ceiling, and feeling a love for wasps. "I am. I'm free. Absolutely free. Of everything."

⚬ VI ⚬

IT was almost six-thirty when Mrs. Alexander got back. She was melancholy. Tiredness from her long active day was nourishing a depression over Syra's leaving that had begun this morning, and that had robbed all the day's encounters and activities of real pleasure. She was coming home to Syra, to their evening cocktail hour, their merry dinner, their talk, their friendship, and because tonight or tomorrow night or the next night might be the last time, she was gripped with a feeling of desolation. Syra's being here and Lewis's death had shown up her life; it was a lonely old woman's life, making the most of little things in order to stave off... "In order to stave off you know what," she murmured with a facetious fatalism, and told herself not to pursue the mood.

She stood in the front hall realizing all this, her packages dumped on the two chairs flanking the telephone table, sifting idly through the mail in the hope of something interesting, small handwritten envelopes or the red and blue border of an air mail letter, neither of which she found. She sighed and shrugged. Then she straightened her shoulders and lifted the bag of groceries from the chair, and humming the Kent commercial tune to lift her spirits, went out through the dining room to the kitchen, experiencing another stab of loneliness as she passed the table set for two with its wineglasses and its centerpiece of bleeding hearts.

Bernice was bent broadly over the kitchen table rolling out crust for a chicken pie. The poignancy of the wide, dogged back, of Bernice's slavelike, automatic performance of this task, and a sudden compassionate recognition of thirty-five years of rolling out piecrusts solitarily and dutifully, dispersed the single-mindedness of Mrs. Alexander's depression and restored her customary perspective. "Well, well," she said gently, "there you are making my favorite thing. We were always going to teach me to make your piecrust, weren't we, and we never did, did we? Now let's face it, we never will. I want a drink," she finished emphatically. "Is the ice upstairs, or shall I take it up with me?"

"It's upstairs," sepulchrally, her laboring back a wall and her dogged pursuance of the task martyred and accusative.

"Well you're not very friendly. What's the matter?"

"I'll tell you what's the matter." The voice rose, the rolling pin clattered to the tabletop, the bulk straightened up, turned. "I'll tell you what she did you ain't going to believe, what's one of the worst things could happen to this house, so don't let her fool you which she will. *I* saw them. I was up putting away the sheets and pillowcases and what do you know if all of a sudden they wasn't down there in the driveway kissing. *Kissing,*" she spat. "Yes sir, kissing. *I* told her I saw them, oh yes indeed I did, and she tried to make out I saw no such thing, but *I* could tell she was a-stir, *I* hit the mark. Now she's a-scared, you mark my words, but she'll pretend she ain't."

"Oh Bernice for goodness' sakes what kind of perfect *nonsense* is this?" Mrs. Alexander's voice was indulgent. Her face was amused and faintly disgusted.

"It's no nonsense. Not on your life. They was looking at each other with cow eyes and holdin' hands and he kissed her hands like he was gonna eat 'em."

"Well all *right*," impatiently. "What on earth's the matter with that? Now Bernice, stop this. This is all just plain silly."

"It is not. And what you don't know," viciously, "is what kind of a person she is because she's such a smooth one she's got you fooled just as sure as I'm here. She stays here spongin' on you and carryin' on with another woman's husband behind your back and what's more she's the snippiest thing and why you can't see it I don't know believe me I don't. It's not one shell steak now it's two shell steaks, and do you know I use more'n a pound of butter a week now, to say nothing of upstairs downstairs, in my lady's chamber, and sleeping till all hours in the morning with no regard for anyone and then expects to be served breakfast at any old hour. But when it gets to neckin' with Mrs. Knight's husband, I'll tell *you* I –"

"Bernice! Stop it!" From Mrs. Alexander's very small body a great force gathered and concentrated in her eyes, which grew dangerously still. "What on earth do you think you're saying." Her voice was soft with fury. "Now do calm down," she said, "and let's hear no more of this–this utter filth. Of course I don't believe it," she said, cold strong fury in her voice but uncertainty in herself, curiosity, faint panic. She put the package of groceries harshly down on the counter. "*Is* the ice upstairs?"

"Yes it's up there like I said. And the two of you'll be having them drinks, and she trying to lie out of it, mark my words, all the time you have one, two drinks and then you'll both be laughing and carrying on and you won't be in no mood to believe it no more. Oh she's a cool one, I'll tell *you*."

Mrs. Alexander gave a slight withering laugh and said "Ugh," softly. Then she said, with the firmness gone from her voice, and wearily, in a trucelike way, "I think *you* need a drink, that's what *I* think."

"I don't touch strong drink and you know it."

No, only gallons and gallons of New York state sherry, thought Mrs. Alexander. Then as though to a child she said, "Now really Bernice, I don't know what you think you saw, or what sort of interpretation you've put on what was obviously some little gesture of friendship, they're firm friends those two, you know. But I don't want you to utter another word about it. I *will* not listen to another word of it."

Tiredly, wanting a bath, wanting a drink, wanting to free herself of a silly depressed uncertainty and suspicion and panic–Syra, of all people, how perfectly unthinkable–tiredly she drew an unsure breath. "Is Mrs. Syra in her room now?"

"She's in her room. With that registerated letter from her husband. I was down in the cellar ironing when he started honking out there, never once let up on the horn till I got up there. Honk, honk. I'm coming, I'm coming I kept calling to him trying to hurry up the stairs. You should'a seen her carrying on this morning while you was away, putting on the victrola and dancing around and out on the verandah for all the neighbors to see, hair all flying around. Mourning my eye. Oh she's pulled the wool over your eyes all right. She goes off every afternoon with him for hours and comes back and stands there kissing thinking you're not here so no one'll see her, and dances like a chorus girl all up and down the verandah, while I stand there watching, oh she's brassy, she's no shame, and she knows I'm watching but does she stop, no she –"

Crash. The pantry door slammed shut behind Mrs. Alexander's outraged back.

Upstairs she stood uncertainly in the center of the worn Oriental rug of her sitting room, bone tired and bitterly distressed. She was in no mood to pull herself together, though she knew she must endeavor to do so, for Syra would appear any minute in the doorway. Depression was one thing, but this unsavory business was quite another. Bernice's nastiness clung to her like a malodor; detesting it, she couldn't free herself of it. She felt soiled and helpless and irritated.

But why? What earthly reason was there to think that there was any truth to Bernice's poisonous tattle? Bernice was obviously jealous of Syra. And of course Bernice wouldn't be expected to know about the social custom of the kiss of greeting or farewell placed lightly and impersonally on an expectant cheek. Everyone kissed indiscriminately these days. It was the new thing, particularly, she had noticed, among country neighbors. *She* didn't do it, she didn't like it. She wanted to choose whom she would kiss or be kissed by. And so, she suspected, did Syra. "You're a kissing friend, Mrs. A., a really *meaning*-it kissing. Not 'hello darling' kissing." Syra had once said this to her, and Syra had meant it.

A wave of new uncertainty swept over her. Syra would not have kissed Rupert lightly and impersonally, this was a certainty. Nor would Rupert have ventured to take such a liberty with Syra on his own. She was sure of this, she knew it in her bones.

She drew a troubled breath and stared at the floor, "from whence cometh no help," she thought wryly. Across the hall she heard Syra moving about in her room, heard a drawer being opened and then closed, listened to the bathroom faucets being turned on, and then after a moment turned off. Threatened and at bay in her own house, she nibbled at her lips nervously, tapped together the forefingers of her clasped hands, tapped the rug with the toe of her shoe.

"Well this will *never* do," she said aloud, suddenly. She crossed quickly to the bathroom and dashed cold water all over her face, lengthily, then combed her hair. She powdered her nose, flicked powder from the front of her dress in a businesslike way, drew a basin full of warm water and sudsed her hands in its comfort. Then she dried them abstractedly, pushing back the cuticle of each fingernail as was her custom when she washed her hands. And now she dropped the towel onto the bowl and marched back into the sitting room and sat down hard in her chair and poured herself a drink from the bar tray in front of it.

She took a fiery sip, sighed, and sank back against the cushions. It was a lovely evening, she saw, serene and tender and

lively as only a spring evening can be. A spot of pink light–the
projection of setting sun through a prism of the mantelpiece
girandole–trembled on the darkened wall behind it, shrinking
and expanding and breathing as though alive. Mrs. Alexander
took another little sip and watched the pink spot grow and float
and dwindle, and then, gradually fade away. It saddened her profoundly. She wanted to let herself go and to weep, though she was
not a weeper. One shock after another, she thought starkly. First
Lewis. And now this. Those long daily walks, just the two of them;
and Syra's growing happiness... I'm shocked, she told herself.

She heard Syra crossing her room to the door, heard the door
open, heard her coming down the hall. Then there she was,
standing in the doorway, her chin raised, her eyes proud, and
with the faintest suggestion of defiance about her that made Mrs.
Alexander know, immediately, that Bernice had been right.

Her heart plummeted. But even as it did, she knew she loved
Syra unconditionally.

She felt faintly relieved and ashamed, and all at once, shat-
teringly exhausted, and she sank back in her chair with a pursed
smile that seemed to say that everything was absurd and so what
on earth was there that was worth getting all worked up about.
That girl is sound as a nut, she said to herself. And she flung out
both arms in an impulsive rather grand exaggerated gesture,
welcoming Syra. "Come on in my dear. I was utterly exhausted
and I began without you. Pour yours, do." But then there was a
silence as Syra came slowly over to the tray. Something was
here, a new caution, in Syra and in herself, so that she felt
obliged to clear her throat fussily, anticlimactically.

In the complete silence, Syra, bending over the tray, raised
her face to Mrs. Alexander's with a vivid searching look. Then
she returned to fixing her drink, and when she had put the ice
into the glass, and then the bourbon, and pushed it around with
a finger, she turned and went over to the rose velvet fireside

chair and sat down in it and took a long swallow of the welcome liquor. And as she felt her hips against the velvet chair, this part of herself stirred with memory and a pulsating message flooded through her whole body, acknowledging it peacefully. This wave of sound delight tended to reassure her.

Mrs. ALexander noticed the softening of Syra's face, and the way her eyes blurred and shone. She had never seen this look of Syra's, but she interpreted it. Anyone could have. She felt a great hollowness, an impotence. And then, in a moment, a pricking of curiosity. And, too, a slight repugnance.

Syra took another long swallow. Murmured, "Yum," unemphatically. Then she flung her hair away from her neck and looked hard at Mrs. Alexander. "Mrs. A., did Bernice tell you that she saw Rupert and me, as she put it, necking?"

Admiration, relieved admiration, dispelled all other emotions, and for a moment Mrs. Alexander experienced only a certainty of her fidelity to this young person. At last she said fervently, "Indeed Bernice did, she launched herself at me the minute I went into the kitchen, she could hardly wait. I hated to have to listen to it Syra. Yes, she told me she'd seen you and Rupert kissing."

"We weren't kissing, Mrs. A. We were standing saying goodby, and Rupert took up my hands and kissed them. That's the *kissing* she saw." Syra's nostrils widened with distaste over the necessity of having to explain herself. "Bernice told me she was going to tell you she saw us necking, so I thought I'd better set you straight, in case she had told you and you wouldn't know what in hell to do about it."

Syra took another, rather hectic swallow. "We were saying good-by. I didn't really know till afterward that I was saying good-by to Rupert. It was quite some time afterward that I realized it. There *is* a close thing, Bernice *did* see a thing that glowed. Oh yes, I think it had gold edges, what she saw. I think

Rupert's wonderful. We've grown very close these past weeks." She looked steadily into Mrs. Alexander's eyes, which seemed speculating, evasive, bleak, stern, yet seemed for the most part well-wishing. She had not known she was going to say what she was saying, and she felt a certain relief, and new courage, as she found this truth, though not whole truth, coming out of herself. It fortified her, and seemed to be making things easier. "There is a close thing that has gotten to be immense, Mrs. A. So much of a one that I feel I must leave tomorrow. Today showed us." She poured the last of her drink down her throat and then lowered her empty glass into her lap, and looked across challengingly and bravely at Mrs. Alexander.

There was a long, long silence. At last Mrs. Alexander said quietly, "Pour yourself another drink, Piglet."

PART SEVEN

IT was time to set the table. To get the ice out. To peel four thin slices of lemon skin and put them on a white saucer. These were little things that Rupert did to make Anne's homecoming, at the end of each long day, something for her to look forward to, little services that gave him pleasure because they gave her pleasure.

He had been sitting for a long time in catatoniclike immobility on the terrace bench beneath the living room window, turned entirely in upon himself, as in sleep, the incredible experience pouring through his blood.

He was reliving it with yet another discovery, with other sweet nuances, when from without, something–perhaps lengthening shadows, or coolness as the sun sank–made itself subtly but imperatively known to him. His eyes had been open. Yet now he felt as though he were just opening them.

Sighing, he saw the evening sky, and heard a robin on the lawn. Anne was not home yet. She was late. He must hurry to set the table, to get the ice out, to peel the lemon.

His heart went thick as clay.

He stood up, an ugly solid panic in his center. How could he be with Anne, look at her, talk to her? It was impossible. False as it had been between them for the past five weeks, this encounter tonight would be false in a new and particularly unbearable way.

And he didn't want to have to mask his rapture. He didn't want to have to hide it, he wanted to keep it vivid and open and the vital part of him that it was; he even doubted that he *could* hide it, for it had taken over the whole of him. He was a new man and it was against nature to have to hide such a great thing, and he probably couldn't, since it must be so evident.

He stood uncertainly beside the weathered old bench, thinking of getting into his car and driving away fast, anywhere, away from Anne. But then he saw that this would be irrational and impractical. And then he began to feel that he could, of course, with an effort, mask his rapture, which was what would have to happen. For five weeks neither of them had made much attempt to mask their mutual alienation, and so tonight would only be a colder variation of the same chill theme. No, somehow, he saw, he would get through tonight, and face decisions tomorrow. Decisions?... His heart sank.

But he didn't think he could bear the deadness there would be between them as they sat down for dinner, and picked up their forks, and chewed in uneasy silence, and lifted their glasses of wine, all without looking at each other. The candles would burn in the middle of the table, the only aliveness in the room. Crushing as a mountain on top of them would be the nothingness between them, where there had once been everything. For a minute he felt that there was nothing in the world so terrible as this—the death of love, worse than Anne's death would have been for him. But. Love? What was love?... Oh, it's Syra I love, he thought eloquently. With her I am what I truly am, what I was meant to be.

He walked heavily down the terrace, tired unto death all at once, and around to the kitchen door, and he went into this kitchen of theirs having a sudden sense of overwhelming sadness and hopelessness as its homely and significant collaboration struck him. This was in a way the heart of their home, and though he had created its attractiveness more than Anne, her presence was very much here. What had he done? Was this his kitchen now? Ah no, it did not seem like his kitchen any more, since it had never been just his kitchen but *their* kitchen, and he could feel that he had destroyed the "their" of his existence. He felt excluded from the heart of his home, and because he had betrayed it and it was rejecting him for his betrayal, it had lost its essence and was nothing, impersonal as a window display.

He looked down at his rough hands. He looked at one calloused palm. Repugnance rose in him at the sight of it, this expression of the aging man he couldn't feel, didn't know, with whom he had no emotional connection whatsoever. Then the dark palm blurred, and in it he saw a young small mound of white breast, soft as velvet, which these roughened hands had touched. He could feel the warm velvet skin, and his palms ached. His heart ached.

He stood uncertainly in the doorway. But then he was seized with a powerful reliving of holding Syra's marvelous spirited thrashing body, and he stood swaying, clinging to the counter. Then the vividness of his sensation lessened, leaving him full of an overall radiance like an afterglow.

He pushed himself away from the counter and then closed his eyes in a slow despairing way. "Oh God," he said flatly, "oh God," and opened his eyes as though he must. Seven-thirty? He couldn't believe it was that late. But the old Regulator clock, ticking impertinently on the wall, proclaimed without doubt that this was so.

The clock and the time seemed a punishment, and he turned away from it deliberately, angry and afraid, because Anne was an hour late. And yet he was relieved. And then the memory of Syra washed over him in a great wave, and he smiled as he went mindlessly to the refrigerator to get out the ice. On the top shelf were four little glowing cups of orange Jello with mandarin orange sections, which Anne had mixed this morning before leaving. "I'm making that nice little dessert for tonight so be careful for an hour or so not to slam the refrigerator door too hard. Okay?"

"Did you put Kirsch in it?"

"Of course I put Kirsch in it."

"Well I only asked."

"Well Rupert, you have a way of checking up on me that gets my goat. If you could hear the accusing note in your voice, as though you were sure I'd forgotten. *Heavens*."

"Well you do sometimes forget."

"All *right*. But I don't want to be checked up on all the time."

Rupert closed the refrigerator door on the four little cups of cold delight, and cleared his throat, and raised his chin defiantly, and in a slow and very splendid way, to conceal his discomfiture, he crossed to the sink with the ice tray held aloft and carefully, as though it were something valuable. He put it in the sink, and then he slowly took a knife from an ironstone jug full of knives, and slowly took a lemon from the fruit tray, and began to peel from it, very slowly and meticulously, four paper-thin slices.

It was now all perfectly clear. Hard, unbearably hard for everyone, but clear. Anne did not love him, and he did not love Anne. Perfectly clear. Now he could see that her terrible tirade the night of Lewis's funeral was important, valuable, a contribution because it had brought their mutual loveless dependence out into the open.

But how could the happiness of fourteen years become suddenly something else? Could violence erupt after fourteen years, if those years had been real and good? He wrenched the lever of the ice tray viciously and knew, without understanding why, but knew deeply, unwillingly, that yes, there could have been peace as well as the building up of violence, both real.

Nevertheless, he told himself, cascading the ice cubes into the ice bucket, he and Anne must separate. Because with Syra he was sometimes himself, the essence of himself. Her quiet gave him quiet. *Urging yourself upon the world...* Anne must be right about that, for now he could feel that when he was with Syra he was always trying to rein himself in, since her quiet, her tranquil absence of any need to impress herself upon him, made almost everything he said and felt seem garrulous and self-centered and noisy and frantically pouring from some urgent need. Ah yes, he was constantly having to restrain himself with Syra. And wanting to, since there was some other sound besides his own that was the point of it all, some other way that she was showing him, something in himself that could give way to something else. Oh how he needed her, how he needed her. He and Anne brought out the worst in each other, that was now tragically clear. Yes, he thought, with purpose and terror, putting the lid onto the ice bucket, when she comes home we will face it. We will face it tonight. And I will have Syra, his heart sang, underneath the determination and the terror.

The telephone rang.

He dropped the ice tray so clatteringly and went across to the telephone with such haste that he was clearly aware now of his concern, surprised by it. He snatched up the receiver. "Anne?"

"Oh? No. Rupert? This is Ava Aranson."

His hand holding the receiver began to wobble horribly, but his mind couldn't yet shape images of disaster, and so his voice was at first unperturbed. "Oh. Ava." And then sharply, "Yes, what is it?"

"I've tried and tried to get you, Rupert. Anne asked me to call you to tell you she's had to go to Boston. She said to be sure to tell you she herself tried this morning to reach you but there was no answer. I tried on and off all afternoon. Then I left the office at six, but it takes me all this time to get home, so I've just this minute gotten here. I guess you worried."

"Worried? Well naturally. Anne's never this late." Relief turned into controlled anger. "She might have called from Boston. What time did she leave?"

"She got the two o'clock shuttle, at least that's what she was aiming for."

"I see. Well of course she thought *you* were calling me, and how would she know you wouldn't reach me? Yes, I see."

"Right."

"What did she have to go to Boston for?"

"Why this Mr. Orientes she did that paper with called to discuss last minute changes, and she thought she'd better go up there and do it properly. The paper has to be sent out tomorrow."

"Ah." Rupert was relaxing and expanding into a gradual realization of his good fortune. "Well, well," he said pleasantly, "so then she plans to return tomorrow?"

"Tomorrow morning. Right. But she said to tell you she might be delayed here a bit to make up appointments she had to cancel by going to Boston. She said to tell you she'll be staying with Eunice at the Fifth Avenue Hotel. 'For a bit,' she said."

"Oh indeed."

"Uh-huh. But she'll be in touch with you. You'll hear from her. I know she'll call you tonight."

"Did she say she would?"

"Well no. But she would, wouldn't she?"

Yes she would, Rupert thought as he put the receiver gently down. He felt uncomfortable. It wasn't like Anne at all. None of this was like Anne. He was shaken. But then, gradually, he felt relief, and began to smile broadly, and was ashamed of himself for smiling.

But then the reprieve he felt began to be spoiled by more flurries of unsureness about Anne. She hadn't called. It was a quarter to eight and she had not called. And tomorrow, instead of coming home, she was staying in New York. For a bit!...

Now, suddenly, he understood. He cleared his throat raucously, making a long-drawn-out sound of it. Then he took his hand and wiped it hard across his mouth. "So," he announced aloud, in tones of bitterness, relief, pique, finality, fear, "that makes everything easier, doesn't it."

Yet his heart soared as he walked away from the telephone. He did his wordless swagger from side to side, smiling idiotically. He felt truant, yet free too; real, matching Syra's realness. He felt light as air. Guilty as a boy playing hooky, and just faintly, silly.

He sat down in a chair by the round table. He saw suddenly that the other chairs were all empty. This seemed tragic to him, and caused his joy to drain away. A faint perfume stole to him from the white lilacs in the center of the table, saddening him overwhelmingly. He leaned abruptly forward and struck a match and lighted the candles on either side of the lilacs and whipped out the match. Then he sank back in his chair, and brought both hands slowly down flat onto the tabletop, quietly. It was all too much for him. He wouldn't go any further tonight.

There was comfort in the feel of the smooth cool tabletop, which was permanent and reliable and which couldn't do anything to him. He closed his eyes and let his hands rest on the table, absorbing the comfort and inactivity of cool friendly wood. Finally, in a few minutes, from complete exhaustion, his head tipped forward onto his chest, and he slept.

❧ II ❧

THE morning was interminable. But finally it was twelve-thirty, and then twelve-forty. At twelve-fifty, thought Rupert, who dealt with time decimally, I'll start out.

He did not feel well. He had lain sleepless for most of the night, and after dozing off toward dawn and sleeping for perhaps two hours had waked precipitately to a gray, still day–a change in the weather that emphasized the change in his life. This morning he could not encompass the changes with any equanimity at all, or with any plan, and while he was often shot through with hot lances of ecstacy, he was for the most part nervous and bewildered and tired.

He couldn't eat. He couldn't put his mind to his work. He did chore after small chore, grateful for them. He drank too many cups of coffee. He performed elaborate, lengthy ablutions. He washed his hair, and found that it wouldn't dry because of the dampness of the air, and sneezed, and worried about sneezing. He listened constantly for the telephone to ring, Anne's call, wanting it and not wanting it. He watched the kitchen clock. And finally the black clawlike minute hand, with a teasing deliberateness that enraged him, moved and settled on the time he wanted to see–twelve-fifty. Ten minutes to one!

He set off down the driveway, his heart pounding. When he got to the mailbox he was suddenly seized with such desire for Syra that his legs turned boneless, and he felt unsteady and faint and had to lean against the mailbox for support. He loved the sensation; was there any sensation to compare with it? He'd forgotten

314

how wonderful it could be. And to have it at this age, at this time of life!... But he was aggravated, too, because it was not an unalloyed sensation, because it had to be interlaced with fear and unfamiliarity and confusion. Why couldn't he be *thoroughly* happy?

The cool air moved his damp hair, and he sneezed again, explosively. He wondered briefly whether it was going to rain, but dared not let himself be diverted from his central obsession by irrelevancies. He could not look at the sky, or the trees, or the birds. He could only wait.

And wait he did. He never wore a watch, didn't own one, because he had complete confidence in what he thought of as his acute and unfailing sense of time. But after a while it struck him that he had waited for more than ten minutes, that it must be past one o'clock. Even long past one o'clock!

He felt a stab of concern. But then he reminded himself that his precious time sense had failed him this morning, and couldn't be trusted in this situation. Every time he had looked at the clock expecting ten minutes to have elapsed, only two or three had. He reassured himself, too, that Syra was casual about time, and was often late.

He fell to waiting again. But he was anxious now, unsure. And then, suddenly, he knew that something was wrong.

He began to shake, hating himself for it. He thought first of going to Mrs. Alexander's, but shied away from encountering her in his transparently fatuous state. Then he decided to go back to the house and call Syra from there, though he felt a faint panic at the thought that as he entered the house the telephone might start to ring, and it would be Anne. But he could not just let it ring and not answer it, because it might be Syra. No, he could not go back into the house.

He decided to go to Mrs. Alexander's.

He squared his shoulders and settled his face into impassivity, and set off up the hill grandly, slowly, and with a great show of casualness for his own benefit, since his heart had begun to pound again absurdly.

Mrs. Alexander, from her desk by the upstairs window, saw Rupert coming up the drive. Like the pope, she thought, he walks like Pope Paul. Only the pope's skinnier. She had just gotten back from driving Syra to the station, and had settled down to paying bills in order to take her mind off everything that sooner or later she was going to have to assimilate.

There was a sudden spat on the window pane, which shuddered. Rain. A threatening black cloud had materialized, was racing toward being presently overhead, and she saw Rupert glance up at it with a quick, timid look, and then compress his face and begin to walk faster. She sighed. She took the letter from the top of the desk, where Syra had left it, and rose, and passed her hand down her front as a way of bracing herself, and then hurried briskly out of the room and downstairs to let him in before Bernice could get to the front door ahead of her.

As she reached the foot of the stairs, she heard the shepherd and shepherdess clock in the upstairs hall strike one-thirty, and she felt an impatience with it, and a queer compassion for Rupert. What effrontery from those two, in their mannered simpering dalliance, to announce that the hour of Rupert's tryst was past; that it was never to be.

She walked along the hall to the front door, and stood waiting, her arms resting across her stomach and the hand that held the letter placed quietly in the other palm. She felt a certain composed dread but a mild excitement too, and she hoped that neither would show.

❧ III ❧

"CAT got your tongue?" Ava, shorthand pad in two hands, pencil stabbed into the hair over her ear, hovered over Anne, who was sitting at her desk, still as stone.

"What time is it?"

Ava twisted her wrist, glanced down. "It's twelve-twenty."

"Only twelve-twenty?" She felt she had been sitting here for a century. It seemed to her it was in another era that she had walked out of Dr. Lovelace's office, and waited on the curb for a cab, and waited in the lobby of this building for the elevator, and walked into this office, and sat down in this chair. But it had been only twenty minutes. How was she to deal with time?...

Ava put down her shorthand pad and went over to the bookcase along the wall. Under the reproduction of a green Cézanne forest, a decanter of sherry stood on a tray with four little gold-rimmed glasses. Ava unstopped the decanter and poured sherry into one of the glasses. "I think I'll have some too," she muttered, and scowling, filled another glass. "Here. Drink this," she ordered, coming back to Anne with glasses in both hands. "Drink up," she commanded. She began to sip her own, but then she set the glass down hard, and dug into her skirt pocket for her package of cigarettes. The hand that held a lighted match to a cigarette, shook.

"Thanks, dear." Anne studied the glass. Then after a moment she reached out a hand and picked it up. After holding it, studying it some more, she brought it to her lips, tilted her head way back, and poured the sherry down her throat in three long swallows. She put the empty glass back on the desk. "Sit down," she said to Ava. She could feel the warmth of the wine seeping down into her stomach. She felt its glow fade down into her abdomen, she could feel warmth spreading *there*, spreading in the fullness of all that was *there*, she could feel it expanding like rays of sun around the presence there of her womb. Oh the beauty of its being there, the beauty of this full, warm abdomen. And three weeks from today there would be nothing there.

She began to shake. She drew a long breath to try to steady herself. "You obviously see I've had a shock," she said, and she turned stricken eyes to Ava.

"Bad news, was it?"

"Very. I have to have a hysterectomy."

"Cancer." This wasn't a question, it was a statement. Ava's non-quibbling eyes searched Anne's.

"No. Oh no. It's for the hemorrhaging. Medication doesn't cure it."

"Well *baby*," Ava cried, and relief loosened and lighted her face, "then that's *nothing*. It's only a nonscary *operation*, baby."

Anne pulled up a long breath and thrust out her chin. She made a movement with her lips that tried to be a smile. "Well," she said. "Yes," she said. And then with great effort, searching for her bright tone, she said, "Of course that's so. But it's been a shock. It was a great shock. No woman likes to lose her uterus. That's the thing really. That's the bad thing." For a second her face was convulsed. "Particularly when you've never used it." Her voice was strangled, holding back tears. "Yes."

Ava got up, she scrubbed out her cigarette, she came over to Anne and stepped behind her, and she put her arms around Anne and brought her head down to rest her cheek against Anne's cheek. "Cheer up, baby," she whispered. "You'll get over feeling this way. Betcha. Everything passes. That's what you're always telling *me*."

The warmth of Ava's young body, the ripeness and the readiness of her promising fortunate young femaleness, flowed into Anne like the most punishing poison, she could feel the triumph of young ready womb and breasts pour into her own body where already there was nothing, where already there was emptiness and sterility and shriveling aging uselessness. But she clung to this blood and breath of femaleness, she clung to the love that was pouring, along with it, into her starvation.

She put her two hands over Ava's, and she whispered, "My dear daughter. What would I do without you?"

❧ IV ❧

"I don't like letters!" Rupert spoke aloud, contemptuously, into the silence. On the marble top of the coffee table, at the height of his knees, the letter lay.

The house was still.

Anne had not come back. Anne had not telephoned.

It was Friday noon. Wednesday night's stillness had accumulated into a greater volume of stillness that was Thursday's more menacing stillness, and the ominous suspension of sound all day Thursday had gathered into a silence by Friday noon that had become to Rupert like an alive pernicious presence that he was living with and listening to, a presence which told him now, conclusively, what the nature of this silence was. Anne had left him. Syra had left him.

"I don't like letters," he said aloud again, wanting the sound of his voice. And he was impressed by the authenticity of those words, and of his voice. "Letters are obfuscating, and they are cruel. Cruel. Letter writers are snipers. Letter writers are cowards." He was still outraged by the letter that lay blandly on the coffee table, the small envelope with Syra's round, strong *for Rupert* written across it. She didn't dare face me and she let herself down and she let me down, because she thought neither of us could take it... This sounded impressive to Rupert, and gave him a short moment of self-admiration.

Sun, which had poured through the east windows of the living room earlier in the morning to fill it entirely, had now receded from the coffee table and the red velvet loveseat upon which Rupert sat, leaving that part of the room sunless. The long red velvet couch in front of the east windows was richly ruby still, and would be, lesseningly, for another few minutes. Beyond it stretched a lawn that was very green in the bright sun. A robin tugged at its worm. Tugged some more. Is anyone ever sorry for worms? Rupert wondered numbly.

A cup drained clean of coffee stood on the table, and a plate with a few crumbs, remnants of Anne's toasted bread which Rupert, with a flush of visceral panic, had characterized to himself as "a satisfying mouthful" as he ate it, and which he had tasted this time in the same discovering and worshipping way that he had when Anne had first begun to bake it for him. Today, one piece of this toast had not been enough, and he had gone back to the kitchen to make another. He was hungry, he couldn't seem to stop wanting to eat. The second sleeping pill had clubbed him into sleep, and he had waked up near noon feeling euphoric and calm in a cottony way. The complexity had been taken out of everything—the sun was bright and he was calm; all very simple. And downstairs, in the kitchen, he was hungry.

There were the bookcases made from the driftwood he had gathered that summer in Nantucket. He had all the time in the world to sit here and do nothing, and look at his driftwood walls. His? Theirs? Terror pierced him for a second. The other loveseat, and the big couch that was losing the sun, and the Italian chairs along both sides of the Italian dining table over by the wall–all these seats were not leading the life they were supposed to be leading, yet they had an animate dignity and cheer and persuasion, as though declaring that they were only temporarily vacant, and soon would be filled again. Rupert felt this.

In the bedroom, the white lilacs on the table beside the bed, which on impulse Rupert had brought in from the kitchen last night, had begun to drop and to scatter tiny white browning flowerettes onto the tabletop and over the rumpled pillow. The bed was unmade. Last night he had not gone up the stairs to his dreaded celibate bed but had crept with terror and seeking comfort into this bed, their bed, where, however, a terrible bout with *timor mortis conturbat mē*, was no easier to deal with.

The sun did not reach this room, since it faced west, until early afternoon. The covers were dragged across the bed and onto the floor, testimony to a hellish night, and such disorder seemed out of place in the neat and churchly white of this serene room. Rupert had created this room. Anne loved it. White lilacs were at home in it. Anne's silver brush and comb, and the silver-topped cut-glass jars of several sizes that had been her Swedish mother's, lay on the scalloped and embroidered dressing-table scarf that had been Rupert's mother's. Two gray hairs in the comb caught the light. A blue jay smote the great glass window, which reflected the sky, and in the living room Rupert jumped.

A cup and a plate are beautiful fundamental things, Rupert thought in his detached euphoria. The euphoria did not emanate from him but from the pill's removal of the fullness of his anxiety, and there was a peculiar numb spot on the top of his head, toward the front. He was beatifically without involvement. And in shock. Yet clear thoughts could appear in his

mind and throughout him, and he had been once or twice calmly pleased by them. Now he thought, almost gratefully: There is
something very wrong, something very wrong indeed. The quiet
of the house, and the quiet of himself, lent this recognition
great weight. It seemed so easy to him to say it and to know it.
It felt peaceful to know it.

He cleared his throat, and brushed white crumbs detachedly
from the front of his black sweater. His eyes were gaunt and
peaceful, staring off at nothing. He wondered whether there was
not, after all, comfort in being alone, and wondered how the
terror of yesterday's aloneness could have changed today into a
kind of melancholy comfort at being alone. The letter on the
table made a clamor he didn't want. Neither Syra nor Anne is
my answer, he thought peacefully, neither one of them. He
sensed that this was a quiet he needed very much, a quiet that
was the absence of *behavior*, of the strain of "relating." Anne's
word... That was the thing about Syra, he thought peacefully,
there was so little strain.

But how could Syra have left me? he thought with a sudden
flareup of anguish that reminded him of how alive that anguish
was. The answer, he assured himself distastefully, was that Syra
was someone who sailed in, then sailed out, another breed,
promiscuous, without probity. She'd ditched a husband, lost a
beloved cousin, and seduced a married man she'd known only
five weeks, all in that short time. She bore no relationship to
that cup and that plate, eternal symbols of nurturing, and to the
red couch with the sun slipping away from it, where people had
sat and should always sit, in a caring kind of social communion
with one another, teacups, drinks in their hands, responsible for
one another, upholding something and keeping this kind of
thing up. Syra was irresponsible, and she brought destruction.
Perhaps she had even brought it, in some way, to Lewis. Syra
would never be responsible to anything or anyone but herself. It

was all there in her letter, in that flip sentence, "It was the perfectly right thing for me at that moment, was it for you?"

He reached for the letter and opened it. Then he sniffed and flung up his head, his eyes cold, his face hurt and haggard and helpless, and wondered why he must read it again. He put it down on the couch beside him. Then he remembered that that was where Syra had been sitting the night of Lewis's service. Only a letter, a piece of paper there now, where her warm, strong behind had been. He could feel those firm loaves in the cups of his hands as he pressed her up into him in that last moment as though he would seal the two of them together forever.

He made a helpless, awful little sound. It can't be true, he mourned, it simply...can't...be...true. He opened his eyes, and with an avid, humiliated expression, picked up the letter.

Dear Rupert,

This morning I woke at 4:30, and wept a thimbleful of tears, and then drifted around the house following the moon from window to window. This is the second letter I've written you since then. The first had to be in the scrapbasket. Even I couldn't figure out exactly what I was trying to say. But now I do know what that is. I mean what I have to say to you is that I think I'd better go now, instead of a week from now, because I have the feeling it won't do for you and me to go on making love any more. I don't usually take it upon myself to decide what is good for someone else. But now I'd really better. I don't know enough about you, or your life, or about myself to know what I'd be doing to you by our making love in the woods every day for a lot more days. I feel in my bones—the only place where I really know what I know—that it was a *once* for us, and must be left that way. I loved our lovemaking. I'll never forget it. It was the perfectly right thing for me at that moment. Was it for you?

You've helped me back to living again, every day we've walked. And yesterday was, literally, the climax of the good thing that grew between us. I wonder if that's what I'm trying to say about leaving today—that what we had, had its climax yesterday. And if we made love today, and tomorrow, it would be the beginning of something else, something mixed-up and mistaken, and, heavens, I know it would be a kind of pointless, hurtful thing, for everyone. And leading to what?

I hope your life will be filled with all blessings, even extra ones than those I am thinking of.

Oh Rupert, I feel as if a cloud hung over me, but I would rather it did, than not. In other words, I mean adoring you is worth paying for.

Good-by. I must leave with a part of me unsung.

Syra

"Right thing at the moment, was it for you," indeed! How ruthlessly she assumed that everything was as simple for him as it was for her. Rupert tossed the letter away from him.

Suddenly he had been sitting here long enough. He jumped up in a nervous way, and went out of the living room and down the hall and into the welcome blaze of a sun-filled kitchen. Without thought, he took a bucket and a scrubbing brush and a bar of brown soap from the broom closet, and went across to the sink and filled the bucket with hot water, then got down on his hands and knees and began to scrub the sunny floor. For the next hour he scrubbed, vigorously and passionately, thinking numbingly of Syra, and of the white of the cleaned wood and the warmth of the suds in the pail and the sensation of the effort of scrubbing in his arms and his shoulders.

The pill had worn off and he was restless, jerky as a live wire. He took his corduroy jacket out of the closet, hanging in its darkness beside Anne's gray-and-white tweed coat with the cuff button missing. Anne!...

He hurried out of the house, with its packed echoes of himself, with its telephone not ringing with Anne's call, or with anyone's call, and with the thin white envelope of Syra's letter, which seemed in an outsize way to fill and to dominate it like Alice grown into a giantess–his house, vacant in the most silent and lifeless kind of way, and yet flooded to overflowing with the vibrations of his own misery. As he closed the kitchen door he wondered if he could ever again get down on his hands and knees to scrub the white floor without seeing the knots and grain of it as Syra's hair, Syra's eyes, a bit of violet leaf on Syra's tooth, without seeing and feeling everything about her as his and now no longer his.

He got into his Volvo and drove explosively away, but then he saw almost at once that all of nature was beautiful and dreadful and had removed itself from him as his house had, that it was no longer his, it was a scene and he was dead to it. He drove to the village with a set face, but once there, he had no heart for marketing, and though he knew he should, he could not bring himself to buy food that no one would cook and that, stacked in the refrigerator and on shelves in a vacant house, would have no usefulness. For a moment, passing the A&P, he ached for the homely normalcy of emerging from there with his arms full of bulging paper bags.

He drove for hours, anywhere, everywhere, because it was better than going home and because he was afraid to go home. He went to a car-wash place and had the car waxed and washed, he stopped for gasoline, having gone way out of his way to find a Shell station, he had the tires checked, he went into a shoe-repair shop and got a shoeshine, a thing he never did, he stopped for fried chicken at a Chicken-in-the-Basket place and then later stopped in a drugstore for a frosted chocolate, buying at the same time a new toothbrush and a bottle of aspirin and a Milky Way. He went to the library and found three Agatha Christies he hadn't read, and also sat down at a table and leafed through a pile of new magazines without seeing what he was looking at. On the way home he stopped the car on Ogilvie lookout, and sat for an hour or so, with the radio going softly, looking off into space, eating his Milky Way. He dozed.

When he awoke, the sun was lowering. He listened to the lift and drop of a robin's bubbling song. He felt a difference in himself, a shifting of intensities and of focus, as though a change had been going on in him in which preoccupation with Syra had become smaller and concern about Anne had become larger. Syra was an ache, but dulled now, a melancholy rather than a gouging pain. She was lost. Gone. He would have to assimilate this fact. It was time to stop despairing, and to start thinking, for distanced from her letter, he was now beginning to admit and to feel its sincerity and its beauty.

He felt evening, the weariness of the day's end, he felt the cycle of the day's beginning and its ending. Immutable. The sun rises and the sun sets. He was an aging man and the dawn of his life was a long way back and now it was evening and he wanted to go home.

In the gold and shadowed evening light, the house had the cumulative stillness of a house long empty. The evening commotion of birds outside only increased this vacuum of silence.

Rupert went numbly from one room to the other, as though seeking something. The kitchen was clean looking, clean smelling, empty, and the Regulator clock ticked dutifully for no one, lonesome as an old guard in the silence and emptiness of a museum room. The fire in the living room was stacked with logs and ready to be lit. The room waited, composed and integrated and hospitable, ready for the social communion it existed for.

The bedroom was softly, grayly white, though with a luminosity from the afterglow of the sunset toward which it faced. The mess of the unmade bed, tangled blankets, crumpled sheets, had no place in its serenity, though it gave some life to the room, and seemed to declare vulgarly that it was the clue to the misery in this house. His study upstairs was awful, too full of himself, of his words and his thoughts and his moods and his fears, too full of everything he knew about himself.

And he did know everything about himself.

He stood on the threshold of his room, of himself, and felt that he was a shapeless but dense certainty that knew everything about himself. He knew that this shapeless but substantive certainty was rooted and unmovable and unchangeable. And he said to himself, that's what it's all about. That's the trouble...

He turned away from it, and came back downstairs. He hesitated in the dark hallway, since there was no room without threat, and where should he go now? But here was Anne's study, with its door open.

A greenish, dark, intense light filled the square little room with its one wall of glass. Rupert went to the desk and sat down at it. Anne's chair... He noticed with a clearness and a shock of feeling that everything in this room was an imitation of him. Had he always known this?... A group of five stones was arranged on a flat piece of driftwood, touchingly stiff and inartistic. He reached over and scooped the stones off, and held them in his palms and studied them for a moment. Then he selected two, a white one and a black one, and put them on the piece of driftwood, the black one in the center, the white one just off center an inch away from it. This good shape and composition and balance gave him a faint satisfaction.

Anne's chair... The warmth from his own backside seemed to become Anne's warmth. It was impossible to sit in the curves of her chair and not feel her curves, and it was impossible to run his palms over the smoothed-to-satin arms of it and not feel her palms to be the palms that had rubbed these arms to smoothness.

He was shaken with a wild sadness, and a yearning toward this woman he had put away from him, whose separateness and difference this desk and this chair and this arrangement of stones proclaimed. He put the five stones back on the piece of driftwood and scrambled them all together. Even that way, he thought sadly, they looked better than the way she had meticulously, and not from anything in herself, arranged them. Poor Anne. This was terrible. How had this come about? But hadn't he always noticed, and been flattered to be copied? At the moment he thought he didn't want it.

What would it be like, he began to wonder, shifting in the warmth of her chair and feeling as though he were contaminating her by such thoughts, what would it be like if Anne had not had to worship him, and if he had not wanted her to? What if she didn't worship him one minute and boss him the next? Just suppose she didn't, just suppose she treated him the way Syra treated him.

What would it be like?... He set a little scene for himself: Anne was walking beside him down the fields and into the woods on a May morning, and she was saying to him, "You look tired, Rupo." She said it cheerfully, without grasp, or without some kind of intent.

"Oh I am. I don't sleep." He said this calmly, without intent too, without a sense of the importance of himself, and feeling free because he didn't want, and wouldn't get, pity from this Anne.

"I wish you did." She said this quietly, as Syra had said it, and her noninterfering way of saying this left him stronger, more real, just as Syra's way of saying it had. It was a calm, free, strong, and uniquely close feeling–this Rupert walking along beside this Anne, two people letting each other alone.

She was enjoying the air and the birds and the trees and the flowers in a matter-of-fact way, not with poetic rapture. Her pure sharp white profile was tilted against the blue sky, it was alive with interest, but it wasn't proclaiming this, wasn't making anything out of it. He, too, was refraining from poetic rapture. He imagined, and even felt, the two of them walking along this way, felt himself keeping to himself, and as a result, the world, and Anne, more visible. The image was so real that he actually began to feel Anne, and to feel himself, as "hands off" each other, and to feel the May morning in an unusually distinct and appreciative way since it was not distorted by the expressive imagination of either of them.

Rupert sighed, and reached abruptly to turn on the desk lamp, for the room was melancholy in the deepening dusk. His fantasy had strengthened him. Some of the load and the pain of Syra had faded away. It seemed that a being together of an Anne and a Rupert without their demands could give him something of the experience he had had with Syra. Ah, Anne is right, he thought wearily and yet with a certain fortified complacency—vanitas, semper vanitas. That is me. I don't really want her to build me up into something I'm not. Or do I?

Suddenly he felt stifled. He cleared his throat in a kind of groan, and in need of action, or release, snatched from the desk a Jensen silver paper knife that had been Anne's father's. The pebbly silver transmitted hereditament to his fingers in such an electric way that Anne and her childhood were suddenly alive in him.

He dropped the knife with a metal clatter in the stillness of only himself in this room, in the stillness of this whole empty twilit house, where the cold fires he had carefully laid two days ago had not been lit. In that distant dark living room, a fire would be leaping and crackling now if all were as it had always been. There would be a light in the kitchen, and pleasantly mingled cooking odors. And sounds. The snap and the tiny busy explo-siveness of something broiling. Anne's footsteps, back and forth, back and forth. The refrigerator door opening, then closing.

Restlessly, he flipped open a leather folder fat with papers, not out of curiosity over what was inside, for he was not a prying man, but only because his hands were responding automatically to his inner pressures. At first he glanced unseeingly at what lay there. Then his heart gave a great clap of fear, for a letter to himself stared up at him. Unreasonably, he thought he was looking at a farewell letter–she hadn't come home, hadn't called, she had left this for him to find.

Then he read the first line and immediately knew how absurd his fears had been. He picked up the sheaf of papers–a carbon copy of the letter clipped to yellow pad sheets apparently much worked over with a red pencil and also addressed to him, he saw. It rattled distressingly in his shaking fingers, and he put it down on the desk to do away with that. It seemed to him like a heav-en-sent communication, and like a living presence in this dead house at last, and he was awed and impressed by its timeliness. Alert, revived, he set upon the typed letter first, his lips parted and his eyes sparkling and with a kind of eager curious delight, like a child with a Christmas package.

He read the short letter through quickly, startled; and then once more. Dead? Anne dead? "Being as I am, dead," "cremat-ed," "obituaries," "guilty bereaved," "predecease my husband," "'Rage, rage against the dying of the light...'" He was stunned, sickened, by all these morbid images of death she had conjured up for him. *Timor mortis conturbat mē* bludgeoned his mind again. He felt clubbed in the forehead by those big black iron words.

Compelled to, but now uncomfortably depressed by this dis-cussion of death, he flipped the typed pages over and started in on the handwritten yellow ones. He read with growing anguish these worked-over pages, these crossed-out lines. He finished the last page.

His hands were shaking as he flipped the turned pages back into place, and let the sheaf of them drop to the desk, and pressed his hand down on top of it as though he would silence it, as though he could hold the reality of it away from him with his hand. For minutes, stupefied, there was nothing in him but incredulity.

But gradually his stunned heaviness livened into a listening. *What have I done to you?...* He heard her letter speak. *Why do I feel that it was my voice that decided us?...*

Rage blasted up through him, brutal rage. He wanted to strike her down. He wanted to howl, to beat his fists on *her* desk, the cruel potentate's desk. This room destroyed him, this chair of hers felt like a poison to this flesh of his that she had ruthlessly, powerfully, for her own selfish purposes, denied fatherhood to. It was monstrous.

For a long time, hours it seemed to him, he sat unmoving, colossal with raging hatred, powerful with it. Hatred raised him way above Anne now, he was huge, righteous up here, and she was little, cruel, evil, down there. At the same time he felt that this was the most awful sensation he had ever had in his life, and he knew that he could not endure being with it. Justified hatred pounded in him and swelled him to enormity, and yet he knew that he hated hatred, and would have to end it.

Gradually the rage drained out of him, leaving at last a vacuum. He began, then, to be overwhelmed with sorrow. He closed his eyes over the tears in them. He pressed two fingers to his eyelids to keep the tears from oozing out, and spilling down onto the page. Oh God, he said to himself, the pathos of this, writing it all out for me and then being too ashamed and too guilty to show it to me.

331

Ashamed? Guilty? Anne ashamed and guilty? Proud and powerful Anne Knight, brisk and bossy Anne Knight, unsure of herself?

Yes, back there she had said it. Or had she? He picked up the sheaf of papers in disbelief and scrabbled through the pages until he came to what he was looking for. He read it again, slowly, painstakingly. "The sorrow and the guilt have never left me, yes, guilt at feeling wrong, deeply even cruelly wrong." And further on, "So here I sit, ashamed of myself."

Anne ashamed of herself? Anne knowing herself to be lacking? *Anne Knight unconvinced?* It was shocking to Rupert to know this, in fact he couldn't know it, couldn't believe it, at first. How could he know Anne this way, when he'd always known her to be the very compelling opposite? He truly couldn't believe it. And yet she opened up suddenly to him as human. He was so relieved. They were together.

And then he knew, in a second's clarity, that he and Anne had from the beginning been together in a way that allowed for no dilution by a child, that they hadn't come together for the purpose of Anne's mothering a child, but for the purpose of Anne's mothering him. And also didn't he really know, he thought, aghast and humiliated, that he would never have gone to work instead of Anne, never have given up staying home in order to write.

Yes. Their childlessness was as much his fault as Anne's. They were reduced to this same low common denominator. They shared this same base fault, and it felt like the strongest and most promising bond he had ever had with her. Which didn't soften the fact that she had committed a crime against him by not giving him the chance to say yes or no to their child. That was forever unforgivable. He could never feel the same way about Anne again. Never. Anne could be brutal–she had brutalized him with words on the day of Lewis's funeral, and she had brutalized him long before that with a terrible deed.

He lifted his head and raised suffering and contemplative eyes to the ceiling. In the angle of the wall and the ceiling was a cobweb securing several black specks that were no doubt the little carcasses of insects that had been caught in it and died there, and that had probably been there all winter long. Irrelevant. Just there. That's the way it is, he thought. He felt a melancholy comfort. He felt that the jangling spears, the battle hymns, the rallying to advance, to conquer, all this razzle-dazzle tumult and shouting of his and Anne's, had somehow fallen crash through the floor and been silenced.

He put his elbow on the desk and sank his forehead into a helpless hand, which gave support and a feeling of the warm living contact of himself, and a kind of comfort to his head, which was weightedly full of the mess and the helplessness of himself and of his proud and powerful and ashamed wife.

But now, slowly, interestingly, his head began to clear toward a simplicity, a single strong sense-thought that suffused him and had a just-born newness to it. He had never felt this before.

He cared about Anne.

He examined this new infiltration—it had been such a clear-cut physical sense of something happening that it had indeed felt like something coming into him from without—and knew that it was entirely new, and he was awed by the solidity and complacency and uneventfulness and the sense of a fact, come to stay, that he felt in knowing something surely, and without any doubt. He cared what happened to Anne. Every other thought fell away, and there was no confusion in him. It was just as simple as that. He cared what happened to Anne, what happened to her, and toward her. He did not want her to suffer because of herself, or because of him. He wanted her to be beyond the suffering of unfulfillment, and arrived in that happy land of knowing the truth of herself that she was now playing such impossible games with in her letter. "There is a happy land,

333

far, far away..." The past sang in him like a gentle taunt. Promises, promises. There is a happy land, yes, but not the kind the hymn promises. There is a happy land, all right, and he had always really known there was. He wanted that happy land just as much for himself as he wanted it for Anne. He wanted it for both of them. But how in God's name, he marveled, did you get there? Syra wasn't here any longer, to lead him there.

Where was Syra?... Tears filled his eyes. She felt close, as though she had not gone.

He lifted his head sharply because of a sense of something, a shift in the density and total silence of the house. A faint sound had come to him, and possibly the faintest refreshment as of cool air coming in through a just-opened door. Then he heard a real sound, the kitchen door closing. And at the same moment he saw a distant glow flare up, the kitchen light being switched on. Then he heard footsteps, Anne's brisk footsteps, tapping across the kitchen.

And then she stood in the doorway.

PART EIGHT

&a &a &a &a &a &a

THE October day began with rain and moist warm air, but in midmorning the sky lightened and the northwest wind came in with a clear and cool suddenness that blew the sweet freshness of Mrs. Alexander's new-mown back fields toward the house and through the open window of her upstairs sitting room, where she sat self-disciplined and uninterested, doing a crossword puzzle. She was expecting Syra today at noon, and she couldn't put her mind to anything.

She looked up gratefully as the change in the weather became apparent to her. The curtains at the open window lifted, swelled, collapsed, and the smell of mown sun-warmed damp field grass invaded the room. She shivered in the sudden coolness and rose reluctantly to close the window against the spirit-lifting fragrance of those cut fields, though she was glad of a little something to do.

She was dressed with particular care today. She wore a navy-blue light-weight wool dress and jacket, and a choker of pearls, and her navy-blue oxfords that had just been resoled, given a new lease on life, as she put it. Her hair, which she had had done yesterday in Deer Valley, was softly waved, and too blue. "She *will* do that," Mrs. Alexander muttered, glancing in the mirror with resignation. She looked once again, as she had done every few minutes in the past hour, out of the window down toward the road, and felt the breathlessness in her chest, and was annoyed. She was nervous, yes. Her anticipation of Syra's coming was a mixture of joy, of reserve, of doubts and lurid suspicions. The meeting last week with Heloise had disturbed Mrs. Alexander deeply, and she wasn't at all sure how she was going to react to Syra, or even how she was going to behave with her.

She clucked her tongue and told herself to stop imagining all kinds of things, and for gracious' sakes to be objective. She stood uncertainly by the window, looking out at the Norwegian maples along the drive, the edges of the leaves yellowing, drying, as though little slow, crisping, glowing fires were eating into the outlines. The sky was a silent burning blue. She felt the depth of light of this autumn day, and the sense of the suspension of time, and a great golden stillness as though the earth had stopped.

She loved autumn. Unlike most old women, she said to herself, and raised her chin.

She thought now, suddenly, of that day in May, five months ago, when she had kissed Syra good-by at the Deer Valley station, and she had a moment of longing for the way everything had been then, Syra here, Bernice here, the house down at heel and undemanding, not spruce the way it was now. She knew that the loss of Syra had affected her far more than she admitted, though she had adjusted to it. But the loss of Bernice she had not adjusted to, and she suspected she never would.

Bernice was gone. Her room off the kitchen had been converted into a laundry, to prevent another such accident as had befallen her on the cellar stairs. It was on her way down those stairs with an armful of clothes to be laundered that Bernice had fallen, her great body thudding down the dark stone steps and lying at the bottom cracked and limp.

She was permanently disabled as a result–she had broken a knee, a hip, and her pelvis–and had had to be put in a nursing home in Deer Valley, where she would spend the rest of her days. Mrs. Alexander visited her dutifully once a week, something she took in her stride, but with a growing abhorrence, for the shabby frame house smelled of old bodies, of bedpans, and of never-renewed, stale air, and the only sounds were querulousness and the incessant drone of the television. The lost, crepewhite faces, the vacant faces that fixed so avidly on her as she came in, the old eyes that looked out of the window at nothing–all this depressed Mrs. Alexander increasingly. But she went. Week after week. And would continue to.

The accident happened in July. Within two weeks a young Dutch couple had supplanted Bernice, and were now in residence in the apartment over the garage. Mrs. Alexander was glad to have a young, able-bodied man around. And glad of Margreit's youth, too. They waited on her quietly and deferentially but never volunteered to talk to her, though they chattered to each other incessantly and in high-pitched voices, in the kitchen. She liked their reticence, it reminded her of the old days when her mother's young Irish or Scotch or Finnish servants had "known their place" this way–wonderfully undemanding.

Margreit was pugnaciously clean, a stereotypical Dutch housewife. This gave Mrs. Alexander great satisfaction at first, for she liked to see this house clean and orderly and shining, as it had been in her parents' day, and in Billy's day. She had her house back. And yet, after the first flurry of satisfaction, excitement almost, at having the old ways back, she began to realize that the house didn't matter that much to her any more, and that she missed Bernice's sulky and devoted companionability, missed the desultory morning chats and evening television watched together. She soon grew to realize that there had been something remarkably relaxing about growing out of the obligation (and how imperceptibly it had waned), to have the house kept up to the mark as in former, energetic days, and that if she could she would have Bernice back, dust, sloth, bad temper, and all.

She wondered whether to go out and bring some tomatoes in from the garden, but then she remembered she'd done that yesterday. At that moment, as though telepathically, tomatoes simmering in Margreit's kitchen sent their autumnal, aromatic, pinching smell up the stairs and into this room, as though announcing lunch. Soup's on, Bernice would have bellowed, standing at the bottom of those stairs. The cream of tomato soup was for the lunch Mrs. Alexander hoped Syra would be in time for, although she knew there was no way of being sure how long a real-estate closing would last.

A wave of expectancy and excitement swept over Mrs. Alexander. She returned with a firm step to her chair, and, restlessly, opened a Florentine leather box on the table beside it, and took out her nail buffer, and set about polishing to a high gloss her short, ridged, bluish nails.

She was sitting in the sun in the wicker rocker by the verandah railing when she heard the crackle of tires on gravel, and looked up to see a dusty yellow car stopping at the foot of the steps. She arose, slowly, squaring her shoulders to compose herself. Syra had shut off the motor and was looking up. Her face was tanned and rosy and her eyes very clear. It was the calm intentness of that face, the lucid undemanding friendliness of Syra as she looked up, that swept away Mrs. Alexander's reservations at once.

Syra! She had forgotten Syra... All the suspicions she had

recently been distorting Syra with were suddenly nonexistent, and she sang out, "My dearest," beaming broadly, and hurried across the verandah and down the steps with her arms wide open as Syra was sliding across the seat and opening the door, and stooping out, with a smiling face turned up.

Syra stood. Mrs. Alexander saw. She caught her breath. And then with a spontaneity exaggerated by a determination to be spontaneous, she flung her arms around Syra and kissed her, too heartily, on the cheek. Against her own corseted rigid front she felt Syra's round soft mound of pregnancy and was unnerved. She made haste to step off from it, from the soft life of that mound against her own fortified and genteel flesh, but was nevertheless determined to stay with the conviction of loving, with the cautious joy she felt as she looked into Syra's face. "Well, well," she said, too brightly.

Mrs. Alexander knew! Syra's wide trusting smile faded slowly away. She had a moment of feeling lost. But how could Mrs. Alexander know? Well she couldn't, she said to herself. She couldn't possibly. It's just my being pregnant, she assured herself. She's embarrassed. And then she gave Mrs. Alexander a curious glance, amused and generous, though wary. I love her, she thought. And she said quietly, "I'm afraid I'm a little later than we thought I'd be. I hope you didn't wait lunch."

"My dear of course I waited lunch. I've been waiting for this lunch for weeks. You don't think I'd sit down by myself at that dressy table without you, do you? But now come in, dearest."

Syra came into the hall that was at once startlingly familiar—warm and alive and current as a friend just met after a long separation—and at the same time fastidiously aloof and strange, as though she not only didn't know it at all, but was being told that she had no right to.

There was the blue-and-gold Chinese runner. And a bowl of yellow marigolds instead of yellow tulips, on the table under the long mirror. It was unreal to be back here, like having a strange dream a second time. Its unrealness was stronger than its familiarity, which seemed to have taken on a life that was not related to her. She almost felt as though she'd never been here, and in a way, she hadn't, not the Syra who stood here now. Her feet felt the soft old rug and liked it, remotely, as in a dream. A figure leapt by her in a wild dance, down the long rug and out onto the porch, while Bernice stood in the darkness of the dining room, watching.

Then that whole May day beginning in this hall and flowing on toward the floor of a forest flashed suddenly into Syra, with the detail and compartmentalization of a Persian miniature in which life busies itself at all levels–its tiny vistas, its floral opulence, its central episode framed by other small squared-off, behind-the-scenes episodes. For a moment, Syra saw that May day in a similar depth and variety–the dramatic events of it moving against a background of towering green trees, and silver brooks, and bright-colored birds, and jewel-like flowers. The day smote her with its beauty and its totality, and its dreamlike pictorial quality. She parted her lips in amazement, turning her face away from Mrs. Alexander.

"You chose a beautiful day to come. Isn't it glorious? I love fall. It doesn't depress me like it does most old women," Mrs. Alexander was saying foolishly. "So, now you're finally out from under all the business of Lewis's house, I hope, all signed, sealed and delivered?"

"Oh yes. Except that I had cut out the clause about subdivision, which I'd decided on the way up would absolutely not do, and I was a fearsome person about it, Mrs. A. They tried everything short of thumb screws, but I would not give in, and pleased with myself I was. I told that Lawyer in whose office I undistinguished myself that he could put away his plans. And I went off in a cyclone, leaving them to think, well, she's on her way to nothing. Personally, I think I helped to lighten their morning by being such a dragon."

Mrs. Alexander, who knew how appealingly innocuous Syra's fearsomeness could be, said, "I'm sure you *made* their morning, my dear."

Syra dove her face into the bowl of marigolds. "Mmm. Spicy. I like that smell. Fall." She was feeling exposed and defenseless in these awkward preliminaries. "I guess the rain outpoured itself last night, and this vile humidity has grown sick of itself, as we have," she prattled. "Such wearying weather. The ancient Chinese were so right to feel that in hot weather it was bad manners to visit or be visited." She jerked her hair away from her neck in her characteristic gesture, and then she turned in a small stately way and directed a challenging and challenged and yet grave gaze at Mrs. Alexander.

This gaze brought Mrs. Alexander back to the Syra she loved. She saw the square-shouldered young woman with the searching eyes, the characteristically nondescript cotton tent of a dress sloping over the thrust-out mound beneath it, the feet, in the same old black ballet slippers, standing unsurely, hesitant with unwelcome.

She stopped fumbling with her pearls. She brought her hands down and composed them across her stomach. "Here I stand chattering away," she chided herself, "and you may want to freshen up, or rest. Are you tired, Piglet? In your condition?" Ah, she had managed to say it... "How do you feel dear? Utterly pooped after all that legal fol-de-rol?" She smiled with a fussy, embarrassed glowing smile. "Oh, it's just heaven having you here again," she said, truthfully, and for a moment, her squeamishness suppressed, she sensed in herself an added depth of feeling toward this enhanced and multiplied Syra. Dignified to begin with, Syra seemed to Mrs. Alexander further dignified by "childbearing." And this first function of woman seemed to have both humanized and depersonalized Syra, to have brought her down to some common fundamental level that made her more humanly particular, and at the same time more humanly general.

Mrs. Alexander was pleased and moved by this feeling, and enormously relieved, and because of this, suddenly her old, gay self. "Now c'm on, we'll go up and have a drink before lunch. Everything's ready up there. Ice and all." She lowered her voice to a whisper. "Wait'll you see the style I'm living in these days."

Settled in the rose velvet fireside chair with a glass of iced vermouth, Syra knew that she was not at ease. She couldn't find the old easy feeling toward Mrs. Alexander at all. This made her unsure, unhappy. She had kept Mrs. Alexander warmly and fondly in her all these months, as a kind of reliable beating second heart. "How is Bernice?" she asked gently. "That was an awful thing to have happen to Bernice, to fall down the stairs like that."

"Oh it was ghastly." Mrs. Alexander sipped her sherry. "Have one of those little cheese-spread things. That's one thing I miss Bernice for, she didn't use all these packaged things, 'I miss your divine pie crust, old dear,' I'm always telling her when conversation peters out, as it always does. Poor Bernice. She's awfully lonely in that depressing place, because nobody likes her very much which is no surprise. It's a hard way to have to live out your last days. I miss her, Syra, I really do. I know she was an awful old bore, but we were good companions. I really liked it a lot better than having these two efficient young things." She put her cut-glass goblet with its amber sherry down on the table beside her, and gave it a little shove. "The older you grow, the less all that sort of thing matters. At least to me." She looked toward the window with sprightly, fine, distant eyes. "What matters," she said as though to the blazing blue autumn sky beyond the window, "is a few close friends. And my garden. And the news on television. And good books. That's about all. It keeps narrowing down." She smiled faintly and humorously. "I wonder what it'll all narrow down to, in the last analysis? I hate having all my interests peter out like this. But now tell me, Piglet, about your ventures. I want to hear all about them. What's your house in Everglades City like?"

Syra described her house. And they went on to talk about this and that, surfacely, with a certain constraint. Mrs. Alexander gave Syra the news of the Road—Anne's operation, her long and harrowing recuperation, Rupert's saintly patience and devotion. Syra told Mrs. Alexander about her trip to Mexico for the divorce. "I feel as though I'd been to half the world," she said, "and then plunk, like an anticlimax, I land in Florida, of all places. But it suits me."

Beyond Mrs. Alexander's head, the yellow maple's great placid glow inspirited Syra, sent into her a melting rapture, which in turn allowed her to feel the velvet chair beneath her and the pleasure of her body sitting in it, and to remember sitting always in this chair during those May days. Those days and today fused into a nonspecific timelessness, and the Syra of then and the Syra of now were coordinated into a third and different Syra, into a surcease from either one of those women, into a nonconsciousness of them. She sat here pleasurably and feelingly, in a kind of identityless trance, savoring her body in the soft chair, and Mrs. Alexander's silver head, and the glorious maple beyond. The baby moved infinitesimally inside her, a sensation that had from the very beginning given her pleasure. She began to breathe peacefully.

"Well I'm sorry you didn't get your Caribbean island. What was the problem there, as Anne Knight would say?"

"The contrast of the haves and have nots, I guess. Everything so touristy, plus the poverty all around the tourists. I found it was something a person couldn't stand, it drove me up several walls, actually," Syra said, and she went on to tell Mrs. Alexander how stifled she had been by it, and how it had offset all the physical gains. She would have stayed in Barbados, she told Mrs. Alexander, where there were plantations high in the mountains, and a wild sea beach, but for the same strangling sense of tourism. And she had liked Tobago, where it was quieter and far less touristy, almost not touristy at all. But she hadn't been able to find a house. And anyway... Her voice lagged, then stopped.

And anyway, indeed, she thought. It was in Tobago that she had found out she was pregnant. She had been climbing the stone steps to the inn for breakfast, passing slowly and appreciatively the mass of jasmine on the bank beneath the dining room windows, when she had stopped, stunned, to be struck with the full knowledge of the coming together of two isolated facts which for the past week had had their own separate, nagging reiterations–she was three weeks overdue, and her breasts were tender. In one moment her whole life was changed. The scent of jasmine, and a green humming bird whirring and stabbing into it, were the perfume and the pulse of shock.

She couldn't absorb the fact of it for days. Because she had never conceived with Georges, she had gradually developed the conviction that she would never be pregnant. She felt she had met another self, a new self, with whom she would have to come to terms. She was appalled at first, frightened, sickened, fascinated. But when the baby moved in her for the first time, she was arrested, then stilled with a new pleasure, totally new. And then as the baby moved more and more, this alive thing became her companion, her own secret companion, hers and no one else's. It was strikingly pleasurable. It even alleviated her loneliness.

Mrs. Alexander picked up her glass and sipped from it, and, as though reading Syra's thoughts, looked searchingly at her.

"Did you never get lonely, Piglet? How is it for you, being alone?"

"I like it, most of the time. I don't feel very lonely, I guess. Not so much lonely as alone. Except in the evening. But enough happens so that a person doesn't get restless. I do let days slide away, and leave important things undone, of course. And oh, the air is benison, it is, it is. I have four pupils from Naples. That's thirty miles away. Two of them drive down to me because they like having lessons in my quiet house on the river. One of them, my sweet every-three-weeks Julian, has a beard and gives me big scratching kisses. And I've had concert engagements there, in Naples, I mean, and in Sarasota. And getting a few things for the house has taken up some time. It's nice inside. There's almost no furniture in it, and that's rapture. I know a few people. And there's a little library bus that canters all over the state, they've grown notable. So I read a lot. And Geneva Cleo keeps me company."

"Mercy, you could have had all of Lewis's furniture you wanted. You don't need to live in an empty house. Who is Geneva Cleo?"

"But I like living in an empty house. Geneva Cleo? She's the baby," Syra said.

"Where on earth did you get that name, my dear?" Mrs. Alexander exclaimed, wishing they could avoid getting onto the subject of the baby though she couldn't skip anything so intriguing as that name Geneva Cleo.

Syra reminded her about the baby sister who had died. Probably because of that name and her mother's love of it, she explained, she had never once thought of the baby as anything but a girl. The "Cleo," of course, was for her mother.

Mrs. Alexander made an exasperated sound with her tongue. "Good Lord, you did tell me that. This memory of mine, or rather, lack of it." She paused. "Well," she murmured, "it's certainly a name no one else will have." And then, because she was getting too near dangerous territory, she said rather hurriedly, "It's a crying shame you had to drive all the way up here. That's an exhausting trip, particularly if you have to do all the driving yourself."

"It got boring. Yes, a person doesn't enjoy droning along for all those hundreds of miles. Better than flying, though, which shrinks me into a fig of fright. And the thing about driving is, I've the car to take back all those cartons of Lewis's papers and valuables you told me are there, after I've moused through them. Simpler than wrapping them and mailing them. I hate wrapping packages. Though I can't imagine what I want with what's in them. Letters maybe. Maybe I'll be glad of them, I don't know. I'll go down later and get them." She was quiet a moment. "And say good-by to the house." Then she said, "Mrs. A., it was simply wonderful of you to do all the auction business for me. I can't thank you enough."

"Well actually there was almost nothing to it. Once Heloise and her nice young couple had carted off all the 'choice pieces,' as she called them, that perfectly terrible Mr. Runieff came in with his staff and took over completely, sorted, put into lots, put on display, and naturally ran the auction. He was the most offensive man. But he did a good job at the auction. Wasn't it fortunate Heloise brought that nice young couple out to look at the antiques, since they ended up by buying the house. And oh, I didn't tell you Heloise was crazy about the crewel bedspread. Remember that crewel bedspread? That ton of bricks? She said it was the one thing she wasn't going to let some customer have."

"Oh she did?" Syra imagined the heavy old coverlet on the double bed of Heloise and Georges, no doubt a treasure of an ancient bed, probably with a canopy. "Heloise Gachet," she murmured, tasting the name experimentally, as though it were foreign food.

Georges and Heloise... Syra had a vision of impermanent connubiality, as though two people were patching up each other's wounds but would eventually run out of bandages. And still, she thought she might not be right about this. Perhaps they had what each other needed. And what was that? she wondered. More, what good was that? Was marriage only a need?

"Piglet," Mrs. Alexander said abruptly, again echoing uncannily Syra's thoughts, "I would love to know that you'd met a nice man and were going to be married. That hasn't happened, has it dear?" she asked wistfully. "Because I do feel," she said, giving Syra a strong bleak look, "that a child needs a father. I know this is none of my business Piglet. But still, it would relieve my mind to know you planned to be married."

"I've thought about marriage a lot in the past months. Yes. Sure. A child should have a father." And then, warming to Mrs. Alexander's sudden warmth, she said, "But no, Mrs. A., I haven't met anyone. And you know, I've no idea how marriage as I see it all around me could be a means of a good kind of man-and-woman being together. But I tell myself that there must be a way. Oh dear, the new moon happened yesterday, and I have not yet crawled out from influence of old one, so my mind isn't working. Or maybe it was that wearisome closing that blasted it, because it's certainly filled, my mind, I mean, with a circus of things, or rather, a merry-go-round of things. Anyway, I think what I'm trying to say is that I'm beginning to think there might be something new and different that used a part of me not now in use, I mean with a man. Someone strong. Not weak. Someone who doesn't have to mesh with me all the time."

She turned privately away, uneasy about such confidences. She looked at the great placid glow of the maple beyond the window, a dazzle of yellow, like an area of sunlight. Slowly, in the faint breeze, single leaves detached themselves and floated, idled, down past the window, and then, in a burly faint gust, a golden shower of them fell together. A sense of her mother was brought to Syra by the sight and sound of this golden passage of time. And in a sudden burst of vision she knew that somewhere along the way she had let go of her mother's hand.

She felt both alerted and soothed by this extraordinary comprehension. She felt curiously interested, vaguely proud, a little frightened.

Then she thought she had been silly to have been embarrassed about confiding in Mrs. A.

"I wish I weren't so turned off about marriage, Mrs. A.," she said eagerly. "And yet, honestly I really have to believe that the fascination and oppositeness of man and woman is what makes the world go round. Well sure it makes the world go crazy, too. But I'll bet somehow that it's also what makes the world go ahead." She smiled, sipping her vermouth. "Maybe that's what Anne Knight would call 'wishful thinking,' I don't know."

With her lips on the rim of her glass, just then she remembered sitting in the courtyard café in Nassau with a cup of coffee in her hand, and seeing the boy and the girl across the street with their arms around each other and their oblivion to everything else in the world but themselves.

She closed her eyes for a second, and smelled a scarlet rose.

Suddenly, and with as vivid a perception as then, she knew that she had not, as she had believed, been witnessing loving only as a bulwark against loneliness. She had thought that the boy and the girl were clinging to each other because they knew they were born to be alone. But no. She felt now, absolutely, that she had been wrong, that that had been her entire view of loving then; but it was only partly her view of loving now.

For a moment she thought she saw that loving went beyond the need to cling together against the inevitability of aloneness. And that maybe two alone people could love more truly that two clinging people. Could it be, she wondered, that loving (unlike falling in love, of course), was something so simple, something so absolutely un-Romeo-and-Juliet-like, so unsplurgy, so under-wrought–not overwrought–that you didn't have a keeping-on *sensation* of it? Was love necessarily a way of being *toward* some-one, or was it simply a way of being? As she had felt with Rupert. And as he had so much wanted to, and had, she knew, felt with her. It had been a very remarkable thing–glittery because they set matches to each other, but at the same time calm and together, like two resting horses standing beside each other in a pasture. Oh yes, she and Rupert had been happily separate though happily together, long before making love, even. She didn't love Rupert in the sense of wanting him for a husband–he was someone else's and he was too old–but she loved *him*, she loved the *man* Rupert, the radiant, good, bursting-with-life and enormously attractive male; though she loved him only mildly, not in the deep gut way she had loved Lewis, but, well,–contentedly, she loved him. With a sure contentment. More than that was needed, she knew. It was not enough. But it had had its glow and its legitimacy, she could feel that this was so. And in feeling this, she realized she was glad that her child was, oh yes legitimately, Rupert's.

Syra sipped her vermouth and thought, and forgot to con-gratulate herself on thinking, and felt some power within herself that she had no name for.

Hearing Syra murmur "Heloise Gachet," Mrs. Alexander had been assailed by the memory of her conversation with Heloise. And now in Syra's long silence, she was overcome with the sus-picion and the dread that had been planted in her that day. "It's a crying shame Syra has to drive up all that distance alone in her condition," she had said unguardedly to Heloise. They were sit-ting in Lewis's two fireside wing chairs, facing each other amid bureau drawers laid bare, overflowing wastepaper baskets, card-board cartons waiting to receive whatever they would receive.

"What condition?" Sharply.

Mrs. Alexander had realized immediately that she had said something she shouldn't have. She could have covered up, easily, with a little fib about some other kind of physical condition, but something goaded her into saying, "Why Syra's going to have a baby." She couldn't bring herself to use the word "pregnant," since it was the clinical word, and therefore too realistic. "Perhaps I shouldn't have mentioned it," she said cautiously, shrewdly.

"*Pregnant!*" The word had exploded out of Heloise. And then, apparently completely taken off guard by the news, she had told Mrs. Alexander that it couldn't be Georges's child, since he had confessed to her that he was sterile. The disclosure had made Mrs. Alexander shudder with embarrassment.

In the next second she knew that Rupert was the father of Syra's child. Dredged up from the reservoirs of her suspicions, even her certainties, that something serious had gone on between Rupert and Syra that day in May, the knowledge that he was the father of her child smote Mrs. Alexander then with shocking force. She had subsequently often held her hand in front of her face and counted off the months on her fingers, then nodded her head judiciously and triumphantly, and with a shrinking-away from Syra. From Rupert, too. She had had a hard time being light and easy with Rupert since that day with Heloise. Yet often she would find some pleasurable little risqué comment coming into her mind, such as, I'll bet dollars to doughnuts that baby's going to have the great big black eyes of Rupert Knight.

"Syra, you haven't told Georges about the baby?" Mrs. Alexander said mendaciously, to her own surprise voicing the knowledge of this unappetizing fact and a driving curiosity about it; though essentially what she was trying to do without knowing it was to lead herself and Syra along with her, to openness. From the very first days of knowing Syra, Mrs. Alexander had been aware of the response in herself to this young woman's perspective. And now, prodded by this, she was pushing herself, perhaps not consciously, to meet Syra on an unconventional and somehow replenishing plane of frankness. "Heloise seemed stunned by the news," she said boldly. "I perhaps shouldn't have told her, I blurted it out without thinking."

"Oh." Syra seemed surprised. "Oh I see. You mean. Oh I do see. Heloise thought..." Her eyes, which had been indolently and pleasurably roaming the walls, flickered, then sharpened into stillness. Suddenly she put her glass down hard onto the table, so hard that the ice clattered. She lowered her head. Then without raising it, and looking out from under her eyebrows, she gazed defiantly and yet with a pleading candidness across at Mrs. Alexander. "It's not Georges's child," she said carefully. "There's no mistake. So he doesn't have to worry. I'll write him and tell him so, if they're worried about it." She raised her chin and continued to look clearly at Mrs. Alexander.

"Oh no, I don't think they're concerned in that sense," Mrs. Alexander said cautiously. Distaste and distress puckered her face. "Heloise told me out and out that Georges was incapable of having a child."

So that's it!... Syra was stunned. Why did he never tell *me*? Oh but, God, throw it away, it doesn't matter now. And Mrs. Alexander knows of course...

For a moment Syra panicked. Yet she managed to say, coolly, "I thought as much. But I would never quite admit it, since Georges wouldn't. Well!" She smiled with an indifference she didn't feel. "I'm glad for his sake he's got a woman he can confide in."

Syra drained the last sip of her vermouth. Then she brought the glass down to her lap and wrapped both hands around its coldness, and peered down into it. She saw ice, and thought

"Ice." Then speaking to the ice she said with great control, "My child is Rupert's."

The shepherd and shepherdess clock chose this moment to strike the hour of one, deliberately, crazily, it seemed to Syra, in order to accent her revelation to Mrs. Alexander of the momentous consequence of that one o'clock rendezvous with Rupert. The two women were silent. Syra looked into Mrs. Alexander's shocked eyes, the defiance and hardness of her face changing slowly into an intentness of such probing sincerity and trust that Mrs. Alexander's eyes wavered. She sat back, and looked away from Syra. The echo of the clock's chime hung in the air between them like an invisible bell, crystallizing and prolonging the difficult silence.

"Well," she said finally, turning to look full at Syra with cold, honest eyes, "I don't know what to say, my dear, except that I've suspected this. I belong to a different generation, where this sort of thing wasn't treated as it's treated today. Anyway," she said impatiently, "whether it's my generation, or it's just me, I find it all simply beyond me. Now look here Syra," she went on, "I'm very fond of you. I know you're a good woman, not a 'bad' woman, in that sense. I don't know, frankly, whether I'll ever get used to this situation of yours. I hope it won't matter to you too much. I hope it won't get in the way of our continuing to be friends. Because I don't intend to condemn you for it, Syra." She paused. Then in a quieter voice she said, "Does Rupert know?"

"No. Of course not." Shock had been growing on Syra's face during this pronouncement. "He must never know. That's why I set the closing for today, after you'd written me they were leaving for Europe yesterday. I mean, so we wouldn't have to meet, which would burn me up in bright flames. I suppose he may eventually find out from someone who's seen me this morning, but he may not connect it with himself, and anyway I can't do anything about it if he does, so I'll relax and hope it will last and

I won't get the broods. Why should he necessarily think it's his child anyway? Just the same, I hope he never finds out. I simply would not like to have his nice life all pulled apart like that."

"Are you very sure?"

"Very sure. What purpose would it serve?"

"I somehow feel he should know. That he has a right to know."

"Mrs. A.," coldly, "it would only torment him. And as for me, I have no need of Rupert. I don't love or want Rupert. Nor he me. There was never any thought of that."

"Well...of course it's up to you. Naturally. But now Piglet," she stood up briskly. "Let's forget all about this business. That was one o'clock and lunch will be ready."

Syra stood up, too. In spite of her knowledge that Mrs. Alexander could not be otherwise, she looked at her with eyes in which hurt vied with reproach. And she said bitterly, in a soft voice, "How can we forget all about it, Mrs. A.?"

"Well my dear, I know *you* can't." Frostily. "But *I* can try."

ᆇ II ᆇ

A crow sent its sharp call into space so dazzlingly stilled that the sound was drawn out into infinity and lost in it. A curtain of orange leaves sifted down past the bedroom window, giving a momentary golden darkness. Anne, bending over the suitcase on the bed, heard the crow's penetrating call and sensed the shadow of leaves. She straightened up and went across to the window.

A migrant flock of starlings, hundreds of them, came in a cloud and descended all over the field. Anne put a hand slowly to her cheek and stared out, moving her little finger to lie across her parted lips. She stood looking out, and could be less anxious this way, seeing the passage of birds and the passage of leaves that told her of tomorrow and tomorrow.

She was glad to be reminded that she'd been lost in anxiety. Getting off on this trip to Switzerland was an obsession with her, and she knew it. Going away with Rupert, and being in some foreign place with Rupert, carefree, on vacation, had the promise in it of a different and perfected relationship, one in which, away from their "rut," as she called it, away from this house, and away from their work, two new, free, enjoying people would come into being. And she longed for this trip to the foreign land they were going to as though it were the promised land.

She was more on edge about this trip than she had anticipated being. The summer stretched behind her, endless and harrowing. After the operation, at the beginning of June, she had spent June and July recuperating slowly from the depths it had let her down into. For weeks, needlessly she felt, she had lain on the chaise longue on the terrace, under the whisper of the great sheltering maple, looking up through the leaves to the sky, feeling weak, "bloodlessly weak," she said to Rupert, "weak as that bird's feather lying on the flagstone."

"Just take it day by day, dear."

"But I'm weak throughout. Not just my body. My will feels transparent and light as that feather. Rupo, I feel so empty. And the very thought of *doing* anything, of putting my mind to anything, sickens me. I can't stomach the thought of getting back to work. Stomach! Ha! That's where I feel it, right here. Oh. I have the feeling I'll *never* get over this *lassitude*, Rupo." My uterus has been taken out—she said this litany over and over to herself—my will has been taken out, all ambition, every bit of it, has been taken out. I'm perfectly empty, she thought, and perfectly useless. Bloodless. There was no more blood to pour from her body. That was gone. And it felt as though *that* were the blood that had given vitality to her arteries, not the blood that was now only circulating to keep her alive, nothing more, and which felt like white blood, not red blood.

I'm going round the bend... She was too proud to say this to Rupert. She was too proud to say this to her doctor.

"Can I get you some iced tea, dear?"

"Oh? No. No. Thank you."

"A drink then," patiently. "Some sherry before lunch?" Rupert was shelling peas, sitting beside her in a folding aluminum chair. And she said to him fretfully, "Besides, Rupo, I have a feeling you're going to be important. I think it's taken some of the *purpose* out of my working."

"Important? Oh I wouldn't say that. No, dear, no." He spaced his words cautiously. Then, "The advance interest *has* been gratifying, of course. I'm surprised. Really surprised." She looked at his widened, incredulous eyes, his lips parted in amazement, and she saw his deep sincerity.

"Well, it's really wonderful. I am glad, glad for you." For a moment she was. "After so long, to have this come to you." Saying this made her feel spent and useless. She looked at the studious, brooding face bent over the bowl of peas, she saw the look of triumphant joy he was trying to conceal.

A stranger. These days she often felt that he was a perfect stranger. She didn't know this man. She even didn't want to know this man. But I love him, she told herself. And she knew she did. There had been no doubt about that, ever since walking into her study that night and finding him with her letters in his hand, and a look on his face that was new, as though agony were being purified.

And something new in his eyes, too. Their eventual reconciliation had opened closed doors, and in the days that followed
she had let all of the fullness of him, and of him and her together, take her over. The fullness was love, she thought, love both
as memory and as promise. And something else, too, she knew.
Energetically she explained it to Rupert. "I sense that our marriage has been a concoction of love along with something else
that clouds it, and that if the best part of it is to survive, we'll
have to really understand what that 'something else' is. I know
we're calling it by all kinds of names these days, Rupo, like, 'the
games we play,' and so forth. It's that, of course, but that's only
giving it a surface identification."

Yes, it was more than that, she knew. For she had begun to
see that she lived uncleanly in her marriage. And she had a
faint buried knowledge, not of what this uncleanness was, but
that it could be exchangeable for a cleanness, and that this
cleanness would be an entirely new way for her.

But then the operation had come. And it felt as though the
faint buried knowledge of an uncleanness exchangeable for a
cleanness had been cut out of her along with her uterus. She
needed will, she needed a psychic energy she was now entirely
without, to come close to an unmuddled feeling about Rupert.
And it was all the more impossible because of the way he was
changing. She felt cut adrift by his difference, in a strange land
with a stranger she didn't know how to behave with.

She looked intently at him, trying to force herself to see and
to know him as she used to. But she couldn't see him, her seeing
wasn't working, he was like someone painted there, a stranger,
shelling peas with maddening patience. "And the lectures dear,
at last for you a real honest-to-goodness lecture tour." She said
this in a spiritless voice that, instead of being sprightly, enthusi-
astic, as she knew it should be, came out this flat way. "You'll

love that, won't you. And the talk shows. *You. On TV.* Won't Mrs. A. and Bernice have a field day, watching you on TV?"

"I'd *enjoy* it, Anne. Of *course.* But let's not count on it. No one has said it's definite, yet. I wouldn't want it to change our lives. I don't want my life to change." He said this almost pleadingly. "I like it the way it is. I really, Anne, do *not* want to be famous. I can sense that you think I *would* like to be. But no. I can so well imagine the misery it would be for me. I *do not* want that. A little acclaim, yes. A lot, no."

She didn't fully believe him. "My how you've changed. You really have changed you know, Rupo." Yes, he had changed. She knew it. She couldn't quite put her finger on how. He was quieter. He was more, what? More serious? Was that it? She was put off by this subtle, indefinable change, puzzled by it, even, rattled by it. She felt him to be strong, and forgiving, and infinitely patient. But this irritated her, often. "Really dear, you're positively saintly, the way you look after my every need." She couldn't anger him. He was really very calm and strong. He, taking care of her? She, the child? He the senior member of this duo? It was disconcerting. She was lost in this new mood.

And she was still lost, too, in the strangeness he had precipitated during those first days of their impassioned reconciliation, when, though crushed about her abortion in a way more awful than she could ever have imagined, he nevertheless confessed that he knew himself to have been a willing partner in their not wanting a child, though he could never forgive her for going about the abortion on her own. She was still shocked and bemused by this confession, made at great cost to his pride, she knew, and how she admired that.

Yet, she had been torn between relief, and, strangely, anger; relief at having been found not wholly responsible, and anger, too, irrational she knew, at this collaboration of weaknesses that had messed up both their lives. It had caused her to find fault with Rupert in a new way–he had been her ally in what she thought of now as the destruction of their lives. Why hadn't he been strong enough to keep her from getting away with what she did to them both? She hated this weakness that had aided and abetted her own. He had done something to their lives that he should not have done. She couldn't stop blaming him for this, and being angry with him for it.

"I would have thought," she said shrilly, unable to stop herself, "that being famous would be exactly your cup of tea."

"No, dear, no." His face tightened.

She bit her lower lip and clenched her eyes shut. Then she opened them, wide. "I'm afraid I'm going round the bend, Rupo." She said this in the shrill, driving voice that had become her new voice, the voice on the edge of hysteria.

Rupert finished scooping the peas from a pod and let them pelt down onto the pebbly green pile in the bowl in his lap. He threw her a quick, frightened look. Keep her occupied if possible, Dr. Lovelace had said. Let her cook as much as she can, for example. Make love as soon as she's ready to. The trauma of losing a uterus is fierce for some women, he had said.

"I understand, dear," quietly, "I understand what a time you're having. I can see it." He thrust a hand over to place it on top of hers, to squeeze it, then to hold it tightly for a moment. "But you won't go round the bend. Not you. Here dear, let's do the peas together."

"You couldn't possibly understand. You're not a woman."

You're not a woman, and you're not me. I feel I'm without any familiar reliable confidence, she could say to him. I feel, I feel conquerable, open to anything, without a defense. I am without a force, I feel impotent, she could say to him.

She reached a white languid blue-veined hand into the basket of unopened peas, picked one up, split it open, leaned across to Rupert's bowl, and thumbed the peas out of the pod.

"Scooped out, like this empty pod, that's me," she said hecticly. But, impotent?

Why had she thought that word?... Terror pricked her. She wanted to disown that word. It had nothing, nothing to do with her. I'm going round the bend, she thought. I'm perfectly empty, and perfectly useless, and perfectly powerless. I am spayed. I am neuter....

So, she was without anything now. She would have to start all over again from emptiness. She would have to start in from nothing, and find something to be. She had thrown away her womb, she herself had ripped it out of herself long ago. Oh yes, she had been neuter long before the operation. She had *never* used her womb, she had used something else.

She sat up violently. She lunged across the chaise longue and grabbed the bowl of peas from Rupert's housekeeping hands, and hurled it, in a spray of green rain, across the terrace. It landed earsplittingly on the flagstone, exploding into flying fragments.

"I won't go round the bend." It was later that afternoon. Muffled by the pill Rupert had given her, she stood in front of her dressing-table mirror and spoke to the woman she saw there. She had taken off her dress, gray-and-white calico, and as she peeled it up and over her head she said into the warm folds smothering her mouth, "I'm sick and tired of gray."

She flung the wad of dress onto the bed and went over to the mirror. The sharp bones of her bare shoulders seemed like knives to her. The bones of her face, though, sharpened and prominent beneath the pearl-white skin, gave her an ease, gave her something to think about, gave her some interest. And then she said aloud, "I won't go round the bend." But she let herself retreat, she took in, beneath the silk of her slip, the diminished now drooping breasts, once so tight and high and beautiful. "Face it," she hissed, "face it," and she reached for the bottom of her slip and ripped it up over her head and flung it away. Look the lion in the mouth....

She stood naked in front of her mirror. The brutal scar was a long welt of bright fuchsia on the whiteness of her body. Face it... Memories of despair stirred behind her muffled mind, yet she saw that she could look at the scar without the vivid despair of this morning's nonanesthetized mind. Touch it...

Always cringing from touching it even with her washcloth, she now brought a hand slowly down to it and ran her finger up along the hard fuchsia ridge. Strangely, now it felt to her almost like the rest of her skin. She scooped up listless breasts in cupped palms, and she saw that this way they looked almost like they used to. An illusion. But they felt soft, even pleasant. Poor breasts...

But then the tiny despair behind the pill's muffling stirred again, and she nearly let it come through, it was so easy, so usual, to do this, to let it say everything; all the time.

"Damn it!" She wheeled away from the mirror and crossed to her clothes closet. She opened the door and stood looking tiredly at the row of dresses hanging there, all gray. Everything gray... She fingered a gray damask Chinese robe. She felt no interest in it. She pushed it petulantly aside. She came to a gray taffeta housecoat. Stopped. Then passed it over with apathy.

She knew then what she wanted. She dived with both arms into the limp row of dresses, spread a path through it, and disclosed another row of clothes behind it. And there it was! A long chiffon caftan, pale green as ice.

She snatched it out. She ripped it off the hanger. She lifted the slithery mass and poured it down over her head, and then, the chiffon floating against her skin, she went back to her mirror and stood and looked at herself, and then took a lipstick from the tray on the dressing table and spread a pale pink shine over her lips. She opened the embossed silver jewel chest and took out a rope of pearls, and looped it twice around her neck. She found earrings, single small pearls, and with a bemused look on her tilted face, she screwed them into her ears.

Perfume?... She reached for the bottle of Tabac Blond. Almost empty. Almost empty for so many years. She picked it up. She hesitated. "I feel like a fool," she muttered. The bottle shook in her hands. She unstopped it, doused her fingers with it, tapped her fingers behind her ears, down between her breasts. She drew a long, shaking breath, almost a sob. I hate this... The feeling at the back of the pill's muffling flared, reminded her that despair was the way it was. She wanted to retreat back to the despair, it was there, it was familiarly, easily there in her shrouded skull.

But she looked in the mirror, forced herself to see the loveliness in the mirror–stirring chiffon as cool looking as ice, warm pearls on pearl-white skin, pink lips (my lips are beautiful!). For a moment she saw that this woman held herself with a kind of straight-spined pride, and that in the long mobile chiffon she looked almost regal. Then she thought: Maybe thinness is more becoming to me.

In a sweep of chiffon, she walked out to the kitchen, and took a head of lettuce out of the refrigerator, and began to wash the leaves in the sink. They're the same color as my dress....

"More wine dear?"

"Just a smidgen." She held her thumb and forefinger an inch apart. The other hand twisted her pearls. "I'm getting blotto."

"Good." He poured the wine into her glass, bending over her. Then, gently, lingeringly, he kissed the back of her neck.

She wanted to laugh. She wanted to say, "This is a seduction scene," and to laugh fit to kill. She bit her lips together to keep from laughing. Then she couldn't keep the laughing in, and out it burst. And she leaned back, and looked up at Rupert, laughing uncontrollably. "I'm sorry dear," she gasped, "but it's all so...pat–the pearls, the perfume, the wine, the kiss. Oh God, it's wonderful, wonderful." She shook with laughter, hysterical now, she couldn't stop.

He smiled, stepped away, rebuked, embarrassed. He went back to his chair, sat down, picked up his glass of wine. He emptied it. Then he cleared his throat, and set the glass down carefully. "I think it's lovely," he said simply. "I think it's fun. We haven't had anything like this in weeks." He widened his eyes, parted his lips. "Even in months." Then he smiled sadly. "Even...in years. I'm enjoying it. Can't you let yourself enjoy it?"

She shook her head. "No. I don't want to get dressed up for it."

"But you look so perfectly lovely. I love looking at you in that dress. Have I ever seen it? It's new, isn't it?"

She began to laugh again, wildly. "Oh no. It's ancient. It's one of the first dresses I bought for us. Before we were married. I bought it at Saks. And you loved it. Oh honey. Oh well."

"'Ah, yes, I re-mem-ber, it well,'" he sang. He shook his head. He gave her a sparkling, a longing look. "Of course I don't, but let me be Maurice Chevalier for a second, anyway."

"I love your voice, Rupo."

"I love you, Anne." He stretched a hand across the table and put it on hers, and began to knead it sensuously. "You're beautiful. You've never looked so beautiful to me."

All desire to laugh drained away. She was able to look at him in a quiet way, and she felt this hand, as she used to, sending love into her fingers and up her arms and into all of her body.

Then she was terrified. I'm not ready for it, she thought wildly. She drew her hand away, and picked up her glass, and looked down at it. She laughed nervously. She shrugged. "More wine, and you can do anything you like with me." Then she tilted her head way back and flung some wine into her mouth.

Rupert stood up suddenly. He came around the table to Anne, he took her glass out of her hand, he reached for her hands, and he pulled her up from her chair, strongly; and easily, she came easily. He brought her into his arms. He forced her self-conscious mouth to stay with his and he kissed her long and deeply. He slid his hands down over the chiffon of her body and pressed her against him. Oh, at last, she thought, but dully, with sadness. And with fear. And yet she could feel herself livening.

"But. The dishes."

"To hell with the dishes. I'll do them later."

At first it hurt, and her feeble arousal was doused, though she believed that joy would come. But joy did not come, and feeling did not come at once. She was shell hard, everything soft scooped out of her, dried out of her, and so there was no longer any point to this. Gradually, in that one spot, localized, she could feel, but it was all in her lower region only, she was working wildly up to something in her hips and nowhere else, because of being a hard shell; but nevertheless working wildly for it to be more than this, to be the overallness it used to be, to have it be a spreading, a sunset, blazing out slow and wide.

But when it happened it was only in one bright little pin-pointed flash, surfacely.

She began to cry, stormily. A lifetime of tears poured out of her. Rupert held her wretching body. She could feel the comfort of her tears wetting his shoulder. Gradually, as the hiccupping sobs lessened, she felt her whole self softening, inside and out, her body and her heart were loosening against him, she felt as though she were melting from her center and pouring into him. She began to feel a faint peace in this softening self that was close to him now, and one with him. She stopped thinking of a scooped-out shell. She stopped thinking.

She stood at the bedroom door watching the rising, shifting flight of the migrant starlings, and knew that she was tense with anxiety to be gone. Her tension had been exacerbated this time, realistically, by a last minute delay in their departure. They had planned to leave Thursday afternoon for Princeton, to spend the night and the next day with their old friends, the Metcalfs, and then to come up to New York for their Friday night departure from Kennedy. But Thursday morning Rupert discovered that the furnace, which had to be left on during their absence, had broken down. And the furnace man who took his own sweet time getting there, as Anne had wildly said, labored ineptly and grimily in the basement so late into the day that the trip to Princeton had to be canceled. It was almost unendurable to Anne. Were her worst fears to be realized? Would something else happen that would prevent their boarding that midnight plane tonight?

She slid the glass door open and stepped out onto the leaf-covered terrace. She was already dressed for the journey, in a new gray tweed suit, new black patent leather shoes, new white jersey blouse—her trousseau. She closed her eyes and lifted her face to the sky, and the sun pressed down onto it. She had a momentary softening away from all the activity of plans and procedures, passports, clothes, suitcases; and a flicker of not wanting to leave the effortlessness of this hot stillness that seemed so infinite, that seemed to be seeping into her and drenching her and weighing her down, and could melt her and depersonalize her and absorb her into its own endless spaciousness.

She realized she was tired. Very. Yet she felt full of purpose, not only the jittery purpose of getting away, but the deeper continual new purpose, like another beating heart, that had begun to stir in her healed and revived body. She was perpetually full of this purpose, exhilarated by it, and by what she called the "insights" it had begun to bring her, at first in trickles, and then, she felt, in great explosions. For the most part these insights, though, were words; she had words for everything. I can sense, she would tell herself (never Rupert), my "basic insecurity." Obviously I have a lack of a "true identity," I reached an "identity crisis" with the operation, no doubt a "midlife crisis." She kept digging for that word "inevitability" and bringing it up for inspection.

She had a new crusade, self-improvement. She went on record with herself that she was going to improve, and by giving herself the image of today's unsuccessful Anne and tomorrow's successful Anne she actually felt, most of the time, hopeful, elated with promises, sure of ultimate happiness, sure of better conditions to come. She saw herself revived and at peace with herself, in contact with the "something else" she knew she was. She felt this, truly. But too, she saw herself restored again through new and admirable qualities to a more powerful pinnacle than ever.

And yet, underneath the same old driving mind was the simple core in which choice was still alive, in which openness to change still vibrated; and sometimes she could hear its needling little warning, telling her that there is not always tomorrow.

She heard a sound in the room behind her, and then Rupert came out of the door onto the terrace. He was in his shirtsleeves and held his tan corduroy jacket in both hands, and had his head already hung to one side in a little-boy, helpless way. "There's a button off this," he said, and pouted out his lower lip. "Perhaps you'd sew it on, dear, before I go to the village." He, too, was dressed for departure, his newly washed dazzling silver hair combed smooth and straight, his cheeks still pink from shaving. His face wore a pleasant, though harassed expression, but his eyes sparkled in their old way. Rupert's face had changed. It was heavier, as the rest of his body was, and it seemed settled into itself in a permanent way, no longer so resilient. There was more serenity in it, and less youthfulness.

"Just look at those starlings!" he cried, and raised a slow grand arm to sweep it across the sky. "What a spectacle!"

"They're traveling, just like us," Anne exulted.

Rupert punched his fist into the air. "Birds of a feather flock together," he cried out, ringingly. Then he swung slowly away and went into the bedroom to deposit his jacket on the bed, and Anne trotted after him automatically. He crossed to the armoire and opened it, and began to peer and to rummage. "Dear?" he said in a moment, plaintively.

"Yes dear?"

"Where would the keys to all the suitcases be? I thought they were all together here."

"Well no dear, they're in the big drawer of your desk."

Rupert smiled sheepishly, but there was true pain in his voice. "Tee-pee-cal."

"Dear if you keep saying it's typical, you'll end up by believing it. Yes? No?"

"You don't know how many times a day this happens."

"Well certainly. You're distracted. Profoundly, deeply distracted. I don't believe in this deterioration business one whit. I think it's chiefly a deep consuming distraction."

"I know you do," Rupert said with gentle sarcasm. He couldn't agree. He knew he was growing forgetful. He knew he was dimmed, slowed down, in new ways. Nature came through to him in a diminished way, as though his ears were deafer to it, his eyes dimming to it, and his sense of smell less keen. Though he knew this was not so, for occasionally something got through to him with an acuteness that made his spirit soar. But in general, a certain energy of emotion was reduced, and he had fewer sharp joys. Rarely did he feel the old elation. "You're forgetful too, you know," he said gently.

"You're telling me, dear. I go into a room and stand there and can't remember what I came in for. Be under no illusion about that." She gave a little laugh, and shrugged her trousseaued shoulders. Rupert laughed too, they laughed together with furtive compassion. "We're getting old," he said.

"No we're *not* Rupo." Sharply. "I simply refuse to think that. It's what I said. Distraction. Look dear," vigorously, "you must not sell yourself this notion. You've hypnotized yourself with it." She stepped briskly over to the bed. "But where's the button, my boy?"

"In the pocket there."

"Which pocket?"

"The breast pocket," testily.

"Oh all *right*. How could I know?"

He smiled suavely. "You couldn't." He walked slowly over to the open door and out onto the terrace. "It's so lovely and peaceful, isn't it?" he said, looking out across the fields. "I almost hate to leave. Even to go into the village."

Anne found the button and walked out onto the terrace, holding it. "Just think, though," she cried, "how glorious it will be in Switzerland. That mellow, golden, horn-of-plenty feeling. The valleys, the harvests. I remember it all seemed Breughel-like to me. And Rupo, those crisp, fresh-baked Ballons, wait till you have your first Ballon for breakfast. Oh Rupo!" She looked up at him with shining eyes. "Let's swing, let's swing!"

He smiled faintly. "I don't know why I can't get excited about Switzerland."

She threw him a swift look, unsure and concerned but withal determined. "But I know you'll love it. And if you don't we can just up and go to Spain. Spain you'll be mad about."

"Look dear, we're going. I'll like it once we're there. It's just that home always seems so much more precious when you're about to leave it. It seems to me we have everything in the world we could want, right here. Everything."

Perhaps he would like it, but he only half-believed that he would. Where were the old interest and excitement in the thought of new adventure? He ached at having to leave this home of his. He had no enthusiasm or energy for the effort and the inconveniences and the strange languages and the strange foods of European travel. Swiss Ballons for breakfast… Helplessly, Rupert realized that he wanted nothing more than to have breakfasts in his own sunny kitchen, with Anne's bread, and Anne's coffee, and the birds coming to the feeder by the window.

His turbulence was such, these days, that he craved the order and permanence of his home that never changed, and he depended upon waking up each day to the familiar routine that unrolled itself pleasurably and profitably within it. He did not want to go away from the one certain thing (other than a newly satisfying lovemaking) that he and Anne shared these provisional days—their home. He was afraid to be alone with Anne in their new precariousness in foreign places, he in his new sporadic but ever-renewable quiet, she with her occasional violent flareups and her euphoria and her lapses into a burdened silence, the acute tension of the past year gone, but no real solidity to take its place.

Memory of Syra had lost its reality. What she had done to him he had depersonalized and internalized, she was his small hoarded treasure. Passion for her had been channeled into a profound, encompassing concern for the rounding out and the fulfillment of his own life. Through her, through what *she was*, he had had the first intimation that he wanted the peace of being the way *he was*, the peace of not having to be primarily and tenaciously involved always with building himself up into something he *was not*. Through her he had gradually understood instead, to strive for the absence of the cover-up of drama and of vanity and for what existed in him without it.

Questions, and all kinds of answers, assailed Rupert's battered head these days and fought there without mercy. Yet whatever the contrariness of the question or the fickleness of the answers, he knew, his guts knew, that what he really wanted was to cease striving to make Rupert Knight appear to be the rarest and the most exceptional of men. He knew he couldn't continue on without this true interest, this existence that was not the dream.

Anne was a vital part of this interest in, this passion for, becoming. He cared for her with a new concerned awareness that had an effect on his ways and that had strengthened and sobered him, and he knew it. Anne weak called for him to be strong. Anne the distraught child called for him to be the adult. Anne faulty called for him to enjoy the superiority of seeming to be faultless. And to a certain extent, strong and adult be became, and also to a certain extent, ashamed of the satisfaction he got in seeming to be stronger than Anne.

During her recuperation, and nourished by the acclaim his book was getting, gradually, he grew into the heavyweight of the household; he, Rupert, was in the mainstream now, not Anne. On top, he would think with solid pride but with a certain smugness, too, which he forgave himself. And yet his new awareness of Anne made him feel happier with himself than he had ever been, happier than he had ever been able to be, because it was necessary to subdue his own loud sound in order to allow this small sound of his interest in her to be heard. He could not think about her if he was thinking too strenuously about himself. And so, more often than he realized, he was quiet in himself.

And the new quality of his caring for Anne persisted, though it showed him very increasingly what the tendency of Anne's kind of caring was–an obdurate compulsion to have and to hold, and to give in a way that burdened him wearisomely. Often he could see her trying to restrain this tendency, and he was struck then with tenderness and irritation and compassion and admiration by the poignancy and seeming hopelessness of her efforts. Sometimes he wondered whether her periods of sad separate quiet were periods of reflection on, and frustration over, the problems of staying in power. For this much he could admit and define about what went on in Anne.

But in an undefined way he also knew, as one sees the threads that compose a tapestry but not the finished tapestry, that Anne could not have allowed him to have the focus of his life be directed away from her to a child he might love more than, or instead of, her. Nor, probably, could she have dared to give herself a real child and then find she had nothing left for her child Rupert. And how could he have dealt with that? But then of course he *had* dealt with it, hadn't he, by collaborating in its not happening?

All this Rupert knew but did not really know he knew. Yet this obscure gestation of knowledge continued to progress in proportion to the dying down in him of the sound of himself that had, for sixty years, so exposed and so emblazoned his fragility.

His passport was in his pocket, and his travelers' checks. His suitcases were closed, and waiting on the sun-flooded kitchen floor. The Regulator clock had just struck two. The taxi would come for them at five. He dreaded the thought that the clock would run down, then stop. The fields were radiantly still. A yellow maple at the edge of the lawn was more than a visual mass of golden light. It pulsed, was alive, effervescent, and Rupert felt that he could breathe it in, and hear it, that it affected him like sound and touch. Heavily, he wondered whether he would ever see it again.

But he drew up a sigh that was an attempt at cheer. "Well, if

I'm going to the village, I'd better get going."

"Hurry back."

"What's the hurry? The taxi's not coming till five."

"I know. But I've got a trauma about getting off, after yesterday. I like you right here, where I can keep an eye on you. I think we should sit sedately in the living room, where nothing can fall on us, ha! befall us, that's where that came from, and eat nothing, so that we won't choke, and wait until the taxi comes to scoop us up and bear us off. Cinderella's coach." She laughed with bravado to conceal her anxiety which she was ashamed of.

"Going away matters that much to you," Rupert said slowly, with real concern and with a penetrating worried look, understanding this for the first time. "I didn't know you were on such tenterhooks." He bent down and kissed the top of her head, and her eyes softened with gratitude. "Don't worry," gently. "I'll be back." He put an arm across her shoulder and drew her to him; Anne, full blown once more, warm and pliant and large against him. His eyes softened. He was content and strong in his vigilant caring for her. Their bodies, beginning with what they both now laughingly called "the seduction scene," had come together in a new and powerfully fleshly way. Now they slept curved against each other, like two animals.

Oh yes, they were together again. For better and for worse. But together. In bed, their bodies in communion and their minds not in combat, they experienced the foundation and the essence of their love for one another. "What more do you need than this?" separately they would ask themselves. "You can't have everything..."

"We have so much dear," Rupert said quietly. Anne was snuggled against him in blissful surrender. And he was steeped in golden time stopped still. He felt a rich complacent quiet, tinged with melancholy.

❧ III ❧

IT had been a startling relief to have Rupert leave. Because of their voices, Anne realized–their voices made such perpetual noise, always the same. Tiring. "I'll be back." His voice would not leave the room. She closed her eyes patiently as though to close out the sound of his voice, which was always with her.

She stood with her eyes carefully closed over this admission. Where had it come from? But I love his voice... She opened her eyes abruptly, to look at things. The sun pouring into the whiteness of the room hurt her eyes. She closed the sliding glass door and with her pink mouth pursed seriously, latched it, there, that one's latched, and pulled the net curtains to subdue the light. Of course I love his voice...

But was she tired of what it said? Oh no.

Or was she tired of the way it kept on and on? No. Not that, really.

Or was she tired of trying to be so perpetually responsive to it? Yes, that was it. She was tired unto death of that, really tired unto death of it.

Some tiny part of her that begged for its own life was taking over, and her lively gray eyes softened, widened so that the faint radiating lines at their corners were erased. Her face, always unmuddled, skin drawn tight over fine bones, looked less like marble now, and more like flesh. She was beautiful as she stood there with the loud sun lightening into silver all her grayness, gray-blonde hair, gray suit, gray pearl skin.

But the suitcase lay open on the bed, ready to be closed. A

374

surge of anticipation seized Anne, and she stepped energetically across to the suitcase, deftly put into it the few things lying on the bed beside it, and closed it, latched it, there, that's latched, and then she went over, in vigorous steps with the sun flashing on bright new black patent leather, to stand centered on the sunny rug, an elbow in one hand, the other hand tapping at her cheek.

There was nothing left to do but wait. The room seemed full of sun but nothing else. She felt its emptiness, its being out of service, and knew that she had left it. She was neither here nor there. Was a room only alive when one wanted it to be? Aliveness was not in this room in any way, but seemed to exist amorphously way off in the blue somewhere, in a blur of taxis, airports, planes, Swiss Alps, martinis, porters, foreignness; she and Rupert on a pink cloud with glasses in their hands. Anticipation nullifies the moment, she said to herself with empty wisdom.

There's no use my telling myself that the moment is what counts, she then told herself, smiling faintly, when I'm all charged up to be anywhere but here.

Anywhere but here?

She looked around the room as though it had betrayed her. But I love this room… A foreign room flashed into her mind–striped wallpaper, brass bed, bolster, swelling quilt–as static as a color photograph in a travel brochure; and for a second she was nowhere.

❧ IV ❧

THE church was dazzlingly white in the still sun. The only sound in the country silence was the sound of her car. The house would come next.

Then there it was, maroon, square, the same, forever sturdy, forever small-ly beautiful, secluded. The maples, their leaves sifting down, towered over it like great spaces of yellow light, and the leaf-covered lawn was a floor of light.

The sign was gone, "Fools' Paradise," and the signpost. Syra turned into the drive and felt Lewis wiped out, gone entirely. The house stood empty of him, so still. It proclaimed his death to her as nothing else had. It was alive, for it had a life of its own, had had long before Lewis came to it, would have long after the next owner left it. Timeless there under the light of the maples, it ignored the interruptive entrances and exits of human life. Infallible in its permanence and dignity, it stood grounded, serene, perpetual, impervious to fallible man. Syra saw all this as empty of Lewis, and now she understood, finally and with a sense of steady anguish, Lewis's departure from this house, this world.

She searched for the key to the house among a welter of objects in her bag, waded across the driveway through a yellow lake of leaves to the door, and fitted the key into the lock, all with a kind of brave confidence she didn't feel.

Good God, I went off and left the place unlocked and the keys, you can be sure, on the nail in the kitchen. Then his laugh... *Good old meticulous me. You let me drink too much.*

You did the same thing to me.

376

Are we drunk?

Soused.

Goody….

She was surprised and terrified by the presence of Lewis. Lewis was inside this empty house. Or some information congesting its empty rooms. Something was in there. She was afraid to go in. She had a feeling that Lewis dead had altered into something that had left human fallibility behind, and that he had become pure and stern as God; and that he could see her clearly, mercilessly, now, without the bias of his needs. She felt suddenly muddled with sin and failure, and frightened.

She opened the door, the warmth of sun on her back. But the sudden stale still coldness inside this empty hall echoed with the opening of the creaking door and then with the striking of her steps on the cold boards.

She stood tentatively. Accusation pounded in this house. She set her bag down on the dusty floor. She shrank with guilt. Her wrongdoing seemed to make this house enormous, to make all the empty rooms expand as though swelling the house to mansion size.

She was stricken with the surprise of all this. It was something new to be found here. And yet she knew it was as old as she was, as old as time, and that its power was justifiably authoritative. It mocked her–small, erring Syra–it mocked the futility of her independence. She felt suddenly sick with fear of it, and she said to herself in a firm voice, "I am now desperately below the waves," as though by declaring fear she could deal with it.

She shook her head, to shake it all away. Then she straightened herself, inside and out. The moment of acute terror passed. Less fearful, and with timid confidence, she brought up her chin and braved the living room.

It was, after all, only a small, empty, silent room. But it felt impregnable to Syra, it felt confidently unresponsive in a stubborn way, proclaiming that it would lend its four walls, and its empty fireplace, to nothing of the present. Instead, it declared to this intruder that she had no identity with it and could claim none, nor had the late owner, who had only been an intruder too, though he had added the mulberry paint and the lavender and pitted old window panes, and the layers of glossy wax on the two hundred-year old floors.

But then all at once the emptiness of the room felt wonderful to Syra. This is a flowering moment, she told herself, and she felt the perfect peace of the room's emptiness, and along with peace felt all living as a great clutter, hectic, disastrous. She tried to remember how the room had felt with Lewis's beautiful things in it, and succeeded only in having a memory of effort and of artificiality and of palpitant unhappiness. She felt that the room had its dignity and serenity in its emptiness, that it had gotten back its own, and that all of Lewis's priceless furnishings had been something it had had temporarily and patiently to put up with. The room said this to her: I endure. But nothing that man does to me endures. He fills me full of his foolishness and his failure and I'm glad for the moment to be rid of it. Syra couldn't help but agree, and to feel the peace of the absence of foolishness and failure.

Inspecting and then hoisting cartons and carrying them out to the car was a long and tiresome job. Midway, it was necessary to lift her guitar out of the trunk to make room for more cartons and on impulse she decided to take it back with her into the living room and to play the Villa Lobos there for Lewis. Once more and the last time here in this house, for Lewis. She heard his voice. "Syra simplifying Lewis." Yes, she would leave in his empty house an echo of the music that had simplified him.

She wedged a particularly cumbersome carton between two other weighty ones, and then straightened irritably. I am not in a state to simplify anyone, she said to herself. She drew a deep, impatient breath, hating all these voices inside her, which seemed invariably to crop up here. In Florida there had finally, safely, come to be only one voice–hers. She drew another breath, a long, easier one. She shrugged, smiling ironically. This has been a very unhappy-making day. I make myself a mess here, helpless. I know it, and will simply try to throw it away when I return to wherever *I* am. That's the way it is...

She heard Mrs. Alexander saying this, in lilting imitation of Walter Cronkite. And her heart felt suddenly heavy and bitter. She told herself she would not go back to say good-by to Mrs. Alexander, but would proceed on, head as fast as she could for the Jersey Turnpike and the route south. She felt as though she had been bludgeoned with Mrs. Alexander's repugnance and rejection, and because of it she now felt tears coming. She tossed her head, slinging the tears arrogantly out of her eyes.

Turning, she walked back toward the house where her duty lay, and how she detested duty. That was another thing about the empty house–it seemed to present her with some kind of impossible responsibility. Walking into the house was like walking into that responsibility. Once she was inside the responsibility would claim her, the doors would slam shut and lock, and there she would be, trapped in it forever.

A sudden swirl of wind lifted her dress and ballooned it around her so that warm air was inside the tent of it for a moment, and then the wind plastered it jovially against her stomach, and whipped it out behind her, before letting it at last collapse into prosaic folds. At the same time in this temporary pleasure she heard the sound of a car in the road which she paid no attention to, and a clucking sort of chirp in the maple above her, and recognized it as Rupert's beloved redwing. Elated, she raised her head gratefully to the bird, the tree, the sky, "the hills from whence cometh my help." That's Rupert's quotation, she said to herself. She was glad it had come into her mind. She remembered walking across Moores' meadow and listening to Rupert dramatically intoning it, but thinking that at the moment her help was coming from him.

Well one thing I *do* know; help is certainly not coming from this house, she thought grimly, and walked into the living room, where she would play the Prelude, and then lock the door, and leave the place forever.

But the living room held something in its silence that stopped her. Steeped in mulberry shadow and dusty sunlight, it was full of something unanswered, or full of something calling to her. For a moment she was perfectly certain that what she was hearing so powerfully was the soundless voice of Lewis's spirit. And though surprised to be thinking this, she wondered whether perhaps after all spirits do live and do communicate and can be heard, and that a sound that is soundless can come through, in a strong and communicative way, when one knows this.

Her response to this possibility was to lose her fear in favor of something more compelling, and to go straight across to the fireplace and to sit purposefully down on the carton which stood in front of it, and to take her guitar out of its case.

You like to perch and be toasted...

She smiled comfortably. Lewis *was* here. Or in her. One or the other, or both. Spirits or no spirits, this room had suddenly become Lewis's again.

And the accusation in the room was gone. The air, or density, of the room had lightened. It had calmed itself, and was now a normal empty room. Lewis hovered here not as a stern and pure and accusing God, but as the old Lewis, yet also purified. She looked up to him, felt humble before him. No doubt but that death had cleansed him. Maybe it was the other way around now. Maybe it was Lewis who was simplifying Syra.

She was on the firebench and the fire on her back was hot, the bourbon in her stomach was hot, and Lewis was sitting in the wing chair. It was perfectly wonderful to know this, to know that such a thing could happen, and to feel that she hadn't lost Lewis. He was the Lewis of her childhood, before he had become silly and shrill. And she was the Syra of her childhood, before she had begun to lose her hold on what she knew. This Lewis could talk to her and she could talk to this Lewis, reverently and without quibbling.

What was so wrong, Lewy? I feel my vast wrong. What was it?

There was no formation in the sound-presence coming into the room with such strength, no dark striations in it, only a palpable voluminous onrush.

But the answer was borne into her by it, or so it seemed to her. I was wrong to feel that your wanting could be as easy as my wanting. Was that wrong? I came because of "ausec," I thought. But as usual I acted from not *knowing*, in my head. I didn't think, that's all. I simply did not *think*. And I should have. I wanted you so badly, no I mean so goodly, but I should have known you well enough to know you couldn't let it happen, couldn't, absolutely couldn't, since you never had, even though I knew you always wanted to. Do you remember the outhouse that summer, when I invited and you declined? And then thirty years later I repeated the invitation, and it killed you. It's hard to do a greater wrong than that. Finally I *had* to believe that I had killed you, but I thought I'd gotten it all straight and excused in my mind, feeling I was right, and you were wrong. But now you convince me, this scary house in such a ruling way convinces me, that I am wrong.

Syra stopped talking to herself. She was watching a sudden shower of yellow leaves rattling against the window pane, like a gust of sunlight. She crossed over to the window and opened it.

Freshness poured in–leaf mold and hot sun and the clarity of a northwest wind, and, faintly, the sweet astringency of goldenrod.

She went back to the carton and sat down on it. She picked up her guitar and pressed it against the swell of her stomach, plucked a string–a furry buzz, reassuring, alive, which palpitated for a long moment.

Silence.

The sound-presence was gone, and the spirits. She was Syra, in an empty room with the sun pouring into it, and all the gusty crisping bitter-fragrance of autumn pushing into it. There was no sound-presence. There was no such thing as spirits. She felt foolish. She didn't like this house. She saw that it was a threat.

Then words explained. They slipped easily into her head and stayed there, clear as light, visible, she could both see them and hear them, and they had the sound, the feeling, of an announcement: Everything this house had made her say was a threat, *its* threat she told herself. Everything she had said belonged to this house, this way, and according to *its* lights, Lewis's lights, she *was* wrong. But the wrong was this house's wrong, and Lewis's wrong. It wasn't her wrong. This house, Lewis, everybody in the world, tried to make her bear the responsibility of their wrong, as well as the responsibility of being in every way like them, and she was sick and tired of it. In a moment of great perception she sensed that the power of this house was that it was all of society versus her small and persistent self, and it wanted to fashion her into one of *them*.

Lewis was gone now. She was alone. She was clear. She thought the fresh air coming through the open window had brought this freshness and clearness into her. She felt ready to play. She brought her fingers slowly across the strings, and this discordant terse music seemed to her to match the brown, bitter-fragrance of the outdoors. Ah this is mine. I am stuck with me–me on a very high, dropping-away-on-one-side path cut along the side of a mountain. Single file. You are not allowed here, Mother, because I cannot hold your hand on a one-person path. It is all right for me to tell you this because we have both always known it, and are both now glad of it.

She began with the utmost delicacy to probe the melody of the Villa Lobos Prelude, lifting it and lifting it with stern honeyed strings. At the top of the long question she paused, knowing herself to be this very thing that she was giving musical expression to, aware that this single, unornate sound was herself; and then she began, in the gentlest most roundedly complete answer, the descent. The music struck the empty room with strong resonance, and *it* was the sound-presence of the room now. Everything that had been in the room before, all the animateness and cloudlike threat of it, was dispersed.

The last note, separate and distilled, pierced deeply into Syra and in terms of sound, of solitariness, and of simplicity told her what she needed to know about herself. She was so thoroughly informed by this note, which was, in a way, the consummation of the ascending question and the descending answer, the period at the end of the sentence, that she had no need to try to put into words the finality and the hopelessness and the peace it gave her. She only felt that she was it–separate, alone, unmothered now, and that perhaps alone in this world she would always be. She did not feel a loss of anything, the moment of the sound of the note seemed complete, and she felt peaceful, a peacefulness without any particular sensation of hope or joy, an overwhelming neuterness as though to be other than neuter, to be quick and vital and individual, one must feel oneself to be like everyone else. No, this house, and Lewis, had forced upon her a perfect knowledge of her unlikeness. And now that she knew that, she could stay with it. Everything from now on would have to come out of that.

❧ V ❧

RUPERT turned into the road, lowering the window so that the baking sun could flood the car. There's still one redwing around, he thought as he raised his eyes to the flaming tree and the rippling sound exploding from it and then the quick black dart of a bird from out of the flame. His eyes softened and glowed. There could be moments of perfect satisfaction like this, from the sight or the sound of a bird. He began to feel an expanding happiness. The road was a mosaic of gold and red and orange leaves–gold road, infinity of breathless gold leaves over head, gold leaves showering slowly down, gold sun flooding his car–Rupert himself became goldenness. And it was in this bursting and disembodied serene elation, rounding the curve by the church and approaching Lewis's house, that he saw Syra.

She was crossing the driveway from the car to the house with her guitar in her hand. And as the surprise of seeing her there smote him, and as he prepared instinctively to slow down and to drive in, in that second he saw the hugeness of her belly, as a sudden breeze plastered her loose dress against its bulge and then sportively billowed and whipped it out around her.

He had begun to slow down, and he was unable to do other than to continue to slow down, though he was in sudden senseless confusion. Syra, in the meantime, her head lifted to some sound in the trees above, her hair tossing in that fun-loving wind, turned in an abrupt elated way and walked toward the house.

Rupert had stopped. He sat for several moments in a clear and resolute panic–Syra was pregnant and the child was his and he must go to her. This instinct was so strong that he shifted gears and started to turn into the drive.

But then his mind cleared, and the house was a maroon house, and the sky was a bright blue, and the car was a yellow convertible with a Florida license, and he was Rupert, and a kind of sensible clarity tempered his panic, and he put his car into abrupt reverse and backed hastily out of the drive, not daring to look back in his terrible urgency to get away unseen. The gears ground, his hands shook, he panted painfully. The car jumped, lurched forward, then shot off up the road, and in a moment he came to Moores' wagon road that turned off and wound around behind the hills into the woods. Seeing it as a godsend, he drove into it and around the bend of the hill and into the shelter of the pine forest.

He turned off the ignition, and the sudden forest silence calmed him. He crossed his arms on the wheel and put his head down onto them and closed his eyes. The world spun, roared. He was in a vacuum that became a cone and then a whirlpool with a smooth dizzying slick surface that took him round and round with it, faster all the time until it began to slow down to allow the words *oh God* to come into his head. The whirlpool slowed down and then wasn't there, and in his head were these words he couldn't speak because he didn't want to hear the sound of his own voice, didn't want to relate to that man and what he had done and what he would have to do, words would make everything immediately real, and how could he deal with that?...

With his eyes closed and the beginning of panic leaving, and his head pressed upon his arms, he could feel the safety of hiding. A fly zoomed in through the car window and droned about his head and then alighted on his freshly washed-for-Europe shining gray hair, buzzing there. He moved his head to shake it off, terror shooting through him at the thought of Europe, going away this afternoon, Anne.

＆

But gradually, in this hiding place and in the hot pine-scented stillness, thought began to be processed through his chaos. A sense of being himself surprised him gratefully.

Whole thoughts, sentences began to disentangle themselves from the scramble of words in his head, as though he were taking cardboard letters from a heap and laying them out into words, and then into sentences: Why didn't Syra tell me? She did not tell me. She does not want me to know. She knows what is best. He admitted these truths and their impact, with a numb wounded weightiness that had somewhere in it a flicker of relief. Syra doesn't want me. I don't want Syra. I want Anne. I want my home. I want my life.

He could feel the truth of these words he was thinking, and he could feel them surrounded and even controlled by the four walls of his home, the walls of his life, a fortress of familiar objects and ways he had built around himself, object by object, act by act, throughout the years, so that the words *Syra does not need me* were superimposed upon the scene of himself sitting in the kitchen in the sun eating Anne's toasted bread. His car with its familiar wheel and its familiar dashboard, his tan corduroy jacket with the button Anne had just sewed on, his freshly washed hair, his able hands on the wheel, the poetry pulsing in his body and mind, all of this was vivid and precious and threatened, and the words in his forehead–*Syra does not need me*–were chosen to vivify and validate it. Yet they were the truth, too, he knew.

Ah, if only I hadn't set out for the village, if only I'd stayed safely at home with Anne as she wanted me to, I wouldn't have seen Syra. I would never have known....

But now he began to be disturbed by sentences that seemed

to him to struggle out of the comfortable mire of the previous sentences into a prominent despairing daring of their own: What shall I do? I have a responsibility. I am the father of her child.

The father...

It was as though Rupert had been struck a blow. "I am a father," he said to himself aloud, puzzled.

The words kept repeating themselves. I am a father. I am a father. Gradually he began to feel a permeating sense of belief, and this brought a vague amazement. Suddenly he was awed.

The man who would soon raise his head and open his eyes was already a different man, and what he would see when he opened his eyes would, in some uninterpretable way, look unfamiliar to him, because of this subtle yet mighty difference he was experiencing now in himself. He had become all men, he was now like all men, fulfilling their first purpose. His sense of this was so total, so, yes, normal, that it was in one way sensationless.

I am a father...

An agony of relief overwhelmed him. I am not the end of myself...

Hard on this wild gratitude for immortality came a memory of putting himself into Syra. And then the knowledge that he had indeed been procreating on that forest floor came over him in a great wave of sensual memory, so that suddenly his body began to stir and to grow with longing for Syra, Syra–her open body taking his seed into it, himself and herself in that wonderful struggle, making a child together.

The miracle of this suffused him, and he saw that this was the completion of lovemaking, the added element that took it way beyond sensual joy and into an act of creation. The miracle of its having happened, to him, to Syra and him together, gave him a feeling of being bound to her, and of wanting endlessly, insatiably, to be in her, the two of them constantly orgiastically one–one flesh, superflesh, with the spirit dictating no less than the senses.

Desire was actually moving in him now, and with it he felt such a resurgence of longing for Syra that he opened his eyes and reached impulsively toward the ignition, to start the car and to go to her. But he held his hand outstretched, inches from the key. It was over with Syra. How could he dream of going there and forcing himself on her? They were totally separated; he knew this. And yet he ached to be with her and in her where their child was, feeling the mound of it against his body, pressing and pressing and pressing into Syra, forever and ever, without end, all those seeds of his that had in her, at the end of his life and in his aging years, become life.

"Well, well, this will never do," he said aloud suddenly, with a conviction that surprised and relieved him. A crushing sadness came over him, a kind of practical helplessness. What a mess he had perpetrated, and what was he to do about it? *What was he to do?* Within the next few minutes he must decide, take action.

A breeze whisking through the little clearing brought with it a swirl of brilliant leaves and a strong hot dose of pine. The breeze died as suddenly as it had come, and after a brief frenzied skittering the leaves were left without impetus, so that they drifted down to earth as though abandoned, some of them coming to rest on the hood of the car, though one of them, on some secret current of air, drifted in through the open window and settled on Rupert's sleeve.

He looked at it. He picked it up and brought it to his nose. It smelled of sun and woods and time. It gave back to Rupert the still, deep, incandescent glory of autumn. He was standing on the terrace with Anne, looking out at the unearthly light of the yellow maple; he was steeped in golden time stopped still. Oh yes. That was the way for him, and that was what his life could be. That was what he wanted. The golden tranquility of autumn, and this closeness to, this verging on, what could come of *himself*. And of Anne. Poor Anne, who *was* the end of herself. He was stung with compassion for her. What he had been given she had been denied. More terribly, what *she* had been given she had denied herself. And though it was now clear how very much he had always wanted a child, he saw, for the first time perhaps with total comprehension, how tremendously, at bottom, she too had wanted one. Perhaps even more than he. She was a born mother. And yes, she knew that now. Too late. That, he suspected, was part of the hell she'd been through, and was just now coming out of–knowing herself to be the born mother she had not let herself be. And that he had not let her be–oh yes indeed.

It seemed to him cruel, suddenly, that this should have happened to Anne and him, unfair and treacherous. And he realized that the greatest imperative of this whole complex mess was to keep Anne from knowing anything about it.

The wild moment of longing for Syra had altogether faded now, leaving in its place a sturdy, rooted conviction that Anne was his life, and that autumn was his life, but more, that *he* was his life, he alone was his life.

But. My child. My child's life. What about that? I must think, he told himself desperately, I must think fast. I have a responsibility to my child.

Like a fist then, a question smote his clearing mind: Why do I think *I* am the father?

There was nothing in Rupert to want or to encourage this thought, but there it was, with all the aggressiveness of fact. Why, fact pointed out needlingly, did he think that he was the father of Syra's child? What on earth had driven him to this immediate conclusion? The child could most certainly be Georges's. The child in all probability *was* Georges's. Or, Syra being the way she was, the child could be any other man's child.

He sat tensed, his heart beating irregularly and loudly, his whole being fighting the idea, and yet having admitted the possibility of it, he was unable to discard it. He sat for a long time struggling between suspicion and conviction—he had known instantly, hadn't he, that the child was his? Why? Was it wishful thinking? Was it a buried longing finally given expression? Why had he been so sure, so instinctively sure, that the child was his?

And how was he to find out?

He hid his face in the palms of trembling hands for a moment, then wiped them down and away with a despairing gesture and a great sigh. He was certain that he would never have any peace until he found out. And yet everything in him warned him not to go to Syra. But how, then, was he to find out?

The answer of course was simple when it came to him. He would go to Mrs. Alexander. If anyone were to know, it would be Mrs. Alexander, though he could understand that she might very well be the last person to have such a fact disclosed to her. But he knew it was his first hope. If she doesn't know, then I will have to go to Syra, he told himself frantically, starting the car and backing it down the road. And if Syra comes while I'm there? And if she hasn't been to see Mrs. Alexander at all? And if Anne begins to worry about my being gone so long and starts telephoning?

Rupert's face was shining with sweat and the blood was pounding in his head as he bounced the car slowly back along the rutted road, and came at last to the main road, and stopped with a bucking jerk, and then started up the hill with a roar of speed.

♣ VI ♣

IN his silver frame, with the serious eyes of the doctor constantly in the presence of tragedy and never inured to it, Billy looked at her and told her not to lose her grip. She was startled to have Billy come to life like this, speaking to her, as it were. Except in her dreams, she hadn't for years had a conscious vivid reexperiencing of him.

She was pierced by a pain she thought had gone forever. Oh why did you die so young, Billy?... She bowed her face into the shaking mesh of her fingers and began to cry quietly, young tears that surprised her and refreshed her. She did not want to stop. Down her cheeks poured years of loneliness and of sorrow for the life she had loved, cut short. And in the midst of her abandon she was amazed, finding it terrible that she had repressed so much for so long, yet curiously happy that such wells of feeling still existed in her old body.

She blew her nose. Then she flung her head against the back of her chair, and dropped tired hands to the chair arms, and stared at the ceiling with bleak eyes that were seeing the whole of everything. Billy whom she loved had been all gain, in spite of the loss of him. The tears in her body told her this again, now, twenty years after his death. And Syra whom she loved was all loss, in spite of the gain of her coming back to renew friendship with innocence and trust. Billy, in-every-way-desirable Billy Alexander, had never been a challenge in any way. She and he, ideally attuned emotionally, ideally attuned situationally, had never presented each other with any circumstance in which either of them could fail. But Syra...

Mrs. Alexander closed her eyes and moved her head slowly, helplessly, against the back of her chair, full of the weight of failure. To have disappointed herself thus at the end of a long life well lived. To have failed in the most important thing. Where was the rest of her? And of what possible use were scruples, since she had closed her careful door on some essential thing? She was appalled over her inability to accept the bald fact of Syra's promiscuity, while knowing in her heart of hearts that she loved Syra unreservedly and admired her as much as anyone she had ever known.

Why don't I just admit it's too much for me? she thought tiredly. Why don't I just realize there's a generation gap that's perfectly impossible to bridge? But she couldn't admit this, wouldn't. She couldn't throw Syra away. It felt like death to her to consider such a thing.

Love for Billy, love for anyone, now appeared not to have been whole. Had love for Billy, remembered with such fresh and vivid pain, been a full and honest love? Was this old woman with her sad and soiled inadequacy a person who could declare herself totally, holding back nothing? What was she, what was her love for Billy, if she could love Syra and at the same time judge her so shallowly and from such unsound principles? Where was the common sense she had always relied on, if her repugnance for Syra's deeds could override her knowledge that Syra was as true as they come, and that her prized independence was allied to that truth?

Mrs. Alexander opened her eyes. Of what possible use was her long life if she was unable at the end of it to declare herself for what she deeply and truly believed, if she was unable to resist being overridden by a part of her she saw to be shoddy? What had she lived for, and what had she been to Billy, if she did not have the power to declare herself for love when it was what she wanted most to do?

Margreit was coming up the stairs. Mrs. Alexander heard her solid quick tread and sighed. She was too beaten to move. But pride forced her to raise her unproud head, and to sit up straight, and to compose her valueless hands on the arms of her chair, and to have a strong gaze ready for Margreit. There were few situations that could rob her of presence.

"Is here Mr. Knight," Margreit said in blonde and blue-eyed and deferent breathlessness, waiting in the doorway. "Does Madam wish to tell he comes up?"

"Mr. Knight! But I thought he'd gone!"

"No Madam. Is here. Yoost now down below."

"My God!"

"Madam not want he come up?"

"Oh my God my dear child, yes. But wait, ask him to wait just a minute. Tell him I'll call down. Go down right away and tell him that." She got up abruptly and hurried to the window. Yes, there was Rupert's black car parked alongside the front steps. She looked at the clock on her desk in panic, dabbing at her hair and her dress abstractedly as though it were disarranged looks, not disarranged lives, that were at fault and could be righted with a few touches. Almost two-thirty. Syra might come back at any moment. And what on earth was Rupert doing here when he should be in Switzerland? She drew a long stabilizing sigh. This was serious business and she must keep her head.

She crossed with a quick firm trot to the door and went over to the stair rail and called down, impatiently, "Rupert, whatever are you doing *here*? Come on up," leaning over her own stair rail, in her own hall, with her own shepherd and shepherdess clock ticking recklessly away behind her. The clock had never seemed so loud to her, so insistent about something. Then as Rupert materialized, clear and distinct it struck the half hour, and she felt a flash of irritation with that penetrating, accusing chime, that simpering wooing pair flaunting their immortal chastity.

Rupert seemed to fill the whole hall with his size and with a heavy purpose that expanded him, gave him a dimension of Rupert-space around his body so that man and aura overflowed the staircase as he mounted it. She saw the silver of his long hair in the shadow of the stairwell, and saw him as Einstein, and noticed, too, that the clock sounded impertinent. For a moment, turning both clock and man into what they weren't, she felt uneasy and almost faint. Then common sense returned. And she noticed his portentousness. "My dear man, why on earth haven't you gone?" And then fearfully, "Has something happened? Is Anne all right?"

Rupert came slowly up, without speaking. On the last step, he still did not speak. She moved toward him and clasped her hands in front of her breast. "What is it, Rupert?" she whispered.

"I think, in your room." He gestured toward the open door.

Certain that tragedy had befallen Anne, Mrs. Alexander turned and hurried into the sitting room, where sun shone brazenly yet stabilizingly, and closed the door. Then she raised stern appalled eyes to Rupert. "Now tell me."

Rupert was pale and his drawn face gleamed with perspiration, and his oriental eyes were flat and hard as matte brown stones. A strand of careful gray hair, blown haphazardly, was plastered along the dampness of one temple, and his unawareness of it spoke to her of desperation. With the door closed behind him he let out a sigh of provisional relief, and smiled a faint smile that was an effort but that softened his face momentarily. "Anne's all right," he said heavily. "We were delayed a day in leaving. Nothing's happened to her. We're both all right. That's not why I'm here."

394

"Well thank heavens," she sighed. "I was terrified." Then she squared her shoulders and looked at him sternly and lied. "I'm about to dash off for an appointment, I'm sorry to say. But what is it my dear? Obviously something's on your mind. Can you say quickly? For I really must go this minute. I hate to be this way but —" She faltered, then said suggestively, "but I've got a very necessary doctor's appointment." She looked at him with an inquisitive boldness to cover her discomfort and to test his credulity. "A sort of little emergency," she added.

"I'm sorry," he said courteously but summarily, as though her physical troubles were nothing compared to his emotional ones. "I'll be brief." He drew a rasping sigh and tightened his mouth. "I've seen Syra. She didn't see me but I saw her."

"You've. Seen. Syra." The echo of his words came out of Mrs. Alexander in slow incredulous alarm. "Oh good God."

"So it's true. Else you wouldn't say 'oh good God.'"

Mrs. Alexander rallied surprisingly. She groped with a shaking hand for her chair and collapsed into it, and then said up to him, with no conviction, weakly, "What's true?"

Rupert sat massively down upon the little rose velvet fireside chair. "It's true, then, that her child is not Georges's. That's what I meant." He cleared his throat long and carefully. Then he looked across at her. "Is that what you meant?"

"Yes, that's what I meant. I'd give anything in the world not to have blurted it out, but out it came."

There was a long silence, a cautious, wary suspension in which one waited for the other to make the next move, and in which the wind gusted softly beyond the open window, rattling leaves in a happy sunny swirl along the roof of the porch. Finally Mrs. Alexander turned around and looked pointedly at the desk clock. "I really must go," she said with no conviction.

Rupert sat forward suddenly. "All right. But first tell me. And believe me," he said quietly, "I have every right in the world to know. Whose child is it? Do you know that? Has Syra told you that?"

"What, may I ask," said Mrs. Alexander shrewdly and settled back in her chair, and stretched her legs out and crossed her ankles deliberately, "what may I ask do you mean by saying that you have every right in the world to know?" She felt curiously on top of this now, though repugnance fought with determination, for she knew what he meant and might be going to have to listen to it, but perhaps not. He was every bit as fastidious as she, and perhaps they'd get away with no more than this skirting around the truth. She looked at him with arrogant and sympathetic eyes. "I know. But I most certainly am not at liberty to divulge this confidence. You must realize that, since you know now that it's illegitimate."

She seemed to see clearly, perhaps for the first time, that Rupert's face had a brooding goodness about it. His great dark eyes, serious, had a look of quiet intelligence that struck her as being more appealing than the radiance they usually had. He was a good man in spite of his self-importance. There was no conceit in him now, no swaggering. Rupert quiet, Rupert humble, was very attractive indeed. Far more interesting than Rupert being dazzling.

He was suddenly very attractive to her, more so than usual and in a sound, interesting way. She wanted him to stay. She felt a need of him, though she never had before. They were sharing something immense, something of the first importance, tasteless and shocking though it was. It was, she thought, like being forced into war and having it be good for you. She felt a bond, rather like growing love, and it felt so much more interesting, so much more, yes, real, than anything else. She and he were in the midst of naked reality. "Real life," she said to herself, moving her lips faintly. Her eyes softened and she smiled at him, though she dreaded what he might say next, and dreaded more the burden of having to withhold from him the knowledge of his child. "Syra is not unhappy," she said gravely. "If anything, she's quite happy, I should say."

"I believe it's my child." Rupert spoke aggressively and gave Mrs. Alexander a lofty eye that refused to be abased, though there was not as much humiliation as he would have supposed in confessing. He'd known in coming here that he'd cast off pride, but now, vulnerable, thinking himself lesser, he felt as though he had lost his bearings. He thought he would never again be a hero to Mrs. Alexander, or a "gentleman," or a "wonderful person." And he said to her, defiantly, "I have a right to *know*, because I know it could be my child."

"It *is* yours." The words came out of her instinctively, and to her great surprise and consternation. But she'd said it, and she felt right about having said it. Why should he not know this great consequence?

"It. Is. Mine," he repeated slowly after her, letting this truth sink into him with all its marvel and awful challenge. It was so. He was a father. It seemed unreal here, with Mrs. Alexander. It seemed terribly inappropriate, and he felt shy and foolish. Philanderer... This room repudiated him and all such goings on. The joy of fatherhood had gone. And belief in it was indistinct.

Rupert flushed painfully. The eyes he raised to Mrs. Alexander were evasive, yet defiant too. But now he saw that her mouth was slightly open, and her eyes were open quite wide, and that she was looking at him with more than curiosity, with a kind of timid interest. Suddenly he had a feeling that he and Mrs. Alexander had arrived together at some common level of openness, or even of interest. He could feel that this had suddenly developed in her and in him and between them. They were allies, that was it. She hadn't rejected him after all. He smiled at her radiantly, with relief and admiration for having surmounted a lifetime of prudery in favor of humanness. He had never felt such respect for her. His eyes flooded suddenly with tears.

"Oh yes it's yours, Rupert." She felt repugnance, relief, a new interest in this splendidly large and handsome *man* who sat there dwarfing her little velvet chair. She felt a sense of romance. And there was a fleeting admission in her of the inevitability and the primacy of physicalness, along with a profound recognition of Rupert's decency and value, and of the conjunction of this with the decency and value of Syra. She felt a sorrow for Anne, and, yes, for herself, along with a sense of something just now glimpsed that she had long ago lost, and might have found for a moment before it would be perhaps lost again. All these emotions mingled furiously in Mrs. Alexander before she lowered her head and looked at her hands and said again, faintly, hoping to keep all this out of her voice, "Yes, it *is* yours." Then she raised her eyes, practical, and growing anxious. "But you must go, Rupert. I lied. I've no doctor's appointment. I just wanted you to get out of here before Syra comes back."

"Because she doesn't want me to know. Is that what you mean?"

"Yes. She most surely doesn't want you to know. She made every effort to get here after you'd left, so that you wouldn't know. Go, my dear man, before she comes. You mustn't meet." Mrs. Alexander stood up. She smiled at Rupert, and crossed over to him, and took his hands in both of hers and gave them a little fond tug, so that he would rise.

He got up slowly, holding onto her hands. She looked severely up into his curious face, which was softened and saddened but which looked down at her with relief and with a trace of interest. Her old fingers felt to him curiously insubstantial, velvety.

He brought their four hands together, put one of hers on top of the other and then encompassed them in both of his own, pressing them hard. "I don't know whether you would understand this, but it wasn't a question of love, not the kind of love Anne and I have, and possibly there's no need to go into this, but, I have a responsibility," he said. "I have a responsibility to Syra and my child." He gripped her hands, held onto them for dear life, so that the single diamond of Billy's engagement ring dug painfully into the tender side of her finger. "Who will look after them if I don't?"

"You know perfectly well Syra can look after herself," Mrs. Alexander said quietly, with heavenly satisfaction letting her hands be held in a man's big grip. "You know perfectly well she has more than enough money. You know perfectly well she's independent as all get out. You know too, what you've just told me, that there isn't that kind of thing between you. So your responsibility, if you ask me, which I think you're doing in part, is to respect her wishes. That's what we all have to do with Syra, since she so truly always respects ours. Wouldn't you say?"

"Yes, what you say is true. It's what I've said to myself. But still, it's not right for a woman to be pregnant all alone. Or to go to a hospital and give birth, all alone. Someone should be with her. She should have someone to look after her. Syra's such a loner, don't you feel, such a loner? But in this case she shouldn't be alone, really, oh I feel it so strongly, so strongly. Someone must stand by Syra."

Mrs. Alexander disentangled her hands from Rupert's, giving these male hands a series of pats as she did so. Then she rested them on his arms and looked searchingly up into his face. "I'm going to look after Syra," she said with perfect ease and with no surprise at hearing these words come out of her mouth. "If she'll let me. I hope she will."

She had wept only a few times in her life, but now tears filled her eyes for the second time this afternoon. And these strange tears as they spilled out of her eyes and down her cheeks were wet and warm and welcome, and she felt that their springing up in her dry hard eyes meant that the springs of life had begun to flow in her again.

Her relief was so immense that she wanted not to speak. She patted Rupert's arms again, and then leaned forward suddenly and laid her head against his chest, and put her short arms around his big bulk, and let herself go in a torrent of weeping.

He was shocked and saddened by this violent weeping. It was terrible to see Mrs. Alexander, who had never had a tear in her eye, giving way like this. But bringing her old small shuddering body more closely and more tenderly against him, he realized all at once that he was glad of it. Hadn't he needed her to do this more than anything else, since it was this that made him feel close to her in a way he had never been? Had he really needed her gay courage as much as this wild humanness? He found himself thinking that he hadn't known she had it in her.

Concern for her began to take over his surprise. What was she crying for? But he needn't know. She was quieting down now. He sensed it had something to do with Syra. He wouldn't ask.

Then he sensed that everything in this moment had to do with Syra, with what she had caused to happen to Mrs. Alexander, and in him, and between them. This knowledge swept over him in a flood of happiness. Suddenly he felt that they were all saved—Mrs. Alexander, Anne, Syra, the child, himself.

Mrs. Alexander had stopped crying. She raised her head and looked at him with reddened, swimming, proud eyes. Then she pushed at him a little, and he took his arms away.

"Thank you, Rupert," she said. She stepped away, and pulled a handkerchief from the sleeve of her jacket and blew her nose noisily. Then she drew up a quiet sigh that was full of peace. "You had better go, my dear. Before she comes." With a return of her old spirit she smiled suddenly, gracefully. "I feel everything's all for the best now. Don't you?"

"Thanks to Syra, yes," he said. Then he hurried to go, but at the door stopped and looked back over his shoulder and said, "I'm glad to know you'll be looking after my child. There isn't anyone else I'd rather think of doing that."

"Well I only hope she'll let me. I'm not sure she will, Rupert."

"Why do you say that?"

"Because I treated Syra badly, Rupert."

"I simply can't believe that, Mrs. A."

"Well, I did. I'm terribly afraid she won't come back here. I wouldn't, if I were her. Now hurry and go, my dear."

He stood uncertainly, wondering about this and distressed by it, held here by sudden incompleteness. Until she said, "Do go," softly.

❧ VII ❧

RUPERT was opening the door of his car when it struck him as insane not to go and see Syra.

He was suddenly in a panic for fear she would have left. He thought he must have lost all touch with humanness, and with the fact of Syra herself, to have had such elaborate reasons for keeping away from her. Syra was here, on this road. She was part of his flesh and heart and mind, she was the best part of him, and it was insane to think he wouldn't want to see her, touch her. Thank her.

Flinging to the winds all his concepts and cautions, and Mrs. Alexander's admonitions, he clambered into his car and slammed the door shut. Only to touch Syra, to look at her, to make her pregnancy real to him. To complete something. To say good-by. And to thank her for his life. And to tell her to hold fast to her own. That was all. Did she know what she had done for him? Did she know what she had done for Mrs. Alexander? It was imperative that she know what she'd given both of them. He was in a panic to get there, for fear she'd go away without knowing what she was for.

He reached out to the ignition key with shaking fingers. But then he stopped. His eyes widened. He sat for a second immobilized. Then with the precipitateness of sudden decision, he flung the door open and heaved himself out, clumsy in his hurry, and tore up the steps, and into the hall calling excitedly, "Mrs. A., Mrs. A.," and raced up the hall stairs two at a time calling, "Mrs. A., Mrs. A., Mrs. A."

She was pushing herself up from her chair with puzzled eyes when Rupert plunged in. She held onto the arm of the chair, unsteady, feeling too old, too spent for anything more today. She had loved everything that had happened with Rupert, but she needed it to be over with for now.

Rupert's eyes glistened, and his smile was confidently radiant and he strode across to Mrs. Alexander and took one hand, and then the hand from the chair arm, impatiently, urgently in his, and pulled her toward him. "Come. If you think she's not coming back here, then come. We're both insane. She's here. We're going to see her. Together. This minute."

She looked at him with tired and stupefied eyes.

"Come on, Mrs. A.," Rupert said more calmly. "We've got to hurry. I've got to get back to Anne, who's probably already started worrying, and of course she must never know. Can't you see what I see, that the obvious, the natural thing for you and me to do is to go and see Syra together? She needs us. We can't just stand here. We must do this."

She pulled her hands out of his, and stepped back a little

with a slack and shocked face, as though to feel what was her own, to step out of the area of persuasion.

"There's no question about the rightness of this," Rupert said anxiously, with less certainty. But then he cried vigorously again, "I'm taking you by force if necessary," and even laughed.

Mrs. Alexander raised her chin, tilted it, and held it stiffly in that pose while she looked above and beyond Rupert's shoulder with stunned eyes that gradually focused, warmed, grew alert. She gasped. She smoothed both hands down the front of her dress in that characteristic gesture of reinforcement, trying at the same time to compose her flabbergasted mouth. When she opened it, the words were ready in it. "That won't be necessary," she said. "I think it's a marvelous idea. I'll come willingly."

An Acknowledgment

I want to express my gratitude to Toddy Sloan for her unfailing interest in the progress of this book, for her generosity in taking the time to read and re-read it, and for her helpful editorial comments.

M. H. F.